Passion is not enough

❦   ❦   ❦

Amanda was warm, so warm. She parted her lips to gasp for breath and Esteban placed his mouth over hers, his tongue intruding into her startled mouth, colliding and entwining with hers. For a suspended moment, he just held her to him and kissed her deeply, yet with such a draining, searing gentleness that she was dizzy and limp, holding onto him for support. Then he guided her head to the ground as he continued the beautiful joining of the kiss. Before she was even conscious of it, he had the button on the front of her riding habit open. The thin silk camisole slipped away and she could feel the warm noonday air on her upper body. Never had she felt like this, anything like this! Amanda gasped in startled delight.

But the warmth of the moment fled and blind panic took its place. Esteban sensed the sudden change in her from melting, hypnotized assent to frozen, frightened rigidity as she pushed him away.

Shame flooded over her in succeeding waves, oddly mixed with hurt and anger, and she thought, "I won't be a whore again, never, I swear!"

Golden Lady

Shirl Henke

WARNER BOOKS

A Warner Communications Company

WARNER BOOKS EDITION

Copyright © 1986 by Shirl Henke
All rights reserved.

Cover art by Max Ginsburg

Warner Books, Inc.
666 Fifth Avenue
New York, N.Y. 10103

A Warner Communications Company

Printed in the United States of America

First Printing: September, 1986

10 9 8 7 6 5 4 3 2 1

For Carol J. Reynard

Without her "poison pen" and flying fingers, this book would never have been written. Friends like her come one to a customer—if you're a very lucky customer.

ACKNOWLEDGMENT

Weaponry and medical practices in the nineteenth century are two highly technical areas about which I am abysmally ignorant, but Esteban was a skillful gunman and Amanda and Elizabeth were skillful healers. For expert advice on both subjects I wish to thank my good friend Carmine V. DelliQuadri, Jr., D.O., physician and weapons collector.

PROLOGUE

Mexico, 1848

Mexico City lay before Esteban Santandar like a ravished woman, still beautiful despite her defeat. Winfield Scott's army of occupation patrolled the narrow alleyways and broad boulevards. High on Grasshopper Hill the blood of fourteen-year-old military cadets stained the fortress walls in mute testimony to the senselessness of war. The lone rider, scarcely five years older than the Niños Héroes, shivered in the thin air as he rode past Chapultepec Castle without looking at it. Esteban was alive and those school-boy defenders were dead. The war was over.

He appeared to slouch in the saddle, but closer inspection revealed that he favored a wounded side, still infected from a slash inflicted by a Yankee saber. He was so emaciated that the remnants of the elegant uniform of a cavalry lieutenant, now bloodstained and faded from dozens of battles, hung loosely on his body. As he murmured a few coaxing words in Spanish to his spare gelding, his voice was low and gravelly, old beyond its years. His unkempt beard could not completely conceal the high cheekbones and sculptured lips of his once-handsome face, now ravaged by illness and disillusionment. Any casual observer would pass the youth by, thinking him merely another vagrant on the long downhill road leaving Mexico City.

Esteban felt as rootless as a vagabond, even though he knew his destination, seemingly endless miles westward for man and beast who were starved and hurting. He was certain of his course but not of what he would find at journey's end. Was Miguel alive? Would he already be safely home, or did he lie, like so many uncounted others, in a muddy grave? After three months in the obscene stench of what passed for an army hospital, Esteban felt almost immortal. If the surgeons and the filth had not killed him, nothing else would. Pray God his brother was made of the same stuff. Only part of his mind troubled over Miguel's fate. Below his pain and hunger lurked the deeper questions that nagged him. What had it all meant? What had he killed for, nearly died for? President Santa Anna? General Valencia? Mexico? He shrugged fatalistically, then winced at a pain in his side caused by the sudden movement. He muttered a string of Spanish oaths and forced his thoughts elsewhere. Perhaps his family in Sonora would give him the answers he had not found in the city. Someone must. He looked toward the setting sun and rode on.

Kansas, 1848

Thousands of miles north on a bleak prairie, another journey west was interrupted by a bitter farewell. Amanda Whittaker watched while shovelfuls of hard, dry earth thudded and then broke into chunks as they hit the blanket-wrapped body. A pale, blond woman in a faded calico dress held her arms about the thin, pinch-faced girl who held back tears as they buried her father.

Cholera. So many had died, good men like Randolph

Whittaker. He left a desolate wife and thirteen-year-old daughter to survive a wagon trek all the way to California. Randolph and Mollie Whittaker had packed up and left Saint Joseph long, hard weeks ago. Along with Missouri they left behind their comfortable cottage, the schoolhouse where he taught, even the grave of their young son, Randy. Everything was gone, faded into the past now. The womenfolk had a wagonload of farm equipment and a small cash nest egg for buying land in California. If they could ever get to California, without a man.

What will we do? The question hammered at Mollie Whittaker as relentlessly as the prairie wind. When the sorrowful old Methodist circuit rider closed his Bible, the mourners filed silently back toward the wagons, their conversation blown away with the tumbleweeds.

Carver Cain, a big, brutish man of vigorous middle years, shambled over to the widow Whittaker and doffed his hat in respect. His huge, bear-paw hands fumbled with the greasy brim, then he reached up to run his fingers through his stringy, red hair before replacing the well-worn headgear.

"I'll be right glad, ma'am, ta help with camp chores, bring firewood an' tend the oxen fer ya. A woman alone cain't do fer herself so easy." He glanced over at the thin, sullen-looking Amanda, and she skittered away from his hairy, odorous presence, feeling threatened.

"I—I'd be obliged, Mr. Cain." Mollie made the reply vaguely, as if she was uncertain of her surroundings.

Shock had been compounded by shock. After Randolph's death at dawn that overcast morning, the wagonmaster had come at once to tell her that she and Amanda must leave the train at the next settlement. Her husband had not even been buried yet, but there he was, explaining that the council had decided to move on now that the epidemic had run its course. Randolph was the last to die. And his widow, a woman alone with only a bookish daughter, couldn't pull her own weight. The wagonmaster was sorry. Sorry! A lot of help that was.

And now here was Mr. Cain, making such a kind offer

of assistance, even if Mollie had never liked him. If Carver Cain helped her, perhaps the wagonmaster might reconsider. She had to think of Amanda. Dazed, she trudged back to the wagon to fall into a deep sleep for the rest of the morning.

Two weeks later, the wagonmaster did reconsider, just as they reached Singleton, the next town on a sparsely inhabited trail. He would let the Whittaker women stay on, but only if Mollie agreed to marry Carver Cain. Numb with grief and desperation, Mollie Whittaker became Mollie Cain. A shocked Amanda watched the same preacher who had buried her father marry her mother to a coarse, loud man who seldom bathed and could neither read nor write. Carver made plain that he was very generous in accepting Amanda as a stepchild. He could use the wagon, farm supplies, and cash, but what earthly use had he for this scrawny, frightened girl child?

PART 1

ARRIVAL

CHAPTER
1

Willow Valley, California, 1852

Amanda was scared. Sweat ran down her arms and soaked her back, making her long, dark gold braids wet and sticky. She was gasping for breath, and even her strong, sixteen-year-old body was exhausted. Stifling the noise of her labored breathing, she lay still, flattened to the hot, dry earth as he searched quietly for her. Carver was in no hurry. He'd waited nearly a year; he would catch her sooner or later. He neared her hiding place in the midst of the patch of wild blackberries. She tensed.

One of her braids stuck out between the dark brambles like a beacon. Carver whirled and invaded the bushes. Amanda heard the sound of tearing fabric as the thorns caught at his rough workshirt. He grabbed the braid, and as Amanda desperately yanked at it, unwilling tears sprang to her eyes. Frantically she struggled until he captured her slim, tanned arm and hauled her out of the thicket. She was too terrified to speak. He shoved her roughly to the dry grass, knocking the wind from her and standing with one foot on her skirt, pinning her like a golden butterfly on a board, waiting to be mounted. Just as he untied his rope belt, she heard the voice of Farrell, the neighbors' teenage son. Carver grunted and stepped away from Amanda, freeing her.

As she watched him shamble away toward the sound of the caller, Amanda sat up and let out a long, slow breath, like steam escaping from the kettle. She stopped shivering, then stood and dusted herself off. He was gone, for now. She picked up her pail. When Carver surprised her, she had spilled the berries hard picked in the heat. *Drat it all anyway,* she thought with fierce anger. *Two hours picking and we needed them to make a pie for supper.* No help for it, she simply retraced her steps toward the place where Carver had found her. Amanda glanced from side to side like a wild thing, making sure he was gone. Then, with a sigh, she began to regather the spilled fruit. As she picked up the last of the blackberries and tossed them into the bucket, a twig cracked. She jerked her body around. It was only Farrell Wellsley. He lived on the next farm and his pa made the awful whiskey Carver and some of the other ne'er-do-well settlers drank.

Farrell smiled his tight smile and ogled her small breasts, prominent against the outgrown calico gown she wore to do chores. "Howdy, Miss Mandy."

"Hello, Farrell." Although she disliked him, his timely appearance had saved her from Carver. She tried to smile as he walked with her toward the house, never offering to carry the pail.

Farrell gazed at her pensive profile as they walked. "What ya woolgatherin' 'bout? Bein' a fancy lady agin," he scoffed.

She didn't slow her stride. Last year in a burst of loneliness she had confided her dream to him. Her family had gone to San Francisco to buy a new plow. They stayed overnight in a cheap hotel, but had passed through a fine section of the fast-growing city, filled with exotic shops and elegant carriages. It was there that Amanda saw *her,* the most beautiful lady on earth, dressed in a blue velvet traveling costume and ostrich-plumed hat. She was being helped out of a barouche by a servant. Everyone paid attention to her. Servants scurried to open doors and gentlemen tipped their hats. She spoke to her escort in soft, modulated tones as she gave him her gloved hand and entered the glass doors of an elegant restaurant.

Amanda never forgot that scene; it was engraved on her heart. She longed to be gorgeously gowned and attended by servants, to be educated and able to converse easily with cultivated gentlemen. Most of all, she wanted to be respected as a real lady of quality. Every time she read her books she was convinced she had the mind and will to succeed. Her mother's faded and cracked mirror even gave her a hint of possible beauty. She dreamed and read, and once made the mistake of telling Farrell, who laughed and called her "tetched in the head."

"Ye're a hardscrabble farmer's kid. Ya'll end up married with a dozen babies."

Amanda had retorted, "I'm better educated now than most *men* in California, and my father was a schoolteacher back in Saint Joseph. I will be a lady someday! You just wait and see if I end up with someone like you, Farrell Wellsley!"

As they neared the house Farrell went toward the barn and Carver. Amanda was relieved; his presence would distract her stepfather and give her another day's reprieve. She was beginning to live from day to day, surviving like a hunted animal. She knew she must think ahead. Could she dare tell the schoolteacher, Mrs. Trudale? Telling someone her shameful secret was beyond her, but Carver's attempts to catch her alone, as he had done that afternoon, were becoming increasingly frequent. She must do something. She mulled on this as she entered the house.

Mollie stood at the stove with Abe hanging on her skirts and Hank in the corner crying for supper. At two years of age the twins were spoiled and crafty, like their father. "Where you been? It be nearly all afternoon and that's all you picked?" After two years of marriage to Carver,

Mollie spoke as he did. She looked worn and listless, her face no longer young.

Amanda looked at her mother and said, "It was hot, Mama. I got all I could. I'll make a pie now so we have something besides sidemeat and greens."

As she began to work the lard into the flour, Amanda watched Mollie's listless attempts at quieting the boys. It never occurred to her to tell her mother about Carver. Amanda and Mollie scarcely talked at all anymore. After Randolph's death and her remarriage, Mollie had withdrawn. Amanda sensed the bare truth—there was nothing Mollie could do except wring her hands—if she knew. Amanda doubted her mother would even believe her. It was so easy for Mollie to stay in her shell. A hopeless knot of misery welled up in Amanda's throat, but she forced it down, fiercely rolling out the dough and slapping it into the old pie tin.

Supper was the same as hundreds before it. Amanda hurried through cleaning up while Farrell and her father went off to Wellsleys and more raw liquor. From the loft Abe screamed, refusing to go to bed, while Hank splashed a spoon in the half-full coffee cup Carver had left on the table. The black liquid spilled on Amanda's dress, jerking her attention from the dishpan to the boy.

"Stop it, Hank."

With his defiant, yellow eyes, he already reminded her of his father as he watched to see if she would slap him. Amanda considered the child, put down her dishrag, scooped him up, and headed for the loft, where Mollie was struggling to put Abe to bed. Both boys listened to their half-sister more than to their mother. Amanda sternly tucked them in with no more nonsense.

After the dishes were done, Amanda was bone weary and wanted a bath. Carver would be at the Wellsleys' most of the night drinking, so she felt safe taking her towel and a piece of homemade lye soap to the creek. She was hot, sweaty, and scratched from the blackberry brambles. A bath was one of her few luxuries, even if taken in a cold creek with coarse soap.

The sun was setting in the west when she returned to the house, hair damp but clean, hanging in shining ripples down her back. She opened the squeaky hinge on the cabin door and entered quietly so as not to wake the boys. Mollie was not in the kitchen. Carver was. She froze in the doorway as he rose, lurching drunkenly toward her, pulling the door closed behind her with one huge paw. The bang of the door jolted her from her trance.

"Where's Mama? You'll wake Abe and Hank."

A slow grin spread across Carver's mouth but never reached his cold, yellow eyes. "They's all down ta Wellsleys'. Seems when I up an' got there fer a toot, th' missus was doin' poorly an asked yer ma ta come set with her tanight. All th' boys went on home an' th' party busted up. I fetched Mollie an' th' boys over ta Miz Wellsley an' come on back ta see ta ya. Ain't safe, ya bein' alone 'n' all."

As he spoke he put his hand against the door, closing off her one route of escape. Amanda backed away from his sour, animal smell as his bulk loomed over her. With surprising suddenness, for so lumbering a man, he grabbed one of her wrists in a tight grip and yanked her back to him. "Now, missie, you 'n' me is goin' ta have us a time."

He twisted one arm behind her back until tears of agony sprang to her eyes. She was silent in her misery, for who could hear her cry? He began to unbutton her calico dress, apparently not wanting to damage it. Amanda struggled, despite the arm pressure. With a grunt of exasperation, he tore it down the front. All Amanda had on was a white cotton shift and pantalets, fragile protection as he grabbed her from behind, taking a small pink-nippled breast in each enormous hand. She felt faint from the pain as he squeezed. He picked her up, threw her over his shoulder, and stalked the few steps to her side bedroom, which was little more than a lean-to with a door cut to join it to the kitchen. Amanda's bed was narrow, covered with a rough patch-work quilt. Carver dropped her, and as she landed she tried to roll off. He stood in the door, calmly taking off his shirt and pants, but when she scrambled desperately for the one small window, he reached out and yanked her back before she could climb out.

He ripped at her pantalets and then fell on top of her. All Amanda remembered of what followed was a series of harsh pressures and sharp stabbing pains. The weight of his huge body snuffed the breath from her as a strong wind douses a fluttering candle. She could neither breathe nor see but could feel, feel his coarse, hairy body rubbing against her. When he pulled her legs apart, she struggled to roll off the bed again, and he slapped her into semiconsciousness. Silently he used one hand to guide his engorged penis into her. She struggled against the bruising pressure, then gasped at the sudden dry piercing. She was too breathless to cry out. Her body was being torn apart as he forced himself into her. Then, mercifully, it was over and he collapsed on her.

Finally, when it seemed to her that his weight might suffocate her, Carver rolled off her, holding her fast to his side. He lay there, replete, while Amanda numbly fought for breath and took inventory of the functioning parts of her body. After a few tentative movements she decided she was alive and could move, if she could get free of him.

"Don't ya go thinkin' ta tell yer ma. It'd shame her ta have a daughter what made up ta her steppa. Word'd git out ya was free 'n' easy an' all th' boys over ta Wellsleys'd come on over fer a sample."

His low, fast threat barely registered before he began to rub his hands over her. She squeezed her eyes shut and made her mind go blank.

When Carver finished the second time, he left her lying there, a broken stick doll, and shambled off to the kitchen table and his jug. Amanda felt the blood running down her legs; she was so weak she couldn't stand. She must have fainted, for when she awoke it was false dawn. No sound came from the kitchen except the slow, even snoring of Carver, passed out across the table and chair.

Amanda forced herself to sit up. Looking at the shreds of her white pantalets nearly made her faint again. They were red with her own blood! She felt her legs, but was afraid to touch the throbbing place between. Swinging her legs over the side of the bed, she silently sat up. With a grimace of agony she held on to the nightstand, then knelt before the small walnut trunk she had brought from Saint Joseph. She opened it, looking for fresh underwear and a faded green muslin dress, her only good one. Amanda trembled as she pulled off the bloody remnants of her clothes and dressed again. Carrying her one pair of shoes, she moved as stealthily as a cat. Her only thought was to get out before Carver awoke from his stupor to inflict more horrors on her.

How she climbed through the window without passing out from pain or waking Carver she would never recall. She just accomplished it and began to walk. As the sun rose and an early morning breeze came up to clear her head, Amanda realized that her only hope lay in getting as far from Carver Cain as possible.

She would go to San Francisco. It was the only answer. The trip took about four days by wagon, longer on foot, but once clear of Willow Valley, maybe she could find someone on the road to give her a ride. The city was big enough that she could lose herself in its throngs more completely than she could in the smaller, rowdier gold camps to the north. Perhaps a girl who could read, write, and do sums as well as cook, sew, and clean could find a decent job there. All she wanted right now was to vanish, to have the earth swallow her up and hide her from Carver Cain and all the people in Willow Valley who would think her a harlot who had seduced her stepfather. At the thought that some might look on her with pity, shame coursed through her. Carver would see that Mollie did not cross him. No protection would ever come from Amanda's mother. Amanda knew her fate was sealed. She remembered the old proverb she had read in one of her books: ''A journey of a thousand miles begins with a single step.'' Thank God the distance she had to travel was far less! Painfully she continued walking, leaving the farmhouse and the valley in the shadows.

It took Amanda five days to reach San Francisco. The first day was a nightmare of pain and terror. Her old shoes tore open, giving her blisters as she walked on the rough, rocky trail that passed for a road. The bleeding between her thighs stopped after a half-hour of walking, but the knifelike pains stabbed for the entire journey. Her green dress was torn and the hem mud-stained. Her hair hung in wild disarray, so she tore a strip of cloth from her sash and gathered it together at the back of her head.

She filched some apples from a tree near the roadside for supper that evening. While enjoying her first meal that day, she spied a wagon lumbering over the slope behind her. Her first impulse was to run and hide in the thickets behind the tree for fear that it was Carver or someone she knew from the valley, but as the wagon neared she realized the driver was an old drummer, one of the itinerant breed who wandered across the western landscape, selling pots, pans, dry goods, and medicinal cures to the isolated settlers. Since the gold rush, everything from picks and shovels to fry pans and blankets was in high demand and commanded staggering prices. If a supplier was near the diggings, he could make a lot of money quickly. The old man in grubby broadcloth pants, flannel shirt, and well-worn boots did not appear to be one of the fortunate. His beard was filthy and mottled with gray, and his hair was long and shaggy. He was a match for the beat-up old wagon he drove and the pair of bony, fly-bitten mules who pulled it.

Amanda stood up hesitantly and shaded her eyes with her hand for a better view of him as he drew up beneath the tree. He grinned at her, then released a vigorous spit of tobacco juice that raised a mud splat on the soggy ground when it landed. He had three well-spaced teeth and eyes of indeterminate grayish color that crinkled up as he began to talk.

"Ya look ta be a mite lost 'n' footsore, gal. Might be yew could use a ride? I'd favor someone ta talk ta 'sides these two ornery critters." He flicked the reins in the direction of his mules.

Amanda approached the wagon, unsure. She was so footsore and tired that the shade of canvas awning across the rickety structure seemed pure heaven compared to the dirt road still radiating heat. The drummer looked at her patiently, sensing her desperation and terror. She tried to smile but could manage only a grimace.

"I'd appreciate a ride toward San Francisco if that's your direction." Since it was the only road for miles, the question seemed foolish to her as she said it. He seemed not to notice.

"Yep, I'm fer thet very place—need new fixin's ta sell. Shipload of prime pots 'n' pans comin' in th' fifteenth. Be proud ta give ya a lift. Name's Jebediah Hooter. Ya kin call me Hoot. Most do." He reached down to give her a handshake and hand up. Guardedly, she took the proffered hand.

CHAPTER
2

Mazatlán, Mexico, 1852

Rodrigo Ruiz slapped a wicked-looking riding quirt against his thigh as he paced the white sand of the beach at Mazatlán. His elegant black leather riding boots were dulled and his roweled spurs were gritty and clogged by the soft sand.

"Just like Esteban to keep me waiting. Nothing changes between us, even after three years. Pah! Three years wasted in universities in Paris and London. He could have gone to Lima or Mexico City for his education, or even Madrid, but he had to leave good Spanish ways behind and mix with foreigners. He'll no doubt come home with even more mad notions than that gringo uncle of his has already corrupted him with!"

As Rodrigo's eyes ranged towards the hill, he spotted a woman nearing the beach. So, May Ling had heard Esteban was arriving on the *California*, too. Rodrigo swore. "We were ever rivals, eh, Esteban, in children's games, in teenage horse races, and now even for women." In his cousin's absence, Rodrigo had enjoyed May Ling's attention. Now it seemed she was ready to return to her earlier love. He bitterly begrudged the fact that she preferred Esteban. *Just a prostitute,* Rodrigo reminded himself; though as she neared her delicate Chinese beauty overwhelmed him anew.

He straightened his flat-crowned hat and began to brush the windblown sand from his skin-tight black jacket and pants. He cut a dashing figure, dressed in the close-fitting dark ranchero clothes, resplendent with silver trim, red sash, and gleaming high-heeled riding boots. His face was hawkish and pale with contrasting deepset blue eyes under thin, elegant brows. His lips and nose were also thin and well drawn, altogether a classic Castilian appearance, complete with light brown, curling hair and a tall, muscular frame.

May Ling noticed his attempts to appear meticulous even on the windswept beach. She smiled to herself. He was so vain about his looks.

"So, you also await Don Esteban's arrival." She inclined her head in a formal bow although Rodrigo had been her paying customer for the past three years.

"Yes, he sent word ahead that he made the crossing at Panama and was booking passage on the *California.* I was elected the official welcoming committee. My cousin Miguel is occupied at the mines in Hermosillo and Uncle Alfredo is getting too old for such a long ride."

He shrugged, a gesture of careless resignation that belied his inner tension. "How did you find out he was coming back?" Rodrigo asked as he scanned the ship bobbing precariously on the churning blue-white waves at the opening of the magnificent bay.

"A boy from the harbor came to our place of business and spoke of his message to you. When I heard the Santandar name, I knew." Her quiet yet almost defiantly prideful way of speaking always irritated Rodrigo. She had no right to such dignity.

"So, my love, we part ways and you return to his embrace just as if no time passed since he last lay with

you. Don't be so sure he'll be interested in the skills of a
Chinese whore in a backwater Sinaloa port city after all the
lovely courtesans he could buy in Paris or London!''

His cruel taunt struck home. May Ling lowered her
head. ''I will want to greet him anyway, Don Rodrigo.''

The *California* had put several large wooden landing
craft into the churning waters and now the debarking
passengers were climbing into them. The Mazatlán harbor
was ringed to the north and south by jaggedly beautiful but
treacherous rock islets, making it too dangerous for the
large steamer to come close to shore. As the boats beached
a few dozen yards away, Rodrigo and May Ling were
joined by several curious townspeople, a vendor of fresh
tropical fruits, and the eternal customs man from the
alcalde's office. Esteban was in the prow of the first boat
and leaped into the knee-high waves as it jarred against the
white sand.

He hasn't changed, thought Rodrigo. His cousin was
still lean, still darkly tanned despite cold northern winters.
Rodrigo had always suspected that the Santandar side of
the family was not criollo, pure Spanish blood, but liberally
sprinkled with base Indian strains. Of course, the dense
shadow of black beard, the curly hair, and the golden eyes
belied this, but it was possible there was at least a taint.
Esteban was dressed for ship's travel in a loose white linen
shirt, tan breeches, and flat-heeled leather boots, a contrast
to Rodrigo's dandyish attire.

Esteban helped the ship's mate pull the boat firmly
aground, then turned as the other passengers were climbing
down, and strode toward his cousin. They embraced warmly,
then Rodrigo held Esteban at arm's length to give him a
mock inspection.

''You look the same, cousin. No more educated than
when you left Sonora. What good did all those damn
French and English schools do you, eh!'' He laughed and
Esteban thumped him on the back.

''I'll tell you all about what I learned, Rigo, but not
until I have a good cold beer, iced from the caves. God,
how I've longed for the taste of real, cold beer!'' Cerro de

la Nevería, or Icebox Hill as the gringos called it, held a series of deep underground caverns where ice brought from San Francisco was stored for cooling drinks and perishable foods for those in Mazatlán who could afford the luxury.

As the two men turned, Esteban saw May Ling waiting quietly, her eyes downcast. He took several long strides up the beach and grabbed her by her reed-slim waist, tossing her high in the air like a doll. Her reserve was gone. She joyously clasped him about the neck as he kissed her and whirled her around.

Placing her gently back on the sand, he held her delicate face, bending down to speak to her. "You are as beautiful as ever I remembered, China Doll." At that old endearment, she smiled and softly stroked his jawline, feeling the prickly growth of beard that defied his razor, even when he had been only a seventeen-year-old boy and they first were lovers.

Rodrigo came up behind them to interrupt. "Ah, so tender the lovers' reunion, but we must get this man a cold beer—"

"Real, Mexican beer, not that evil brown soup the English drink warm," Esteban laughingly interrupted. With one arm around his cousin and the other around May Ling, Esteban Santandar began the long climb up the beach toward the public square in Mazatlán. He was home.

As dusk fell quickly into the clear, star-bright night of the northwest coast of Mexico, Esteban and Rodrigo were finishing their evening meal at the Canton Royal. May Ling cleared away the empty dishes. Her uncle Lin Soo owned the Royal. He had come to Mazatlán in 1840 and quickly discovered that the hostlery business was good and that operating a whorehouse and gambling place on the premises fattened his profits even more. After 1849 many gold-rush argonauts came overland to Mazatlán and embarked by steamer for California. The steady stream of "nieces" and "cousins" imported from Canton increased as the demands for exotic prostitutes grew. May Ling was one of these imports, sold by her real family to Soo's agent.

She entered the private room where the cousins were leaning back in their chairs, replete from a surfeit of the Royal's excellent cuisine and a great deal of iced beer. She put more beer on the table quietly as the men reminisced about the past and argued. Rodrigo and Esteban always argued.

"If you had stayed home, you would take pride in your heritage, not live like a—a Yankee merchant!" Rigo had no need of cruder epithets; but the concept of business alone was a staggering insult to a ranchero. Most criollos did not soil their hands by engaging in mining, trading, or shipping—the very way Esteban's uncle Frank Mulcahey had become rich in southern California. Of course, marrying into the Santador family helped a struggling young Irish immigrant's standing, too. That and the discovery of a rich silver vein on Santandar land. Even Esteban's older brother Miguel now oversaw the management of the mines owned by Mulcahey and Santandar together.

Knowing his family's stiff-necked dislike of upstart men without pedigrees, men who worked in business rather than ranching, Esteban smiled tolerantly at Rodrigo. "Rigo, you should've come with me and left those boring tutors at the ranch. You might even have learned to like some things about those gringos, especially my uncle."

Warming to his subject and angry with his cousin's half-tolerant, half-teasing response, Rodrigo rose from the table and paced across the floor, his high-heeled boots clicking against the hardwood. "I don't think I would ever have anything in common with your uncle or any of those Americans in California or the other states you seem so fond of. They are our enemies! We fought a war against them!"

"I was with General Valencia outside Mexico City when Santa Anna left us to be cut to pieces. I still carry the scar across my side from an American saber. A stupid nineteen-year-old should never join an army—least of all one led by a cowardly bastard like Santa Anna. Northern Mexico is probably better off being ruled by the Americans now. God knows, our government in the south is still making a botch of everything." Esteban sounded weary.

"I was in the army and suffered the defeat with you. It doesn't matter about our generals. I'm a Mexican and proud to serve under my flag and defend my country and heritage!" Rigo's voice rose.

"Just because I'm fed up with our political corruption and military blunders doesn't mean I'm not proud to be Mexican. I am a Santandar and I take pride in my heritage, just as you do, Rigo." Esteban's voice began to show some irritation.

All the while they argued, May Ling silently and unobtrusively refilled their glasses from a pitcher of cold beer. With a curt nod, Rodrigo dismissed her and she silently carried the tray out of the room, leaving the large pitcher of beer for the two men.

Rodrigo realized he had gone too far. Esteban and his brother Miguel had been severely wounded in the thick of the fighting. Rodrigo had seen relatively little action and emerged unscathed. He put up his hand in a gesture of resignation. "I'm not questioning your patriotism, just your interest in gringos and Europeans. They're influencing your life too much, that's all. If you're such a good criollo, why not study in your own country, eh? Why travel all over the United States and Europe?"

Esteban sighed. "I learned a few things while I was abroad, Rigo. This country is in trouble. Britain and France hold millions of pesos in Mexican debt. If we don't get a responsible government in Mexico City and begin to repay our debts, the European powers could occupy the port cities of the east coast. That's a much larger danger than losing the war to the Americans. Even that was completely the fault of Santa Anna and his idiotic personal vendettas with his own generals. If he'd organized his troops and cut the American supply lines..." He shrugged in disgust. "I don't think there's much hope for our system.

"The British have some 'crazy ideas,' as you call them, and they've not had any revolutions lately. A small handful of aristocrats can't hold the rest of the population under their thumb, not in England, France, *or* Mexico—not in the nineteenth century. Times are changing everywhere, whether or not you like it, Rigo.''

Rodrigo threw back his head and laughed harshly. ''Tell me, cousin, when will you sell all your lands and give the money to the poor? Maybe you're more religious than you think, eh, man? Your father's wealth paid for your fancy education in Europe.'' He stood, fists on hips, eyes glittering, almost challenging the indolent-looking man at the table.

Both of them were well on their way to being quite drunk. May Ling had replaced the pitcher of beer regularly throughout the dinner and afterward, even as she regretted the obvious. Esteban would be in no condition to spend the night with her after his reunion with his cousin.

Esteban shook his head to clear it and laughed abruptly. ''Look at us. We grew up together having these same arguments. Now we haven't seen each other in three years and what do we do? Start the same old fights!''

At this, Rodrigo came over and sat down at the table. ''You're right. Some welcome home, a lecture. I'll tell you what, if you still love to race as much as you did before you became a university man, we'll have a race tomorrow. We can leave for home after you get your ass whipped. I have the fastest new chestnut and I brought several of my best mounts from my father's ranch, the big black and a golden palomino. You choose any of the three and I'll ride one of the others and I bet I beat you by at least a length.''

Esteban responded at once. He had always loved horse racing and in England he had acquired a few new riding tricks that should make him a match for Rodrigo, despite his cousin's constant practice in the saddle. ''Let's make this interesting. What will you wager? I brought back six cases of good French burgundy that I'll put up. I know how you love the wine the French make, even if you do scorn their politics. Ah! I have it!'' At this point Esteban snapped his fingers and rose to face Rodrigo. ''One of those splendid horses of yours. I was trying to breed a sorrel of mine with a palomino to start a line of golden horses before I left. I'd like to increase my breeding stock. You put up the palomino. If it's half as good as any of the horses Uncle José had when I left, it's just what I want. Agreed? Who knows, I might even go into business breeding horses. I've been thinking about what I want to do when I get home."

"Agreed." Rodrigo did not hesitate. Esteban had not ridden any of the three horses and probably had little chance to ride while abroad, so Rodrigo did not hesitate to accept the wager. The burgundy would taste sweet.

The next morning dawned warm and clear, and a strong ocean breeze off the bay cooled the open stretch of ground where the race was to be held. Rodrigo, cursing beer and his cousin's perverse penchant for the vile brew, held his throbbing head as he stretched out under a pine tree. When he had awakened at ten, Esteban had not been in his room. They had agreed to meet here at eleven. *Damn, where was Esteban?* Just then Rodrigo heard the laughter of a man and woman blending together. Rounding an outcropping of boulders on the high road overlooking the ocean in the distance, Esteban came into view. The wind whipped back his curly black hair, and he showed no after-effects of last night's drinking spree. May Ling held tightly to him, sharing the stable horse he had ridden to the race site. Coyly she looked at Rodrigo as Esteban swung her down from the horse as if she were featherlight.

That son of a bitch spent the morning with her! That's why he wasn't in his room! Rodrigo thought furiously; but carefully he schooled his face to impassivity as he rose and walked toward them. He nodded at the horses his vaquero held across the clearing.

All three were magnificent. The chestnut was the biggest of the three, gleaming like dark bronze in the sunlight. The black was completely unmarked, not a white hair on his perfect ebony coat. The third horse, the palomino, was a perfect specimen, bright gold with a pure white mane and tail. Although not quite the size of the chestnut, it was sturdily built and had the calmest manner.

Esteban walked around the horses, carefully checking them, soothing them with low Spanish endearments as he moved about. Meanwhile, Rodrigo strolled over to May Ling, who had stayed by the rented horse. "So you got him to come to you, eh, love? It won't last. He'll use you for now and then take off to Alta California or Sonora, and you won't see him for half a year. Now, I, on the other hand, am always in and out of Mazatlán. You made a poor bargain, choosing my cousin over me. After he's gone, if you're a good little penitent, I might take you back, even set you up with your own place, get you out of your uncle's *establishment*."

His sneering reference to the work she did at the Canton Royal did not produce the desired effect. May Ling, her eyes still fixed on Esteban's dark form as he moved amid the horses, said calmly, "I know, Don Rodrigo. He told me he could not stay here. After he is reunited with his family in Sonora, he goes to see his American uncle. I am practical. He does not want a mistress to travel with him. If you still want me when he is gone, I will be most agreeable to your kind offer."

Before she could say more or Rodrigo could reply, Esteban strode over to them. "The palomino is excellent for breeding stock, but I'll take the black for racing. I've seen him run, if you remember, Rigo."

"Ah, but you haven't seen my new chestnut run, cousin. That wine will not leave the rotten taste in my mouth that your accursed beer did!"

"Don't uncork the bottles yet, Rigo. I want that golden horse. Let's get to it."

The course of the race was agreed upon and both men mounted. By this time a sizable crowd of spectators had gathered. Bets were made with excited gestures, and oaths filled the warm noon air.

Esteban, despite his appearance, felt little better than his cousin and regretted the late-night drinking bout—and this race. He also regretted having told May Ling that the youthful idyll they had shared before he left for Europe could not be resumed. He had gone to her room early that morning, feeling he owed her an explanation, but when she held out her arms, he had forgotten his resolve. *She's still a skillful little seductress,* he thought with a rueful grin. That, of course, meant that he had had even less rest than Rodrigo.

But now, this idiotic race! Yet, Esteban realized that the race could be a good thing. Even if he lost, the wine was no tremendous forfeit. If he won, the palomino was a superb piece of horseflesh for breeding flashy-looking horses for sale in both Mexican and American markets. It was an idea he'd been toying with and one of the things he wanted to talk to Uncle Frank about.

Esteban swung himself into the saddle of the nervous black stallion. He'd seen the horse a few times before he had gone to Europe; then, it had been barely old enough to race. Now it was an edgy mount, but devilishly fast. The difficulty lay in controlling him. Of course, Rodrigo's chestnut was an unknown quantity.

A rancher friend of Rodrigo's gave the signal for the race to begin by dropping a red scarf. Both the chestnut and the black were off in a flurry of dust. The course was only about ten miles, ending at the starting point after making a wide swinging loop over a coast road and back. It was fairly smooth, making speed, not surefootedness or endurance, the essential ingredient.

Knowing from long experience with his boyhood companion that Rodrigo was one to start too quickly to maintain a pace, Esteban held back the black to gauge the pace of the chestnut and choose the moment to push. For the first couple of miles, he merely kept a few lengths behind the chestnut, watching Rodrigo work the horse. It was fast and had a long stride. *Rigo was always too eager,* Esteban thought. *Here's to that new stud palomino!*

As they reached the last part of the course, the chestnut slowed as Esteban watched from behind. Finally, feeling the tension held in check in the black, he let it go. In the last mile, Rodrigo, sure of his wine and already thirsty in his hangover, was rudely surprised to feel the approach from behind. The wind beat against his side as the black, with Esteban leaning far over his long neck, opened up and seemed to glide by Rodrigo's chestnut and over the finish marker.

By the time they dismounted, both men were drenched with perspiration and the horses were lathered. It had been a close race and the crowd was congratulating both riders. The vaquero from Rodrigo's ranch led the exhausted animals away, but the men were not so fortunate. It was more than an hour later when they finally saw the shade of the Royal's cantina and a cold drink.

After cooling off and quenching his thirst, Esteban headed upstairs to change for the long ride ahead of him. Rodrigo had decided to stay in Mazatlán to enjoy the pleasures of the city for a few weeks more. Now that his troublesome cousin would be gone, with one of his best horses, Rodrigo could count on May Ling's undivided attention. He knew of a small house on the outskirts of town that he could rent cheaply enough. It would be comfortable for him as often as he visited the city. Since he spent little time on his family's ranch, he would be here frequently. He would make arrangements with her "uncle" tonight.

The farewell between the cousins was jovial, with many promises to visit each other's ranch. Yet, as he headed his small entourage up the northern coast road, Esteban felt saddened that their boyhood companionship was a thing of the past. His association with his uncle and the time he had spent in California while a young teenager had widened the gap. The war had served to make Rodrigo even more distant. *Strange*, Esteban thought, *since Miguel and I suffered so much more*. Now, after three years' absence in Europe, the breach seemed irreparable. *Some things are just inevitable*. Esteban sighed and turned his thoughts from his cousin to his parents.

CHAPTER
3

Esteban found Rancho Santandar had not changed at all since he had left it in anger and frustration three years ago. It was located in the incredible beauty of the southern Sonora subtropical wilderness, an outpost of wealth and civilization in a lightly inhabited land of jaguars and Mayo Indians. The state of Sonora was itself isolated from the rest of Mexico by the Sierra Madre Occidental, jaggedly beautiful mountains running north to south down through the state. Just so, the wildly blooming subtropical desert country where Sonora met Sinaloa was isolated at the narrow neck of land between the mountains and the ocean. The ranch was situated on a gently rising slope where its blindingly whitewashed adobe walls and red tile roofs were the dramatic capstone for surrounding hot springs, cactuses flowering with purple and pink morning glories, and a wide range of evergreens from scrub mesquite to hardy pines. The blue and lavendar backdrop of the Sierra Madres completed an awe-inspiring scene.

The ranch was an outpost of safety and a feudal kingdom in its own right, with hundreds of people working the livestock, tending gardens, and keeping the house and grounds in smooth order. Bunkhouses for single vaqueros, small clusters of single-room adobes for married couples, livestock corrals for horses and cattle, a blacksmith shop, and even a small winery spilled over the surrounding terrain.

Estaban surveyed the ranch as he rode in, scarcely conscious of its beauty, for he was deep in thought about the imminent meeting with his family. Absently he nodded to the ranch vaqueros who bade him *buenos días* at the end of their six-day trail ride with him from Mazatlán. He handed the reins of his mount to Juanito and walked toward the cool, inviting arches of the front entry.

Suddenly a small, gray-haired woman darted from the interior of the entry and fairly flew toward him. Doña Esperanza was overjoyed to see her younger son return home at last. He hugged her fiercely, and she returned the embrace. Then, her eyes devouring him with maternal possessiveness, she looked for the inevitable signs of malnutrition and neglect that so long an absence must have caused.

"Esteban, my son, you are pale and too thin, but you look splendid to these old eyes! Three years and so few letters. For the past weeks since we heard of the ship's arrival, I counted the days. I wanted to go, but your papa would not hear of the journey for me. He is too protective of me. He..."

"Mama, slow down and let us both catch our breath and get out of the hot sun," Esteban interrupted her and gently began to lead her inside. "Old eyes, indeed! You are prettier than all the women in Paris. How have you been? Your letters never mentioned your own health, you know."

"Ah, I am well enough, but I fear your eyesight is failing—I have more than enough wrinkles for a woman of forty-five."

"To me you will always be the fairest, you know. I missed you and Miguel. How is his hip?"

"It pains him more than he admits. He wanted to make the trip to Mazatlán when he heard of your arrival, but there was a mine shaft cave-in last week. No one was killed, thank the Blessed Virgin, but several men were hurt and the timbers had to be made safer. Miguel takes the safety of the mines very seriously and felt he must oversee the operation. He begs you to come up to Hermosillo and visit him and Inez as soon as you can get away from your duties at the ranch."

"I will soon, Mama. Are he and Inez expecting that first grandchild of yours yet?"

"No. I fear Inez may be barren, Esteban. It has been nearly two years. . . ." Her voice trailed off sadly and she looked at her second son almost pleadingly, taking his hand in hers. "If you and Elena would only . . ."

"Would only what?" A harsh bass voice interrupted the two figures in the front *sala*. Don Alfredo, tall and thin, hair iron gray and eyes jet black, a hawkish, imposing man, strode into the room. "We will make the arrangements between these two final tomorrow, do not fret, my dove." Don Alfredo patted his wife on the shoulder gently and then fixed his obsidian eyes on his younger son. The look was full of the same mixed emotions that Esteban's golden eyes reflected back at his father—love, pride, intense frustration, and anger. The two men embraced, their long, spare frames dwarfing the tiny woman who stood next to them.

"So, what have these fancy French and English taught you—how to ride a horse better, judge the grade of silver from a vein, choose the best stud for prime cattle? Eh? Or perhaps you learned how to wench and gamble and drink their wine even more proficiently!"

At his wife's small gasp of indignation, Don Alfredo threw back his head and rocked with laughter, grasping his son around one shoulder while bending over to plant a kiss on Doña Esperanza's cheek. "Dear one, you know the wild oats young men must sow. Even your saintly Esteban," here he rolled his eyes, "must be allowed the indiscretions of a young buck. But now he is home, finished with

school, ready to take his place with his family, where he
belongs.''

As he talked, the old don ushered both wife and son
through the *sala* toward the massive winding stairway that
led to the second floor. ''Lupe has your rooms ready and
I'll send Manolo up with hot bath water. Rest and refresh
yourself. When you're ready, come to my study. We will
talk then, man to man.''

Glad of the dismissal, hot and weary, Esteban did long
for a bath and siesta before confronting his father. Also, it
was better for them to talk without his mother present. She
was always upset when they argued. He bent down and
kissed her lightly and then sprinted up the stairs toward his
old rooms, his long legs taking the low, wide steps two at a
time.

Estaban felt much more presentable. He changed his
traveling clothes for tight-fitting black pants and a short
jacket accented by a ruffled white linen shirt and red sash
at his waist. High-heeled, intricately tooled leather boots
gleamed on his feet, completing the picture of Hispanic
elegance. His father was a stickler for traditional dress. *At
least I can please the old man that much,* he thought with
a sigh, and knocked on the massive oak door. The wrought-
iron hinges, oiled to perfection, made no sound as the door
swung open and he entered the lion's den.

The perfunctory questions about his stay abroad were all
neatly covered over predinner brandy. He inquired about
the cattle shipped and profits made in Hermosillo at the
mines, about the health of his old companions who rode
for the rancho as vaqueros. Finally, as he lit the expensive
black cigar his father offered him, Esteban looked squarely
across the big oak desk at the ramrod-straight old man
sitting behind it.

''We do have to talk, Papa, you're right about that,'' he
said as he released the fragrant smoke in clean, airy puffs.
''Before you begin with your plans, how about listening to
mine? I've had a long, boring ship's passage across the
Atlantic and up the coast to think about it.''

"And, of course, all your uncle Frank's advice flowing in letters across the Atlantic to you for these past three years," his father interrupted dryly.

"I don't deny he made me an offer before I left for Europe. A damn good one. I told him I needed time to sort out my own problems and thoughts after the war. Besides, anti-Mexican tensions were running too high among Americans in California just then. But now I want to learn what he can teach me. If I can work in the coastal shipping trade, I can forge a link between our products here in Sonora and rich, new markets in California."

Don Alfredo snorted with obvious disgust, but Esteban continued. "You know there's been a gold rush—even Sonora isn't that isolated! People from all across the world are flocking to California, many of them across our own state. Some of them become very rich, but even those who don't strike gold still must work and buy essentials—food, clothing, lumber and other building materials, and livestock. The needs of a burgeoning population can't be imagined unless you've been there and seen it."

"And I imagine Frank has seen it and reported this to you?"

"I saw the beginning of it myself when I was there in 1849 for my farewell visit. Papa, I'm an experienced traveler, I speak three languages fluently and can learn any others I'd need, and I know ships and I know livestock, especially horses. I want to see what I can do under Uncle Frank's guidance."

"So, you no more than set foot here and you're ready to take off again, chasing all over those accursed United States—good Mexican land they stole from us at sword's point! What about your obligations here? Your brother is not well. He can scarcely handle the mines. Who is to take over the ranch when I'm gone? Esteban, you are twenty-four years old. It's time—"

"Papa, you're barely fifty-one and strong as a jaguar. You'll live another thirty or forty years. So, there is plenty of time to worry about your ranch. Besides, I hardly think

Miguel would appreciate your consigning him to the ranks of the retired.''

"That brings up another matter—grandchildren.''

Esteban slumped back in the chair. "Inez and Miguel have been married only two years. You and Mama took that long to produce my elder brother. The least you could do is have the good grace to allow him the same courtesy.''

Don Alfredo stood up and leaned belligerently over the desk. "No more of your foreign-learned impertinence, young man! Inez is from a good family, but it is likely she is barren. The doctors even confirm it!'' He threw up his hand in disgust and walked around the desk. "You are old enough to be married and taking on your share of family responsibilities. The Montoyas are coming for a fiesta tomorrow night, in your honor,'' he added when Esteban opened his mouth to protest. "You have not seen Elena since she was a child. She's a very beautiful young woman now, of the best family, our oldest friends. Also, she has four brothers. Need I remind you what that implies?''

Esteban's eyes took on an amused glint. "I hardly think the lovely Elena would be flattered to hear herself referred to as a brood mare likely to bear prolific numbers of male children!''

"Can nothing be serious to you!'' The older man's voice rose dangerously. Then, seeing the cigar clenched between his son's teeth and the stubborn set of his jaw, he decided on another tack. "God in heaven, Esteban, I implore you, at least be civil tomorrow to Elena and her parents. There has been an informal understanding between us about your betrothal since you and Elena were children. Look at the girl, talk to her. She's a beauty. You must think of marriage someday. Your days of being a playboy are over, and you could do far worse than a Montoya! Besides, your mama has gone to much trouble for this fiesta. You must not hurt her.''

Esteban rose and ground out the cigar in a crystal ashtray on the desk. Then he set his brandy snifter on the side table and turned to his father. "I don't ever want to hurt Mama or you. I will be a gracious 'guest of honor' tomorrow and dance with Elena dutifully. Just don't force anything. I haven't even seen the girl or talked to her in three years."

Esteban came onto the balcony that ringed the courtyard, open on the west side to catch the cool breezes. He leaned on the balustrade and watched the scene below as it filled with the cast of characters for the night. The central courtyard was hung with brilliant lanterns. Candles winked their golden lights across the table that dotted the sides of the patio, making a pattern on the white linen tablecloths set among the small, flowering trees that grew against the walls of the house. Musicians were tuning up their instruments, and the guests, all resplendent in formal evening clothes, were filtering in. Those who lived close enough came already dressed for the occasion. Those who lived more than an afternoon's journey away hurried inside to change. All planned to stay the night, dancing till dawn. Then all the guests would sleep late, eat a huge repast, and start on their way home.

Esteban caught sight of Elena Montoya, and her parents, Don Diego and Doña Maria. They hadn't changed at all, but their daughter—Esteban was taken aback. Elena was a classic Castilian beauty with thick black hair piled high on her petite head. Her ebony eyes and creamy skin were a startling contrast, and her demure white dress trimmed with red embroidery did little to hide the lush figure that had been formless baby-fat three years earlier. *If she leans forward, that dress won't hold her,* he thought, chuckling to himself as he took advantage of his view from the heights. Then he slowly descended the stairs on the east wall of the hacienda, indolently aware that all eyes turned to observe the guest of honor.

Elena had been watching him also. *God, he is even more splendid than I remembered.* Elena's mother and father hugged the young man they fondly hoped would be their son-in-law, while Elena coyly watched, biding her time. When Esteban turned, he took Elena's hand, kissing it gallantly before raising his golden eyes to gaze deeply into her dark ones. Her pale skin flushed pink and she looked down, batting her thick lashes as she had been practicing on all the boys of the neighborhood. Esteban was no boy and her girlish actions did not enthrall him. However, as he assessed her physical charms, he found them more than acceptable.

"When last I saw you, Elena, you were a child. Now the child is a beautiful young woman."

"I find you little changed in three years, Esteban, but that is also for the better," she said.

Estaban could see that her boldness shocked her, but he only chuckled and asked, "Would you do me the honor of dancing with me?"

The musicians had just begun to play a soft, slow, formal piece, suited for the opening of the night. Under her parents watchful yet benevolent eyes, Esteban guided Elena onto the patio to begin the dancing. They made a striking couple, he tall, lean, and dark, she tiny, voluptuous, and flushed with triumph.

"How is it to be home after so long in cold, foreign countries, Esteban?" She looked up into his face as they danced.

"Europe is not so very cold as my countrymen think, although I admit the sea air when we landed in Mazatlán was wonderful."

"Ah, the farthest I have ever traveled in the world is to Mazatlán. It is so beautiful I'm not sure I'll ever want to go elsewhere—of course, except for Mexico City," she added in a burst of enthusiasm.

Realizing she was only sixteen and had led a sheltered life, Esteban smiled tolerantly. "Mexico City is indeed beautiful. I'm sure someday you'll see it."

She made a small pout. "Only if I take my dueña along with me, I fear. I am never left alone a minute. Do you think you could take me from under her hawk's eyes for a little while?"

Esteban threw back his head and laughed at her chafing under societal restrictions and at her apparent naîveté.

When the dance ended, they made their formal bows

and he escorted her toward the tables, which were heavily laden with food and beverages. As they chatted, her vapid provincialness became increasingly evident to him, as did her conventional flirtatiousness. *She wants this match just as my parents and her parents do*, he thought almost grimly.

Her beauty and fresh, unpracticed air, which had at first attracted him, became stale as the evening wore on. It was all a choreographed scene, the watchful eye of the dueña, the beaming mothers, the young girl's downcast eyes and fluttering movements—all prearranged. He was becoming cynical. What else did he want? The brilliant salon conversation of the educated women in France? The high-minded debating skills of aristocratic English bluestockings? Certainly he must marry in his class, and Elena was undeniably beautiful and appropriate for his position. He loved his mother and could hope that, with age and the experience of raising a family, Elena might mature into a woman of his mother's warmth and common sense. What made him so skeptical? Did he fear that a woman, even with his mother's qualities, would bore him to distraction?

God, I have been abroad too long. I need time. I'm just not ready for marriage and neither is Elena. She's only sixteen. That's too young, even for a woman. He would have to make his father understand.

That was easier hoped for than achieved. The next day all the guests left, including the triumphant Montoyas, sure of their quarry when Esteban and Elena talked together by the courtyard fountain. Later, in Don Alfredo's study, Esteban informed his father of his feelings about marriage at this time. The explosion was furious.

"Have you no sense of honor? No pride in the Santandar name? We have pledged you and Elena since childhood, Don Diego and I. It is agreed, as is always the custom. You, with your foreign ways and ideas, cannot go against your birthright! You owe this to your mother and me. This ranch will be yours—your children's, if you ever sire any legitimate ones! You must see to your duty!"

With his father's obsidian eyes flashing at him, Esteban

struggled to rein in his own volatile temper. *One of us must keep his head. I can't let this end as it did three years ago. I'm not a confused boy anymore,* he thought desperately.

Taking a long breath, he spoke calmly to his father. ''I am not turning my back on responsibility to the Santandar name. I will marry and give the estate its heir, Papa. But I just arrived home and I want to reacquaint myself with the ranch, my friends, and look at the business prospects we spoke of. I need time to get my bearings. Elena is just sixteen. She's rich and beautiful. Surely her parents can't worry about marrying her off quickly before suitors run out! She can wait. I must wait. I'll learn the ranch operation and visit Miguel and see the mines. I want to go to see Uncle Frank and Aunt Ursula and discuss the horse breeding and sales with him—just a brief stay and then I'll come back to Sonora and work here. Isn't that a good beginning for us?'' Earnestly he looked at his father, who had been pacing back and forth across the thick woven rug in front of the huge study windows.

The old man sighed and looked at his son, recognizing the same iron will he himself possessed. *He has his mother's eyes, but in stubbornness he is my son,* he thought, realizing that Esteban was no longer the war-weary, defiant boy who had left him in anger three years ago. He was a man now, with plans of his own. The old man could compromise, and with luck eventually he would get his younger son to marry and take over the ranch; or he could force the issue and drive him away forever. *Frank Mulcahey, you haven't won the war, just a skirmish,* he thought and shook his head in agreement as he clasped Esteban's hand.

For Esteban, the trip to Los Angeles was tedious. After heading overland to Santa Cruz de Mayo, a tiny port town on the southern Sonora coast a day's hard ride, he caught a sailboat to Mazatlán, then booked regular passage on a steamer up the Pacific coast along the beautiful Baja California waters. When finally he reached Port Vincente, an hour's ride from his uncle's city residence in the sleepy town of Los Angeles, Esteban was glad to be at the end of his journey. Yet, he was apprehensive about confronting his uncle with a business proposition that would involve cooperation between Frank Mulcahey and Don Alfredo. The two brothers-in-law scarcely tolerated each other, and it was fortunate they lived so far apart.

When he walked into the *sala* of their spacious hacienda just outside the city, Aunt Ursula came to greet him immediately. She was tall and thin and had the same severe features and black eyes as her brother, but her face was more delicate, softened by laughter and gentility. Gravely, after the fierce welcoming hug, she held her nephew at arm's length to inspect him. "You are a man now. Really grown. Europe was good for you."

Señora Mulcahey did not make pronouncements lightly but considered and weighed each word. For a Mexican woman, even of the upper class, she had been extraordinarily well educated, always slipping in to listen to her brother's lessons with tutors and reading his history and philosophy books, things no ordinary female would have dreamed of doing. When she met the big Irishman at Mass in the Hermosillo Cathedral, it was as if she had been waiting just for him all her spinsterish twenty years. She knew that he possessed the qualities she wanted in a husband, unlike any of the young rancheros her parents kept insiting she marry.

Now, looking at Esteban, she could see that he fit no better into the family mold than she had. *Yet, we are blood and bone Santandars,* she thought with a sigh.

Flashing his most beautiful smile, Esteban said, "You haven't needed to change a bit, even if I have. At least I'm physically well and not the pale, sickly wretch you fretted over three years ago."

"You look splendid and well you know it, you vain young man. But how do you feel? Have you worked out all the troubles with your father?"

At once his countenance gave away the answer, but he replied, "We have a compromise of sorts. When I arrived home I spent a few months at the ranch checking its

operation and visiting Miguel and Inez in Hermosillo.
Papa and I agreed my marrying Elena Montoya could wait
if I settled down to business. I'm twenty-four and I know
it's time to work at something. Besides wanting to see you
and Uncle Frank, that's part of the reason I'm here.''

"How is your brother?''

Esteban's face mirrored the gravity of hers at the mention of Miguel. "He's in constant pain. I fear the injury
will never get better but only worsen with each passing
year. He drives himself hard to please Papa, as he always
did. Inez frets about him but can't get him to rest or follow
doctor's orders. I—I'm almost afraid the war may claim
another casualty this long after it's over. God help me, I
hope I'm wrong!'' His eyes showed the terrible fear he had
felt ever since he had seen his brother two months earlier.
The thin, wasted face and cruelly limping body were
barely recognizable as those of Miguel Santandar, the bold
cavalry lieutenant.

They talked more about his father and mother, his time
in Europe, and the Montoya family and Elena. Even the
renewed rivalry with his cousin, Rodrigo, came up when
Ursula asked about "that wild Ruiz boy you and Miguel
-used to play with.'' Ruefully he related the bet won from
Rigo on the beach road. Both Esteban and Ursula were
deep in thought when Frank Mulcahey burst in the room.

His booming voice rang out across the *sala* where his
wife and nephew were sitting. "Sure and it's the wanderin'
world traveler returned from the edge of the earth! You
haven't let those Sassenach fops turn your head against a
good Irishman, have you, lad?'' Tall and beefy, with light
brown hair and bright blue eyes now twinkling in pure
delight, Frank Mulcahey could be a formidable sight on
occasion. Now, he was simply overjoyed. Esteban was
back!

The two men embraced fiercely with the thumping
enthusiasm of long camaraderie. "I see your ugly face
hasn't changed one mark on the map of Ireland,'' Esteban
said when he could get his breath after Frank's bear hug.
His uncle's hair was flecked a bit more liberally with gray

at the sides, and the laugh lines around the arresting blue eyes were deeper, but the incredible mass of energy Mulcahey radiated remained the same.

"After all that schoolin', sure and you must be ready to work for a livin'? Else you'd not be here, but bettin' on cockfights with your cousin Rodrigo in Sonora." Eagerly he looked into the cool, golden eyes and waited for a reply.

"Yes, you know my mind, it seems, even before I do. It's been a long trip, Uncle Frank, and we have a lot to talk about." And talk they did, far into the night, about the family, the political situation in Mexico, the gold rush in California, and about business, especially about business. Frank Mulcahey's holdings were vast: cattle land, a hide and tallow company, a lumber mill, several dry-goods stores, a coastal shipping line, and a Sonoran silver mine. The gold rush and its resultant influx of population had dramatically increased the Mulcahey fortune in the past four years. Yet, for Frank there was always another challenge, another new idea to experiment with, another project to undertake.

Esteban told him of the race with Rodrigo and the base of breeding stock he now had accumulated on his section of the Sonoran ranch. Several neighbors had been breeding a particularly impressive strain of palominos, large and true golden colored with pure cream manes and tails. The rate of producing the perfect color was uncommonly high—well over half the time. In the months after his homecoming, Esteban had acquired sizable numbers of the stock in addition to the stallion won easily from Rodrigo.

"It's the perfect kind of horse to sell to rich Yankee miners and other men who are successful because of the gold rush. The horses stand out—they symbolize gold. They're big and flashy. With the training my men can give them, we can sell one prime saddle horse for a fortune. I have several men from the ranch who have been with the family all their lives who can work on that end. What I want to do is learn the shipping business. How do you move livestock and other goods up and down the coast?

Where in the process could we arrange to move prime horses to American ports?''

"A rare item for the rich, those horses . . ." Frank's eyes began to dance as he rubbed his hands together, warming to his nephew's proposal. "Do you have any idea of the wealth a few men are makin' in the gold fields? And those sharp enough to take advantage of the basic needs of the mass of luckless miners? One dry-goods merchant arrived in San Francisco with almost all his stock sold before the ship docked. All he had left were canvas and rivets. It's a fortune Levi Strauss is makin' in miner's work pants! This is a mad place, lad, and an even madder time we're livin' in! Yes, tomorrow we'll be goin' to my office in town. You'll learn the ins and outs of the coast trade from Panama to Port Angeles. Of course, my steamers and small sailin' boats are no fancy transatlantic vessels with gentlemen's quarters. It's not luxury you're lookin' for, is it, lad? Or even too much of comfort, I hope!''

Esteban threw back his head and gave a raucous laugh that was uncannily like that of his uncle. Esteban Santandar could turn easily from Mexican haughtiness to Yankee earthiness. The two men balanced each other.

"No, Uncle Frank, I expect no luxury—*ahem*, havin' lived the life of impoverished student in heathen lands for these past three years, it's hardy I've become." He mimicked his uncle's brogue perfectly, much to Frank's consternation.

"You've a confounded good ear for languages." Of course, that would work to a decided advantage in many of the multilingual port cities from Central America to the Pacific Northwest. *I wonder if he knows any Chinese?* Frank mused to himself. He should have asked.

CHAPTER
4

San Francisco in 1852 had a population of fifty thousand and averaged around thirty new buildings, two murders, and one fire a day. Possibly never anywhere at one time and place in history had such colorful and divergent forces come together to create a city and a legend. In the late 1840s it had been a tiny Mexican hamlet called Yerba Buena. Then came the gold rush, beginning in 1849 and stretching through the 1850s.

San Francisco became the nucleus for much of the expansion into the California interior. It was the seaport nearest the great gold finds on the American River. It was also the stronghold of Yankee traders and the debarkation point for many would-be war heroes who were eager to conquer Mexican land for the United States. The Mexican War was a quick and profitable exercise in manifest destiny for land-hungry Americans.

As the wealth from the gold rush trickled down, along with some disillusioned individuals who didn't strike it rich, the city became a hodgepodge of many languages, cultures, and occupations. Chinese coolies and French prostitutes rubbed elbows with escaped slaves and freed blacks from the American South. Southern gentry, fallen on evil days, were forced to endure the crudities of Italian cardsharps and "pikes," the midwestern dirt farmers. German musicians and butchers competed in the same business milieu as Jewish grocers and dry-goods merchants. New England seamen, long familiar with the sleepy port of Yerba Buena, now transported many of their Yankee kinsmen, pale schoolteachers and stern Protestant ministers of the Gospel, attorneys and physicians, to California, where they hoped to strike it rich. From distant Australia came penal-colony escapees, called "ducks," who set up a dangerous underworld in the infamous area known as Sydneytown, south of Telegraph Hill. There the cultured and the crude, the fabulously wealthy and the newly impoverished, European and Yankee, Chinese and Kanaka (Hawaiian), mixed together to weave the colorful interracial tapestry that had been begun in 1776 when the Franciscans arrived and founded the fateful settlement.

Lyla Deveroux had arrived in San Francisco in 1846 along with a boatload of Mormon saints and sundry farmers, as well as individuals bent on less honorable pursuits. She fell into the last category. Born Delphina Drummond in 1803 in a slum section of New York, Lyla had changed her name, occupation, and residence often in the more than forty years before she finally washed up on the San Francisco Embarcadero.

Although she had been born to poverty, Lyla's quick intelligence had convinced her at age twenty that if she was going to be more than a broken-down hooker panhandling change at age fifty, she'd better learn to do more than what any common harlot could do. A series of wealthy, educated, older men kept her in her early years, and she learned how to dress like a New York socialite, speak several languages fluently, serve tea like a Boston society matron, and read classical literature from Plato to Shakespeare. Her establishments in New Orleans and then in San Francisco were designed to cater to the polished tastes of rich men.

Wealthy businessmen, ranchers, shipping-fleet owners—men, whatever their occupation, were still men. Lyla reasoned that if they wanted a cultivated woman in a refined atmosphere, they also wanted a beautiful woman in bed. She provided both in one. With a setting of white lace curtains, elegant crystal gas lamps, crimson damask sofas, French handpainted wallpaper, and thick Brussels carpets, Lyla's in San Francisco became a quietly passed byword for a first-class brothel. By 1852 it was located on Stockton Street in an elegant neighborhood amid rows of stately mansions owned by respectable families. Part of the paradox of San Francisco during the gold boom was that the righteous double standards of the Victorian nineteenth century could tolerate the decadence of a parlor house existing in the midst of respectability. It flourished discreetly.

When Amanda and her new champion, Jebediah Hooter, arrived at Stockton Street, the drizzle that had dampened the day had abated. In the dusk, the beauty of the houses and yards was still visible to the girl. The mansions were tall and stately, some of Georgian style, others of Dutch colonial. The lawns looked manicured. Amanda had never before seen grass clipped and weeded and marveled at its even verdancy. Hoot swung the team toward one large house, a three-story brick with lights softly beckoning from the front windows. It was set back off the street with thick hedges and dense vegetation on both sides of the wide lot, giving it an aura of seclusion. He pulled around to the servants' entrance in back and stopped.

"Ya wait here, honey, whilst I see who's about." Hoot climbed off the wagon and went to the large oak door. To Amanda, even the rear servants' entrance was a grand door. Hoot's knock was quickly answered, and he entered.

Amanda felt very alone and awed by the beauty of the surroundings, which contrasted with her own muddy, dank appearance.

She began to talk to the mules, Baker and Bitsy. "This

place sure is grand, that's no lie. Hoot didn't exaggerate one bit." The cool night air suddenly enveloped her as the last faint rays of the sun sank in the west. She shivered in her damp clothes. Hoot had told her what business was conducted in this house, and she shivered again, worrying about what might be expected of her here.

Suddenly the door opened and a shaft of bright light cut into her reverie. Amanda gasped and sat up straight, trying desperately to smooth out the skirt of her pitiful dress. Voices came nearer, and a soft, low female one said, "Hello, Amanda. I'm Lyla. Hoot's told me about you. Come in and let me get a look at you. Then you can speak for yourself." The tone was cultivated and pleasant, yet brisk and businesslike. Miss Deveroux was not one to waste time.

Clumsily, for she was stiff and cold, Amanda climbed down from the wagon and followed Lyla into the lighted back room. Once inside, Amanda could see the woman more clearly. She looked to be in her mid-thirties at first glance, but a second look convinced Amanda that she must be somewhat older. Her hair, piled high on top of her head, was a lustrous reddish brown, and her eyes were clear blue and soft. Her figure was tall, yet fine-boned, and the skin exposed across her hands and collarbone was a very pale, clear ivory. She was dressed in a low-cut gown of pale gray silk trimmed in dark blue. Obviously the house was open for customers tonight.

Lyla made an equally thorough inspection of Amanda, beginning with her bedraggled long braids, bright green eyes with thick golden lashes, and tawny skin hidden under a film of mud. She took note of the slight but blooming figure, the swell of breasts encased in the too-small, smirched muslin dress. Her final glance at Amanda's feet led the girl to quickly try to shuffle her ruined shoes under the hem of her muddy skirts. The split uppers were more off her feet than on them.

Sensing the child's embarrassment, Lyla smiled gently and motioned for Amanda to sit down. Then Lyla looked over at Hoot, who had been shuffling about while the two females took each other's measure. He had told her briefly of Amanda's past. Although Amanda had never been able to tell him the whole story, he had pieced it together from the few sad details she had confided.

"Hoot, why don't you go into the bar closet and have a drink on the house while your young friend and I chat." It was a gently phrased command, as both the old man and the girl recognized at once. He bobbed his head and vanished.

"Now," Lyla said as she seated herself directly across the small oak table, "we can talk woman to woman."

Amanda gulped and forced herself to return the steady blue gaze. "I need a job and a place to live, Miss Deveroux. Hoot said you might be able to help me. I'm strong and healthy and a good worker. I can cook, sew, do washing, and I read and write. I'm good at mathematics. I'll do any honest work you can give me." She finished, almost out of breath. Had she put too much emphasis on the word *honest*?

Lyla smiled faintly and said, "Amanda, do you know what this place is?" The question, phrased so directly, took her off guard. She nodded. Lyla went on, "Well then, you know I have lot of young women working for me. Fifteen, to be exact, not counting domestic help. You'd have to get along with them and do chores for them."

Amanda nodded. "As long as I don't have to have anything to do with the men." She looked squarely at Lyla. There, that had to be clear for openers!

The woman appraised the girl and admired such courage in one so young and forlorn. She was like a wet, fierce kitten, yet her speech was clear and grammatical, and intelligence shone behind her bright green eyes. *What's the matter, old girl,* Lyla thought to herself, *are you seeing yourself thirty years ago?*

"No, Amanda, you would have nothing to do with the men. I just want you to understand that this is a parlor house."

"Where do I fit in, then?" Amanda was still uncertain.

"I can use some extra help doing the marketing, helping the cooks, and doing morning pickup—that is, picking up the bed linens out front of each door and taking them to the cart by the side door where our Chinese laundryman collects them each day. Also, dishes, glasses, and food on trays must be cleared and brought to the kitchen. The parlors must be dusted and swept clean every afternoon. Mostly they are light chores my cooks and housekeeper can teach you. In return, you can have Sunday mornings and Thursdays off. I'll furnish you with a small room on the third floor, all your meals, and five dollars a week. Is that satisfactory?"

Amanda had never seen five dollars in her life, and the work seemed far lighter and cleaner than the filthy drudgery of the farm. She stood up with as much dignity as she could muster and said, "Miss Deveroux, your offer is handsome. I would be pleased to work here."

Lyla smiled as she rose, appraising the girl's mud-spattered appearance. "Let's get you a bath and change of clothing. Hoot told me you might be hurt, and I want our doctor to examine you."

Amanda was thrilled at the prospect of the bath and clean clothes, but a doctor, a man, examining her in that shameful place where Carver had hurt her so! She paled and began to protest.

Lyla, sensing the nature of the girl's fear, took her sternly by the arm and led her to the door. "I don't think you'll find our doctor hard to talk to. Just get into the bath and soak till you're clean and warm. One thing at a time. And I'll have some food sent up."

The room beyond the door was smaller, with darkly stained wood cabinets on each side. Amanda could see a large stock of bottles through the glass fronts. Hoot was at the far end of the room on a stool by the marble counter top, a glass of amber liquid in his hand. He gulped, coughed, and rose. Taking in Lyla's proprietary, almost sisterly air toward his Mandy, he sighed in relief. Thank God, it would be all right!

Amanda was introduced to Hetty, the housekeeper, a

tall, thin woman with a fierce scowling face and no-nonsense clothes. She had black hair pulled tightly into a small knot at the back of her head. "Come," was all she said, and before Amanda realized what was happening, she'd been ushered up two flights of polished oak stairs to a small, neatly furnished dormer room with a large window set in the tilting ceiling. A cheerful braided rug lay on the polished floor, the checked green curtains matched the bedspread, and a beautiful little brass kerosene lamp stood on the small bedside table, casting off a welcoming glow. The walls were painted white and reflected the greens and golds of the materials and brass in the room. To a farm girl who had spent over three years in a lean-to where the wind whistled through the chinks of bare logs and rain blew on her quilts in the winter nights, it was paradise.

Amanda wanted to jump on the bed and bounce up and down like a child, but she remembered her soiled clothing. She stood gazing with a rapt expression all around the small room while the bathtub and huge pots of water were brought up by a large, muscular Kanaka. Hetty oversaw his filling of the hip bath with nods of approval, testing the bathtub for temperature from time to time as he made repeated trips with more water. When the bath water met her approval, she dismissed the servant and turned to Amanda.

"Get in the tub and take a good scrub. Soap, shampoo, and body oils are in the nightstand. Towels are in the closet. I'll bring a shift and robe for you tonight, along with a dinner tray. Miss Deveroux will see you later. I'll have a breakfast tray sent up at seven o'clock in the morning. The women may sleep late, but the housekeeping staff does not." With that she turned abruptly and left.

Amanda checked the closet uncertainly and pulled out the biggest sparkling white bathtowel she'd ever seen. The nightstand also yielded a treasure trove of scented soap and an unfamiliar, wonderful lemon-smelling liquid that she assumed must be shampoo. The moisture oils gave directions for application after the bath and smelled delicately of citrus and spice. So beautiful! There was even an extra pitcher of warm water with which to rinse her hair.

She luxuriated in the bath and untangled and shampooed her hair, then rinsed and dried herself, being especially careful of the sore place between her legs. No more blood, thank God! The hot water soothed her abused flesh. She wrapped the towel around her body and sat carefully on the bed. Just when Amanda felt she might fall back on the soft covers and doze, Hetty returned and placed a covered dinner tray on the nightstand and a white linen nightrail and matching heavier robe on the bed.

"Miss Deveroux will be in to see you in a half-hour," Hetty said abruptly, and left.

Amanda quickly donned the nightclothes and then uncovered the food. It was very inviting, a thick, hearty chicken stew, slices of fragrant, crusty bread with butter, a dish of fresh blackberries with cream, and steaming hot coffee.

Just as she was finishing the coffee, Lyla knocked and glided in at Amanda's response, carrying a mirror, a hairbrush, a comb, and a pair of small white house slippers. "I think these will fit you. Let me help with your hair. It must have been hard to shampoo so much." She began to separate and untangle the gleaming golden masses of hair down Amanda's back. As she worked, she asked questions. What did Amanda like to read? Who had taught her? What did she want to be? Did she have any family back east?

Under the gentle ministrations of the older woman, Amanda relaxed and her background, dreams, and hopes spilled out in girlish enthusiasm—Saint Joseph, her papa, the lady in the carriage here in San Francisco. However, she said nothing about her mother, the trek west, or Carver. She pushed that to the darkest recesses of her mind.

When a knock on the door interrupted the conversation, Amanda's gleaming, waist-length hair was almost dry. She looked like a small golden and white statue poised in the midst of the bright green bedcovers. The door opened and a young woman with light brown hair and brown eyes came in carrying a small leather bag. She removed her gray cape, dropping it carelessly and revealing a slightly plump figure in a wilted dark wool suit. Lyla smiled. "Amanda, this is Dr. Elizabeth Denton. She will examine you while I attend to some matters downstairs." With that perfunctory introduction, she left the room.

Amanda was too surprised to do more than gape as the "doctor" sat down beside her on the bed. "Let's talk about what happened to you a little. You're not the first young woman who has been raped. Lots of others have gone through the same experience. The important thing is to get it out in the open and talk about it. Then, I'll make sure you've suffered no injury that requires treatment. After that, you must get on with your life and learn to put the past behind you. You're not guilty of anything, and nothing should hold you prisoner—no fears or shame or any bad feelings."

As she spoke, Dr. Denton took Amanda's hand. The softly delivered but genuinely impassioned speech was not new to her lips. Amanda realized that Dr. Denton had seen many girls in trouble and that she cared about them. She looked into the doctor's kindly brown eyes set in a plain face that compassion made warm and serene.

"Are you really a doctor? I—I mean, it must have been awfully hard to get them to let you in—the medical schools, that is."

Elizabeth Denton smiled and said, "Yes, it was. However, I was always strong-willed. I wasn't the first woman to be certified a physician in this country, but there are few of us, and prejudices are still very strong. People here in the West, where physicians are scarce, accept more easily. Also, women in Miss Deveroux's business who want a treatment and not a sermon have found me more sympathetic than my male colleagues." She smiled and looked at Amanda. "Now, may I examine you? I understand your feelings, but I have to see if you are injured."

Amanda could accept a woman examining her, and she liked Dr. Denton. She stood up and took off the robe, then hesitated, unsure of how to proceed. The doctor helped her stretch out on the bed and gave her a gentle but thorough examination, asking questions as she went along. When it was over, the doctor smiled and said, "You are young and strong and have sustained no severe physical injuries. The thing to worry about is how you feel about what happened. That is, that you don't blame yourself or hate all men because of what one evil one did." Leaving Amanda to ponder her words while she dressed, Dr. Denton went in search of Lyla. A few minutes later the two women returned, and Amanda was ready to tell her story.

"I don't know how I feel about men, in general, I mean. I loved my father, and I think Hoot is one of the kindest people I ever met. I know my"—she hesitated at the word *stepfather*—"my mother's husband was to blame, not me." This initial release sent her into a long monologue about the past three years' events, ending with the horror of Carver's assault and her flight from Willow Valley. Once the pent-up fears and hates were out, along with a torrent of tears, Amanda's natural strength seemed to reassert itself.

Throughout her recitation, both women sat beside her: the doctor on her left, Lyla on her right, as if the three of them were joined against the outside world and its cruelties. As Amanda stilled her sobs, Dr. Denton rose and gathered up her bag and its equipment. She turned and told Lyla, "Put her to bed and let her get a comfortable rest."

Then she took Amanda's hands in hers and said gently, "You will be fine, and I'll be around to check on your progress in a few weeks. Remember what I told you. Good night."

As the doctor left, Lyla got up and picked up the empty food tray. "I'm glad to see there's nothing wrong with your appetite. Keep it up. You need to regain your strength. If you need anything in the night, just knock on the door by the stairwell. That room belongs to Hetty's assistant, Mina. She's a lot more approachable than my chief housekeeper!"

At these words Amanda smiled. "I am so very grateful

for all you've done for me. I want to pay Dr. Denton out of my own wages. You've already done so much."

Lyla's eyes danced. "Don't worry about the doctor's fee. In my business I have frequent need of a good physician, and we have a satisfactory agreement for regular reimbursements. Just rest now. Good night, Amanda."

Lyla walked down the stairs and entered her own elegantly furnished private apartments. Dr. Denton was sitting across from the square oak file desk where Lyla kept her records. Motioning the doctor to remain seated, she sat down behind the desk.

"Is there any chance the child could be pregnant?"

Elizabeth looked at her friend and said, "I'm afraid it can't be ruled out, but it is very unlikely, given the time of the month when she was attacked. I'm leaving some medication that should help induce a good heavy flux within three to five days. It's an Indian herbal that most of my colleagues don't approve of, but then, they don't have babies forced on them by their stepfathers, either. You put this in her food for the next three days and let's see what happens. There's no use traumatizing Amanda any further by intimating the possibility of pregnancy until we are sure."

Lyla nodded and took the vial from Elizabeth. "I could use a drink. Now that you're off duty, care to join me?"

"I hate to turn down a good invitation, but I'm not off duty. Mrs. Larnatt is due anytime now and I'd better stop on my way home and see how she's doing."

"Dr. D, you are a wonder and much better than San Francisco deserves."

Elizabeth Denton laughed. "If only the rest of my patients paid me as promptly as you do, I could live without their gratitude." Then she bade Lyla good night and headed on with her rounds.

Two days after arriving at the parlor house, Amanda had a heavy and early "monthly." Both Lyla and Elizabeth were silently relieved.

Amanda loved her new job. She helped market, cook, and dust on the first floor, but except for morning pickups of trays and linens outside the doors, she saw little of the second floor. The domestic staff, of which Amanda was a part, lived on the third floor and comprised a small world in itself, presided over by the cold, efficient Hetty. Mina, her assistant, Kano, the dishwasher, Kathleen and Susie, the Irish housemaids, Sophie, the cook, Fran, her assistant, and Burton, the huge French Creole who served as bouncer, completed the staff. Burton was a dour man who spoke little English, disliked Americans, and had the nighttime responsibility of evicting any troublemakers. He was six feet four and weighed 240 pounds. His very presence assured that there was seldom any disturbance at Lyla's.

On occasion, however, a customer would create a ruckus and need to be subdued. Amanda had only been working there for a little over a month when an altercation occurred. The timid assistant housekeeper, Mina, was summoned by the prostitute Eleanor to fetch clean linens. It seemed a customer had suddenly become indisposed all over the sheets! By the time the flustered little woman arrived laden with linens, the drunk had revived and become abusive.

"Dammit, I paid fer ya, honey and when Lem Tucker pays top dollar, he gits his money's worth." His loud uncultured voice sounded grotesquely out of place at Lyla's.

Amanda tiptoed from her third floor room to see what was going on. Clad in her nightrail and robe, she perched on the top step of the back stairs. From her vantage point behind the railing, she watched the scene unfold in the open doorway of the big room below.

An expensively dressed buffoon of a man, tall and lanky, staggered about the hallway. Eleanor tried unsuccessfully to soothe his ruffled feathers. Mina, trapped in one corner of the room, clutched the sheets like a shield to her flat bosom.

Tucker brushed Eleanor aside and lurched toward the bed. "Wassa' matter. Git yer job done. I paid fer thet 'lady' 'n' I mean ta have her." As he put his soiled hands on Mina to yank her to her task, she let out a squeal of terror. When he swatted her a clumsy, glancing blow, he staggered and fell onto the bed, pulling the shrieking maid with him.

Mina was freed suddenly when a tall slim stranger plucked the hapless drunk off the bed. Esteban Santandar had been on his way out of Willa's room when he heard the melee. Following the noise and smell of the enebriated Tucker, he quickly intervened. The drunk shrugged himself free of the stranger's restraining grasp, then let out a bellow of rage and took a roundhouse swing at his antagonist. The younger man easily dodged the clumsy blow. Not wanting to soil his hands by hitting Tucker, Esteban neatly tripped him with one foot. Lem collapsed in a sticky heap on the floor, once more relapsing into blissful unconsciousness.

By that time Burton had reached the room and quickly gathered up the peace disturber, removing him with silent resignation.

"Thank you so much," Eleanor purred. She had tried to catch the eye of this mysterious, handsome foreigner downstairs, but unfortunately, she had ended up with Tucker.

Esteban flashed a dazzling smile as he walked to the door. "My pleasure, Ma'm. Good evening."

"What's your hurry? That dreadful man paid and then wasn't able to, ah, enjoy the merchandise. I'm free...." She let her voice drop to a suggestive whisper.

He cast a speculative glance from Eleanor to Mina, who was hastily stripping and remaking the bed. It wouldn't take long, but he was due back in Los Angeles and Frank's ship sailed on the early tide. "Sorry, baby. It's a tempting invitation; maybe next time I'm in town."

Amanda took in the entire exchange and throughout it her eyes never left the stranger. He was positively the most beautiful man she had ever seen! His clothes were as impeccable as his manners. He was elegantly dressed in a rich dark brown suit and snowy white shirt. After he had raised Eleanor's hand, kissed it and sauntered down the hall, Amanda still sat staring in rapture after his retreating form. His sculpted features and sunny smile were in dramatic contrast to the lumpy, drab men who populated the streets of San Francisco. This man was cultivated, graceful, charming, like a prince from some distant kingdom she had read of in her story books. It never occurred to her to question what he was doing in a place like Lyla's.

The next day, Amanda overheard that the stranger was a wealthy Mexican businessman. She treasured her first girlhood crush, and dreamed of the day he would return. Weeks flew by. Her knight appeared in her girlish dreams, rescuing her from danger, always the gallant savior, smiling and noble. Each night she dropped off to sleep, eagerly anticipating their tryst.

Her nights were free for dreaming, but her days were more than filled with new and exciting people. Gradually, as she became used to the job, Amanda got to know the prostitutes. Their shifts did not exactly coincide, but contacts were inevitable. The first one she met was Rita, a small, black-eyed girl of Spanish extraction. One morning as Amanda was gathering the linens, none had been left outside room 12, despite the late hour. Working up her courage, she knocked and held her breath. Surely all the gentlemen callers were gone from last night! After what seemed forever, a sleepy-eyed, diminutive Rita, clad in a red silk wrapper, came to the door and smiled as she lit a slim cigarillo. Amanda was taken aback. She had never seen a woman smoke before, but the other girl's contagious grin reassured her. She waved Amanda into her room, pushing a wealth of black hair back from her face.

"You must be the new waif Lyla took in. Why, you are almost as old as I am! And all you do is pick up and cook? Think of how much more fun and money you might have doing my job." As she spoke she appraised Amanda's abundance of long, golden hair held back in a simple ribbon and the slim curves that were revealed by her yellow cotton day dress. Rita quickly pulled the linens off her big double bed, separated the sheets from the satin spread, and rolled the sheets up, thrusting them at the still-dumbstruck Amanda.

"You don't want to be with men, eh, niña? Pity, but someday you learn it can be not so bad. How did you get here?"

Amanda was not sure how to respond to the accented, rapidfire questions and interjections but was quite desirous of having a female friend near her own age. Rita was friendly; it did not matter that she was a prostitute.

She smiled and said, "I'm Amanda Whittaker, and I came west with a wagon train from Saint Joseph and settled in Willow Valley. That's four or five days outside of town."

"I am Rita Valenza from Madrid. I came to California on a steamer from New York. What a cold, gray city! Lyla's Place is wonderful. Do you like it here?"

"Miss Deveroux has been kind enough to give me a job, and I do like the work. Compared to farm chores, this is easy work. And I have days off when I can go to the lending libraries, and I get to read Miss Deveroux's books, too. I want to learn all I can about the world. I even got to attend the opera last Thursday in Miss Deveroux's private box. We saw *The Magic Flute* by Mozart and I was thrilled. Do you ever go to the opera or see plays?"

Rita shrugged. "Before she would have me, she made me show off my manners and education. My papa was a banker who lost his money in bad investments. My education was a proper one for a Spanish girl of good family, but an education without a dowry is meaningless in Madrid. So, I found a protector, an Americano who took me to New York and to the opera." She finished with a pause and a smile. "Sometimes I like it, if there are fine young men who admire me and offer to buy me dinner in the best restaurants. Usually dinner means other gifts and great fun. I suppose I don't see the world as you do, Amanda."

For all her sophisticated dialogue, Rita's laugh was a girlish giggle and Amanda took to it instantly. "I think we shall be friends and I can teach you many things—about men, fun, and money. No ?'' She cocked her head saucily at that last inflection.

Amanda put up her hands in mock dismay as she laughed. "All I want is to be your friend and to learn Spanish! The rest can wait."

Now, for the first time in her young life, Amanda had another young woman for a friend. Rita was eighteen to Amanda's sixteen. They could share dreams and fears, frustrations and laughter. The two often met on Thursdays when Lyla closed down the house ("for a day of rest and recuperation," she said). They went for walks or carriage rides around the city. Amanda became more familiar with San Francisco, its beauties and drawbacks. With a natural flair for languages, she also picked up Spanish.

One day after shopping for a new gown for Rita, she and Amanda emerged from the dressmakers, where they had waited for a rainstorm to end, to find the usually muddy street a quagmire. One local wit had posted a sign on Kearney Street stating: "This street is impassable, not even jackassable." He was quite correct. Both women eyed the deepening mud in which even mules were struggling to slog along, and resigned themselves to hobbling from one piece of broken hardware to another along a precarious "bridge" through the mud until they could clear higher ground and get a hack. These improvised bridges were in reality a series of sunken pieces of flotsam and jetsom discarded or haphazardly dropped by passersby. Items such as iron cookstoves, bathtubs, and even an occasional piano were sunk in the mire, forming a semisolid passage across the swamplike streets. For all its gaslights and glitter, there were still primitive aspects to San Francisco.

Rita and Amanda had almost crossed the wide, muddy street to signal a hack, when disaster struck. Rita had persuaded a driver to stop and get down from his carriage. He assisted her into the cab and was reaching for Amanda's hand when a big wagonload of logs careened toward them.

The teamster driving the wagon lashed his mules furiously

and his inventive oaths filled the air as he struggled to slow the slide of the heavily overloaded wagon. The hack driver unchivalrously dropped Amanda's hand and leaped onto the side of his vehicle, clinging like a leech as the mules and wagon skidded by. Amanda was forced to throw herself blindly to the other side of the road or be crushed under the flailing hooves of the mules. She cleared the wagon's path with only a split second to spare.

The burly teamster continued on his way, chomping on his cigar without a backward glance. Amanda felt unladylike words begin to form on her lips, then stifled them in a strangled gasp of helpless fury. She would not sink to his level and use such language!

Sink to *what* level? She looked down at herself as she rolled over in the stinking mire. Her once pale peach muslin dress was now a mass of dark brown slime adhering to her body with some suspicious lumps clinging to it here and there. She had landed headfirst in a deep pool of unidentifiable origin, part mud, part sewage, and God only knew what else! She pushed one long strand of hair out of her face and it hit her shoulder with a resounding smack. After experimenting with moving her feet, she realized that the muck had permeated her new slippers and was oozing between her toes. Oh, misery!

On the third try to escape from the suction of the pool, she succeeded, only to find her feet flying up in the air once more as the slime won round three. Now her aching derriere told her she'd suffered injury as well as insult!

By this time the hack driver had managed to wade across the street. Standing on the edge of the abyss, he gingerly offered her a hand up! When she grasped it overeagerly, instead of freeing herself, Amanda succeeded only in toppling him in with her, sending them both sprawling in the mire. By the time they finally managed to extricate themselves and reach the safety of the hack, Amanda's restraint was fast slipping away.

On the way back to Lyla's, Rita had serious problems keeping a straight face as she viewed her friend's plight. After starting out so splendidly, the day had ended ignominiously. She paid the hack driver and turned to offer Amanda assistance into the house.

"I certainly hope you gave him no tip after the way he dropped me in the mud to escape that wagon!" Amanda shook off her friend's offer of help and walked spraddle-legged up the driveway. Weighted down with mud, her full skirts and petticoats were incredibly heavy and made walking nearly impossible.

"It was not his fault, Amanda. And he did try to pull you out, poor man." Rita grimaced to avoid a bubble of laughter, recalling the picture of the skinny hackie sprawled on top of the shrieking, choking girl. "You will feel much better after a bath."

"A bath! After this I'll have to wash in the bay, and I'll probably stop up the channel with all this mud. Oooh! Just let me get to my room and change before anyone sees me. It's almost dark and customers will be arriving."

Rita smiled. "And of course, chiquita, you must do your famous disappearing act before you are seen, dirty or clean." Trying to take her friend's mind off her misery, Rita asked, "Has there never been a man in that big house whom you fancied, Amanda?"

Amanda considered a moment and slowed her awkward stride, then shook her head, not wanting to share her dreams.

Rita braved the front entrance despite the late hour, but the mud-encrusted Amanda was taking no chances. Tortuously she slogged toward the kitchen door.

After requesting bath water from the bug-eyed Kano, who gaped after her in amazement, Amanda limped to the back stairs. She reached the second floor, then, hearing Helen Staffer's lilting soprano voice, she lowered her mud-covered head and made a desperate lunge for the next flight of steps and the safety of her third-floor sanctuary.

Just as she whirled around the corner, eager to place a foot on the first riser, she connected with something very solid. *Smack!* It was a man's chest, a tall man, judging by the location of the buttons on his cream linen vest. Now his entire pastel suit was liberally imprinted with the mud from Amanda's person. And to her horror, Amanda recognized him as the Mexican who had rescued Mina from the drunken Lem Tucker.

Two strong hands reached out to steady her as she reeled backward, but not before she collided with the woman who was standing beside him. Helen Staffer, Lyla's senior lady of the evening, let out a furious shriek as Amanda's muck-covered hand inadvertently smeared across her shoulder and down the side of her blue silk skirts.

"You idiotic child! Make your mudpies outside and stay the hell away from me or I'll wring your scrawny little neck!"

The man let out a deep resonant laugh in response to the picture the three of them presented. The unrecognizable wreckage of what he perceived to be a girl raised its head like the Loch Ness Monster, eyes flying wide in the brown face, the little mouth opening in a sudden O of horror. The prince of her dreams now stood before her, indelicately marked with her unique stamp!

Before he could say a word or Amanda could register further humiliation, Helen took matters into her own hands, striking the girl a sharp blow to her face.

Great masses of slimy hair slogged forward and wrapped around the girl's face and neck. Goaded beyond control into a blind fury, Amanda reached two grimy sets of fingers out in claws to rip Helen's artfully piled hairdo.

Helen was cruel and sneaky, always unpopular with the domestic help as well as the other prostitutes. All Amanda's suppressed fury at the teamster and cabbie exploded. "You nasty bitch! I'll make a mudpie out of you! Damn you—"

Again that deep rumbling laughter came from the stranger as he stepped in to separate the two clawing, thrashing females before any real damage was done. At least he suspected the young one was female. Of Helen, he had no doubt. He pulled her back and stilled her wildly gyrating arms by embracing her from behind while he murmured suggestively, "Let the kid go, Helen. We'll send for some hot water. Then we can have a nice, long, luxurious bath. What better excuse for me to scrub that delectable little . . .'' His voice faded as he pressed his lips directly against her ear and whispered.

Amanda stood frozen in consternation and humiliation.

Helen's eyes lit up and she dismissed the girl with one passing remark: "Just so my ruined gown comes out of her pay, darling." She turned in his embrace and gave him a fulsome kiss, then began to swish seductively down the hall toward her room, with him following.

They gave Amanda no further consideration, but she gave them plenty. She would never forgive Helen, the vicious harlot. And as for him! Oh, he was just like all the other customers here, a lewd, lecherous—man!

As he closed the door to Helen's room, Amanda heard him ask, "Where did that filthy urchin come from? Off a garbage scow?"

The filthy urchin fled up the stairs to the third floor and barricaded herself in her room. Too muddy and miserable to touch the bed, she threw herself in a fit of self-pity on the braided rug and sobbed unconsolably until a soft tap brought her head up.

"C-come in," she said with a hiccup.

Lyla stood in the doorway and took in the sight of her young charge, a smile tugging at the corner of her elegant mouth. "Well, Rita said you had had a 'slight accident,' but I think she understated the situation just a bit. No matter, bath water is on its way up." Gently she helped Amanda shed her rapidly stiffening clothes.

"Best get out of these while you still can," she said dryly, peeling the pantalets from Amanda's legs. "Once they set, you'll wear them until the spring thaw." She chuckled; then, sensing the girl's distress, she said consolingly, "It's not the end of the world, Amanda; I'll buy you a new dress and shoes. There's no harm done that a good bath can't fix."

"Oh yes there is," Amanda wailed. "Lyla, you'd have been proud of me. I didn't swear or yell at all when that beast nearly ran over me or when the cabbie dropped me in the mud."

"I'm sure I would have," Lyla replied gravely, rubbing

the chilled girl with a towel, trying to scrape off some of the mud.

"But don't you see? When Helen slapped me, I just went berserk. I cussed her something awful and ripped her hairdo."

Lyla smiled archly. "I rather imagine Helen could use a good smack now and then, not to mention a sound cussing out. I won't let her retaliate, if that's what's worrying you."

Amanda shook her head as Lyla toweled it free of mud. "No. It isn't really her, it's *him*. He was there and saw me act like a hoyden!"

"Him?" Lyla raised one faultlessly plucked eyebrow in query. "Who is this 'him'?"

"I—I don't know his name." Amanda flushed furiously. "He was with Helen, and I got mud all over his beautiful suit. He laughed and called me a filthy urchin! Oh, he's just like all the rest!"

The woe in her voice touched and surprised Lyla. So, her fearful young charge had finally found a man to beguile her.

"Why is it, dear, that I suspect you've seen the fellow before tonight?"

Amanda lowered her head as if silently pleading guilty to some heinous crime. "He was here the night Eleanor had that drunken man in her room. He rescued her and Mina."

"Ah, yes, that young Mexican fellow. Well, child, no one will ever fault your taste in men."

Indignantly Amanda protested, "He's not 'my taste' anymore, I can tell you!" She was still torn, unsure whether his behavior or her own mortified her more. "Well, I'll never see him again. That is for certain."

"Maybe so, maybe not," was Lyla's cryptic reply.

Although she did not tell Amanda, Lyla was much relieved to see the girl interested in a man. Let her suffer with a schoolgirl crush now. Perhaps, in time, the ugly shadow of Carver Cain would recede. This was a hopeful beginning.

The months passed and the handsome Mexican stranger did not return. As her activities and education accelerated, Amanda had less and less time to consider him. By year's end, she thought of him only as a vague, bittersweet memory placed lovingly away with the jump ropes and dolls of her childhood.

Lyla became increasingly taken with the ambition and intelligence of her charge. Her systematic project of polishing and educating a shy, awkward girl to become a confident, beautiful woman was netting impressive results. Between reading, attending the opera and theater, and becoming acquainted with the lives of the women who worked in the house, Amanda was getting a full if highly unorthodox education. She still shied away from much contact with men after living there for over a year, but Lyla never intended to have the girl join her professional staff. Yet, with all her dreams of being a lady, how could Amanda graduate from a bordello to a respectable marriage? Indeed, marriage was the only answer for a woman desiring a secure life in the male-dominated world of the nineteenth century.

Given the shortage of women of any sort in the West, it was certainly not unheard of for even the lowest-class street woman to marry respectably. Occasionally a wealthy and susceptible miner would fall prey to a smooth and clever "soiled dove." More than one San Francisco society matron had a questionable liaison or two somewhere in her past, and in the open and boistrous society of gold rush California, much was accepted or at least tolerated that would have rocked New York or Boston to its soul.

Lyla's plans for Amanda seemed to be working out rather well by the end of her first year at the parlor house. Not only was Amanda the polished, graceful, educated lady she desired to be, she appeared unafraid of the shadows that loomed upon her from Willow Valley. *Indeed*, Lyla mused one day, *I guess I found the daughter I thought I'd never have after . . .*

Amanda came flying into the room to interrupt Lyla's reverie. "Lyla, I just heard Lola Montez is coming to town! Do you think I could go see her? I'll get all my chores done and the books up-to-date.''

Actually, over the past year, as Lyla's affection grew, she had gradually cut Amanda's menial chores, substituting such things as keeping books and helping with selections at the dressmaker for the women. Except for her innate love of cooking, Amanda was not expected or asked even to go into the kitchen anymore. She did so, and picked up linens, only to have an occasional chance to visit with Kano, Sophie, and a few of the women who worked on the second floor.

"So, you want to see the famous spider dance of Lola Montez?" Lyla laughed heartily. "I knew Lola Montez back in New Orleans. Her talent was nil then and hasn't improved since. But if you think it would be fun, you can go—properly escorted by Dan Wagoner or Ray Wall."

Amanda made a mock grimace as she thought of the two available and adoring young men who often took her for carriage rides and escorted her to the theater. They were both homely, harmless, and really quite nice, if boring. But to see Lola Montez! Her young heart sang!

PART 2

NIGHTMARE

CHAPTER
5

Ray Wall escorted Amanda to the music hall. Both of them were thrilled by the huge, raucous audience anticipating the dramatic entrance of Lola Montez with artificial spiders flying from the whirling layers of her Spanish dress. The dress and dance were no more Spanish than the woman, as Rita had scornfully told Amanda, but it did not really matter.

Just as the curtain rose, Amanda heard a commotion at the back of the hall. Looking behind her she saw Burton, his massive bulk dwarfing all the seated and standing patrons as he quickly pushed by them, searching for her. Something in the pit of her stomach contracted as she rose and moved toward him. Something must be wrong at the house. Lyla!

Earlier that evening Lyla had not eaten supper with Amanda as was her usual habit. Every Thursday night when the house was closed for business, she would share a quiet meal in her apartment with Amanda and an occasional guest, sometimes Dr. Denton, sometimes one of the young men who escorted Amanda. However, on this particular night Lyla had sent a note to Amanda, saying that she had a headache and was retiring early and that Amanda should "enjoy the talents of Miss Montez and have fun with Ray." Because she was so excited by the night's festivities, Amanda had set aside her misgivings, even though Lyla had been rather tired and subdued for several days.

One look at Burton's dour Gallic face confirmed Amanda's worst suspicions. She was out of her seat before Ray had time to take her arm.

"It's Lyla, I know it. Is she ill?"

Burton's terse nod was confirmation enough to send Amanda running toward the exit and the waiting carriage. The ride back to the house seemed to take hours. Burton broke his habit of answering questions with monosyllables, and trying to reassure the frantic girl, he told her what he knew.

When the women had departed for their night off and most of the household staff were retiring after the dinner clean-up, Mina had found her employer unconscious on the floor of her office. The noise of breaking glass from a decanter had brought the assistant housekeeper in to inquire. Luckily, Lyla had knocked it off the desk as she passed out, otherwise no one would have found her until the end of the night.

Mina had called Hetty, who had sent Kano for Dr. Denton, and then had gotten Burton. When he had come to move Lyla to her bed, she had still been unconscious. As Hetty was undressing her and applying cold compresses and smelling salts, Lyla had regained consciousness several times and asked for Amanda. That was why Burton had come for her.

As soon as the carriage pulled up by the front walk, Amanda leaped out and dashed up to Lyla's bedroom. Elizabeth Denton, clad in her ever-practical dark serge suit, was taking Lyla's pulse. She looked up and silently gestured for Amanda to sit next to the bed as she continued her examination. Lyla looked as pale as the ivory silk curtains that covered the big bay window across the room. Her complexion looked as dry as antique lace and her breathing was light, fast, and erratic. The doctor rose and placed the covers back on her unconscious patient. Silently the two women moved into the room adjacent to Lyla's bedroom and sat down together.

Holding Amanda's hand, Elizabeth began, "Lyla has suffered a paralyzing stroke. How much damage has been done is hard to tell this soon. I'll have to watch her progress over the next days and weeks. Sometimes patients recover completely, with enough rest and careful exercise. But sometimes they stay in a comatose state until death, or regain only partial speech and use of their arms or legs or both. I just don't know yet. There is so much we don't know about the causes of these blockages of blood flow in the body, especially as it pertains to brain function."

Amanda struggled to digest this and to quell the hysterics she felt rising within her. She took a deep breath and asked the doctor, "How long until you have some idea if she'll recover?" She could not bring herself to consider the other painful possibility.

"It will take at least forty-eight hours to see if more strokes occur. If not, the chances for stabilizing her condition will improve. She might regain some speech and ramble while semiconscious. Amanda, you are the daughter she never had. She needs you now as she has never needed anyone. Don't condemn her or be repelled by her past." She assessed the girl with her level gaze and seemed reassured by Amanda's reaction.

"Never, never would I turn away from her! She saved me when my own mother deserted me and left me to Carver Cain. Lyla would never have been so weak, never have let life beat her or given up. She's a fighter and so am I. I won't let her die!"

Elizabeth nodded. "You have to be prepared for the worst, however. She might just slip away from us."

Amanda got up and walked to the bedroom door. "What can I do to take care of her? Show me."

*   *   *

The whole staff rallied in response to Lyla's illness. Even the irresponsible, flighty housemaids, Susie and Kathleen, worked overtime, and the house bustled with calm if strained efficiency. The women kept their usual hours for customers and the music played in the front parlor as if all were well.

Lyla had regained consciousness the morning following her seizure, but could not speak or move. Amanda worked tirelessly with Lyla, massaging her atrophied muscles, changing her bedclothes and linens, and trying to get her to talk. Only her eyes showed that she had comprehension of what went on around her. Amanda's days were spent in constant efforts to stimulate Lyla's mind and keep her from giving up. Dr. Denton came daily and attempted some speech therapy, which she taught Amanda. Both women talked to Lyla as if she could answer and was in full control of her intellect. The work and routine comforted Amanda, and as Lyla gained strength, everyone was hopeful of a full recovery.

Perhaps not everyone, as Amanda discovered one morning three weeks later when she entered Lyla's apartment and found Hetty sitting at Lyla's desk going through the books. By this time Hetty's stern countenance no longer held terror for Amanda, who immediately demanded, "What do you think you are doing? *I* handle Miss Deveroux's bookkeeping."

Hetty sat back in the cushioned chair and surveyed the indignant girl who looked like a glowing wraith with the morning sunlight reflected across her long, golden hair. "Helen and I have been talking and have made some decisions, Miss Prim and Pure."

Amanda stiffened at Hetty's tone and her reference to Helen Staffer. After more than a year of living under the same roof Amanda continued to feel uneasy around Helen. Rita said she was cold as ice and used everyone. She kept to herself and made no friends, but she had worked for Lyla since the place had opened, and her seniority gave her a place of respect. Despite the fact that she was in her late thirties, she was one of the best with the men.

Amanda was suddenly nervous and said, "What should you and Helen have to do with Miss Deveroux's business? We're making money and everyone will be paid as usual."

"Not so fast, missy. You think you and that female doctor can just run the show neat as you please from here on out. Well, I've got news for you. You can't. Lyla is incompetent and her property has to go to next of kin for proper management." She added in righteous afterthought, "Until she regains her health, of course."

Amanda interrupted, "What do you mean 'next of kin'? Elizabeth Denton and I are the people nearest to her in the world. Who can better take care of her?"

Hetty smirked and shoved several papers across the desk. "I was just getting these out of the records so I could take them to a lawyer. You will see it's all legal as you please. Although she didn't much like me or feel like family to me, I am Lyla's nearest living relative. That's why she gave me charge of the housekeeping all these years, and long, hard ones I've had to work, too. Now it's my turn to be lady of the manor, and Helen will run the girls for me. She'll talk to you and settle up."

Amanda looked at the papers. One was a baptismal record for Delphina Drummond; another allowed Delphina Drummond legally to change her name to Lyla Deveroux.

"I don't see how this makes you Miss Deveroux's relative," Amanda declared.

Hetty pulled a third sheet from the stack of papers. "Read this."

It was a marriage certificate for Walton Waite to Hester Drummond. So Hetty Waite was Hester Drummond Waite. "But just because you had the same last name . . ." Amanda began.

Hetty pointed to the space for the witnesses' signatures. "'Delphina Drummond, cousin'" she read, a hint of triumph in her cold voice.

It did seem on the surface that Hetty might be Lyla's nearest kin. A letter dated May 8, 1847, from Lyla to

"Cousin Hetty" granted her request for passage money to travel from New York to San Francisco after the death of her husband. That was the same time Helen Staffer had applied for the other kind of job in Lyla's place. Hetty had had plenty of time to get to see just how deep her loyalty to Lyla ran. Both women had indeed worked for Lyla long and hard, Amanda sadly concluded. But where did that leave Lyla if they did not really care for her? *And,* a small voice niggled, *where does this leave* you *if they take over?*

Amanda handed the papers back to Hetty and said, "Why did you wait for three weeks to spring this on me? What are you going to do?"

Hetty took the sheaf of documents and put them in a folder. Then she walked in her brisk, stiff way around the desk and stopped in front of Amanda. "I was just waiting to see how bad she is before I went off and tried to shake things up. Now it's clear she won't recover for a long time, if ever, and somebody's got to take a hand. It's my right and duty. I'll take these to Attorney Powers and he can see it's all legal."

As Amanda stood, stunned, a solution hit her in a flash. If Lyla took Hetty in just because she was kin and never much cared for her, as the letter implied, wouldn't she have left a will specifying who would be in charge of the house and business? Lyla was a good businesswoman, too good to leave it to chance that Hetty could take over. *I'll get Dr. Denton. She'll know what to do. Maybe Lyla talked to her about a will or a lawyer who would have the power to stop Hetty.* Amanda fled the study, calling Burton to fetch the doctor.

That evening Elizabeth and Amanda tore the office apart, searching to no avail. "I know she made a will," Elizabeth told Amanda, "but Lyla is so superstitious that she wouldn't give it to the lawyer—she said she might as well climb into her coffin and have done with it. She had it drawn up only a few months after you came to live with her. She said everyone she loved would be provided for. I thought she meant you in particular and didn't ask for details. How could I have been so careless as not to ask her *where* she put it?" Elizabeth chastized herself.

Amanda put her arm around the doctor's shoulders and said, "No one even knew Hetty was related. We all assumed Lyla had no family. No one could have foreseen this. It's not your fault. Anyway, we were all so busy just taking care of her that we couldn't take time to think of legal matters."

Ruefully, Elizabeth smiled at Amanda. "I rather think Hetty thought of it the very night she sent for you and me. I'd bet a cure for cholera that she was in here and found the will that night and destroyed it!" Her usually soft brown eyes flashed as she surveyed the office. "All Lyla's other important records are here. I'm sure she left a will. Her worst mistake was trusting that odious cousin of hers."

Amanda ventured, "I don't think she exactly trusted Hetty, she just underestimated her. It's easy to forget her. She's so efficient she just sort of fades into the background. I imagine Lyla never dreamed Hetty could scheme this way. And I'll bet Helen Staffer put her up to it! Rita told me that Helen had big plans to run the house when Lyla retired. We laughed about it then, but I'll bet she was just waiting her chance to use Hetty. Helen used to work in the same section of New Orleans as Lyla, but not in as good a house. That's how she came to know Lyla. When she ended up in San Francisco, she heard of Lyla's Place and asked her for a job. I bet she found out about Hetty's being kin that long ago and the two of them have just been biding their time."

Elizabeth sighed. "It does make sense and, if true, the will is surely gone and we have no legal recourse. In any court, without a valid will to the contrary, Hetty would be in control. If we accuse her, she'll lie. I guess the next move is up to those two. Perhaps they will just run the place as before and care for Lyla. There is a slight chance she might recover enough to put things right. We'll just have to wait and see—and guard her carefully!"

Amanda looked up suddenly, her throat constricted with fear as she gasped, "You don't think they'd murder her!"

"People who destroy wills are capable of anything."

Amanda agreed with the doctor's assessment and said sadly, "We'll just have to wait it out and safeguard her. Tomorrow I'll talk to Helen and see what changes she wants to make in the operation of the house. Let's just hope she'll keep everyone on so we can protect Lyla. Hetty said she'd leave Helen in charge. She's worked enough!" Amanda's ire rose as she recalled the earlier conversation with Hetty. Behind the anger was fear, for Amanda realized that, unlike the doctor and the other household help, her position near Lyla was in danger. She was like a daughter, yet she was not kin and had no claim. A useless waif taken in and educated to "lord it over her betters," as Hetty had said. And next morning she would learn what her fate would be. *I won't leave Lyla so they can hurt her. They won't force me out*, she thought desperately.

Despite her firm resolve, Amanda was exhausted and frightened as she bade Dr. Denton good night at Lyla's door after they checked on their charge. Dr. Denton and Amanda arranged for Kano or Mina or one of the maids to be with Lyla at all times when they were not. None of them liked Hetty or Helen. Elizabeth trusted the presence of a witness would prevent an "accident" happening to the helpless woman in the bedroom! With leaden feet, Amanda climbed to her third floor room for a restless night.

Amanda awoke with a feeling of vague dread as the cold, gray light filtered into her room like an evil shroud. At first she was unable to focus on why she felt so terrible, until the previous day's events came back in a rush as she climbed out of bed. She sat on the bedside, mulling over her coming confrontation with Helen Staffer as she rubbed sleep from her eyes. After a scant few hours rest she was bone tired and still groggy.

Hardly a way to meet someone as formidable as Staffer,

she mused wryly. Shaking off the gloomy morning's leth-
argy, Amanda rose and began her toilet.

As she walked down the hall of the second floor it
seemed longer than ever before. The doors seemed bigger
and more ornate, and even the thick, ruby plush carpet
seemed to swallow up her footsteps. *It's almost as if the
place were trying to envelope me,* she thought, then
pushed the irrational fantasy from her mind. In front of
room number one, she stopped. Helen's was the first door
at the top of the front entry steps nearest the downstairs
parlors. Amanda had never been inside Helen's room, but
knew it was larger and decorated more lavishly than the
rest of the women's rooms, a sign of her prestige and the
senior position she had enjoyed for years. A brief vision of
her in Lyla's apartment flashed before Amanda's eyes and
she fought down the urge to flee. *I must stick it out and
keep her from getting all Lyla's worked for,* she thought as
she knocked softly and then more forcefully on the oaken
door.

"Enter," a cold, clipped voice replied. Amanda did as
she was bid, closing the door behind her and staring the
imposing Helen Staffer in the eye.

Helen's narrow gray eyes lightened to an almost eerie,
whitish silver when she became angry. They were flashing
a dangerous metallic glint now, but her voice was cool and
controlled as she told Amanda to sit down in a chair next
to the small, elegant French writing desk where she sat
like a queen. She artlessly arranged her dove-gray silk
morning dress in folds, then picked up a pen from the desk
and began to play with it. Her long, slim, almost bony
fingers glinted white in the dim light feebly streaming in
the window. She wore several rings, one a square-cut
emerald and another a ruby of exceptional clarity. Amanda
was almost hypnotized by the green and red lights they
cast in the dim room.

"Well, Amanda, what are your plans?" She tilted her
elongated, elegant head, almost like a spider watching her
victim, as she awaited Amanda's reply.

"I beg your pardon?" Amanda was taken aback.

Helen's high, clear laughter sounded false; then she suddenly stopped and looked coldly at the young woman before her. "You knew perfectly well it would come to this. You can't stay here for free as Lyla's live-in nurse-maid. We have an ample staff to care for her. You never did earn your keep, and you cost Lyla a pretty penny, educating you, dressing you, and giving you all the amusements of the idle rich for the past year. Now that Hetty is owner of this house, I'm in charge. I will be until Lyla recovers . . . *if* she recovers."

At this pause, Amanda stood up and flashed a look of withering scorn at the polished shell of a woman in front of her. "I *earn* my keep and always have since Lyla Deveroux took me in. She has always treated me with the greatest kindness and I'll not desert her now to the ministrations of a couple of silly, flighty maids or the tender care of her 'dear cousin Hetty,' who'd cheerfully see her dead! And you, she took you in and gave you a job and now you sit here talking as if you can't wait for her to breathe her last! I won't leave her! She needs me to care for her and love her!"

Before Amanda could go further with her highly emotional outburst, Helen's silvery eyes flashed white. She pounced. "Fine, you want to stay and I will allow it—on one condition. Keeping books and doing marketing and morning pickup are not nearly enough to earn one good dress or a trip to the opera for you. You can stay and hold your dear Lyla's hand, if you work out. I'm no hypocrite. I earned my money in this house from the first day Lyla took me in, and I owe her nothing, do you hear me, nothing! But you do owe her, and there is only one way for you to pay your debt. . . ."

As her implication sank in, Amanda's knees turned wobbly and she grasped for the drapery at the windowseat. Weakly, fighting surging nausea, she sat down on one of the hard, blue velvet cushions. "I can't! Lyla promised Hoot that I'd never . . . she never meant for me to have anything to do with the customers. You know she kept me away from them deliberately." Her hands drew into tiny fists and she hid them in the folds of her dress. She was desperately cold and out of breath.

Helen's thin lips smiled coolly, revealing long, even teeth. She rose and walked across the midnight-blue Persian carpet to stand in front of the terrified young woman. "It's your choice. If you think you're too good to do the kind of work that supported Lyla and all the rest of the women here, so be it; but I can't afford to keep on dead weight. I never harbored a desire for any children. Neither did Hetty. Pack your things and go." She turned in dismissal and began to walk away.

"Wait! You can't just throw me out! What will Lyla think? It will upset her desperately if I'm not here. If she knew you forced me to . . . to work on this floor, that would make her furious too. You—"

"How you handle Lyla to keep her fragile health intact is up to you. I don't care. All I care about is the efficient operation of this place. You don't have to tell Lyla where or how you work. You can be with her and urge her on to health, if you perform satisfactorily for me." It was clear from the quiet, venomous humor in her voice that Helen did not for one moment believe that Lyla would ever recover.

Amanda began another tack, desperately trying to find a reasonable escape from the unthinkable. "What makes you think I can earn any money from men? I've never been with one except for once, when my stepfather raped me. I know I'd be terrible and they'd laugh at me. But I could do all the books and supervision that Hetty doesn't want to bother with. She said she was retiring. Someone has to do her work—"

Before she could finish her argument, Helen interrupted impatiently, her beringed hand flying in a gesture to take in Amanda's body. "You really are a fool if you think you'd be more use to us as a housekeeper than a harlot!"

Amanda, already shaken by her long-buried admission about Carver, winced at the last vulgar expression. Her head, already aching from her troubled night, began to pound.

Helen laughed. "I do believe you don't realize your own assets. Although I hate to admit it, my pampered darling, you are one ravishingly beautiful bitch! With that mass of fire-gold hair done properly, and lower-cut gowns to accent that elegant cleavage, you'd be a sensation. Fresh and innocent, well spoken, and actually educated, not a fake like Willa or Elaine. You, thanks to Lyla's tender tutelage, are the real article. Yes, the men would love you and pay very handsomely for your company. I can hire anyone to keep house. If you want to stay on, there is only one deal I'll make with you."

Amanda got up woodenly, letting all Helen's words sink in. Helen took her by the shoulders and walked her to the large, gilt-framed oval mirror across the large room. Two pairs of eyes, one cold gray, the other deep green, stared into its reflection.

"Look at yourself as I see you, as men will see you," Helen said mesmerizingly, gripping Amanda's shoulders. "You can make a fortune. Who knows, you might even snare a rich protector who'll hire a live-in nurse for your dear Lyla. You just have to learn to play your cards right and get over the fear that one bad experience with a man caused. Believe me," she went on almost soothingly, "the kind of men who come here are nothing like any filthy, pawing dirt farmer."

At that invocation of Carver's visage, Amanda blanched. She straightened her shoulders and shrugged free of Helen's grasp. "You leave me with no choice at all, do you, Helen? When do I begin?"

Helen made no effort to hide the triumphant glitter in her eyes as she said casually, "Oh, first we'll have to have a few lessons in, ah, deportment and charm for the customers. Then you must have a considerably more sophisticated wardrobe. We'll begin tomorrow. Spend today clearing your things out of that hideous third-floor servant's loft and bring them to room eleven."

"Room eleven is Willa's."

"Was Willa's," Helen corrected. "She quit three days ago. Found herself a gold miner with a generous streak.

He may have had good sense when it came to the gold claim, but his taste in women left much to be desired.''

Willa was a tall, rather coltish girl from Kansas, singularly unsophisticated for a place like Lyla's, yet so soft-spoken and kind that she had always been popular with the customers and most of the household. The coldly elegant Helen obviously felt herself well above Willa.

It's good she got out. Now I get to take her place. I'm glad it's Willa's room, not Helen's cold, blue palace that I'll inhabit, Amanda thought as she moved toward the door. "At least, eleven is a lucky number."

Luck was to have little to do with the following months in Amanda Whittaker's life. The first days were ones of intense activity, mind-numbing in their rush, as she was outfitted for her new profession. Helen spared no expense at the dressmaker, having Amanda clothed in clinging, silky evening gowns in a rainbow of flattering colors. The lacy see-through lingerie was frightening—Amanda trembled at trying it on, for she could visualize having to wear it in front of men. Along with a new wardrobe came lessons in how to walk down the front staircase dramatically to attract customers' attention and how to talk to the men. This was a classy parlor house; no vulgar language was tolerated. Rita taught her the proper phrases and gestures to use in discussing "business" with her customers. It was a game of innuendo and ritual.

Then, there were the cards. Amanda had never learned to play before, but Tom McVea was to be her teacher.

He was the general overseer of the entertainment room. A professional cardplayer and dealer, he amused the women and patrons with card tricks when not dealing faro or other games. There was no popular card game he did not know and none he was inexpert at playing. His biggest draws, however, were his card tricks, especially his famous "house of cards."

One afternoon when Amanda entered the parlor for her daily lesson, she was amazed to see Tom at the faro table in one corner, deep in concentration. He absently motioned

her to an adjacent chair and continued constructing an
enormous three-story house of playing cards, room by
room, each card deftly leaned against or laid upon the
others in the precarious structure. Amanda watched, holding her breath, spellbound as she awaited the inevitable
crash. After several minutes, he deftly raised his hands
above his head, as if someone were pointing a gun at his
midriff, and smiled.

"Well, this time ol' Tommy did 'er real proud." His
Alabama accent was slow and heavy and his grin infec-
tious in his seamed, dissipated face, which the casual
observer tended to underestimate. When he was sober,
Tom McVea was the best professional gambler in northern
California.

"That is amazing, Tom," Amanda ventured in a low
voice, still barely daring to breathe.

He chuckled and let out a long, whistling breath. The
"house" collapsed with a soft whooshing gust, all the
cards face down on the table. "That's the trick, ya see.
Gettin' em ta fall when ya want and all the same way.
Made, mebbe, lemme see, three thousand in dust bettin'
against a miner last week. Owns the Lodestar Mines off
America Creek. He could afford the loss. 'Sides, he rightly
enjoyed the performance. Sometimes the durn fools bet me
on how many cards'll land face up when it falls. Even
what suit or number'll come up. Nice way ta make pocket
change. A man with gold ta spend enjoys losin' it on the
most unlikely odds." His eyes were almost merry as he
scooped up the deck in one smooth motion and then spread
the cards out in a straight flow across the green felt table.

Amanda shuddered as she pondered how her own "house
of cards" had crashed about her. Her "debut" was fast
approaching, and with it her absolute dread increased. She
tried her best to be cheerful in front of Lyla, never giving
up hope for her recovery. She prayed that Lyla might at
least regain the power of speech in time to rescue her from
entering the profession, but she feared that would not
happen. As the day grew nearer and her apprenticeship
was almost spent, Amanda accepted the fact that Lyla

would be paralyzed for months yet, if she ever recovered at all, far too long a time to save her.

Rita, Helen, and the other women assured Amanda it would not be painful as it had been that first time with Carver. Yet, no one could assure her it would not be degrading and ugly. She kept that fear locked away inside herself. She did not want the other prostitutes, many of whom genuinely liked her, to be hurt by her disgust for their means of earning a living. She would lie awake alone at night in room eleven on that hated second floor, and listen to the faint noises filtering in from the adjacent rooms. The walls and floors were thick and she could actually hear very little. It was not at all like the rickety cabin where Carver and her mother had been so close and Carver so noisy. Yet, her terrified imagination magnified faint noises. It was difficult to sleep, and her dreams were filled with vague, shadowy men. Often she awoke, covers kicked off, drenched in icy perspiration, her heart hammering.

Amanda had another recurrent, nagging nightmare during the weeks of her training. What if her Mexican stranger reappeared at Lyla's? She had not seen him in over a year and had almost forgotten that painful childhood infatuation. Almost, but not quite. Sometimes she imagined she was downstairs, and he was asking to be introduced to her. Of course, he would never connect that mudstained urchin with the beautiful woman she was today, outshining even Helen. What would it feel like to go upstairs with him as Helen had? To entertain him in her room, her bed? With a cold, sad dread, Amanda was certain she did not want to know. She had enough shattered dreams already.

Helen had been almost kind with her own peculiar, aloof brand of solicitude. Gentleness did not come naturally to her. Greed did, and she was obviously expecting Amanda's rare and striking young beauty to bring her high fees from customers. When she summoned Amanda to her room a second time, and instructed her to wear the dark green velvet gown the dressmaker had delivered just days before, Amanda knew her entry into the profession was at hand.

When Amanda entered the room, Helen opened a bureau drawer and took out a small case, thrusting it into Amanda's trembling hands.

"Well, don't just stand there. Open it. They will set off the dress and your eyes perfectly. Yes, hmm, quite a debut."

Amanda gingerly opened the case and gasped. Carefully she removed an emerald pendant, huge and square cut on a gold filigree chain. Emerald earrings lay alongside it. They were for pierced ears, on simple gold posts. Helen had had Rita pierce Amanda's ears and now Amanda knew why. She winced as she recalled how one tender lobe had become infected and Dr. Denton had to be called to treat it.

The doctor was another subject that pained Amanda's waking and sleeping hours. Her outrage at the younger woman's fate knew no bounds. Indeed, Amanda had never seen the gentle, strong Elizabeth so furious as when she heard Helen announce smugly to her the new status Amanda would assume. Elizabeth threatened to take the girl out of the place and adopt her, but Amanda quickly assured the doctor that she must stay with Lyla and this was the only way.

After a long and ugly scene between the three women, it was settled to Helen's satisfaction. Dr. Denton left that day, looking as if she had been kicked and beaten. Just watching her retreat down the hall, shoulders slumped and steps dragging, had caused Amanda tremendous pain.

Now Amanda stared at the earrings, thinking of the past month's events. Helen abruptly interrupted her troubled reverie, "Tonight you should be ready to come down to greet the callers by eight. I'll send Susie up with a tray first. Then you can dress. One of the girls can help with your toilette if you need it."

As Amanda moved woodenly toward the door, jewelry in hand, Helen blazed one last warning. "If you want to stay here and not end up in one of those cribs down by the waterfront, you'll remember that I don't want any girlish hysterics or cold, stiff ice-maiden act when a man takes you upstairs. He'll pay top dollar for you and every customer here expects his money's worth."

Amanda turned, her knuckles whitening over the dark jewel case as she gripped it in anger. "I have had ample lessons in what is expected of me with the customers, and I'll perform to suit you, Helen. In fact, I'll probably make a great deal of money for the house." She threw back her head, and the show of bravado seemed to surprise Helen Staffer, who gave a look of grudging respect at Amanda's words and gesture.

With her hand on the door, Amanda made a last comment. "Oh, I expect to see the books every week. I know I should get fifty percent of my fees minus my room and board and other expenses. I kept the books here for a year and I know how much everything costs. I'll remember how many customers I have each week. Don't try to cheat me!" With that she was gone.

Once out of Helen's presence, Amanda's forced resolve carried her to room eleven at the other end of the hall. Inside she collapsed on the bed, shaking but dry-eyed. Several minutes later she collected herself. *Well, here I am, where I'll be earning my living shortly*, she thought wryly. *Rita had to face this and so did all the other women here. If they could, so can I. I survived Carver Cain. Nothing could be worse than that. At least men here have to bathe to gain admittance. Rita's always telling me that working in a good house is preferable to life on the farm. Probably she's right. But, Helen or no Helen, I'll never end up in a crib on the waterfront! And I'll never stay here, either. Someday I'll save enough money to get Lyla out, and we'll go somewhere else and live in peace.* Amanda forced to the back of her mind the thought that Lyla might not live that long.

CHAPTER
6

It was the best of all possible worlds for a man of twenty-six. Esteban had excitement, the challenges of making money, traveling to new places, manipulating people to do his bidding, and, of course, meeting women, easily had and as easily forgotten. He felt pride, not embarrassment in the fact that his fortune was self-made. The heady sense of freedom was also a good feeling. He owed his training and opportunities to Frank Mulcahey, but after several years of hard work he was financially independent of everyone, especially his father.

Of course, the emotional ties to his Mexican family could not be broken, nor did he want to break them. He wanted only breathing space. Esteban contemplated this one starry night as he sat on his patio overlooking the magnificent Sinaloa coast. He had purchased one of the loveliest houses in Mazatlán last year, when his share of profits had been especially good. It was set high on the cliffs, jutting out into the bay. He loved having his own private retreat away from his family in Sonora, as well as away from the bustle and confusion of the United States.

"Your thoughts are deep, my love. Share them?" Solange gracefully glided into the wrought-iron chair next to him on the porch. The thin gold-silk wrapper she wore outlined her flawless figure. Although she was past thirty, Madame Fabres looked younger and took great care of her clear ivory complexion and deep chestnut hair, now artfully falling down over her partially revealed breasts in a profusion of soft curls. She had just risen from bed and looked languid and disheveled, yet cool and elegant.

Madame Fabres had been born in Marseilles in less than elegant surroundings. She had married a much older, wealthy man and cultivated the finer things in life. Solange had attended the most stimulating and witty salons in Paris, exchanging ideas with the brightest lights of the day. When Monsieur Fabres passed on to his reward, she was a rich, young widow. She loved to travel and had discovered the incredible beauty of Sinaloa and its port city of Mazatlán on one of her earlier voyages.

As a student Esteban had shared an uncomplicated liaison with her in Paris. When she reencountered him more than four years later in Mazatlán, they renewed the relationship. It was easy; neither he nor she demanded more of the other than sexual enthusiasm and stimulating conversation. Almost unplanned, she became his mistress, living in the seaside villa and welcoming him home when he returned from business trips.

Strange, she mused, how the tenor of the relationship had changed. In Paris he had been a brooding university boy and she a sophisticated wife with a rich, absentee husband. She had led and he had followed. However, neither one had been romantically attached, and he was hardly the type to be heartbroken when she left Paris for Vienna in the fall of 1850. She had thought of him occasionally after that, wondering how he had turned out. He had shown great promise as a lover. Now, he had fulfilled that promise. He was also the patrón, the rich, cosmopolitan businessman, in his element here in Mazatlán.

She lived in his house, openly. Gone were the days of
trysts in her Paris apartment. Not that she needed his
money or lacked for rich male admirers in Mexico or
Europe, she reminded herself. Yet it was comfortable with
him. He had no plans for marriage, and she had no
illusions that she would ever again be a wife. She wanted
freedom and her own identity. This time with Esteban gave
her a man to enjoy, one with a complex and facile mind,
open to allow for her own opinions, with no emotional
ties. Even in France, harbinger of sexual liberalism in the
nineteenth century, such men were rare. Also, here in
Mexico, he was one of the few men who spoke fluent
French, a skill she enjoyed almost as much as making
love.

After sitting in the quiet of the tropical ocean breezes for
a few minutes, she questioned him again. He appeared
deep in thought since he had returned from Rancho Santandar
last night. "Why the pensive mood? Do you want to talk
or think alone?"

He looked up from his glass, its crystal prisms reflecting
the amber liquid against the candlelight. "I'm sorry, Solange.
I didn't mean to ignore you. Maybe I do need to talk.
Only, I don't know where to begin." He shook the glass
from side to side, watching the contents coat the crystal
interior, his eyes matching the amber depths.

She reached over and pushed a stray lock of black hair
off his brow. "Begin with your last conversation with your
father?"

He smiled up at her. "Yes, my father." He sighed,
stretching his long legs out in front of him, crossing his
bare feet at the ankles. He had on a pair of light cotton
pants, his only concession to dress since arising from their
bed. Despite the fact that they had just spent the afternoon
making love, she found his hairy chest and almost naked,
lean frame distracting. Nevertheless, she could sense his
unease and wanted him to talk it out.

"Doesn't it all begin and end with my father and my
family, my duty . . . ? We had the usual discussion—oh,
hell, argument. Each time I'm home, he pressures me

more about the Montoya alliance. I tell him Miguel and
Inez will produce the Santandar heir. Yet, each year
Miguel becomes more ill and the chances lessen. I have a
duty to my family, I know that. But, dammit, Solange, I
like my life now. The next step is to sell or factor out the
business in California. They want me in Sonora year
round. Of course," he smiled looking up at her, "I could
keep this place and you could live here as long as you
want."

"But you would marry a chaste girl, raised in the
strictest criollo tradition, and breed children to populate
the southern half of Sonora." She laughed gently and rose
to put her arms around him. "With all that time spent on
children, who'd have time for business in the United
States?"

Gruffly he laughed. "I realize I must marry a girl from a
good family, make the acceptable alliance. Elena Montoya
is really quite beautiful and . . ." he threw up his hand in a
futile gesture, "quite proper."

"And quite boring and coy, perhaps even a bit stupid?
Not a salon wit. However, love, virgins never are, alas.
Can you imagine my confronting Don Alfredo as a
daughter-in-law?"

At this he rocked with laughter. "He'd die of apoplexy
on the spot! Godless, immoral Frenchwoman! But you'd
never bat your lashes and hide behind a fan. With you,
love, I'm never bored after bed."

"Ah, yes," she took up his teasing tone, "but be
honest, Esteban, you'd want a virgin wife, mindlessly
faithful and obedient. You can keep a mistress easily, yet
you want no doubt about whose children you bestow the
Santandar name on, do you?" She shrugged one shoulder
in a Gallic gesture indicating that it was a foregone
conclusion.

"Of course I want to be sure of my own children! The
only way is to marry a girl raised like Elena. I do wish she
had an occasional idea, though—at least, beyond what
dress to wear to the next ball!" He, too, shrugged in
resignation.

"You can't have it both ways, my love. Your Elena and I exist in different worlds. Women with brains and spirit are not likely to be content to sit home while their faithless husbands philander off with any woman who takes their fancy. Indeed," she continued banteringly, "women like me are not likely to marry at all unless it's on *their* terms. Besides, you've already seen how impossible it would be with Don Alfredo as my father-in-law! I like our present arrangement better."

"So do I," he said and drew her into his arms, kissing her neck lightly. Opening her wrapper, he revealed stark white breasts to the brilliant moon. As he began small nibbling kisses down her shoulders and over her nipples, she gave a husky laugh and gasped in pleasure, running her hands up and down his hard, dark back. Slowly, in the dancing moonlight reflected off the waters below, they began to undress each other. The wrapper fell in a golden whisper at her feet as Solange pulled the tie string on his pants, working them down his slim hips. The breeze, cool and strong off the ocean, caressed their nakedness and they moved into the soft glow of candlelight beckoning them from the bedroom adjacent to the patio. Together, locked body to body, they languorously slid onto the bed. His dark frame lay side by side with her pale one. Slowly, they writhed against each other, savoring the difference in texture and scent, taking their time to let the tension build. Then he rolled onto his back, taking her on top of him. Her legs spread wide to receive him and they rode fiercely, sweating in the warm night. When she arched her body in a gasping climax, he held her hips down against him hard and pulsed into her slumping frame. Her head next to his, Solange kissed him softly.

Finally, she spoke. "I know what I must do. I'll go light a dozen candles at Saint Mary's Church for Inez and Miguel to have six sons, the first within the year. Then your simpering Elena can wait."

She could feel the rumbling chuckle through his chest while his laughter built. "Some chance, that. If I ever knew anyone less religious than I am, it's you. Another shortcoming of mine even my mother frets about." His face darkened at the thought. "She really does light candles for my soul. But no one can give another person faith, any more than a god can render Inez fertile—or give Elena a brain." He added that last as an afterthought. They both collapsed in laughter, tinged with a bit of hopelessness for the situation.

"Tomorrow I leave for Los Angeles and then go up the coast to look at some timberlands and a sawmill Frank may buy. Also, I'll scout the marekt for selling horses at the price I want. When I get back, I should make a decision about my life. I'll be twenty-seven years old—in my own eyes I'm a success, but in my parents' eyes . . . My mother wants grandchildren. I don't know. This trip will give me a chance to think."

Solange was thoughtful after she summoned the maid and instructed her to bring a light meal onto the patio and change the sheets. They ate in companionable silence. When they finished, the servant cleared the dishes and informed them that their baths were ready. After the girl left, Solange spoke. "You know, love, you are really two men."

He looked across the small patio table at her, a question in his sherry-colored eyes. "I've wondered about that myself. Was it the war and the way it turned out for me? Or the time in Europe?"

"I don't think your personality is due to anything that recent. You spent half your childhood with your Yankee uncle, living in an American culture. You want to work, to travel, to meet all kinds of people. You are like an American or a Frenchman. You want intelligence displayed in everyone you deal with. Even with the men on your ranch, the sailors, all the menials who work for you, you listen, considering their opinions. You believe in the ideals of the Revolution of 1848—or at least a part of you read Mr. Marx and thought it fascinating."

At this he snorted. "Marx is a fool, appealing but unrealistic. I couldn't run a business if I gave away my wealth, could I?"

She waved her hand in dismissal. "Yes, but you want things done more progressively, for every man to have a chance. You can compete and succeed. Isn't that what this is all about—your own land, businesses, freedom from your father—being your own man?"

He shrugged in acknowledgment as she pressed on, "Yet, the other half of you is part of this land, your family name, the tradition that traces your pure Spanish bloodline back over five hundred years. You scoff at a church you were baptized in, will marry in and be buried from, but you will go through the motions because your family demands it. You still feel you owe them loyalty. You agree with their values—at least as far as the duty to please them. You'll marry a virginal criolla even if you would wish her to have more spirit and intelligence than your class system ever permits.

"Yes, Esteban, you'll marry her, expecting her to be pure, obedient, and certainly fertile, and you'll have lots of children and send them to church with their mother. All the while you'll be bored and looking for diversions like me. Not me, for in a while I must leave, but you'll always be searching for something or someone. I don't know if you'll ever find it, or her." Realizing she had said more than she intended, she stopped abruptly and looked at him. "I perhaps go on too much, my love? I'm sorry. You must deal with your problem, not I."

He sighed, tossed the napkin onto the table, and reached to light a cigar. When he exhaled the fragrant smoke, he smiled at her and placed a slim, dark hand over her long, pale fingers and squeezed them gently. "No, you are exactly right, I fear. God help me. I still hope my brother will provide another generation of Santandars, but where does it leave me, even if he does? Even if I escape Elena? What do I want in the long run? The provincial Mexican criollo, the Yankee trader, the European college boy— they're all jumbled up inside me and I'm getting too old for all the damn confusion." He rose from the table, walked inside, then turned and faced her from the door. He flashed his whitest grin, boyish and appealing. "For now, though, I'll just coast. Who knows what can happen in a year?''

''Who knows what can happen in a year?'' That fall those words came back to haunt Esteban. The worst that could happen did. Miguel died. As Esteban stood on the cool, sunny hillside, a short ride from the main house of Rancho Santandar, he watched the shovelfuls of earth fall into the abyss, the open grave where his brother's coffin lay. Where had the years gone? He remembered Miguel and himself as boys, laughing, sitting in the classroom with their tutor, attending Christmas Mass with their mother and father. Miguel had been the quieter of the two, less brilliant, but far more disciplined than Esteban. Yet, despite all their differences in personality, they had shared a closeness in childhood and youth. On that chilly hillside, Esteban felt bereft. Where had the time with Miguel gone?

Don Alfredo supported his weeping wife. The old man looked far more than fifty-three. The Santandars had lost an infant son in his first year, when Esteban was three, then two daughters were stillborn. Now, one of their two surviving children lay buried in the hard Sonoran earth.

Esteban remembered the past six months, perhaps nearer a year, that his brother had fought the increased pain. Miguel had fallen from his horse. The fall was not a hard one. For a well man it would have meant nothing more than indignity and a few bruises. But for Miguel, his hip shattered, it was agony. Finally, blood poisoning set in and he died.

Esteban was home when it happened, helping his vaqueros with the foaling of a new colt, a perfect palomino. Life during death. Thinking on this, Esteban saw no consolation.

Miguel had not reached thirty. Esteban was now twenty-seven. There were no young Santandars. Time was running out, and as he looked around at all the mourners, Esteban knew his duty. When the sad old priest pronounced the last words, he took his mother's arm on one side while his father held her other arm and the three of them trudged slowly toward the carriage.

The Ruiz family, Doña Esperanza's relatives, could not

reach the ranch in time for the funeral. Don José, Doña
Dolores and Rodrigo were expected within a few days.

The Montoyas, Don Diego, Doña Maria, and Elena,
living next to Rancho Santandar, were present at the
burial. In the past several years, Esteban had seen as little
of Elena as possible. His visits home were usually
unannounced and he begged off as many social events as
possible, retreating to his small house on the Santandar
land to work his horses. Esteban and Elena's engagement,
it was tacitly agreed between the two fathers, was to be
postponed but not canceled.

However, Don Diego had been approached by Don José
the previous spring. The Ruiz family fortunes were in
disrepair because of the high life Don José and his son
Rodrigo loved. Don José wanted a good match for his son
to recoup the family fortune. The Montoyas were well off,
and a hefty dowry from Elena would certainly fatten the
thinning Ruiz purse. Despite the old and honored Ruiz
name, the Montoyas were resistant, most especially Elena,
who still had her hopes fixed on Esteban. Aiding her cause
was the strong friendship between her father and Don
Alfredo as well as the slightly unsavory rumors about Don
José and Rodrigo.

After nearly three years of Esteban's shuttling back and
forth from Sonora to California, however, the Montoyas
were becoming impatient and feared Don Alfredo might
never get his willful younger son to settle down. Now that
he was financially independent, it appeared even less
likely that he'd accede to his parents' wishes. Despite
Elena's tearful protests, Don Diego and Don José had
seriously discussed a dowry only a month prior to Miguel's
untimely death.

Now that Miguel was dead without an heir, the situation
had changed, and no one was more aware of this than
Elena. Her thoughts were not of Miguel, but of his
brother. Esteban could procrastinate no longer. He must
marry as soon as the mourning period was over, and Elena
wished to make it clear to all just who the young man
would marry.

Now the Montoyas and Santandars were assembled in the grief-stricken house. If she was careful, Elena would have Esteban at bay before her family left. In the last few years, Elena had grown up mentally as she had matured physically in the earlier ones. Not only was she beautiful at eighteen, but absolutely ruthless. Gone was the coy, flirtatious girl with vapid notions about true love. Elena saw Esteban as a rich, well-traveled man, independent of his family. If they married, he could take her places she'd only dreamed about, show her all the glitter of balls, horseraces, theaters—in short, all the glamour and wealth she craved. And he was still the most magnetic, handsome man she knew.

When Rodrigo had begun to court her in the past year, he had told her much about his cousin, all, he hoped, to show her Esteban's hopeless fall from grace, his crass Americanization and licentious, irreligious ways. Far from disillusioning her, Rodrigo had increased his rival's appeal to the calculating young woman. Rigo, she knew, would marry her for her dowry and then go to spend it in Mazatlán and Mexico City, leaving her alone and pregnant on the Sinoloa ranch. No, she much preferred the prospect of Esteban. He was no prudish, provincial criollo.

The Montoyas would leave at the end of the week. During the days following the burial, as everyone went about wrapped in his own private grief, Elena schemed. She was a decorous model of the sorrowing maiden, dressed in blacks and grays that enhanced the beauty of her rich dark hair and black eyes. One could look well even in mourning. She must be discreet, yet manage to get Esteban's attention focused on her for at least a brief period. Finally she conceived a plan. Timing and the location of rooms and windows in the hacienda were critical. She planned her move for Friday evening, for Esteban could then approach Don Alfredo and her father the next day.

Esteban had the room on the farthest end of the north wing, overlooking the central courtyard and fountain. Elena's room was in the south wing, with her dueña in watchful attendance. The dueña was her mother's spinster great-aunt and quite elderly. Late in the evening she would be asleep and easy to escape, especially if her bedtime milk were laced liberally with the headache powders she always carried.

Early Friday evening, Esteban's deep reverie was interrupted by Elena, who collided with him in the main hallway to the *sala*. Esteban had avoided everyone and not talked to Elena in several days. Begging her pardon for bumping into her, he noticed her tear-streaked face. She made a subdued curtsy with downcast face and asked his forgiveness. Before he could reply, she had slipped past.

Esteban was overcome with guilt about his estrangement from his family, particularly the distance between him and Miguel. He had been able to think of little else since his brother's death. After the collision with Elena he quickly forgot the incident and went to his room, where a servant brought a light supper. All week he had not really talked to his father. His mother had spent almost all her waking hours praying in the family chapel. He had joined her there on a few occasions to give her what comfort his presence afforded, but he felt an alien intruder on his knees in a church. Yet, it seemed to make her soul rest easier to see him go through the motions, so he gladly did it.

Tonight he was exhausted and wanted only to be alone in his room. It seemed he couldn't think even of the day ahead, much less make any plans for the future. After he finished his meal, he paced restlessly around, his long form casting flickering shadows on the courtyard below. By midnight, when the household was asleep, Esteban was still awake, as he had been every night that week. Sleep brought dreams, troublesome ones of the war, blood and pain, and Miguel's death. He sipped brandy and smoked the thin black cigars he used to love, one after another, not tasting them.

The night was windless. The silence was interrupted by an occasional animal cry and the barely perceptible musical tinkling of the courtyard fountain. It was in this moon-dappled, quiet setting that Elena waited. When she was finally sure that all the servants and family members were asleep, she moved across the courtyard toward the north end where a small ornamental pine stood with an iron bench beneath it.

Her heart leaped in her breast. She could see that directly overhead Esteban's light was still burning and his shadow moving across the window. He was awake! Since the night was still, his door to the veranda and the windows on the west end of his room were open.

She took her seat on the bench and then looked at the closed, dark windows next to Esteban's room. Miguel's old room. No one slept there now. Below in that north wing was the library, also dark and vacant at this hour. No one else was likely to hear.

She began to sob, bringing tears to her eyes at will, a skill she had developed to use on her father. As the only daughter in a family of sons, she had learned early how to win male sympathy. Very gradually, watching for movement at the lighted window out of the corner of her eye, she increased the volume of her crying. The instant she perceived a shadow move toward the veranda above her, she subsided to silent shoulder wrenching.

Esteban's morose thoughts were interrupted by a small, low sob carrying from the courtyard into the northwest corner of the house, where his room was located. It penetrated his consciousness gradually because he was so self-absorbed. When he finally heard it, he walked to the veranda and peered into the dim moonlit courtyard. At first he couldn't pinpoint the noise and, indeed, barely heard it. He was about to dismiss it as the sound of night birds or small wild animals that often disturbed the Sonoran stillness, when he caught a small motion on the patio bench next to a pine. A hunched figure sat there, racked with now-silent weeping. Looking closer, he could see the delicate profile of Elena.

His first impulse was to leave her alone, but then he recalled her tear-stained face earlier that afternoon. She had never been prone to displays of grief and indeed had not been particularly close to Miguel. He doubted that she was crying for his brother. Why then? Slowly and quietly he crossed the veranda to a narrow staircase at the end and made his descent. She should not be out here alone, unescorted by her dueña, of that he was sure.

"Elena?" The low, gravelly voice she knew so well cut the silence from behind her. She was already aware of his approach but did not betray it. At his questioning tone and the sound of her name, she whirled on the cold iron seat and gasped.

"Esteban! I—I'm sorry if I disturbed your sleep. I was sure no one was nearby. That's why I came to this quiet place in the shelter of the tree, to think. . . ."

"To think or cry, little one? You were crying this afternoon also. Why?" He sat on the bench a discreet distance from her, making no move to touch her.

"Oh, it's just the sadness of Miguel and—all the family's sorrow," she answered too quickly.

"You never were so close to my brother that his death, however tragic, should drive you out alone in the night to weep. There must be more."

She carefully twisted the small lacy linen square in her hands for a minute and then looked at him, tears streaming down her cheeks, glistening silver in the moonlight. "I . . . yes, Esteban, there is more. You always could read me, even when we were children. I—don't know how to say this. It's so, so humiliating. My father has been pressing me for many months to marry Rodrigo Ruiz!" She rushed out with the last sentence as if it took great courage to say it. Then, lowering her head and continuing to twist the kerchief, she went on, "Rodrigo has been courting me, but I have put him off, much to my father's displeasure. But last week Don José came visiting. I—I overheard them talking about a dowry, making final arrangements, Esteban." She looked up and put her hand plaintively on his arm. "My father is buying me a husband! Don José wants my money. He and Rodrigo are land-poor and spend above their means. They want only my dowry. I'm being bargained over like a prize heifer!" At this she again subsided into sobbing.

Esteban's natural cynicism about women and their tears

put him on his guard. *I wouldn't put it past the little minx to have arranged the whole thing,* he thought to himself, half-amused, half-irritated. He'd seen enough glib and clever Frenchwomen dissolve into teary fits until their men dutifully did what was so ardently desired. Mexican women were certainly as clever at indirect games. *Still, if she is being forced to marry Rigo, I am sorry. He is as rotten a prospect for a husband as I.*

He said, "Elena, are you quite sure your father would *force* you to marry Rigo if you really didn't want to? You were always able to wind him about your fingers as a child, I recall."

"That was then, this is now. Anyway, I'm nearly nineteen years old!" she cried in despair.

"So very old, little one," he said with a chuckle.

"Do not laugh, Esteban. I must marry soon or I will be an old maid."

"Are there no better young men around here? It seems to me you always have a gaggle of swains at your feet at each bullfight or fiesta. Surely one of them would be suitable?"

Fiercely she shook her head. "It is not for me to say anymore. I should not be here and we both know it. If my dueña should catch us, it would ruin me." With that she leaped up and fled sobbing across the courtyard and into the other wing of the house.

He stood there bemused, watching her vanishing form. "Probably, I've been handled," he said softly to himself, disgusted. Well, some part of his future was beginning to clear. He sighed and trudged back upstairs to his room. At least she hadn't entrapped him in a mad embrace so that her dueña or father might catch them. Maybe she was telling the truth and was afraid of being forced to marry Rigo. Who knew? She obviously had waited for him and still wanted to marry him. He had to marry someone. Why not Elena?

I'll talk to Papa in the morning and see what Don Diego has told him about Elena and Rigo. With that settled, he blew out the candle, slipped out of his clothes, and fell quickly into an exhausted sleep.

Esteban awoke the following morning feeling sick. He raised his head off the pillow, then lay back abruptly, feeling the effects of too much brandy and too many black cigars. As he contemplated the throbbing in his skull, he wondered if he'd swallowed half the scrapings from his riding stable last night. The taste in his mouth was foul. Ugh! Then he rolled over and remembered the late-night episode with Elena and groaned anew. Well, there was no further avoidance possible. He'd just have to talk to his father and Don Diego. Slowly he climbed out of bed and prepared to face what promised to be a very long day.

Bathed, shaved, and somewhat renewed, he went downstairs to confront the two older men, only to be informed that they had ridden out to look at a prize bull. It was nearly noon, Esteban was reminded with silent reprimand by the head stableman, old Pedro, who had lifted Miguel and Esteban onto their first ponies when they were very small boys. The señores would be back in an hour or thereabouts. Not wanting to jar his aching head any further, Esteban decided quickly against riding out to find them. He retreated to the house to wait and ponder.

On his way across the wide yard from the riding stables to the hacienda, he heard hoofbeats and looked up, expecting that his father and Don Diego were returning early. Instead, he was surprised and delighted to see the Mulcaheys. They could not have had word of Miguel's death this soon, so the visit must be a routine business trip for his uncle and a chance for his aunt to see her family. Esteban intercepted Frank and Ursula on the front lawn to inform them of the tragic news before they encountered his mother or Miguel's widow Inez.

The rest of the early afternoon was spent in subdued conversation as Frank and Ursula offered what comfort they could to Esperanza and Inez. After an hour or so, Esteban took his aunt and uncle upstairs, and sent a servant to attend to their room and arrange for baths before dinner. It was a long voyage from Los Angeles to Santa Cruz and they were exhausted from the trip.

Never one to be put off, Ursula stopped Esteban's retreat after he got them situated in their room. "Esteban, you're very preoccupied. I don't mean just about your brother's death. You're waiting for your father and Don Diego to return?" Her deep black eyes penetrated his calmly. She seemed to know his moods and feelings far better than his own mother or father. At times it was disconcerting.

Frank walked over from where he had tossed his jacket on the bed and added to his wife's query, "What's tearin' at you, son? I know you loved Miguel and it was a shock, him dyin' the way he did after all this time, but there is more...."

Esteban closed the door and came into their room. "Yes, there's more." He switched to English now. The servants understood none and his family little. It was just as well that no one overheard their conversation. "I do feel guilty about Miguel—oh, not his death. I guess I've seen it coming since I got back from Europe. It wasn't exactly a shock—it's just the distance. The damn distance between us! He was everything I cannot be to my parents, dutiful, traditional—he fit in and I don't. Maybe I never did. When Juan came riding out and said Miguel had died after that fall, I felt . . . oh, hell, I didn't feel anything!" At this point he stopped pacing and ran his fingers through his hair, then clenched his fists and pressed them down against the oak table, hunching over it in misery.

Ursula glided over and stood next to her tall nephew, placing her arm around his slumped shoulders. "This numbness you speak of, it's natural, Esteban. You've grieved for so long without even knowing it. I saw it when you first came back from Europe."

He turned abruptly, and the tortured look in his sherry eyes was shocking. "It isn't just that—the growing apart. I've been eaten up this week by my sense of duty. My goddamn duty! I'm a Santandar. The last Santandar, if I don't succeed where my brother failed. *That's* what I've really been grieving about! Jesus, I hate myself!"

Frank put his huge, meaty hand on Esteban's shoulder, guiding him to a chair. They all three sat down around the table. "So, me boy, and that's out now. Good. You're not the first man to balk at the halter." Ursula started to speak, but Frank silenced her with a quick gesture of his hand. "I know I'm not from the pure, blue-blooded stock as you two are, but I understand family duty." Looking at his wife gently with a slight twinkle in his eyes, he went on, "After all, lad, I married into the midst of you Santandars and had to fight like hell to be doin' it."

He leaned back and regarded the two of them, their dark hair and sculpted faces so in contrast to his fairness and rough, beefy features. "I assume your papa has a proper young woman all picked out and waitin', as soon as a respectable period of mournin' is over, of course. By any chance it wouldn't still be the lovely Montoya child, would it now?" At Esteban's resigned nod, he went on, "Ah, I thought so! All the right papers on that filly—best family, old friends, convent-educated, and watched by her dueña every wakin' minute." At this juncture, recalling the past night, Esteban managed a half-wry grin, but said nothing.

"She is a beauty, that I'll warrant, lad," Frank added, remembering the introduction earlier that afternoon in the *sala*. He scarcely recalled the sheltered, shy child of earlier visits, for now she was a lovely woman.

At this point Ursula did interrupt the two men. "Elena is beautiful and properly raised, but she would bore Esteban to death inside a year."

"Well, Tia, what do I do? You both see the trap. I can't just sail off anymore. Whatever my other shortcomings, I am proud of my name and I do love my parents. And there's certainly no one else I'd wish to marry."

"Part of the problem, bucko, it seems to your old uncle, is that you're not wantin' to marry at all—is that it?"

Esteban sighed and stretched back in the chair. "I guess it's all that marriage and family means—being tied to this hacienda, the whole way of life here. The Montoyas fit in so well. Elena fits in so well. She's not witty and educated like my 'bluestocking Tia Ursula,' " he said, smiling as he nodded to her. "But she is the best, logical choice. Hell, I'm twenty-seven years old, good at making money, racing horses, and whoring." At this last, he looked at his aunt, but she laughed as he anticipated she would, so he went on, "I have to commit myself to this land and this place someday. I always knew that, and now with my brother's death, it is time."

"Are you sure you can make this marriage work, Esteban? That you can really live with Elena and be a good father to your children?" Her level gaze required an honest answer.

"I have to," he replied grimly. "And, if I don't arrange something with my father and her father soon, old Don Diego may marry her off to Rigo."

"And that would bother you, lad?" Frank asked with a twinkle.

"I don't think she'd be any better off with him than with me, that's for sure."

"That's hardly a valid reason for marrying the girl!" Ursula cut in acidly. She had always remembered the Montoya daughter as a shallow, sneaking little cat, manipulative, just like her mother, Maria.

Esteban rose and walked toward the window. "It's not as good a reason as pleasing my father and mother. And, as I said, I don't have anyone else in mind. She wants the match. We grew up together. Lots of marriages work out from weaker foundations."

"You'll be goin' back to California with us to handle the horse deal in San Francisco, won't you, lad?" Frank also stood up and watched his nephew.

Esteban turned. "Yes, although nothing can be arranged in any official way until a decent interval of mourning is past."

"Well, lad, whatever you decide, it'll work out. Besides, there's nothin' like sea air to clear the cobwebs from the brain and help a man fix his bearin's. That's when I reached the decision to whisk your aunt here from under the noses of you Santandars."

At this invidious comparison between herself and Elena, Ursula rose and put her hand protectively over her neph-

ew's arm. "Give yourself time for the natural numbness of
grief to wear off. Frank is right. The trip is a good
diversion. Twenty-seven is not such a very old age that a
few more months can matter."

When Don Alfredo and Don Diego came into the study,
wiping the dust from their boots and discussing the merits
of various methods of breeding prize bulls, they found
Esteban sitting by the window in his father's big leather
chair. "Well, what is this? You wished to talk to me,
son?"

Esteban rose and faced the two of them. His father was
taller than Don Diego by several inches, as well as leaner
of frame. Don Diego was a portly gentleman with the fair
complexion and light eyes frequent in Mexican Creoles.
His earnest smile and genial manner were always disarming, in contrast to his old friend Don Alfredo's haughty
sternness.

"Should I leave the two of you to talk?"

"No, please, Don Diego, this concerns you also. I wish
you to stay."

The three men sat down, and the ritual of cigars and
brandy was observed. As they exchanged small talk about
the unexpected arrival of the Mulcaheys, the morning's
ride, and the Montoyas leaving the following day, Don
Alfredo's black hawk eyes never left his son's face. He
waited expectantly.

Esteban smiled and said, "I understand you are considering a match between Elena and my cousin Rigo, Don
Diego." The silence was deafening for several seconds
while the flustered older man gathered his wits. Such
bluntness! Estaban's American uncle and Alfredo's sister
were a terrible influence! He smiled nervously and cleared
his throat as Don Alfredo watched ominously.

"Don José and I have discussed such a match, yes. You
know, Esteban, that your father and I had always hoped
you and Elena might wed, but in the past several years it
seemed less likely. The Ruiz family name is a fine old one,
as well. It would be a good match." He eyed the young
man and waited like the chess player he was. Then, "How

did you learn of this matter, if I may ask? It has hardly been common knowledge."

"Elena," was the laconic reply. "She told me you would force her to marry Rigo and that she didn't want to."

Don Diego's face became even more florid than usual. "That young lady had no right to speak of such a thing to you directly! What's becoming of this younger generation, I'll never know! I suppose she was alone with you at the time, as well!"

Esteban waved his hand in a placating gesture. "It was all quite proper. We simply collided in the hallway yesterday and she had been crying. I found out why. That's all that happened."

"If so, then why speak to me of it now?"

"Would you force her?"

Don Diego was a poor liar. He rose and sighed, then paced the floor. "You know I could deny her nothing she wanted since she was a babe. Alas, it seems as if the one thing she wants most, however, I cannot furnish her." He paused, looking at Esteban squarely. "Has she led you to believe I've become a tyrant in my old age?"

Realizing that his first instinct regarding Elena's duplicity was right, Esteban smiled ruefully. "Not exactly, Don Diego. I understand what you and my father have wanted for all these years—that the houses of Montoya and Santandar be joined together. It is time I marry, and Elena would make a splendid wife, I'm sure. I know my duty as the sole heir of this family line. But there is the matter of timing. We must wait until the period of mourning for my brother is over. Then, I will speak to you. In the meanwhile, I just wished you to know of my feelings and beg you to hold off any plans regarding a match with Rigo."

At this point, Don Alfredo, who sat back taking in the exchange silently, stood up and cleared his throat. "Good! This is how I hoped you would come to your senses, Esteban. But, Diego, my son is right. We do mourn for my elder son and the proprieties must be observed. My wife is prostrate and it will take some time before arrange-

ments can be made. Would you be kind enough to wait
with no formal announcement?''

"Yes, certainly I would. I know my daughter would,
also. She has always had many suitors and held them at
bay by herself. She can do it for a few more months
unaided!'' He smiled broadly. If it was not official, at least
it made firm their earlier understanding.

Dinner that evening was a formal affair, with Doña
Esperanza foresaking her chapel long enough to supervise
the setting of a full table. When Esteban and his father told
her of their earlier conversation with Don Diego, she
smiled for the first time in the weeks since Miguel's last
illness. Esteban consoled himself with that thought as he
sat across from Elena.

She was still dressed in gray, as custom dictated, but her
coiffure was elaborate and her gown cut elegantly. She was
a beautiful, scheming child, he thought. His aunt's words
about the years of boredom came to him, but he dutifully
pushed them to the back of his mind and went through the
ritual of the meal. That ocean air beckoned him.

The following morning, he rose early and made arrangements to go to his section of the ranch and prepare the
horses and vaqueros for the forthcoming trip. He had no
chance to speak to Elena that morning, and in the afternoon the Montoyas took their leave for home as planned.
What Don Diego told his daughter, if anything, Esteban
never knew.

CHAPTER
7

Night. Music. The noise and clatter of silverware and dishes at the buffet. The crisp click of chips landing on the felt card tables. Male and female laughter blended together. Fine cigar smoke. Amanda's senses took in a welter of impressions as she slowly moved down the front stairs, dressed as Helen had commanded. The gown Amanda wore was simply cut of forest green velvet, so heavy it needed few petticoats to add fashionable fullness. Its simplicity seemed to add height to her five-foot-four-inch frame, and the low neckline was sculpted around her breasts to show off their beauty discreetly. The emeralds she wore caught the deep green of the gown and of her eyes, accenting the outfit perfectly. Her hair, brushed to lustrous highlights, was caught in back of her head with a few artful curls piled on top and the rest spilled down her back in a waterfall of gold that ended at her waist in soft waves. She was young and vulnerable, a picture of innocence and arresting beauty.

Helen was waiting for her at the foot of the stairs, almost licking her lips in anticipation of the revenues to be derived from her newest protégée. Elegantly gowned in pale blue silk, her dark curls carefully arranged, Helen was very much the businesswoman in charge.

Smiling as if Amanda were a long-lost daughter, Helen took her ice-cold hand and helped her down the last three steps into the main foyer, guiding her past the open stares of admiration from several newly arrived patrons and into the entertainment parlor. Tom was dealing at the faro table and a sizable crowd had gathered to watch the luck of the players. The men, Amanda noticed, were mostly middle-aged or older, and all were very well dressed in expensively tailored, dark wool suits with gold watch fobs and gemstones gleaming on their hands. Some had mustaches or beards; some were clean-shaven, but all had the attention of a fine barber and manicurist. Sighing inwardly, Amanda thought, *At least they'll be clean.* She knew that loud, boisterous behavior was not tolerated. Lewd comments to a woman were likewise frowned upon, unless she indicated that she regarded such intimacies as entertaining, and even then, any exchange of sexual wit had to be discreet. After an arrangement was made for a trip to the second floor, there were far fewer restrictions. *What would a man* say *to her after he was done?* Amanda wondered, half in fear, half in curiosity.

Helen introduced her to a series of men around the crowded room. Amanda nodded, offered her hand, and made the appropriate responses. Finally, she was left to converse with three graying men who were obviously fascinated with the new filly. One jowly, coarse fellow chomped on an expensive cigar and eyed her with open, if silent, lust. The other two engaged her in polite small talk until the taller of the two, a thin man with fine silver hair and a pencil-thin mustache, excused himself and moved toward Helen. Amanda wondered if he was making an arrangement for her or merely checking on her price.

Amanda smiled, talked about inane things, laughed, and waited. "Gimlet eyes" with the cigar hovered over her, saying little, just watching like a fat cat about to pounce. Apparently he would not be her first customer, thank God.

Helen glided back into the room accompanied by the slim, elegant man. "Mr. Sawyer has made the necessary arrangements, Mandy." With no more ado, she drifted off leaving the two together. How Amanda hated the shortening of her name! It had been decided by Helen that it suited her new occupation better. "Not so grave and formal," said Helen. Hoot's endearment became Helen's malediction.

Almost gallantly Mr. Sawyer offered her his arm and they sauntered toward the foyer. Determined not to show discomfort or "girlish hysteria" and incur Helen's wrath, Amanda smiled and forced herself to consider how much better this quiet man was than leering old "cigar breath." Of course, he, too, would get his turn sooner or later. She suppressed a shudder. Mr. Sawyer was a banker and spoke of his business and its expansion in the past three years of the gold boom. He had approved the loan for the new opera house, now opened, and asked if she had ever attended.

Amanda replied, "Yes, I've been there several times. I saw *Norma* two times and loved it so. I'd enjoy going more often but my work keeps me here most nights." There, it was openly said and she felt better. The admission of her new status in life was made.

Unaware of the significance of her remark, he replied, "I can arrange to take you out for an evening at the opera, anytime you wish, my dear. Perhaps I'll discuss this with Miss Staffer later?"

Amanda nodded, aware that Lyla's customers often took the women to operas, concerts, fine restaurants, and then, of course, returned to the second floor for the completion of the evening. It was flattering to have a beautiful woman on one's arm in public, even if she had been paid for. In a city where beautiful women were in short supply, it became a frequent practice for the few who could afford it.

As they walked into the other parlor and approached the buffet, Amanda knew she could not eat. However, Sawyer

was in no hurry and was obviously intending to prolong
his enjoyment of her company before consummating the
deal. She took minuscule portions of the terrapin soup,
smoked oysters, and roast pheasant. Sawyer brought her a
glass of French champagne that she gratefully accepted to
calm her nerves.

The rest of the night was not as bad as Amanda had
feared. George Sawyer was no great lover, but then Amanda
had only Carver as a comparison. Sawyer was considerate,
patient, and greatly admired her beauty. Indeed, as he
undressed her in room eleven, he seemed to be in awe of
her slim perfect contours and dazzling golden coloring,
almost like an art critic admiring a piece of sculpture or a
rare painting. She grew tense with dread as he took his
time undressing her and gazing raptly at her body, but
when he quickly shed his own elegant clothes and lay
down on the bed beside her, she was even more frightened. He allowed himself one more survey of his prize.
Then suddenly he thrust himself into her, spent himself in
a climactic shudder, and rolled away from her. While she
put on a satin dressing gown, he dressed with meticulous
care, his clothes as immaculate and unwrinkled as if he
had never removed them. Now he smiled at her and spoke
for the first time.

"My dear, you are a treasure of great joy and beauty,"
he said, kissing her lips lightly. "I will let you know
about the opera as soon as I can get the very best seats. I
hope you'll enjoy it. I'm sure I shall." With that, and her
slight, smiling nod, he was gone.

The room seemed suddenly empty as she sat down at
her dressing table and began to brush her hair, staring
vacantly into the mirror. "Well, 'Mandy,' so far so good.
If George Sawyer is a fair sample, it won't be painful or
rough. Thank God he didn't hurt me as Carver did! He
actually spoke to me about going to the opera. No words
of false love—no lewd referring to what we did, either."
She shuddered a bit despite the fact it had not been so
terrible, physically. Still, her body had now been bought

and paid for. She was officially and legally a whore. Willow Valley, be vindicated!

The weeks that followed were a blur of ugliness interspersed with brief flurries of enjoyment and terrible nights of humiliation. George Sawyer did indeed take her to the opera. Several other of the wealthiest patrons paid handsomely to escort her to glittering theater performances and fine restaurants. In between, the nightly routine never varied except for Thursday and Sundays, when the place was closed. She would dress in an elaborate gown, groom her hair, and wear jewelry she had only dreamed of in years past. She would descend the stairs, enter one of the parlors, and meet the clients. The beautiful clothes, elegant carriages, and well-dressed gentlemen taking her to glamorous places became almost a routine in itself, as joyless to Amanda as the sexual unions on the second floor. She was "Mandy," the fancy soiled dove, lady of the evening, an expensive whore. There was no soul, no life, no feeling in her.

At first the customers were quick, polite, and precise, knowing they wanted her beauty and gentility even as they wanted sexual gratification. With minimal encouragement and participation on her part, she found her looks and manners carried it off for her.

Part of her mind was still desperate to hold on to her girlhood dreams. Many nights as she made her careful toilette and then took that long walk down the front stairs, Amanda thought about the stranger, her tarnished Prince Charming. The deeply buried dread that he would appear in the parlor one night still haunted her. Most of the men were like George Sawyer, older, in poor physical condition, not particularly attractive, and inept as lovers. Would it be any different with a handsome young specimen like her Mexican businessman? Probably not, she surmised, having had a few younger attractive men, all Yankees, as customers. They were as repellent to her as the coarsest old men. She could not bear to think of her exotic, dashing stranger pawing her like all those others.

After about two months of older men using her rather

perfunctorily but politely, she encountered Moss Lysle, an oyster-fleet owner and self-made millionaire who aspired to the ranks of the socially elite. He was about forty-five, vigorous and thickset, by some standards attractive, with a trimmed goatee and thick, iron-gray hair worn longish but expensively barbered. He took one look at Amanda from across the room and walked directly to her to discuss terms, a breach in etiquette for Lyla's, but forgivable if done quietly. Mandy went upstairs, her "parlor face" firmly in place, thinking as little as possible, but resentful of his speed in taking her off to the second floor. With no chance for small talk first, she could not gauge his wants and likes. It made her nervous.

Using the smooth, light tone she had practiced, Amanda turned to him once inside her room and said, "You seemed in quite a hurry downstairs. If you like, I can have supper brought up after, or perhaps some drinks. We could talk for a while and if you wanted . . ." She left the suggestion of "seconds" unspoken.

He did not even glance up at her, but began to strip off his expensive clothes, casting broadcloth coat, silk shirt, trousers, and the rest on the floor and across the furniture, helter-skelter. Suddenly, realizing that she stood frozen in the middle of the room, he paused and gave her a curt look. "Take your clothes off. I already seen how you look with 'em on. And forget the drinks and talk. I don't talk to whores, especially when I'm paying as much as you cost, sweetie. Stop the innocent young act! I got two daughters your age who *are* innocent, and I know the difference between good morals and your kind, Mandy."

Even the way he said her name made her wince. It took all her willpower not to lash out at him, scathing him with his own hypocrisy. "Good moral daughters," indeed, whose father frequented parlor houses and bought a trapped girl the age of his own children! Carver, her flight, Lyla's stroke, Helen's blackmail—all of it came rushing before her eyes as if she were drowning, coming up for the third time. Then she brought it under control, realizing that a scene would avail her nothing but Helen's wrath. She quickly stripped off her clothes. Without a word or change in facial expression she climbed into bed and lay down. He was rough and he took his time, dragging it out. It seemed to her that he wanted to degrade her even further than his speech had. However, that was not possible.

Nothing that happened subsequently was as bad, not even the times when she was required to perform oral sex or the frightening incident where a customer attempted to whip her with his belt in order to bring himself to erection. The physical aspects of selling herself were never as bad as the picture she had in her mind of her station in life—Mandy, a high-priced prostitute: "I don't talk to whores."

After that first terrible slam, the same message was to be conveyed to her in a multitude of ways by other customers. Rita told her she had to develop skin an inch thick. "Who do those holy Joes think they are?" Lorna said indignantly one afternoon when Amanda was especially bereft. Most of the women had a peculiar camaraderie, buoying one another's spirits and discussing the various men, their quirks and weaknesses. Some even discussed their own lovers. A few enjoyed sex with men, but not with customers. Never with customers. That was against their own rules.

Amanda secretly wondered how any woman could find pleasure in a man's embrace. With a few it was painful, with the rest it was simply a degrading exercise. Was it different if you gave yourself willingly and did not charge for it? Men were such hypocrites, using women for their pleasure. Then they would turn around and call the women immoral and scorn them.

If only she could live free of all men. She realized there were a few good ones like Hoot and Kano, but she was sure she wanted no physical relationship with a man, not even her beautiful dream prince. Even marriage seemed tainted to her now. Look at her own mother. What difference if a woman lay with one man who supported her or with hundreds? No, Amanda concluded, she would be free of all physical entanglements someday. Her earnings in the first several months were considerable. In time, if she saved, she might be able to open a small restaurant or perhaps a dressmaking shop. She could support Lyla and let Helen have the accursed parlor house!

The night that Amanda met Paul Mueller began quite ordinarily with her usual routine of an elaborate toilette. She wore a pale apricot, watered silk dress and topaz earrings. She went through the usual motions of mixing and flirting in the entertainment room, even getting several men to bet with Tom McVea on his house-of-cards trick. The cigar-smoking fat man who had leered at her so unnervingly that first night had become a regular customer in the past months, and he was as crude and rough as Moss Lysle. He was expected again tonight and she was dreading it.

Across the length of the room, Paul Mueller watched her turn and saw the brief flash of anguish in her dark green eyes. His breath caught in his throat as he watched her graceful movements and delicate smile. It was as if his beloved wife had been brought back to life. Amanda's golden hair, haunting green eyes, and smile moved the old man greatly. If he and Marta had had a very beautiful daughter, she would look like this girl. He moved across the crowded room toward the piano where she stood sharing a glass of champagne with several patrons while listening to Eleanor play. The piece was classical and quite well executed. Some patrons enjoyed good music and Paul Mueller was one.

Mueller born in Berlin, had immigrated from Prussia as a very young man, spending many years in New York and then moving to San Francisco in the late 1840s. The son of a butcher, he had learned his father's trade and first made his living working in a German sausage shop. Despite his humble origins, he had been raised with a genuine love of music. Indeed, whenever Beethoven, Tchaikovsky, or any other great composer was played at the opera house, Paul was always in his private box. Since the success of his business on the west coast, he could afford to indulge his love of the arts. When the Metropolitan brought a production company of the opera *Norma* to perform in San Francisco, Paul was their major patron. He was also a major contributor to the Germanic Philharmonic Society and was responsible for getting Rudolph Herold, a protégé of Mendelssohn, to accept the post of conductor.

Now, seeing Amanda obviously appreciate the lovely Beethoven sonata Eleanor played, he felt he had an opening for conversation with her.

As the piece concluded and Eleanor got up from the piano to let Lorna play a light, popular ballad, Paul bowed in his formal, old-world manner before Amanda. "May I present myself, Fraulein. I am Paul Mueller, honored to make the acquaintance of such a beautiful young woman who enjoys Beethoven." He kissed her hand politely and waited for her name.

Somewhat taken aback by such formal behavior, Amanda first observed him to see if it was yet another subtle form of mockery reserved by rich men for the women they bought. His clear blue eyes, however, were earnest and almost wistful. He was genuine! All her instincts told her so. "I'm very pleased to make your acquaintance, Mr. Mueller. My name is Man—Amanda." Why at the last minute she used her real name instead of the hated professional one, she was not sure. It was simply instinct to do so. She smiled the warmest smile she had in weeks as she observed him.

Paul Mueller was sixtyish, stocky yet very dignified, with thinning gray-blond hair and long full sideburns. His dark broadcloth coat and gold jewelry were obviously of the best quality, but understated in an era of conspicuous consumption. His smile was engaging and went from his full mouth to his bright blue eyes. Ebulliently, he gestured with blunt fingers and heavy arms as he talked, and his jovial, animated conversation was refreshing to Amanda, who had been smothered by elegant, glib men who talked sotto voce and were self-conscious of their every movement. Paul threw himself into life.

They talked first of opera and classical music. He invited her to attend the Philharmonic and confessed his amateur

status as a cello player in several chamber-music groups.
He also sang bass with a choral group of German men.
Amanda had always loved to sing and told him of her
enjoyment of the city's numerous musical groups. At
Lyla's she had a really fine piano available for her use and
Eleanor was a qualified teacher. Amanda was not at all
skillful, but she had the chance to learn to play!

"Ah, I too have a fine grand piano in my home. How
my Marta loved to play. She filled the house with such
beautiful music. She . . . But you don't want to hear the
reminiscences of an old man for his dead wife, my child.
We should talk of the present and happy things." By this
time they had moved to the small private alcove in the far
corner of the buffet parlor that allowed for quiet conversation.

A cardinal rule of the business was never to pry into a
customer's private life, only to listen sympathetically to
what he volunteered. Yet, the long, earnest conversation
that had just transpired led Amanda to venture impulsively,
"Did your wife pass away recently?"

Paul took no offense but answered, "*Ja*, it will be only
a year next month. She was ill for so long and so brave
through it."

"I'm sorry for your loss. You must have loved her very
much. I lost my father to a sudden illness, cholera, when
we were coming west in a wagon train. Sometimes I think
the speed of the taking may be a mercy." Her confession
violated another strict rule for a high-class prostitute: never
bore a customer with your personal woes. Yet, the conversation
seemed so natural with Paul Mueller.

He smiled and took her tiny, delicate hand in his big,
blunt one. "Either way, it hurts, *nein*? Yet, life goes on for
the living. So I tell myself finally, Paul, you go to work,
you come home, you go to your chamber music or to sing
with the others, yet always you come home to that empty
house. One day I think to myself," and he tapped his
temple with one hand as he spoke, "Paul, you should meet
a woman—not the stuffy old prunes at the opera with their
lorgnettes wrinkling their long noses, all sticking up in the
air, while their tight corsets make it hard for them to

breathe. *Nein*, but someone young and laughing." At this juncture a smile curved Amanda's mouth and she almost giggled, remembering just such frowning women looking with disdain at her.

"So, you came to Lyla's to find laughter and beauty?"

"I am not so sure what I hoped for. I must make a confession, *Liebchen*, if you promise not to laugh at a foolish old man." Amanda nodded gravely and he went on. "Never in my life do I visit this kind of place." At this juncture he raised his hands placatingly. "Not that I am virtuous or mean to say the ladies here are not, but I am married very young and am so happy, I never think . . . well, I have several friends take me aside this past year and tell me what I am missing. So, I come to see. What do I see?" Again, the expansive gesture. "The place is very beautiful and so are the women, but so, so . . ." He hesitated, at a loss for words to convey his feelings. Sheepishly, he confessed, "They are sophisticated and smooth, *ja*, so sure of themselves and also the men. Me? I do not know what to do or say. I am about to leave when what do I see but a young angel who loves Beethoven and looks so like my Marta. No, not really so. You are far more beautiful than Marta was at your age, but the golden hair, green eyes, and the smile—that, that is my Marta, I think. I hope you do not mind my foolishness."

Touched by this, Amanda quickly assured him she did not mind but was flattered by the comparison. It seemed obvious to her that he would not be a customer, but the evening had been so enjoyable she did not mind the loss of money.

Paul was aware of keeping her company all night without paying the usual fee for services and felt he must make restitution. Not being sure how to proceed, he asked her advice. "You must bear with my lack of knowledge, my dear. I keep you all night from other, younger men. After all this talk, I feel I know you. But I know I cannot enjoy a young woman's favor. No more than I enter the door, I know it is a mistake. If it had not been for the sight of you, I would be gone long. But this is not fair to you. May I pay the usual cost, just for the joy of this talk?''

Taken aback at his earnest plea and obvious awkwardness in the delicate situation, Amanda countered, ''Please, Mr. Mueller. This has been so wonderful I don't want you to feel I need anything more.''

''Then, I will arrange to take you to the opera, to dinner, to hear my Philharmonic—this I know I can arrange and pay for. My friends who come here, they tell me this. Would this be pleasing to you?''

Seeing a golden opportunity for such outings with no dreadful bedding afterward, but instead the delightful company of this man, Amanda was beside herself with joy. It seemed too good to be true! Then she hesitated. ''It is very expensive and most men pay for . . . for more than my company.'' She ended with a blush and lowered her eyes.

''And I am thinking you do not enjoy the 'more,' humm?'' He took her delicate, lowered chin in his blunt fingers and tipped her face up to look at him. At her affirmative nod, he went on, ''Amanda, I am a very rich man. I can afford to pay for the company of all your ladies in the room if I wish it. All I ask is that you allow me the honor of escorting you. Not to worry about cost.''

Amanda's routine at the house was significantly different from what it had been before Paul became her only patron. She still rose early each morning in room eleven, but not with the sick, sour dread of remembrance from the night before. Rather, her memories were of outings to the Philharmonic, concert halls, fine restaurants, and even of elegant dinners at Paul's home, which was becoming increasingly familiar to her. She lit up the quiet halls with her laughter and youth. After years of the hushed silence of the sickroom, Paul was overjoyed to see his once-lively home again the site of gaiety. It was well worth paying Helen Staffer's fees.

Amanda still visited Lyla each morning and worked with the frail woman. It had been over eight months since the stroke, and Lyla's condition had not improved. Amanda was deep in thought one morning as she prepared to enter the sickroom. In the outer office she encountered Dr. Denton.

"Good morning. You certainly seem preoccupied." Elizabeth Denton was smiling.

As Amanda returned the greeting, the doctor could see the difference the past few months had made in the young woman. True, she was tired and worried, but the sickening dread of working in the house had been lifted by Paul. Elizabeth was so grateful to him that she could have kissed him, if her naturally reserved nature and his sense of propriety had allowed.

"How is Herr Mueller these days? I saw the two of you driving in the park in his beautiful barouche the other evening when I came back from the Phillips place."

Amanda blushed and smiled, thinking how ironic it was that after all the months and customers, she should feel embarrassment over her innocent relationship with Paul. She was still angry that he must continue to pay Helen, but the greedy woman had been adamant. Mandy was her top employee and commanded high fees. If she were not in the parlor for other men, someone had to pay. If he was so stupid as to pay the exorbitant prices just to squire the girl about, that was his concern, but Helen must be compensated or Mandy was out on the street.

"Paul is fine, thank you, Elizabeth. I was so glad when you were finally able to have dinner with us and meet him. You really do need more time off, you know."

"Nonsense," the older woman brushed aside Amanda's concern. "I thrive on twenty-four-hour calls and I'd be bored to death if I ever had a full night's sleep! You're the one who is not getting enough time off. Between watching over Lyla like a mother hen and keeping all the rest of the staff on the alert for her safety, you scarcely have time to enjoy Paul Mueller's delightful company, much less sleep! Has he said any more to you about moving to his place? I really think you should go away from here."

"Yes, he still wants me to pack up Lyla and have us both move to his house. I know he means well, Elizabeth, but I can't do that to Lyla. She would be so afraid of such a sudden change of scene, and she doesn't know Paul. If she even guessed the reasons for my meeting him and why I live on the second floor . . ." She let her sentence trail off and moved to the window. "No, I can't take the chance of shocking her into a relapse. Anyway, she worked so hard for this place. It's all she has, and I know it would kill her to see Hetty and Helen take it over. I just can't, Elizabeth."

The doctor sighed and crossed the space between them to place a comforting hand on Amanda's shoulder. "This has really been the worst of all for you, you know. It takes a unique brand of courage."

"That's really quite a compliment, considering the source is a woman who fought her way through medical school, practically with a scalpel at her throat!"

Both women laughed to ease the tension, then the doctor set her bag down on the desk and began sorting through it, getting items in order before going in to check Lyla.

One cool, foggy fall morning, almost a year after Lyla's stroke, Amanda woke to a sharp tapping against her heavy oak door. She was filled with anxiety as she gathered a silk wrapper from the chair and pulled it on with quick, jerky movements. When she opened the door, Mina stood waiting, her thin, usually cheery, birdlike features contorted in fright. She was twisting her hands in her apron as she said, "Come quick! It's Miss Deveroux—she, she's bad, real bad all of a sudden!"

Lyla's room already seemed filled with the presence of death when Amanda burst through the door and moved to the bed where an openly weeping Kano was restraining the convulsive movements of his employer. The huge, dark Kanaka was incredibly gentle as he held the white, tissue-paper skin and bones of Lyla's hands. Amanda carefully disengaged Lyla's grip on Kano and took the hands into her own. She looked at the ghostly face and saw a mask of death. The recognition in each woman's eyes was instantaneous. Lyla was dying.

For weeks she had been struggling to speak, with little

success. Her inability to swallow and digest much solid food had so weakened her that breath for her voice was almost too great an expenditure. Now, as if in one last, desperate effort, she struggled to speak by sheer force of will. "Amanda... in my desk—under top right draw—will... yours, all yours—" She moved her eyes around as if indicating the whole house.

Amanda's heart wrenched, yet she was grateful, realizing that Lyla never knew the perfidy of Hetty and Helen, who had found and destroyed the will. "It's all right, Lyla. I'll get the will later. Now you must try to relax until Elizabeth gets here."

As if she knew time for saying good-bye to her old friend was not to be granted her, Lyla gripped Amanda's hands harder. "Like a daughter..." The words were slowly spoken and almost inaudible as Amanda bent closer to the dying woman's lips to hear.

"Love you, Aman—" The long, sighing last breath was low, soft, and very final.

When Dr. Denton entered the room she found a dry-eyed, calm Amanda still sitting with her hands encased in Lyla's. Mina, Kano, and nearly the entire staff were present. Many of the women were weeping loudly, while Kano's tears rolled silently down his round cheeks. Helen was not there, but Hetty stood back in one corner, as if she sensed her final victory yet was afraid to flaunt it in front of all those who loved her cousin.

Later that afternoon, after all the arrangements were made, Elizabeth took the frighteningly quiet Amanda and ushered her into the kitchen, where Sophie made them both sit down and drink hot, strong coffee. The doctor was worried about Amanda.

"Amanda, I checked everything. She died naturally. Kano and Mina were with her and you were there before them. There was nothing anyone could do. Yesterday, when I examined her, I could see signs—not of anyone's poisoning her or doing anything to precipitate the final stroke, just slow, inevitable weakening that finally reached a critical point."

"I know. I'm sure Helen and Hetty didn't have a hand
in her death. Oh, Elizabeth—I'm so grateful she never
knew what they did! She spoke to me when no one but
Kano was there. Even he couldn't hear—she . . . she told
me where the will was, that she left the house to me.
Thank God she still thought it was safe! She never knew
about me, what I've become . . . she said, 'My daughter.'
She loved me. Oh, Elizabeth . . ." A year's desperate
anguish spent itself in the young woman's fierce torrent of
weeping. Finally, Amanda released her agony.

"At last, at last it's over, Amanda. You have your whole
life in front of you, and it does not include parlor houses."
The doctor held the younger woman and let her cry.

Elizabeth Denton was right. Within three days of the
funeral, Helen marched up to room eleven to give a new
ultimatum to Amanda. To her shock and amazement, the
younger woman was packed, putting her last few toilet
articles into a reticule. She wore a somber but beautifully
cut gray traveling suit and had her masses of golden hair
tucked severely under a small, neat, gray plumed hat. As
she pulled on her gloves, she smiled serenely at Helen.
"Well, it's yours, the whole house and especially this
vacant room. I'm sure you can find a far more willing
employee than I. Of course, she won't earn what I could
bring in, but that is your problem." With a snap of her
reticule Amanda marched past the manager, who, for once
in her life, was agape in silent shock.

Finally, recovering herself, Helen stalked behind Amanda
like a harpy. "I suppose you'll become Paul Mueller's
mistress? Always better to let one man keep you in style
and have your own house, I say. Don't think for one
minute anyone here believed your fairy tale about his
being like a father to you—ha! Maybe like your stepdaddy
was a father to you!"

At that hissing, vicious remark, Amanda whirled full tilt
at the bottom of the front stairs, in sight of Rita, Kathleen,
and several other women who stood frozen in shock. The
slap Amanda gave Helen knocked the older woman backward against the newel and left a clear red imprint on her

carefully powdered cheek. Her meticulously arranged hair flew from its pins and scattered in tangles around her shoulders. Before Helen could even pick herself up from the stairs where she had slipped, Amanda was out the front door and climbing into a waiting carriage. One of Mueller's men entered now and neatly sidestepped the disheveled Helen to collect the luggage. Amanda had said her farewells to Rita and her other friends the night before. She would never set foot in a parlor house again.

PART 3

AWAKENING

CHAPTER 8

As Paul Mueller's protégée, Amanda's dreams came true. She had her own glorious sunlit room on the mansion's second floor. It was decorated in pale green and apricot gold with a sunken marble bathtub in the adjoining dressing room. The fixtures were gold and the carpets thick Brussels imports. As if the luxury of her living quarters were not enough, the whole house was Amanda's to command.

On the first day of her arrival, as she stood dressed in her gray mourning suit, Paul introduced her to the whole staff in his most formal European manner. She had met a few of them earlier when visiting, but now she learned the names and duties of all. She was to be treated as his daughter, the new head of the household, in charge of the entire domestic staff. If any of the servants were shocked at this news, their loyalty to Paul made them adhere to the announcement with rigid courtesy. Actually, as the weeks and months wore on, Amanda won them over with her unassuming kindness. Her relationship with Paul was much speculated about below stairs, but no one could fault the propriety of their behavior. The house, so sad and quiet since Marta's death, was once again alive with the sounds of music and laughter.

One of the first expeditions Paul insisted Amanda make was a clothes-shopping spree. The elaborate evening gowns and sumptuous negligees she had owned at Lyla's were left behind. Amanda took only a small number of modest day dresses and some simple underthings. The rest seemed reminders of a past she desperately wanted to erase from her memory. Understanding her desire for a new beginning, the old German called one of the best modistes to come to the house with her array of samples. By midsummer, Amanda had a complete wardrobe, all appropriate for a young lady. No more lacy pegnoirs and satin dressing gowns filled the wardrobe, but rather, delicate batiste nightrails and simple linen dressing robes. Amanda, always conservative in her taste, even at Lyla's, now was scrupulously careful to dress as a young lady of the upper class, modest and innocent.

Given her unorthodox arrival at Paul's home and installation as young protégée of no blood relationship, there were limits on Amanda's social acceptance. Paul took her to the opera, riding in the park, to stage plays, and on carriage trips to the Embarcadero. They dined at all the most sumptuous and elegant of San Francisco's restaurants.

Paul himself had never been interested in society, nor had he attended the balls and other parties given by the elite. When Marta was well, the two of them had frequented the Philharmonic and the Teutonic Society. Otherwise, their life had been simple and home-centered with a small circle of friends. While he amassed his fortune on the California coast, Paul had not mingled any more than necessary for business purposes with his fellow millionaires and their rarefied social strata. He felt no need to justify Amanda and her background to the staid matrons who dictated entrance to high society.

After setting the housekeeping in order, overseeing the cleaning of the mansion, and supervising the replanting of the neglected flower beds, Amanda realized that nearly a season had passed and Mueller's mansion was indeed her home.

When the quiet old German appeared in public with his beautiful young lady, women whispered behind their fans and men turned their heads to admire Amanda. A few men knew her from Lyla's, but, given the tolerant atmosphere of the day, there was no open condemnation. Someone started a rumor that she was Paul's niece from back east. When the story reached their ears, they enjoyed a good laugh. However, the idea of weaving a respectable past held more appeal for Amanda than she cared to admit. People tolerated her, especially Paul's close friends who knew their relationship for what it was. Yet, the nagging feeling that she was whispered about made Amanda uneasy. Once in a great while, at the opera or in a restaurant, she would recognize a patron of Lyla's, and Paul would feel her involuntary stiffening on his arm. Would the old customer denounce her before the public gathering? Always the question haunted her. Of course, given Paul's influence and the obvious source of a patron's firsthand knowledge about parlor-house whores, such men never acknowledged her, except to nod or smile formally. Sometimes she imagined they leered, and she was sure of their lecherous thoughts, but Paul calmed her fears and reassured her that they could never touch her again.

Amanda found an inner core of toughness in herself. She was no longer the terrified child who had fled Carver Cain. Her years at Lyla's had formed her, and the nightmare year as Helen's best-paid whore had forged her determination to outdistance any pain or degradation life might ever inflict on her again. Now free of the parlor house, she was secure in a new identity; no longer Mandy, she was Miss Amanda Whittaker, and she had put behind her all the foolish girlhood dreams of a knight in shining armor.

But who was Amanda? She often pondered that as she lived her new life with Paul and Elizabeth, listening to fine music at the opera and tending the sick patients as a volunteer in the doctor's office. She knew she was a survivor. After living through Carver and Helen, how could she be anything else? Yet, for all her education, her refinement, her beautiful clothes and elegant life, even for all her useful work at Elizabeth's clinic, Amanda was restless.

Men admired her and many courted her, young, well-to-do men who offered her honorable marriage, but she could love no man. As long as she lived in San Francisco and felt the leers of old customers, she would not be free. Amanda held up her head and cut them cold, but, like ghosts, they held a part of her in hurtful thrall. Something inside her still whispered, "Who *is* Amanda?"

The one fixed star in her turbulent universe was Paul Mueller. His wit, charm, and breadth of interest never ceased to amaze her. He played cello with the Philharmonic, sang in the Bach Society Chorus, and composed on the fine piano in his conservatory. What delighted Amanda most of all was the spirited camaraderie between Paul and his musician friends. They would gather on chilly fall and winter evenings to play and sing with such robust abandon that Amanda often felt the roof would rise. Although her voice was untrained, she had a good ear for music and a strong, clear alto voice, pleasing in choral singing.

Paul did not confine his friendships to fellow Prussians or even to German-speaking people. He was fluent in French and he and his vintner friend, Henri Moreau, could converse in either language with equal ease. He also shared a common heritage in music, art, and fine wines with his Italian friends. One Tuscan, Arturo Zella, was a frequent guest at the dinner table, and he, Henri, and Paul would argue long into the night over the virtues of Italian opera, German symphonies, and French wines.

There were over one hundred foreign-language newspapers in San Francisco, which indicated the ease with which a San Franciscan could meet someone from virtually any part of the globe. It seemed that Paul did just that. Amanda found, much to her delight, that she shared Paul's natural flair for languages. With tutorial aid from him and his friends, her conversational French and German were developing quite nicely within the year, and Arturo even praised her Italian, although she knew it was far from fluent. From her days with Rita she had developed passing fluency in Spanish.

Dr. Denton, who had encouraged the friendship between Amanda and Paul, was a frequent visitor. When she could find a luncheon or dinner time free, she would meet them to catch up on the news of her young friend's exciting life. Amanda, in turn, was so fascinated with Elizabeth's medical knowledge that she would go to the office on Portsmouth Square and assist with simple nursing chores. She learned a great deal about basic first aid, hygiene, and even pharmaceuticals helping the doctor mix her own medications. Possessing the strong stomach and common sense of a farm background, Amanda found she was a good nurse and enjoyed helping the doctor.

For all the activity and fun in her life, she was surrounded mostly by Paul's friends, charming and kindly but older. Sensing that a woman of scarcely twenty years should see more of people her own age, he arranged for the brewmaster's son to dine at their house, the ship captain's younger brother to take Amanda riding, and the opera manager's nephew to escort her to the lending library. Paul's well-intentioned plans went for naught. Amanda played the gracious hostess, but preferred the safe company of her mentor and his associates. Finally, after a year had passed, Paul turned to Amanda at breakfast one day.

"*Liebchen,* I think long into the night about your being surrounded by old people—me, Henri, Arturo. You are only twenty. You need young escorts, a chance for a life of your own. Do none of the young men you meet please you?" He leaned forward with a twinkle in his eyes and took her hand from the coffeepot to hold it in his large, blunt one. "You know, someday I hope to bounce a granddaughter on this old knee."

Touched, Amanda smiled and cast down her eyes, withdrawing her hand from his to pour more coffee and stir it as she collected her thoughts. "I am so pleased that you think of me as a daughter, honestly I am, Paul, but as for marriage . . ." She let her hand drop from the saucer and began to fidget. "I—I don't think I ever could marry any man—that is, I don't think anyone would want a girl from Lyla's for a wife."

Paul, in a typical gesture, threw up his hands imploring the heavens. "Ach, Gott, mein Kind, don't you realize how little that means in this time and place? In Boston we do not live! In Saint Joseph we do not live! This is San Francisco, a wonderful, wild place. A young woman with your beauty, your education, your own good self, Amanda— many fine young men would give the whole earth to marry you." He bent over her chair and put his arms around her shoulders.

"Never would it matter to them about what you had to do in the past. Your whole life is in the future. Why, just yesterday I come out of the bank and who meets me with a big bear hug! Doug McElroy, all six feet and more of him—me he practically lifts off good mother earth! 'How are you, Paul?' says he, pumping my hand as to wear it off my arm."

At this juncture, Amanda had to giggle in spite of herself. She knew the young Scot's exuberant nature. He had been an occasional visitor at their house in the past year. Before he had reached thirty, McElroy had become a millionaire in the gold fields.

"He asked for you, Amanda—'How is she?' says Doug. 'Is her hair still so golden? Her eyes so green? Her face so beautiful?' Ach, I tell you, Doug McElroy does not care about your past. He would gladly marry you. I know he is not polished and refined, but you could work on that. He is a fine young man, Amanda."

Paul's earnestness left her feeling defensive and churlish as she put up obstacles to his suit for the Scot. Indeed, she liked young McElroy. He was brash and outgoing, rather inclined to vulgar displays of wealth, yet good-hearted. She regarded him as a sister might a troublesome younger brother. Despite the fact that he was nearly seven years her senior, he seemed callow. Life had not dealt him the harsh experiences it had Amanda.

He was willing to be generous, to forget her past. She knew this because several months earlier he had taken her riding and talked very bluntly about her background. Most of Paul's friends were aware of Amanda's sad story, he informed her. Because he planned to marry her, he wanted her to know he did not care that she had worked at Lyla's.

Her first impulse had been to slap him and ride off, but then she recognized the inept earnestness in his look. He had not meant to taunt her with her soiled past. He was a plain-speaking man who was setting his suit out in the open, the only way he knew how. The pleading look in his pale blue eyes, gazing at her from under the tousled thatch of rusty hair, made his guilelessness clear. She told him gently that she was honored by the proposal and by his honesty, but that she did not think to marry, at least not yet. Now he was back in town, apparently renewing his courtship with Paul's blessing.

"I know he would never hold up my past to me, Paul. I know he wants to marry me, but I don't love him. I'm not sure I can ever love any man that way—to be married, that is." At this point she blushed furiously, and Paul, always aware of her deep sexual fears, gently patted her clenched hand.

"Amanda, *Liebchen*, you will feel this not so much someday, this hurt inside. A kind, loving young man could heal those wounds. Those ugly memories can only fade if you give yourself a chance to see that all men are not like your stepfather or the customers at Lyla's. It is very beautiful and good when you love. Just think on it, *Liebchen*."

A dark, handsome visage with a dazzlingly sunny smile suddenly flashed into her mind. He had seemed the perfect man for her, yet he too had come to the house. He was like all men; he too would spurn a woman who had done what she had.

Paul gave her a reassuring squeeze on the wrist and rose to leave the breakfast room for his morning appointments.

"For now, just have fun and mingle with the young people. It will all work out in time."

She gave him a parting hug. "I don't know what I would do without your advice—be a frightened old spinster sitting in a corner with her cat and her knitting, no doubt."

Paul gave a snort of disbelief as he went through the door. Amanda sat down with her coffee, now cold, and stared into the cup as if trying to read the future. If only he were right. Perhaps time was the key. She had spent the past seven years in incredible turmoil, moving across the country and having the whole fabric of her life repeatedly rent asunder. This past year with Paul had been like discovering a haven in a hurricane. Was she really trying to bury herself with Paul's older friends? Could she ever desire a man?

Amanda had asked herself that question ever since she had lived at Lyla's and begun to discuss previously taboo subjects with Rita. Rita, who loved men, was not at all shy in describing the delights of a young, well-formed male body to a mute Amanda, whose only experiences had been with Carver Cain and then as a paid professional. Amanda had been surprised to learn that several of the women at Lyla's had lovers. Most, however, looked upon sex as a means to an end—money and security. If they did not find it the traumatic, fearful thing that Amanda did, neither were they thrilled by it. Nevertheless, when Amanda reflected upon her mother and father's love, on Paul and Marta and what they had shared, she knew there must be more to physical relations than the ugly rote motions she had been forced through.

Am I a complete misfit? Will I never feel what I should? Or aren't good women supposed to feel anything positive about sex? But then, I'm not a good woman, so how can that even matter. . . . Lately these musings came more often to her, and the morning's conversation with Paul set her mind adrift once again. There was always a knot of fear deep within her, yet there was also a persistent restlessness that she did not understand. She wanted something, had strong physical urges that she could not put a name to. Sighing, Amanda resolved to be friendlier to some of the nice young men Paul brought home. *I just have to lose my inhibitions, that's all.* Deep in her heart, she never believed she could.

It was Steamer Day, June 15, 1855. On the Embarcadero crowds milled as the long-awaited mail was brought from the ship and hauled to the small, squat building that served as a post office. Carriages and fashionable open barouches were parked everywhere as people wended their way past the obstacles. Some were dapperly dressed city fellows in suits, some impoverished workers who left the gold fields and sought menial jobs in the city. Many were dressed in the typical argonaut garb of plaid flannel shirt and stout canvas pants, already becoming known by the manufacturer's name, Levi's. Though it took twelve hours or more before the mail was sorted, lines were forming at the post office. Many people came just to watch the spectacle of the crowds and feel the excitement. Children ran and chased one another while dogs barked and foraged for scraps thrown by careless picnickers on holiday. In addition to the mail steamer, other craft jammed the piers, but to those far from home nothing was more important than news of their families.

Amanda loved the spectacle and promise of Steamer Day. She rode with Paul in their large carriage to take in the adventure. The top was down, since the weather was exceptionally sunny and beautiful that day, and Amanda's parasol lay forgotten at the side of the velvet seat cushions, allowing the sun to caress her face. Watching it gild her hair with fire, Paul thought her as eager as a young child, untouched by tragedy. Also admiring her slim curves in the soft, apricot muslin day dress was Doug McElroy. His breath nearly stopped when she whirled her head to pass a comment to Paul over the din of the crowd. Her hair, caught loosely at the nape of her neck with an orange ribbon, was a brilliant cascade flying about her like fireworks. Doug was lost, dreaming of running his fingers through the dense, golden masses and holding her close to see the gleaming smile she would bestow on him. His reverie was interrupted by Paul's question, obviously being repeated in good humor.

"You are interested in buying some good-blooded horses, Doug?" At the nod from the redhead, Paul continued, "Perhaps the boat that now docks down the quay will interest you."

Doug tore his eyes from Amanda and looked across the milling scene in front of him to where Paul was pointing. Amanda also followed his gaze. A small transport steamer was unloading its cargo about five hundred yards away, well clear of the Steamer Day confusion. The cargo was a string of beautiful horses. They pranced onto the wharf, skittering nervously as they were led toward the haven of dry land. The animals were magnificent, even to Amanda's untrained eye. Golden with cream-colored manes and tails, they were as dazzling in the sun as she was. Intrigued, the three spectators wanted to get a closer look.

Doug, who had "accidentally" run into Paul and Amanda on their way to the wharves, was mounted on a sorrel of no particular distinction. He had certainly been in the market for some flashy horseflesh of a size that better accommodated him. One of those magnificent palominos would be just fine, yessir, just fine.

"Let's head over and check this out, Paul. Do you have any idea who's shipping them? Wouldn't want to appear too anxious and drive the price up." The frugal Scot in him surfaced occasionally despite his vast new wealth.

"Mind if I ride in the carriage with you?" Doug asked. "It might be easier to maneuver." Actually, he had other reasons for the request—to get off the mangy little sorrel and to sit closer to Amanda.

Paul nodded and, as McElroy situated himself next to Amanda, replied, "As to who sells the horses, I think I recognize his agent—the young man by the rail of the ship in conversation with the captain. He will probably make all sales for his uncle, Frank Mulcahey. It is with Esteban Santandar you must deal, my friend. Do not let his Latin name fool you—he drives as hard a bargain as any Scotsman.''

Although she had seen Mexicans in the streets of San Francisco, Amanda had encountered only those of lower classes, sad remnants of the men who had ruled California. The wealthy Hispanic population had retreated into a closed society, proudly turning its back on the upstart newcomers. Many had moved south, forced off their lands by American laws. In all the welter of Italians, Germans, Frenchmen, Swedes, and other Europeans and Americans she knew, Amanda had seen only one genuine Mexican aristocrat.

In the carriage, three pairs of eyes were drawn to a slim, dark man, tall and hard-looking next to the short, pudgy steamer captain. As they neared the pier, Paul motioned for their driver to stop the carriage. Paul and Doug turned their attention to the horses, but Amanda did not take her eyes from the man who was descending the gangplank after bidding the captain farewell. He was very dark, with almost shoulder-length black curly hair and thick longish sideburns. His face was clean-shaven, but evidence of a heavy beard showed through in the bright sunlight. Despite his swarthy sun-darkened complexion, his eyes were arrestingly light, a sherry-gold color under dense black brows. His forehead was high, his nose prominent and straight, and his lips were the most beautifully sculpted she had ever seen on a man.

Amanda sat frozen. It was her knight in shining armor from Lyla's! Even after three years she would have recognized that magnificent face anywhere. All those long-forgotten memories surfaced in a sudden bubbling rush. When she had first become infatuated with him, it had been from long distance, when she was a traumatized child living in a sheltered dream world. Now she was a woman grown, keenly aware of men, but no man of all those she had known affected her this way. It was like going back in time, yet it was not. Then she had seen a smiling, handsome young face, an elegantly dressed Prince Charming. Now she was aware of him as male and magnetic, calling something deeply buried to startling life within the core of her. Suddenly the day became unaccountably warm.

She watched his pantherlike progress down the gang-plank, noting the tight buckskin breeches hugging his long legs as he strode to the wharf. His sheer white linen shirt was simply cut and open almost to the waist, clinging damply to the thick black hair of his chest in the noon heat. Every lean hard muscle on his spare frame flowed smoothly as he walked toward the last horse taken from the boat. He patted the beast, crooning into the golden ear.

Suddenly, the whole scene before her erupted into chaos and noise. A man dressed in the flannel shirt and denim pants of a miner lurched into the throng of nervous horses. Flapping his arms and shaking a large jug of corn whiskey, he hefted it in the general direction of his face. The already nervous beasts began to rear and sidestep restlessly as the drunken miner bumped and jostled his way through their midst, yelling and whooping as he drank. The three stock handlers holding the string of horses reacted quickly, using their hats and hands to herd the horses together into a tight knot and catching the trailing lead reins that had been pulled free in the melee.

While his vaqueros calmed the horses, Esteban dragged the man from beneath the flying hooves. Drawing up his ample girth, the miner shrugged free of his rescuer and spat on the ground contemptuously. "Ya didn' have ta do thet, señor. I kin manage fer myself real good." His eyes, unfocused in his drunkenness, were made even more grotesque by a strabismus that sent the left one wandering off toward the ship while the right one fixed Esteban with a baleful glare. He braced his feet and continued, "I jest wanted ta git a look-see at your horseflesh. Never seed horses so yeller. Fixin' ta buy me one 'a them critters. I got plenty cash—"

Before he could continue, Esteban cut him off curtly. "My horses are not for sale to a drunken lout with no more sense than to run into them while reeking of cheap whiskey. If they had stampeded, you'd have been trampled

to death, *señor*.'' The irony of the Spanish address was
doubled since the speech was delivered in cold, clipped,
unaccented English.

"Why, ya Mex bastard! High 'n' mighty greasers think
ya still own Californey?'' With that he lurched into a
roundhouse swing at Esteban, who sidestepped the larger,
slower man and then, with a couple of fast, well-placed
blows, flattened him. Stepping over the inert form with no
more concern than he would show a swatted fly, Esteban
turned his attention to the still-wickering, frightened horses.
Rapidly, in Spanish, he instructed the vaqueros to get them
off the dockside and away from more harm. One saddled
horse stood off to the side, perfectly quiet through the
fracas. It was Esteban's own mount. In one liquid motion
he was astride the big golden stallion and riding off well
ahead of the herd.

"Well, guess our business will have to wait till he's in a
better mood,'' Doug said with a shrug. "Can't say I blame
him for knocking that great oaf flat. Those horses could
have been injured, or at least have killed that drunk.''

Amanda turned her eyes from the road where Esteban
was disappearing over the horizon to pay attention to Doug
and Paul. Flushed at her obvious fascination with the dark
stranger, she shifted her eyes down to the carriage floor.
Sensing Paul's troubled gaze on her, she looked up into his
face. Doug was still intent on the fight, staring at the
unconscious miner. He did not notice the silent interchange
between Paul and Amanda.

After he climbed down, Doug grasped the reins of his
sorrel and untied them from the back of the carriage. "I
have to get to the bank to meet Peterson at one o'clock, so
guess I'll have to go. If you know this fellow, Paul, I'd
appreciate your letting me know when and where he'll put
those horses up for sale. If the price is right, who knows?''
A twinkle gleamed in his eye at this point and he grinned
at Amanda. "I might even buy two of them, one for me
and one to match a certain golden lady I know.'' With that
he turned and rode toward the downtown district, laughing
as he bade them farewell.

Distractedly, the two in the carriage watched him go. Paul turned to Amanda. "His name, *Liebchen*, as I said a while ago, is Esteban Santandar, and he is the son of one of the richest men in Sonora, Mexico. His uncle, who he has many business dealings with, is an Irish immigrant, Frank Mulcahey. Mulcahey owns a cattle ranch a few hundred miles south of here. Also a hide-and-tallow company, several lumber mills, and a coastal shipping line."

Trying to ease the tension, Amanda said brightly, "Well, it sounds as if this Irishman has done almost as well as a certain Deutschman I know."

Paul smiled. "Yes, and so has his nephew. The young man has a good start at a fortune of his own. He is his uncle's partner in the lumber business and acts as a supercargo and agent for shipments of livestock and silver from Mexico to the coast cities of California and the Oregon Territory. Now, even, he raises and sells prize blooded horses. A very busy young man."

"You seem to know quite a bit about him and his family." Amanda was intrigued.

Paul realized her obvious interest in Santandar but was uncertain of how to proceed. "Everyone who conducts business, *Liebchen*, especially cattle-selling business, is of interest to me. Also, a little shipping I dabble in from time to time." He grinned. "I always make it my business to know the business of all my competitors. Sometimes we work together, sometimes we try to beat one another to a customer or a market. The only way to stay ahead is to know every man who is rich enough to compete, or useful enough to help you."

"Oh, and which is the Santandar family?"

"Both," Paul affirmed, and added gravely, "And much more, Amanda, much more. They are one of the oldest, most aristocratic families in Mexico, a land where a title and a bloodline still mean much. They are criollos, born in Mexico but of pure Spanish blood. They live by a closed code as different from our open, boisterous San Francisco as night from day. *Liebchen*, I . . . I notice how you look at him—and I am glad to see you show at last an interest in a young man,'' he put in quickly as she flushed and looked away. How to explain without hurting her, she who had already been hurt so much? Paul doggedly plodded on in his low, gentle voice, ''Amanda, I want you to meet the right young man. It is good, ach, so very good that you do, but not *this* man. He is exotic and different to your eye, very pleasing, *ja*?''

''I . . . I don't know how to explain it, Paul, I just saw him and couldn't seem to stop staring. I'm sure you're right. I simply never saw anyone with his coloring, so striking-looking, that's all. He took my eye, but that's a foolish fancy, I know.'' It was a sixteen-year-old's infatuation, she thought, but she could not bring herself to dredge up the past at Lyla's, even for Paul. She continued to fidget with the closed parasol in her lap as they traveled slowly homeward.

Her agitation was evident, yet Paul knew he must make her understand why he discouraged her interest in Santandar when she had shown none in any of the other young men he had brought around. He cleared his throat and proceeded. ''A very complicated thing this is, *Liebchen*. This man, his family, they are of another culture, a world apart from Americans. The women there are raised with dueñas, older women who watch them. They are never left alone from childhood to marriage. Always they are chaperoned. The rules are never broken. A man and young woman of the upper class have their marriage arranged by their families. These men are fiercely possessive and so rigid in their behavior—ach!'' His hands flew up in his characteristic gesture of disgust. ''Never do they allow any freedom, even to breathe, to their wives and sisters. Absolute purity is essential in a bride—also, the best blue blood, descended from Spanish dons, and, of course, lifelong practice of their one true religion, Roman Catholicism.''

Amanda smiled weakly. ''What you mean to say, Paul, is that I fail to qualify on all three counts. I have no pedigree, I'm a heretic, and I certainly can't claim to be a virgin. So, Señor Santandar would never look twice at

such an unworthy subject,'' she finished, trying for a
lightness she did not feel.

Paul wanted to pass over the awkward moment, yet was
afraid she might still hold the fascination in the back of her
mind. He continued in a serious vein. ''Any Mexican of
Santandar's class is completely ruthless, Amanda. Their
code is never broken—if any woman of his family is
dishonored, if even a hint of any scandal touches her, he
will fight a duel, kill the man who did it. If the woman is
fortunate,'' he shrugged in a resigned gesture, ''she will
be quietly sent to a convent for the rest of her life. If he is
a really vengeful man, he might publicly disgrace and
denounce her.''

A strange wave of black humor swept over Amanda at
this point, almost as if all her past were coming up before
her eyes. Suppressing a nervous laugh, she said, ''I
suppose it would be very interesting for me to be engaged
to such a Mexican man. Can you imagine my intended
husband calling out half the richest men in San Francisco?
Mission Dolores would be as crowded as the Embarcadero
on Steamer Day with all the men who 'dishonored' me.''

At this point Paul wanted to silence her self-castigation
and comfort her, fearing an outburst of tears. However,
before he could do more than pat her hand and open his
mouth to speak, Amanda broke in.

''It's all right, Paul. Honestly it is. I know what you are
saying and why you brought it up now—to keep me from
being hurt. It's just that—damn men and their petty self-
righteousness! They can go to parlor houses and use all
sorts of women—I imagine the splendid-looking Señor
Santandar has had more than his share of young girls from
his father's ranch, not to mention the pick of the most
expensive women in any fancy house from here to Mexico
City! Why doesn't that count? Why doesn't it, Paul?''

Glad of her anger instead of the self-pity and guilt of a
moment before, Paul nodded in agreement. ''To me she
talks! Me, who never but once saw a parlor house!
Amanda, I agree with you. But it is not only the men who
make up such foolish rules. Remember all the good ladies

who agree—every man who sets two standards was taught one set of rules for men, another for women, by a woman, his mother! *Ja*, the world is a very foolish place, but then," he stopped and tweaked her nose, "it is the only place to live in we have. Besides, not all men live by such a code. This is a wonderful, new country. So big, so free, Amanda. People from all around the earth, here they come to start over. Many men in San Francisco don't care where you came from, *Liebchen*, or what you were forced to do in the past—they will love you for what you are, and that is what counts. Look here in our wide open, wild city and you can find a good young man."

"Like Doug McElroy?"

"*Ja*, like Doug McElroy. Many girls of the greatest purity, best bloodlines, and truest religion could do far worse." At this he laughed, and Amanda was cajoled into joining him, her anger spent as quickly as her fit of guilt had been. Yet, as they pulled up in front of their huge stone mansion, Amanda's thoughts did not dwell on Doug McElroy's earnest blue eyes and russet hair, but rather on golden panther eyes below black shaggy brows.

After his "welcome" to San Francisco at the Embarcadero, Esteban was in a foul humor. He rode in the noonday heat to the area outside town where Frank Mulcahey had a small ranch. The trip from Los Angeles had been long and the coastal waters unusually rough for that season. Finally, after getting the horses safely on land, that damn gringo drunk had nearly stampeded the whole lot! Esteban thought grimly that if it were not for fear of injury to one of the animals, he would have let the bastard be trampled to death. All he could think of was to check the arrangements at the small waystation his uncle kept for penning livestock before a sale. Then he wanted to get to town and have a long, refreshing bath. God, he stank of horses, sweat, and salt spray.

As he rode, he thought of their earlier conversation before he left Ursula and Frank in Los Angeles. He chuckled, remembering the surly, chauvinistic gringo at the wharf. Aunt Ursula understood how to turn American materialism into Mexican profit. They had discussed the largest sale to date of Esteban's prize palominos. She suggested running large public notices in the San Francisco newspapers and posting handbills around the city, advertising a big show and race and inviting contestants to compete with the magnificent Sonoran horses.

Esteban could still see her black eyes and calm face as she impassively explained the logic to her amused husband. "Why not take advantage of the love of ostentation these Yankees have, now that they've discovered gold? They have to find new ways to spend so much and to outdo each other. Remember, Esteban, when you were a boy and we traveled to New York? Remember the rich 'old' families of the best lineage and how each built a house grander than the next? Each had a stable larger and showier than the next?" Her thinly veiled disdain of American "aristocracy" and its crass displays of wealth was apparent, but her rich Yankee husband was not bothered in the least by it.

"Now, my love, are you sure these new millionaires out here are every bit as competitive as those back east, eh?" His eyes were twinkling. "Our usual method of holdin' simple auctions after postin' notices has always worked before and right well, too!"

"Yes, *querido,* but why not outdo the Yankees at what they take so much pride in? Make more money from them than ever before! Everyone, Mexican or American, loves a show. Give them a real one, with charro suits and fancy silver saddles, all the trimmings. Put the horses through their paces, show their training, how well they can run. Draw a crowd and then, sell dearly." Her usually grave face was lit with triumph as she looked from Esteban to her husband. Frank let out a whoop and looked at his nephew.

"What say you, lad? You'd be puttin' on the show. Think you could handle it?"

"Yes, I think I can, especially if it means higher prices for the stock."

Yes, he could, he mused to himself as he dismounted in front of the long, squat building that served as bunkhouse and office for the small crew that ran the operation. He quickly settled the details of feed and quartering for the livestock with the small, rotund manager, Jim O'Hara. Then he turned his mount back toward the city. A bath, some cold beer, fresh food, and, maybe, a woman. Yes, after his deprivation on the voyage, that was in order, but not necessarily in *that* order.

Amanda perused the *Alta* over her morning French toast and coffee. Paul was polishing off his usual poached eggs, spicy sausage links, and black bread. The past week, since the incident on Steamer Day, Amanda had been thoughtful and quiet. Doug McElroy had called twice, but she had no heart to see him and had sent down her regrets.

Paul watched her across the table as he carefully cut his food, eating methodically and neatly. "You have been much too quiet, *Liebchen*, and you go nowhere this whole week long. Today I must spend the morning in the office, but after that I will be free from appointments for several days. What would you like to do? The opera? Perhaps luncheon at that new French restaurant Henri told us about?"

She peeked over the top of the newspaper, her face a delicate picture as she flushed slightly and crumpled the pages to her side, apparently absently. "Oh, I just read there's to be a big horse race and sale at Mission Dolores tomorrow. Do you think we might go to that?"

He looked levelly at her and said, "Is this race, by any coincidence, put on by Señor Santandar with the beautiful golden horses?"

Her deepening flush gave away the answer, but she quickly interjected, "Doug was interested in buying one of the horses. I imagine he plans to go. We could ask him along." Knowing his fondness for the young man, Amanda hoped it might persuade Paul to go.

He rose and came around the table, planted a kiss on her brow, and said, "Well, if you think he really wants a horse, we might go. You send him a note this afternoon and we'll discuss it tonight, *ja*?'' With that he was off.

Amanda knew Paul was unhappy about her attraction to the man on the wharf and even more so about her rejection of McElroy. How could she explain these things to him? To herself? She didn't know. At first she dismissed the whole incident of last week from her mind, as he had urged her to do. But, try as she might, Doug's presence was still stifling and she felt she did not want to face him. At the same time, a small kernel in the back of her mind held the image of a dark, lean visage with flashing sherry eyes that came to her each night as she dozed in her solitary bed.

Uncomfortable about having engineered the outing, Amanda decided to see Elizabeth Denton and talk about her feelings. Expecting shocked reproof, or no better than Paul's concerned tolerance, she found the doctor roundly pleased.

''Amanda, that's wonderful! I was wondering how long it would take you to notice how nice men can be—at least, a great many of them.''

''Oh, he's not like a 'great many' of any of the ones I've ever seen before,'' Amanda blurted, then reddened and amended, ''I mean he's a foreigner, from a very wealthy family. Paul says they're very snobbish and concerned with pedigrees and that I can't ever think of even meeting him, much less getting involved with him.''

''But you can't get him out of your mind?''

''It does seem like a silly schoolgirl fancy, doesn't it? I mean, with someone so suitable and earnest as Doug McElroy waiting eagerly for me, wanting to court me, I shouldn't be so foolish.''

''Nonsense! Every woman has the right to be attracted to whomever she pleases, 'suitability' be damned!''

At this, it was Amanda's turn to be shocked and delighted. ''Why, Dr. Denton, you say that with the conviction of one who has been in love. I thought medicine was your love, never a man.''

''Believe me, Amanda, it's always better for any woman, no matter what she wants to accomplish in her own life, to have feelings and needs—yes, even a need for a man. After all, it's not a one-way street, you know, only for men to need women. Those women, the scarred ones at Lyla's, who use men and feel nothing, they're cheating themselves as surely as the foolish women who marry for money or convention. Everyone needs someone."

Her soft eyes grew moist and she spoke quietly. "I loved a man once, a young medical student. We met in school and planned a practice together after graduation. He was a very wonderful part of my life—still is, even though he died before we could realize our dreams."

She paused a minute and then went on. "What I'm trying to say, Amanda, is that you shouldn't live in the secluded, protected shell you and Paul have built here. He means well with McElroy, but you must let your own instincts guide you."

Amanda put her small hand on the plump one of the doctor and gently squeezed it. "You are a dear and understanding friend. If what Paul says is right, my dream prince will cut me cold, or at best make an indecent proposition to me. That will tarnish his glamour, believe me! I must get out and see for myself, mustn't I?"

Elizabeth confirmed this and, while urging caution as Paul had, nevertheless encouraged Amanda to take a chance. It was all right to find a man attractive. After Amanda's terrible ordeal at Carver's hands and the time working at the parlor house, Dr. Denton was disturbed at the girl's total withdrawal from natural, feminine behavior. Paul's overprotectiveness and well-intentioned nudges toward young men whom Amanda disliked only made matters worse. She had to find her own way.

The sun was fiercely hot and a light breeze was blowing from the bay as Esteban prepared for the day's festivities. Quite a crowd was gathering, many of them well dressed, riding in expensive carriages and carrying on with the exuberance of those newly rich and eager to show it. He was resplendent in a black charro suit, heavily studded with silver, which fitted him like a second skin. The stark white shirt and red sash around his slim waist added to the dramatic effect. For the show horses, which would be put through their paces as gently trained saddle mounts, he selected heavy, ornate Spanish saddles to complete the picture of glitter and wealth. All his vaqueros were dressed in elaborate costumes. The spectacle would be a dazzling display of silver ornaments and golden horses.

The race would be the finishing touch to the day's show. Only a few potential buyers among these rich men would have the skill or desire to race their horses. Most just wanted magnificent mounts for themselves and their ladies. However, he had spotted a few sporting men who owned racing stables. He counted on making impressive sales to them after taking a bit of their money. He was certain that his Don del Oro, or Sir Gold, would leave their Australian thoroughbreds behind in the race. He had had Frank's local men check out the competition and time the horses that were to race against him today. It was well to be a careful businessman, Esteban thought to himself. Yes, this was going to be a very profitable day.

Amanda fairly glowed in a light green riding habit, chosen with great care. She loved to ride and had indulged herself with the beautiful mounts from Paul's stable over the past year. Doug, who was an occasional companion on those equestrian outings, gazed entranced at the young woman who rode beside him today. Her outfit matched her green eyes, and her golden hair was artfully piled into bouncing curls clustered under a tilted green hat. Paul rode in the landau behind them as they approached the mission track on horseback. The conversation on the ride out had been desultory, with Amanda preoccupied and Doug so enamored that he was surprisingly tongue-tied.

The sight that greeted them at the track was one of dazzling color and movement. Carriages were everywhere, filled with lavishly dressed people. Many had come on horseback, and their blacks, bays, chestnuts, and whites milled in constantly changing patterns of colors. Most resplendent of all were the Mexican riders in elaborate silver and black with their ornately carved saddles. The burnished gold of the palominos gleamed vividly in the morning sun. Buyers and gawkers all inspected the merchandise carefully.

Amanda sat straight on her small chestnut filly, nervously smoothing her skirts and scanning the crowd. When the striking Mexican came into her line of vision the rest of the crowd seemed to dim. He was mounted on the largest horse she had ever seen, the same palomino as he had ridden that day at the wharf. Its golden hide gleamed almost as brightly as the white teeth in Esteban's flashing smile. Every lean, muscular contour of his long frame was clearly visible beneath his close-fitting suit. His black hair curled damply over his forehead. The white lacy shirtfront contrasted with his dark complexion, and his golden eyes seemed to match the color of his horse.

"What a splendid animal," she said softly.

Doug, his attention returning to her from the distractions of the melee, followed her gaze to Esteban. "What did you say, Amanda? I'm sorry, I didn't hear in all the din."

She looked away quickly and stammered, "Oh, just that that big golden horse is the most impressive I've ever seen, that's all. I'm not familiar with the breed."

Doug, who fancied himself an expert on horseflesh, proceeded to explain to her that palominos were not actually a breed but merely a color line that breeders strove to replicate, usually by mating a palomino with a sorrel. However, the rate of replication usually came out at no more than a fifty-fifty chance for a new golden horse.

Amanda nodded dutifully in response to his lecture and let the whole day, alive and vibrant around her, soak into her soul. It was so good to be out in the sun, to be young and healthy and alive! It had been a long time since she had felt so excited!

As the show started, Esteban took charge, describing in clear, unaccented English the fine points of breeding, training, and handling the horses. His vaqueros put them through their paces as he spoke. The horses responded to knee pressure and verbal commands. Quirts and spurs, or a heavy hand on the reins, were unnecessary. The men showed their horses' skill as Esteban answered questions. There were quite a few women in the crowd, many of them on horseback. His charm and physical attractiveness made several of the more forward of them join in the questioning with great enthusiasm. Amanda shyly held back and watched the show, by now quite impressed with the palominos as well as their owner.

As the demonstration progressed, Esteban realized it was coming off even better than he had planned. There were more women than he had been led to expect. A number of them were fairly young and attractive. He knew this would work to his advantage, especially if they had rich husbands or fathers to indulge them by purchasing horses. As he looked across the confusion of the crowd, he saw a woman mounted on a good chestnut filly, but he observed the quality of the horse only incidentally. Strange, he mused, he was not ordinarily attracted to fair-haired women, yet this one was truly remarkable in an understated, refined way. No doubt she was of a good Yankee family. Her hair was golden and blazed fiery in the sunlight, framing a face acquainted with the California sun. Unlike so many ladies, she obviously didn't bleach her complexion or go about with a parasol to keep it wan and porcelain-pale. Its light tawny gold accented the delicacy of her features. He let his eyes wander down her graceful throat to the gentle curve of breasts and slight waist. The fullness of the riding skirt hid the rest of her, but he let his imagination compensate. Yes, she was distinctive and very lovely.

Feeling Esteban's warm gaze upon her, Amanda let her attention stray from Doug's conversation. Startled green eyes collided with amused sherry ones. Flushing furiously, Amanda looked away quickly and fastened her attention back on Doug's discourse. Damn, she was as flustered as a schoolgirl! It had been long years since Amanda had been affected by a man's lascivious gaze. After all, she had lived by inviting it for quite a while. Still, here she sat blushing like a fourteen-year-old girl with her first beau.

She fidgeted with the reins of her filly and tried hard to pay attention to what McElroy was droning on about. She would not look, but she knew the man's sherry eyes were alight with mirth.

Arrogant, conceited womanizer! Amanda forced herself to be calm and collected, smiling dazzlingly at Doug. She was more animated in her conversation with the poor Scot than she had been in many months.

Esteban watched her discomfiture and naïveté. She wasn't coy, he decided, but honestly shy and indignant at his bold perusal. One of his potential customers distracted his attention by putting a slim, gloved hand brazenly over his. She leaned across her horse to expose her overstuffed bosom as she spoke.

"Señor Santandar, I must tell you how desperately I want one of these horses. I think I've convinced Papa, but if you were to assure him of how safe they are . . . After all, they are so big!"

She gave him a winsome look, her soulful blue eyes promising much more than she spoke. Marilou Peterson's father was a wealthy banker who denied her nothing. After she introduced him to her doting parent, Esteban negotiated his first sale of the day.

Amanda and Paul had walked to a small copse on a slight rise to get a good view of the upcoming race. They sat in the shade and watched the proceedings until Doug rode over to them, mounted on the outstanding palomino he had just purchased. He had bought one of the largest ones, impressed by its size.

"Amanda, you must take a quick ride around the race course with me before they get ready for the run. We have nearly an hour. Just wait until you see what this animal can do with me in command." He was like a ten-year-old with a new toy at Chirstmas, childishly delighted and eager to show off.

Paul stood and admired the horse, patting him. "Why not, Amanda? Ride now with Doug. I will take my rest here in the shade and save for us a place for the race."

Outmaneuvered again, she smilingly rose and untied the

reins of her filly from behind the carriage. After Doug
helped her mount, he swung atop the huge beast he had
just purchased. Amanda did agree that the size of the
animal fitted him far better than did the small sorrel he had
ridden to the mission. Quickly, however, she realized that
although his size and the palomino's might be compatible,
their temperaments were not. Doug attempted to control
the animal with brute force, pulling cruelly on the bit in its
tender mouth. He was nervous and very anxious to appear
dashing in her eyes. Trying to subjugate the horse in this
way was a mistake.

"Doug, those animals are superbly trained. They can be
managed easily by verbal commands and knee pressure.
Remember the way the handlers did it?"

She tried to get him to relent in what was shaping up to
be quite a battle of wills between man and beast. Amanda
was becoming less and less sure who was the beast, when
suddenly the great golden horse, goaded by such painful
treatment, made a lightening lunge just as Doug loosened
his grip on the reins. He struggled to regain his iron hold
on the horse, but in the process Amanda's smaller mare
was hit broadside and then flayed by the great hooves. The
palomino reared up and dumped its rider unceremoniously
on the ground. The chestnut took off with a start before
Amanda realized what was happening. She stared, aghast
as McElroy flew through the air then she raced after the
runaway. Once free of his burden, the palomino stood
perfectly still and began to graze innocently.

Although Amanda and Doug had ridden a good way
from the crowd, Esteban had watched their progress from
a distance. He saw the man mishandling his new mount
and then the collision and flurry that set the mare off.
Dismounted, he began to reach for Oro, then stopped short
and watched the spectacle in fascination. The slim girl was
quite a rider and had a natural way with animals. Within a
hundred yards, Amanda regained control of the terrified
horse, bent low over her neck, and brought her around to a
neat stop. Then she began to croon softly to the mare,
patted her neck in reassurance, and trotted her calmly back

to where the burly redheaded Scot was gingerly picking himself off the rocky earth. Amanda's hair had come loose and her hat had blown across the track. Her hair fell to her waist in a thick, golden cascade. She swept it behind her with a careless gesture as she dismounted.

"What a lady," Esteban said, whistling to himself, then adding a few choice epithets in Spanish for her stupid escort. That jackass could have gotten her killed! He could never have crossed the crowd and reached her in time to prevent a spill if she had not handled things so well herself.

By this time quite a number of people had seen the mishap and were flocking over to see if anyone was injured. Amanda quickly assured the solicitous men clustered about her that she was fine. Apparently, so was the placid palomino, which was grazing contentedly nearby. She went over to him and picked the trailing reins from the ground, then looked at his mouth. It was bleeding!

Of all the stupid, pigheaded, Scottish stubbornness, she fumed inwardly, soothing the horse, which seemed to be quite content once free of McElroy. *No wonder they ride runty little Shetland ponies in that godforsaken Scotland!*

Paul rushed up, pale and puffing, to assure himself that his *Liebchen* was safe. Doug was hideously embarrassed. However, he was even more afraid to blame the gentle golden horse when a slip of a girl could control him so easily. He subsided into a monotone note of apology, scarcely meeting her accusing gaze.

Wanting desperately to redeem himself in her eyes, he said, "Amanda, you seem to have a way with this great beast and he obviously loves you. I make him a present to you—a golden horse for a golden woman."

Knowing the cost, Amanda was embarrassed to accept so expensive a gift from him, but she feared that if she refused, he might be angry enough to have the beautiful animal destroyed. The crowd gathering around took up the spirit of the gallant offer, urging her to accept.

Paul nodded his approval and Amanda knew there was no alternative but to be in debt to the Scot for the gift. She thanked him and hugged the proud golden neck of the horse. The crowd cheered.

This minor celebration was interrupted by the announcement of the big race. Amanda, Paul, and a badly limping Doug retreated to the vantage point by the trees where their carriage driver had reserved them a good view.

As the contestants lined up, the judge checked off each entry. There was a field of ten horses whose owners were able to qualify for the contest by paying a very high fee. All the animals were of good bloodlines, several from southern California and three imported all the way from Australia.

Esteban carefully watched his opponents handle their mounts while he sat relaxed in the saddle, ready for the starting gun. Just before it went off, he raised his eyes to the small knoll where the lady in green sat. He saluted her with his hand raised to the brim of his black, flat-crowned hat, and when his eyes caught hers, she returned his gaze. Their eyes locked and held until the judge's commands took Esteban's attention back to the race.

At the crack of the gun the big palomino plunged off, yet only kept pace with the other three frontrunners, seemingly content to glide effortlessly in fourth place. Esteban knew that on this track the leader, a rangy buckskin, would quickly tire. The other two would take a bit longer, but because of Oro's long stride and his tremendous speed, he could easily overtake them near the end. The buckskin slowed and the two trailing him passed by. The gray and the black stayed neck and neck until the last quarter circle of the course. Then, without effort, the big gold simply left the other two behind and streaked over the finish line, a good four lengths ahead of the nearest competitor.

The crowd roared its approval, bets were paid, and a hot but happy Esteban trotted the palomino into the thick of the milling crowd to receive congratulations. He removed his hat, wiping his brow with his sleeve. Rivulets of perspiration flowed down his temples and shirtfront. The damn black charro outfit was not at all suitable for California at noon.

He may have felt uncomfortable, but to numerous female eyes he was certainly more than presentable. Marilou Peterson was quickly at his side. People clustered around to discuss the race. A number of stable owners were there also, most eager to make a deal for such an incredibly fast beast or one of his offspring.

Amanda watched Esteban dismount and vanish into the press of people, but not before she saw that cow-eyed Peterson girl plant an exuberant kiss on his cheek. *Such a display in public*, Amanda thought disdainfully. Paul watched her and was thoughtful. Doug, nursing his aching backside, was oblivious to everything.

CHAPTER 9

Only an hour remained until curtain time at the opera and Amanda was not yet ready. She sat at her dressing table gazing into the mirror, seeing nothing, thinking much. A few hours earlier she and Paul had come close to an argument.

"You know, *Liebchen*, Doug wanted to escort you tonight," Paul had said. "Why do you make it so hard? He feels terrible about the accident with the horses yesterday and wants to make it up to you. It is not like you, Amanda, this holding a grudge."

Amanda was still furious with McElroy after she had visited their head stableman that morning and seen how he had to treat the palomino Doug had injured. Yes, she did hold a grudge! She flashed a glare past Paul's beseeching gaze, out the window toward the stables. "I realize how 'sorry' Doug is, and it was most generous of him to give me the horse, even considering that he can't ride it. Paul, you should have seen what he did to the poor animal's mouth! And I kept telling him, if he'd only listened, that horse was so well trained he didn't need to use force. He's a pig-headed Scot and should stick to buggy riding!''

Paul smiled and then sobered. "Amanda, you and I both know we do not talk of horses, but men. Doug was trying too hard to impress you and it failed, but that does not change his heart, or make him a bad man. He is in love with you, *Liebchen*. He wants to marry you. Is that so bad?''

She paced across the thick Turkish carpet silently and fiercely as Paul talked. When he finished, she whirled, her loose golden hair flying like a mane. "It's very noble of him to love a reformed whore.''

Paul's gaze became stern. "Why do you do this to yourself, Amanda? You are not and never have been a whore. The tragedy of your past is just that—past. Doug knows this and wants to marry you. That is the important thing. Anyway, you know, *Liebchen*, if pasts were really scrutinized, half the fine ladies of San Francisco could not escape censure. Better it is, I think, to marry a man who knows you for who you are and loves you.''

"But I don't want to marry him, Paul. I don't love him. I'd always know, don't you see, no matter how kind he was—I'd know he accepted me *despite* my past. I'd always have to carry that knowledge, burned into me and into him, too.'' She wrung her hands and sat down abruptly on the small gold sofa behind her, looking for all the world like a frightened, fierce kitten.

She looked down at her hands, clenched into small fists, crushing her lace handkerchief. Softly, her head still lowered, she went on, "Besides, the whole thing is pointless. I still don't think I could ever marry, be a wife. I certainly am not attracted to Doug that way. I don't think I ever will be, to any man.''

Equally as softly, Paul replied, "Not even to Esteban Santandar on his golden horse?''

Abruptly her head jerked up and she flushed as she met Paul's kindly eyes. Was it sadness or pity she saw in their depths? Or both? She tried for a light smile, which wobbled away. "Oh, Paul, that's just a silly girlish fantasy. You saw, didn't you, how he was surrounded by drooling women at the race? He never looked twice at me. And he's such an arrogant beast anyway. I'm in no danger of even being noticed by the dashing caballero, much less of receiving a proposition or, even less likely, a proposal. So, dismiss him from your mind and so shall I."

As the coach pulled up in front of the opera house, Esteban stepped out and helped his aunt Ursula from the vehicle while Frank followed. The Mulcaheys had arrived a week earlier than planned. They rarely came to San Francisco, but they had all agreed to meet here a week after the horse sale for a few days of recreation. Then, an unexpected offer to purchase some timberland came to Frank and he and his wife decided to come sooner. Esteban was delighted. He had been in San Francisco only a few times himself. They could all three enjoy the sights and entertainments. The magnificent new opera house was an excellent place to begin.

As they were not patrons, they could not secure box seats, but neither the Mulcaheys nor Esteban minded. From the floor, the glitter and glamour of the huge, ornate building was stunning. The brass gaslights and cut-glass fixtures gleamed, adding brilliance to the golds, reds, and blues of the house. The thick carpets absorbed the noise of hundreds of excited voices. In the outer lobby, men smoked expensive cigars and women stared through diamond-encrusted lorgnettes. When the signal for curtain was given, Frank and his nephew stubbed out their cigars and escorted Ursula to their seats.

As the audience was growing silent, Esteban swept his eyes up toward the boxes at the side of the room. A flicker of gold caught his glance and he looked back at one front box near the stage on the right. Entering late was an older, thickset man accompanied by a beautiful young woman. He looked more closely, his sherry eyes focusing intently across the distance of the huge room as they did out on the vast plains of Sonora. Yes, it was the golden-haired woman from the track. The one who rode magnificently and blushed delightfully. He remembered their eyes meeting then, how the green riding habit had curved around her delicious, slim body, and the way her hair fell below her waist when her hat was lost.

Tonight she was dressed in a bronze silk gown, cut modestly low, yet of such soft material that its dancing lights accented each gentle swell and hollow. Topaz jewelry complemented the beautiful mane of hair, piled high in a riot of curls atop that delicate head. The picture was sensually warm, all golden and bronze, with her tawny skin set off to perfection. He stared at her and wondered why he had ever preferred dark women. Indeed, he wished that he might see how the rest of her looked, once stripped of all those ladylike layers of clothing. His erotic musing was cut short by the lowering of the lights and the rising of the first-act curtain. The audience was plunged into darkness, but he could still feel the glittering heat of bronze, almost like a caress.

All through the first act, Amanda would not have noticed if the lead soprano shattered the crystal light fixtures when she hit high C or whether the baritone sang completely off-key. Just as they entered their box, she saw *him* on the main floor, seating an older but most striking-looking Mexican woman. When he raised his gaze and scanned the room, she forced herself to be composed and look only at Paul. She could feel his rapacious stare and perversely delighted in it, being positive that he did not realize she was aware of his presence. No more schoolgirl antics. She was in control. Then why, a small inner voice chided, did her heart keep such a wantonly fast pace, and why couldn't she concentrate on any part of the beautifully performed opera in progress on the stage? Her mind kept returning to prickle over the question of who the woman with him was. She was quite handsome and obviously of good family. Amanda also noticed that he was dressed differently, not in the silver and black of a Mexican aristocrat but rather like a wealthy American businessman. He wore a cream-colored linen suit of the latest fashion, with an elegant gold pocket watch and chain. The clothes were tailored to perfection, strikingly like those he had worn that mudstained evening at the parlor house so long ago.

When the lights came up at intermission, Paul turned to Amanda, who had been staring absently into the darkness, not watching the lighted stage. She blinked at the sudden illumination, and he smiled at her. She looked rather like a little girl caught at the cookie jar.

"Would you enjoy to go to the lobby for some champagne, *Liebchen*? You seem in need of something to waken you. Is the performance so dull then?"

"Oh, no, not at all, Paul. I was just resting my eyes in the dark for a moment, that's all. I'd love a glass of champagne, even though Henri says they serve inferior wine here."

At this they both laughed, and Paul said, "Henri thinks any wine he did not produce is inferior. Now he makes better than even his own France!"

As Esteban crossed the lobby with Uncle Frank and Aunt Ursula, he looked at the squarish, graying man who carried two champagne glasses toward a destination outside the press of the crowd. "Who is that man, Tio? He looks familiar. The one carrying the two glasses over there."

Frank noted where Esteban indicated and smiled. "Sure and don't you remember a good customer, aye, and competitor? That's Paul Meuller, lad—one of the biggest producers of beef cattle in northern California. Also pork and seafood; he owns Mueller Meats and Delicacies and a good interest in a dozen other businesses, like hide and tallow and dry goods. I've sold him some prime livestock, but since he went into growin' his own beef for the slaughterhouse, he's eliminated the middleman, sad to say. A fellow immigrant, German, a good man."

Frank was about to ask why Esteban was interested, but then he saw Paul hand Amanda the glass. "Ah, it's his lady, not the old gentleman you're interested in." His blue eyes twinkled as he took in the beautiful woman in bronze silk who stood across the floor. "Sad to say, lad, I've never had the pleasure. Mueller and I haven't really seen each other or done any firsthand business in quite a few years. I don't get to San Francisco very often. He was married, but his wife was an invalid, and the last I heard, she died. Maybe he married again.''

''No, that one's not an old man's darling. I saw her the other day at the track with Mueller and a young, very stupid admirer.'' What was it about her that fascinated him so? He could recall that day at the track in every detail.

As the two speculated, Ursula came up to them to tell Frank that some old friends they had not seen in several years were at the opera that night, and the conversation turned to other subjects.

Amanda watched them from the corner of her eye as they talked. They were all striking, the woman and the two men. She wore dark blue, with her black hair coiled high on her head, and obviously shared Esteban's nationality and aristocratic bearing. The big fair-skinned man was boisterous and flamboyant of gesture, but not rowdy as so many of the newly rich miners and other San Francisco millionaires were.

''Paul, who are those people over there with Señor Santandar?'' She felt daring as she asked the question, daring enough to meet the high and mighty Esteban Santandar and his companions. She would be in command, and the devil with Esteban's boldness, Paul's protectiveness, and anyone else who crossed her!

Paul looked at the Mulcaheys. Despite his annoyance at seeing Santandar again in Amanda's line of vision, he was pleased. ''Ach, Frank and Ursula Mulcahey, *Liebchen*. She is Ursula Santandar Mulcahey. The big Irishman is her husband, and she is the sister of Don Esteban's father.''

''Really, Paul, I thought you said the illustrious Santandars never married Yankees.'' Amanda was beginning to enjoy herself.

''This is the only case I know where it has happened, believe me. Ursula is a very unusual and strong-willed woman. Frank was, even twenty-five years ago, a very rich and persistent man. Her family accepts the marriage, but they are not close to him. The Mulcaheys live in Los Angeles and seldom go to Sonora or San Francisco.''

"Then how do you know them?"

"We do business, what else? Before I expanded to raise my own livestock, I bought from Frank. He also ships many items for my emporiums, mostly dry goods. A hard bargain he drives," Paul said approvingly.

Her eyes took on the bright gleam of green bottle glass polished to a high luster. "If you are old business acquaintances, why not introduce your 'niece' from back east? I find I have an irresistible desire to meet such an illustrious and unconventional family." Amanda could scarcely believe her audacity.

Paul frowned and said, "Amanda, I do not think . . ." but before he could finish, Frank Mulcahey approached, hand outstretched to Paul, an engaging grin lighting up his face.

"Why sure and it's been at least two lifetimes, Herr Mueller, and you keepin' this fair young thing all to yourself. Where's your sense of fair play, man? You must introduce her to me wife and nephew and meself, of course."

In spite of his trepidations, Paul had always liked Frank Mulcahey and his wife, who was genteel and kind, without the haughtiness of so many well-born Mexican women. The two older men shook hands warmly and Paul presented Amanda. "Frank Mulcahey, an old business competitor and a most skillful one, please meet Amanda Whittaker from Missouri."

As he took her hand, his blue eyes gleamed. "Sure and it's a pleasure, Miss Whittaker. Are you also from the old country? They make some incredibly lovely women in the Germanies."

"No, I was born in Saint Joseph, Mr. Mulcahey. My father married Uncle Paul's sister when traveling abroad." The lie was glib and came quite easily. Paul looked faintly startled, but Amanda remained calm as they chatted. Soon Ursula and Esteban came up to greet Frank's friends.

The introductions were simple and friendly, in Frank's jovial, take-charge manner. When Esteban took Amanda's hand, he raised it briefly to his lips, all the while looking into her eyes. It was a traditional European gesture, often aped by Americans with pretensions. Many rich patrons at Lyla's had kissed her hand, but none had a remotely similar effect on her. Was there the faintest hint of laughter sparkling in the golden eyes as he smiled and acknowledged the introduction? Thinking back to all that had passed before, Amanda felt the pulse in her throat begin to grow unsteady. Calling on all her reserve to hide her feelings, she found it far harder now than it had ever been in the parlor house. Was it easier to hide repulsion than attraction? Damn the man! This time she would show him and Paul that she was in charge of the exchange.

"I'm delighted to meet the man responsible, at least indirectly, for my owning a beautiful palomino. Of course, it was Mr. McElroy's horsemanship that created the need for his giving me Sunrise." The allusion to Doug's unceremonious dumping brought laughter to both young people. Esteban proceeded to explain to his aunt and uncle about the incident at the track.

Ursula solicitously inquired about McElroy's health, and Amanda assured her, "He's quite recovered physically, but his pride was dealt a swift and terrible blow. That may take more time to heal, I fear."

Esteban interjected, "Sunrise—an appropriate name for the animal. Did you choose it?"

"Yes; he was so golden in the early light this morning when I went to our stable to see how he was. It just seemed perfect. He's superbly trained and a joy to ride. I've never had so gentle a horse. I compliment your skills as a stockman and trainer, Mr. Santandar."

"And I, Miss Whittaker, compliment your skill as a rider. An excellent horsewoman deserves a horse such as Sunrise." Turning to Paul, quite formally, Esteban inquired if he and his neice would have dinner with him and his aunt and uncle the following evening at the International Hotel. Frank and Ursula quickly echoed the invitation.

Before Paul could frame a reply, a smiling Amanda assured them that it would be a pleasure. She made a point of directing her acceptance to Ursula.

As the intermission ended, Esteban again took Amanda's hand and saluted it quickly with his lips. "Until tomorrow evening, Miss Whittaker?"

Although her composure was not quite complete, she hid the fact well as they returned to their box. She felt almost triumphant. So, he was turning on the charm. Well, why not? Paul Mueller was a highly respected man in San Francisco. However, a secret voice nagged at her through the final act, Mandy was not a respectable woman.

On the ride home, Paul was alternately morose and pleading. "I think very carefully, Amanda, about this dinner tomorrow. Maybe we should send word and cancel it. It is not a good idea."

Ingenuously, she looked at him in the flickering light of the carriage as they moved down gaslit streets toward home. "But, Paul, I thought you really liked the Mulcaheys. Surely you don't think their nephew will behave improperly in a public restaurant?"

He grunted in disgust. "It is not him but you I worry about, as you know well. You are too interested in such a one. Oh, he is proper and charming to 'my sister's daughter from Missouri.' He does not know you, Amanda, and he would not appreciate you for yourself if he did."

At these references to her duplicity that evening and her background, Amanda colored. "Paul, I know how it seemed, but I just wanted to see if I could do it—be a real lady with a respectable past and good family name that even Don Esteban couldn't resist. I'm just playing a game, a little harmless flirtation with someone who doesn't know where I came from. It won't last, I know. He'll leave. You said yourself the Mulcaheys hardly ever come to San Francisco. What can it hurt?"

Sadly, Paul regarded the flushed, beautiful girl across from him. "You mean *whom* can it hurt, don't you, *Liebchen*?"

"Paul, you know I'm no more serious than he is. He'll

make an arranged marriage to a Mexican aristocrat and I'll never marry at all. We've discussed that before. He'll only be here a week or so, hardly enough time for a silly fascination to turn to bitter unrequited love.'' She broke off with a light laugh at her own melodrama and took his big, square hands in her small ones. "Don't fret, *Uncle* Paul.''

That night as she tossed in bed, her words came back to mock her. Why was she doing this, playing such a dangerous game? She knew, no matter how she tried to convince Paul otherwise, that Esteban Santandar had a terribly compelling effect on her. She had never before been sexually attracted to a man. After Carver and then the degradation at the parlor house, she had always been sure that that side of her nature was dead, if indeed she had ever possessed it. Now she knew a perverse pleasure in finding that she could feel. Elizabeth was right—it was good to be a healthy, normal young woman.

Yet, being who she was, Amanda knew she was courting danger in pursuing her attraction to Esteban. She should play it safe with Doug or someone like him. Yet, there was a part of her, deep within her heart of hearts, that longed for a clean, new beginning. *A new beginning like the one you wanted, Papa. You lost your chance in Kansas. I lost mine in California.* Could she begin again in the isolation of Sonora? Unanswered questions tortured her sleep, and a dark, handsome face filled her dreams, his golden eyes promising. . . .

The dinner the next evening was delightful. Frank and Paul entertained the group with tales of their early days as immigrant businessmen in Mexican California. Frank's lilting Irish charm and Paul's old-world German buoyancy served as perfect background for an evening of laughter and good company. Amanda was impressed with Ursula Mulcahey, whose quiet yet strong presence was obviously appreciated by her husband. Those two, from such different worlds, clearly adored each other.

Paul watched Esteban charm Amanda, all very properly and formally. Yet, his eyes and smiles spoke volumes. So did hers. Paul had never seen Amanda so animated, so glowingly alive, even when she was with their closest friends. Paul had felt pleased when Amanda lost her sad, haunted look after a few months of living at his house. However, as he watched her with Esteban, he realized that he had never really seen the young woman she might have been had she never known Carver Cain or Lyla's Place. Amanda laughed and sparkled like a rare golden gem, without artifice, pure and beautiful.

The following day, as Paul and Amanda took breakfast, he was thoughtful, she vibrant. In the midst of the meal, Albert, the butler, brought a card for Amanda that had just been delivered by a boy from the International Hotel.

Paul watched her face as she opened it. "It's from Esteban. He thanks me for the delightful evening and asks to take me riding this afternoon—with a proper chaperon, of course," she added impishly. "So formal and proper, these Mexicans."

Paul looked at her and took a drink of his strong, black coffee. A bit of acceptance came into his manner. Or was it resignation? "And you will go, *ja*? Properly chaperoned, of course."

Amanda watched Esteban ride up to the house on that massive golden horse of his, even bigger than her Sunrise. Esteban was dressed simply in dark tan trousers and short jacket, cut in the snug, well-tailored fit of Mexican fashion that he wore so well, but without the elaborate silver adornment of a formal charro costume. He wore soft, brown kid boots and a flat-crowned hat. His white shirt was unruffled and open at the throat. He looked as natural in the simple riding clothes as he had in the showy charro costume at the track, or the elegant evening clothes at the opera. Why did she notice so many little things, details of his dress and manners, that she had been unaware of with all other men?

When she came downstairs, Amanda realized that her time spent dressing was well worth the trouble. She wore a deep peach riding habit of the finest raw silk, dull in finish but softly clinging. Because of the slight breeze and the unseasonable coolness of the afternoon, she let her long masses of gold hair hang down her back, bound simply with a dark orange ribbon. No more silly hats to blow away. The effect was one of warm, tawny sensuousness, completed by the light apricot fragrance she used shampooing her hair. As Esteban greeted her in the entry hall at the bottom of the mansion's circular staircase, he was pleased and lingered just a second longer than usual over her hand.

It was a beautiful day for a ride, sunny and clear. True to his word, Esteban had arranged for a groom to ride with them, at a suitable distance behind yet in plain view. They would have their first chance to talk privately on the outing. They rode away from town and out along an open stretch of coast with a splendid view of the bay in the distance. At first they discussed the opera, the social season in San Francisco, the weather, the banal subjects a young couple just acquainted might be expected to discuss.

"That day at the track when your friend was unseated, I was quite impressed with how you handled that chestnut filly. She had a bad scare and could have broken her neck and yours. Not many people can communicate with a horse so well. I bet you've always had a way with animals."

Amanda laughed as she patted Sunrise. "I was always bringing home stray cats and dogs, once even a starling with a broken wing. Papa said we ran a menagerie. Elizabeth says that's why I'm good with her patients."

"Elizabeth?"

"Oh, yes, Dr. Elizabeth Denton." At his look of male chauvinistic incredulity, she went on firmly, "She is a *real* physician and a very fine one who graduated near the top of her class in medical school back in Philadelphia. She has a small clinic on Portsmouth Square and treats those who can't afford to pay as well as those who can, which is more than I can say for some of her male colleagues!"

He laughed and threw up his hands in surrender. "All right, I stand corrected. There is such a thing as a female doctor. Do you help her in this clinic?"

Once again defensive, Amanda answered, "Of course.

She's taught me and I'm a good nurse. My father died of cholera when I was very young. I hate to see people suffer and be unable to help. There are so many new discoveries in medicine, if only the doctors out here would keep up with research and read about new techniques. Dr. Denton gets regular shipments of medical journals and new books as well as all the medicines she can afford to buy.''

He grinned. ''You obviously admire this paragon of virtue. If ever I fall ill in San Francisco I shall call upon Dr. Denton and you to minister to me in my hour of need.''

''I spend as much time as I can helping her on her rounds and in the clinic. I'm afraid I'm not very social, even though Uncle Paul has many friends from all over Europe. His best friend Henri is a vintner from France. We have wonderful musical evenings and I have a weakness for fine restaurants, but I wouldn't trade the work I can do in the clinic for anything.''

''Perhaps I'll have to meet your Dr. Denton. Where I grew up, women of your class would faint at the sight of illness or blood. It's remarkable that American ladies can be so resilient.''

''I'm not a fainter. Neither is Elizabeth, obviously. I've assisted her in actual surgery only on a few occasions. That's the really hard part. Uncle Paul frets and is overprotective, but I want to be useful.''

''Somehow, I can't ever imagine you as useless or merely ornamental, even though you could pour tea for your uncle and just sit and be beautiful.'' His gaze was warm, and the compliment pleased her.

The ride was over more quickly than either of them wanted, but as the sun began to dip lower toward the Pacific, he brought her home, agreeing to escort her to Dr. Denton's clinic the following day.

Most of Elizabeth's patients were poor and had never seen the opulence of Lyla's Place. Amanda was known only as a wealthy lady friend of the doctor's. She felt safe bringing Esteban to meet Elizabeth at her office. No one there would recognize ''Mandy.'' The clinic was a part of her life she would always be proud of, and she felt compelled to share it with him.

The minute they walked in the door, Elizabeth recognized the man her young friend had so haltingly described to her only days earlier. There couldn't be two specimens like this one! That a man of his background would consider it proper for a woman to be a physician and to allow another younger woman to volunteer her time in a public clinic treating the indigent elevated Esteban sharply in Elizabeth's estimation.

At one point she mentioned a brief period of study in Scotland and the fine medical school in Edinburgh, to which he replied, "A bitter, cold, damp place, though. I was persuaded against my better judgment to go grouse hunting with some school friends from London. We spent the wettest, most miserable week of my young life in the hills outside that city. I could have used your professional services for the cold I developed. It nearly killed me."

Elizabeth laughed. "Yes, it is a nasty, unhealthful climate, unless, of course, you're a Scot."

"Europe is a fascinating place to study and visit, but this is the part of the world where people should live. Like my Spanish ancestors, I want to feel the caress of warm sun on my face, preferably all year round." As he said this he looked at Amanda's lightly tanned hands, as she continued to roll bandages. The day before on the ride he had complimented her on her complexion, admiring the sun on her face. She looked up and blushed. The brief exchange was not lost on Dr. Denton.

Esteban made his farewells, reaffirming his acceptance of dinner at Paul and Amanda's that evening. His aunt and uncle would accompany him, and, if she had no emergencies, Elizabeth was to come also.

When he was gone, Amanda looked at her friend and said, "Well, don't just keep puttering with your instruments. Tell me I'm crazy to even bring him here or keep up this hopeless association. That's what Paul keeps insisting. Part of me knows he's right, too. Yet, for this brief time

before he returns to Mexico, I am enjoying myself."
Hesitantly she continued rolling bandages.

Elizabeth, too, kept working, but she smiled and said,
"I'm not so sure Paul Mueller is such an infallible judge
of character. Your Don Esteban seems far more tolerant of
me and my practice here than most American men are,
including that ignorant young Scot Paul's so fond of."

At the mention of Doug, Amanda smiled. "Yes, he does
think it indecent for me to work here, and even for you
to."

"Esteban Santandar may be from a rigid, class-conscious
background in Mexico, but he has traveled quite a bit and
even, I think, may have read a book or two." Elizabeth's
eyes were dancing as she regarded Amanda.

"He's had quite an unusual life, as you'll find out
tonight. He spent a good part of his youth in Los Angeles
with his Irish uncle, and he's traveled all over the United
States. He went to school in Paris for several years and
lived in London, and he speaks fluent French as well as
Spanish and English." Amanda seemed breathless with
information.

"His lack of accent is remarkable," Elizabeth commented
dryly. "Of course, he doesn't look American, but to hear
him speak, you'd think he was as Yankee as any banker on
Portsmouth Square."

"That's because he's spent so much time in our country.
You should hear Esteban imitate his uncle's Irish brogue!
It's wonderful."

Elizabeth was aware that Amanda was unconsciously
looking for an ally. Perhaps she wanted permission to let
this very tentative relationship go on, despite Paul's warnings and legitimate fears. The man was obviously attractive and not at all the rigid Latin type she had expected.
Perhaps it might work out. God knew, Amanda deserved a
chance. She also needed a friend who understood.

"Amanda, I'm not going to side with Paul and give
warnings or urge you to settle for Doug McElroy. I like
your young man. He's handsome, charming, and educated. But you must decide how to handle it if anything

serious happens. I can't tell you that everything will work out splendidly if you continue to see him. He may get on his boat and sail off, never to return again. Or he might even ask you to marry him.''

When Amanda protested, Elizabeth silenced her with a gesture. ''The point is, you must consider all the alternatives and plan what your response will be. I can't put my seal of approval on him, and Paul won't. Neither of us really knows him. Maybe you don't either. Does he know about you?''

Amanda shook her head miserably.

''I'm not saying you should confess all your background to him, dear. Maybe it isn't necessary that he ever know. Many a man has gone through life happily ignorant of his wife's past. Just so you think about it carefully. Whatever you decide, and whatever happens, I'll always be here.''

Amanda was deeply touched by Elizabeth's support and compassion. As the two women went to the waiting room and ushered the first patient into the office, both had tears in their eyes.

CHAPTER
10

In the following weeks Amanda and Esteban spent as much time together as his schedule permitted. They shared dinners at Paul's house with Frank and Ursula and went to fine restaurants in town, chaperoned by Paul and the Mulcaheys. The Mulcaheys were surprised at their nephew's apparent fascination with the beautiful Americana. Ursula realized what pressures the Santandar family could bring to bear on one of its own. When they had left Sonora after Miguel's funeral, it had be tacitly assumed that an alliance between Elena Montoya and Esteban was forthcoming. No matter how enticing this time spent with Mueller's niece, Ursula was afraid that both young people would be hurt.

One morning after a dinner at the Mueller house, she broached her fears to Frank in their hotel room. "Amanda is a most beautiful young woman, but . . ." She stopped in mid-sentence, unable to frame her thoughts, pausing in brushing her long, black hair. She sat at the dressing table

gazing in the mirror as her husband came up behind her
and put his big hands around her thin shoulders.

"But she's a gringa, you mean?" He smiled sadly at
Ursula. At her immediate move to protest, he interjected,
"Now, love, I know you have a soft spot in your heart for
us gringos—at least some of us—and I know you like the
girl. I understand what you mean. Who should know better
than the two of us what it means to break family tradition,
especially when that family is Santandar?"

He paced restlessly across the floor. "I worry, too.
Dammit! I like that girl and I respect her uncle. They're
good people, bright, involved with life!"

"Not buried in an ancient Sonoran feudal system, you
mean? Yes, Amanda is very quick-witted for one so
young. She is also very lovely. I fear that's her fascination
for Esteban. He's seen enough beautiful women, God
knows. He's also known enough witty, sophisticated older
women of dubious morals like Solange Fabres." At the
mention of that name, Frank's face reddened into a shocked
admission of knowledge about the Frenchwoman and his
nephew.

"Oh, Frank, honestly, do you think I don't know she's
his mistress?" Ursula laughed at his consternation. "Men
think they protect their wives from such knowledge, but
only when women are foolish enough to pretend they don't
know what's going on."

He raised hands in supplication. "Just so you know,
love, that I'm a reformed man since I met you, and that's
the good Lord's own truth!"

Matter-of-factly, she began to brush her hair again,
saying, "Of course, I know you don't keep a woman."
Her eyes flashed a mock warning. "You don't need to, as
long as you have me. But we both know Esteban is
different. He's always been restless and always found
women easy. Up until now, I think he assumed he'd marry
someone like Elena and keep a more interesting mistress as
well."

"Portrayin' him as a typical philanderin' criollo is hardly fair, love," Frank defended his nephew. "After all,

he's always known that some women have minds of their own. He grew up around you.''

She smiled fondly, remembering the boy Esteban. ''I think he always thought of me as someone in a category all by myself. Still, I'm a Santandar, part of the tradition, the family. And family is sacred, even to my cynical young nephew, no matter how much he feuds with Alfredo or scoffs at the church. He expects to do his duty, even if he hates it. That's why I fear they may both be hurt. He can't marry her, Frank. She's not Mexican, she's not of a noble family lineage, she's not even Catholic, for heaven's sake! I don't want them to become involved and then have him leave her to face censure here alone.''

At this, Frank's face darkened like a bay stormcloud. ''You don't think he'd dare dishonor a girl like Paul Mueller's niece! He knows the difference between her and a woman like Solange, God in heaven!''

Attempting to placate him, Ursula said, ''I don't think he'd set out to seduce her. No. But they are young and obviously so very attracted to each other, and the strict chaperonage of my country isn't the custom here. So much is different. I just don't know. . . .''

If Esteban had known of his aunt and uncle's conversation that morning, he could not have been any surer of his motives or course of action than they were. What the hell was he doing, spending all this time squiring around a young, virgin Americana whom he did not dare touch? It was unthinkable, yet when he was near her his thoughts continuously went in that direction. Ever since their first meeting at the track, he had lain awake at night in his solitary hotel bed and tormented himself with thoughts of that gleaming, tawny body. At the track he had admired her and would have gladly seduced her into his bed with no qualms. He had sensed her attraction to him, and he was practiced at such matters. However, after meeting her uncle and their friends and seeing that she was not like the European women he had known, he was confused. She was as beautiful and sensual as the most elegant courtesan, yet innocently unaware of her allure. She was as intelligent as his aunt Ursula. A free, open spirit the likes of which he had never seen before. He was not sure he could take her and then just walk away with no regrets.

Damn all these sudden, foolish scruples! She was not a child. She must be nearly twenty years old. If Americans cared at all about purity for their daughters, they would have dueñas and strict social codes as they did in Mexico. What he passed up, that blundering, inept Scot would probably gain by default. Of course, he was forced to concede that the Scot would also marry her, something he could never do.

So, I'm playing with fire, dancing around the beautiful, golden Amanda like a damn fool moth. She was a flame, drawing him nearer, not in conscious seduction as had many women in the past. No, if he wanted her, he would have to be the seducer. He was sure she was attracted to him but had never thought of anything so unconventional as being his mistress.

I have to marry Elena and that's the end of it. I all but gave my word. Yet, a small nagging voice in the back of his mind said, *You didn't give your word, did you?* However, even if he had not, he would doubtless marry Elena anyway. It was his duty. Whatever passed between him and Amanda was a separate matter.

If Esteban was perplexed and the Mulcaheys were worried, Paul was despondent. He understood Amanda's dreams about living in a faraway place where she would be a lady—that mythical world she had created during her impoverished adolescence. She vehemently denied that she was pursuing her dream when he broached the subject. The social occasions with the Mulcaheys and Esteban were just a renewal of Paul and Frank's old business friendship, she insisted. Her transitory fascination with Esteban would end soon.

Almost two weeks after the first occasion, Esteban again arranged to take Amanda riding in the countryside. However, when he arrived at the house to meet her, she was in the back of the foyer hugging and talking excitedly to a scruffy old drummer who was apparently the owner of the

bedraggled peddler's wagon drawn up at the side door.
The man was small, wiry, and none too clean. He must
have been at least sixty years old, if the grizzled hair and
beard were any indication. When the butler announced
Esteban, she grasped Hoot's calloused hand and marched
the old codger across the hall.

"Hoot, this is Esteban Santandar, the man I've been
telling you about. Esteban, I want you to meet an old
friend of our family who, ah, chaperoned me across the
country to Uncle Paul after my father died. This is Jebediah
Hooter, who is like a grandfather to me."

The two men sized each other up as they shook hands.
The elder noticed the curious yet friendly look in the
younger's eyes. Esteban's glance traveled from Hoot's
grizzled countenance to the beautiful young woman.

*I'll jist bet this young man would love ta' know how me
an' Miss Mandy met up, yessiree,* Hoot thought.

He knew without her even explaining that this man was
different from Doug McElroy or any other gentlemen
callers he had met on his infrequent stopovers at Paul
Mueller's. Yes, this one was something special to his
Mandy. Hoot was protective, but he sensed that despite the
young man's obvious wealth and education, Esteban did
not disdain a firm handshake with Amanda's "grandfather." That was a good sign—not a dandyman, no matter
his looks.

"Hoot just pulled in this morning. We've not seen him
in nearly six months. He sells supplies in the gold camps
up on the American River."

"Not so much as a while back, girl. The small mines 'er
peterin' out. Not much call fer my stuff. I'm makin' farm
rounds in the valleys now. More settlers down ta th' real
business hereabouts. Them that's got sense God gave
geese—good land's fer farmin', gold er no gold."

"What kinds of farm supplies do you sell, Mr. Hooter?
My uncle and I own a shipping line that brings in seed and
iron tools for farmers. Perhaps we could offer you a good
wholesale rate."

"Dang, if thet don't beat all—ya look like a picture-book dandy an' ya talk like a Yankee trader—boy, yer all right! We jist might talk us a deal an' thet's no foolin'.''

They adjourned to the kitchen, where Amanda proceeded to fix her adopted grandfather a hearty breafast. The cook had gone marketing and someone had to feed Hoot, she explained to the horrified butler, who planned to bring one of the housemaids downstairs to take over the menial chore. Esteban watched in silent mirth as Amanda fixed the haughty Albert with a no-nonsense stare and told him that she had fixed her father's sausage and eggs when she was ten years old and even Uncle Paul found her cooking most adequate.

It was no idle boast. Her skills in the kitchen, a thing unknown to wealthy Mexican women, amazed Esteban. He thought fleetingly of Elena, who had most likely never seen the Montoya kitchen in her life. His fiancée suffered by comparison with the woman before him. He watched the small, delicate hands deftly fork sizzling sausages in a huge iron skillet, scramble a mound of fluffy eggs, and brown big wedges of bread smothered in butter. When finished, she efficiently stripped the cook's apron from her green riding habit, the one he remembered so fondly from that day at the track. Since she and Esteban had already eaten, they shared only coffee with a ravenous Jebediah Hooter.

After breakfast, Hoot insisted that they go for their planned ride while he unloaded some items he had brought for the Mueller household. He had to settle accounts with other merchants in town but promised to be back for supper with them and Paul. Steadfastly, as always, he declined to spend the night, insisting he had friends near the wharf who always expected him. Amanda had suspected for some time that he had a lady friend at the waterfront, but she never asked.

Amanda did not deem the presence of the groom necessary because the strictures of San Francisco society were not rigid. However, realizing that Esteban might misinterpret it to mean that American women, even of good families, were loose in morals, she did not protest when he went to the stable and had the boy mount up to follow them.

"You certainly made friends with Hoot. I'm pleased you like him and he likes you. He's very dear to me."

As they rode through the quiet residential section, he studied her glowing face alive with childlike happiness at the morning's events. "Amanda, you never stop surprising me. You accept people for their goodness of heart. You never judge them by their looks, manners, money—or even conventionality, as Elizabeth made clear the other night. While we were in the kitchen and I watched you, it seemed so right and natural for you to take over and cook. Just as natural to stare down Albert. No mean feat, that."

She flushed and realized how out-of-place such activities and associations must seem to someone of his culture. "American women are probably different from the women you're used to, but I guess you might call what we have pioneer spirit. Uncle Paul is wealthy now, but he earned his fortune in this country. My parents were not well-to-do, but even if they had been, I suspect I'd have been one to sneak down to the kitchen anyway. Does my liking to do simple chores displease you?" She looked at him levelly, deciding to face at least one issue squarely. She simply could not be a vapory, posturing grand dame with a lorgnette and smelling salts!

He threw back his head with a hearty laugh and said quickly, "Quite the opposite! I found myself comparing your wonderful American resourcefulness to my erstwhile fiancée's helplessness. I doubt Elena would know a skillet from a flat iron. I admire your willingness to cook, work at the hospital, or care for a horse who was abused—the head stableman told me how you helped him treat Sunrise. You're quite a woman, Amanda." The sherry eyes were warm and obviously admiring as he looked at her.

Feeling self-conscious as he turned his dazzling smile on her, she grasped a change of subject from midair. "You've mentioned your family briefly, but not a fiancée." Once the words were out, she could have bitten her tongue! She had no claim on him, no right to question whom he married. Yet, once he confirmed in words what she had always suspected, it stabbed at her—Elena. "I mean, I understood from your aunt and uncle's remarks that family ties are important in your country and your parents have probably made all the arrangements." The more she said, the more deeply she enmeshed herself. Damn!

He rode on, his eyes riveted straight ahead, yet seeing nothing in front of him. After what seemed an eternity to Amanda, he spoke. "I should tell you about the Santandars. You know about my aunt and uncle, but you don't know about my father." He then proceeded to tell her of his lifelong conflict with his father over the role of patrón, of Miguel's death without heirs, and of his informal agreement to marry Elena Montoya.

"She is probably the very best match I could make—old family, *pureza de sangre*, close friends of my parents. She's convent-raised, quite beautiful, and comes from a healthy family noted for producing sons. Alas, she's also spoiled, selfish, manipulating, and vapid. Since she left the nuns, I doubt she's read a book. If all the peons on her father's *estancia* were dying of plague, she'd complain because no one ironed her dresses. Hell, that's not really fair. I'm blaming her for my disgust with our whole social and political system, and that's hardly her fault."

Glad to get the topic of conversation away from the awkward area of his impending marriage, Amanda seized on politics and social philosophy, favorite subjects of hers.

"I think your time in Paris must have radicalized your thinking. What well-brought-up young man whose father is one of the biggest landowners in Mexico would be disgusted with his country's social system? Did you read Rousseau? Voltaire? You have 'the best of all possible worlds,' you know."

He snorted, half in derision at himself, half in enjoyment of her. "My classmates at the Sorbonne filled me with the ideals of the Revolution of 1848, but I hardly think Napoleon's weak nephew will bring the French any better social or political reform than Santa Anna's brought us. I do believe in what your Mr. Jefferson called a 'natural aristocracy.' Frank Mulcahey's living proof of it. So's Paul Mueller. Both were born poor and both, through their own talents and hard work, became successful. They took their own risks, made their own lives.

"I don't like the chaos I've seen in my country. The war with the Americans was senseless. Mexico was foredoomed by rotten mismanagement to lose California and Texas and the lands between to the Yankees. But we could have kept them out of the south. God, at Chapultepec, fourteen-year-old schoolboys died while Santa Anna retreated rather than share the glory by uniting his army with Valencia's! My own brother really died there, or started to die. Stupid, all so stupid.''

Amanda sensed his pain. "I don't think any war is sane, really. I've read that our war with the British during President Madison's administration was a horribly stupid waste. Napoleon in control of all Europe would have been a much greater danger to our country than the British navy, yet we indirectly helped that power-mad man when we fought England. No matter how bad its mistakes, your country has no monopoly on senseless wars, Esteban.''

They pulled off to the side of the road where the view was particularly lovely. He dismounted and helped her from her horse. "I think we should put women like you in charge of politics and there'd be no more wars.''

They both laughed at the improbability of women in charge of governments. Then she said, "You were wounded in the war, too—quite badly, from what your aunt said. Yet you don't blame us for that or your brother's death?''

"No, I don't, although there are many in my family who will never forgive the Americans. Uncle Frank didn't get a warm reception in Sonora. I've always been caught in between, I guess. I spent so much time as a child with Americans, my uncle and his business friends, that I could never see this country as a place full of villains. Yet, I didn't want the Americans invading my homeland, either. I had to fight. Strange, the older I get, the less clear things are. My war experiences led me to question our government and army. My time in Europe led me to question our social-class system. But I'm proud of my family name and honor."

"Perhaps that's why you had to work so hard to prove yourself. To be independent of your father, so you could face him on his own ground. Your uncle isn't modest in describing how well his nephew took to the lessons he taught. You've made your own success, too, just like my uncle Paul or your uncle Frank. I think," she said, dimpling, "you're one of Mr. Jefferson's 'natural aristocracy.'"

Her slight pressure on his arm as they strolled along the bluff caused him to feel the warmth of the day even more. He looked down at her, watching the sun streak her unbound hair with riotous fiery highlights, and felt a sudden wave of desire that swept all abstract ideals from his mind.

Just then the stable hand led his badly limping mare up to them. He explained that when they rounded the last turn in the coast trail, the animal had picked up a sharp stone in her right front hoof. Expertly, Esteban examined the beast and told the young man to begin walking her back home since she was too badly injured to ride.

As soon as the boy vanished around the bend in the road, Esteban turned to Amanda and said, "We should return, too. Without a chaperon, in my country, your uncle could call me out for improper conduct."

At the thought of her gentle, pacific Paul involved in a duel of honor, her mouth quirked and she let out a giggle. "Somehow I don't think he'll consider it necessary. Besides, we're not in your country now. This is the United States, and we're scandalously liberal. You seem a perfect gentleman, so I'll trust your appearance. Also, we have to eat our wonderful lunch."

With a flourish of his hand, he indicated a copse of pine trees situated on a knoll overlooking the ocean. There was grass and shade. Quite a perfect picnic spot. He tethered their horses while she spread a cloth and set out cheese, baked chicken, strawberries, crusty bread, and a bottle of Henri's best white wine. As she arranged the food, she was aware of her increasing nervousness. This was really daring. They were far from town and quite isolated. She should not have suggested they eat before heading back. He was engaged to another woman and she was in danger of becoming just a foreign dalliance. Despite her self-chiding, when he sat down beside her she was glad that they had the time and the beautiful day to share.

As they ate, he described his business ventures up and down the coast and Rancho Santandar, his birthright. "It's beautiful there, Amanda. Wild and stark. You can hear the jaguars cry in the night sometimes. Huge purple and white blossoms cover the cactus plants in the spring. The sky is clear and so blue it almost takes your breath away with its brightness." As he talked, his eyes took on a warm, golden glow. The anger and frustration of his earlier conversation about his father and the war seemed to evaporate.

She cleared the picnic food and replaced the remains in the hamper, all the while watching the transformation in him as he spoke of his home. It sounded like a beautiful, exotic place to her, all tropical and sunny, not gray and cold like the San Francisco Bay area was so often in winter. She would love to see it; indeed, she could envision it as he spoke. Then his words jarred her.

"I would love you to see it, Amanda. Southern Sonora is like you, all green and golden, caught in the fire of the sun." As he spoke he leaned nearer, taking a mass of her hair and letting it fall through his fingers, watching the afternoon sunlight turn it fiery with brilliant highlights.

As he touched her, she was conscious of the smell of him: leather, tobacco, and an unknown male scent she had never been aware of before. He wore none of the cloying colognes her rich customers had used. He smelled clean and appealing. Her eyes moved almost unwillingly to his long, lean frame stretched on the ground beside her. Afraid to face those hypnotic sherry eyes, she gazed at his throat and then down to his chest where his shirt opened and a wealth of thick, black hair grew against his dark skin. She wanted to touch him, to stroke that hard, furry surface and feel the muscles ripple under her hands through the thin material of the white shirt. Forcing her mind away from such shocking thoughts, she raised her head and he captured her face with his hand, delicately holding her chin so that she faced him, her lips only inches from his.

Her eyes were huge, dark green pools, filled with surprise and almost benumbed by the images that he had inspired. Amanda trembled as he drew her to a reclining position against him. She was aware of his every touch as one arm circled her waist and the other held her head, the hand gently tangling in her hair. She could feel his warm breath as he moved his lips down her throat, softly kissing a trail that led back up to her earlobe, her temple, her eyelids, and then gently to the edge of her trembling mouth.

Without being sure of how it happened, she found her hands clinging to his body, one clasped to his shoulder and the other buried in that black forest on his chest that she had so wanted to touch moments before. Her breathing was erratic, as if she had just run a great distance. She was warm, so warm. She parted her lips to gasp for breath and he placed his lips over hers, his tongue intruding into her startled mouth, colliding and entwining with hers. For a suspended moment, he just held her to him and kissed her deeply, yet with such a draining, searing gentleness that she was dizzy and limp, holding on to him for support. Then he guided her head to the ground as he continued the beautiful joining of the kiss. Gradually, he caressed her arm and moved down her side to hip and thigh, then back up to her breast, where he gently kneaded with a soft circular motion, so that she arched involuntarily against his hand. Before she was even conscious of it, he had the buttons on the front of her riding habit open and was reaching inside for her breast, the nipple hard with need. The thin silk camisole slipped away and she could feel the warm air on her upper body. Then he broke the kiss and moved lower to place his dark head against her breasts, gently licking and teasing first the one, and then freeing the other from the silk, doing the same to it. Never had she felt like this, anything like this! Amanda gasped in startled delight.

Esteban was lost in passion, thrilled at her unpracticed yet ardent response. He pulled the length of her body to him and again moved to draw her mouth to his while his arm now cupped her buttocks and pressed her lower body against him, at first gently, then more insistently in slow rhythm. She could feel his pulsing erection, straining against the stiff material of his breeches, probing against her, toward that place. The warmth of the moment fled, and blind panic took its place.

Suddenly, everything came back into perspective for her. She knew little, indeed was virginal, in the ways of gentle wooing. Yet, what that hard staff meant she knew only too well. All the pain of Carver and the ugly copulations in the parlor house washed over her. Amanda's body became rigid in terror. She did not want that, no matter how drawn to this man she was. No, never that, never again!

Esteban sensed the sudden change in her from melting, hypnotized assent to frozen, frightened rigidity. It was obviously no coy act. She was terrified. He could see it in her wide green eyes, almost black with fear as she pushed him away. Then, when he released her, she rolled over, turning her back to him in a protective, fetal position. As he fought to control his own ragged breath, he could see her slight body racked with suppressed sobs, all the more poignant for their quietness. God, what had he almost done? Another few minutes and he knew he would not have been able to stop! He thought he should be angry with her for accepting and then rejecting his advances, but he was not. She wanted him. He felt sure of that from the first kiss, yet she was afraid and knew it was wrong for them to lie together. He knew it, too, now. There was an honesty about her as well as an innocence. The girl sobbing silently on the ground next to him was no tease, putting on an act in hopes of snaring a rich husband.

Gently Esteban reached for Amanda and gathered her up despite her flinching withdrawal. He helped her to stand, steadied her trembling, and then let her turn her back to him as she buttoned her habit.

"I'm sorry, Amanda." He said the words softly, clenching and unclenching his hands impotently at his sides. He desperately wanted to take her in his arms and comfort her, but knew that would be madness. No, he must take her home and then have time to think. Never in all his twenty-seven years had he been so miserably confused and full of conflicting emotions.

The ride back was begun in painful silence, in stark contrast to the opening of the day. Amanda was both frightened by what had almost happened and at the same time deeply ashamed for having let it go so far. She could not look at Esteban after she turned from fastening the buttons of her habit with clumsy, trembling hands. *What must he think of me? What am I? How could I let him practically undress me?* The questions hammered in rapid-fire succession in her whirling mind as he very carefully helped her onto Sunrise and mounted Oro. They began to retrace the trail back to the city.

Shame flooded over her in succeeding waves, oddly mixed with hurt and anger. *Even if he doesn't know where I came from, I'm still an Americana, a gringa, a nobody with no noble family, not like his convent-pure Elena. With me he could do whatever I'd allow.* And still within the raging turmoil of her mind, a clear voice whispered, *And you allowed it, Mandy. . . .* She considered the day and her foolish insistence on having the unchaperoned picnic. Her thoughts heated as she realized how much she had enjoyed his touch, wanted it, how much she had been drawn to him from that first sight on the wharf. Now it seemed an eternity ago. She almost laughed aloud, thinking, *First I feared I'd never feel anything for a man after leaving Lyla's. Now I fear I feel far too much for this one! But I won't be a whore again, never, I swear!*

As for Esteban, he too was deeply immersed in his own thoughts, cursing his stupidity for so badly misjudging a situation. Damn, he was no groping schoolboy, pawing any pretty girl who would let him. He knew when and

whom to try it with, and Amanda Whittaker was not the
kind of girl he should ever have seduced, no matter how
drawn to him she might seem to be. That was the root of
the problem: he had sensed her initial response, right from
those furious, flustered blushes that first day at the track.
She was not coy or manipulative, not able to turn her tears
on and off like Elena. *Maybe that's the problem, if I want
to be honest. I'm so damn drawn to her, too, I lost my
usual judgment. She's a passionate woman yet an innocent
girl from a good family. I've never met any woman at all
like Amanda before. I want her and know I can't have
her . . . a woman like Amanda deserves an honorable marriage, not a quick tumble on the grass.* As he rode and
ruminated, the thought kept surfacing, unbidden, *But you
could marry her. . . .* Then, looking at the pale, drawn
features of the golden-haired woman riding beside him, he
smiled to himself. *She'd probably tell me to go to hell
right now if I did ask her!*

He couldn't broach the subject of marriage. He was bound
to Elena, to his family, and he needed time to think. As he
fleetingly imagined what the reaction of his parents would be
and then considered the Montoyas', his mind refused to move
in that direction. He needed time away from Amanda, away
from San Francisco. Gauging her reaction, he decided she
needed time, too. How could he explain his predicament to her?

Then it hit him, the remembrance of mentioning Elena in
their earlier conversation. *You idiot,* he told himself, *you tell
Amanda you have arranged to marry a woman from a fine
Mexican family with your parents' blessing one hour, and the
next hour, you try to seduce her!* He cringed. Never before
had he done anything so inept. But then, he realized in a
rush, never had he been in love before! That almost jolted
Esteban off his horse. He suppressed the thought. Love was
schoolboy stuff. He never expected to be in love with a
woman, only to marry one and produce the necessary heirs to
carry on his family line. This was ridiculous. He had to get
away and think, clear his mind over some salt air as he had
three years earlier before he began to work with Uncle Frank.
He had succeeded then; he would succeed now.

CHAPTER
11

Amanda's initial panic subsided and, with it, some of her anger. As the outlines of the city appeared below them, she realized that she looked a fright with her tear-red eyes and mussed hair. She wasn't even sure how well she had rebuttoned the front of her habit. Paul must not see her like this! He usually arrived home around five and it must now be at least four. She had to get home and compose herself before she faced anyone. Rather than taking the long way around town to reach home, going through pleasant residential neighborhoods, she wanted to cut through the area below Telegraph Hill, not the most savory place but far quicker. Just as she was turning over in her mind how to explain her haste to Esteban, he interrupted her thoughts.

"Amanda, there are things we need to talk about, things I need to explain to you, but first I think we both need some time apart, to sort out our feelings. I apologize for my actions this afternoon. I . . ."

Furiously she cut him off, thinking he was just trying to

wash his hands of the whole botched affair. He wanted to get on his ship and sail away! "I will be quite all right, thank you, Señor Santandar. I don't need any time at all to 'sort my feelings out'! However, you may have all the time you wish!"

With that she pulled sharply ahead of Esteban, intending to leave him in her dust. His first impulse was to catch her, pull her off her horse, and shake her, but he quickly thought better of it. He would give her time to calm down. She had a right to be upset. For now, he would just follow her home at a distance.

As they approached the outskirts of the city, she abruptly pulled off the wide, tree-lined boulevard they had followed out of town and headed directly toward the outer perimeter of Sydneytown. What the hell was that damn fool girl doing? Esteban wondered. He saw the glint of her golden hair and the palomino horse swallowed up quickly around a street corner. She vanished down a narrow, dirty lane filled with the cheap grog shops frequented by the ducks—Australian penal-colony escapees. Esteban suddenly became frightened that he might lose her in the twists and turns of back alleys in a city where he was unfamiliar.

Amanda was too upset to know her directions clearly, having only the general idea of a shortcut home. Once she got between the narrow, wooden buildings, she became disoriented and immediately realized that the area was far more squalid than it looked from a distance. She stopped Sunrise to search for some higher landmark to get her bearings. Just then, someone grabbed her hand and the reins resting on the pommel of the saddle, quickly pulling her off the big horse. She screamed once, but a bony, foul-smelling hand covered her mouth and held her close to the owner's grimy body.

"Aah, a right pert little canary," said a wheezing, nasal voice with a thick cockney accent as he held Amanda's twisting, frantic body close to his emaciated frame. He was surprisingly strong for one so thin, she thought in terror as she thrashed to get free.

Another, deeper voice said, "Mate, it's share and share

alike, Oye says, an' gov, Oye wants a share o' that sweetmeat!'' The man confronting her was taller and quite fat, with grease oozing from his red, blotchy face. She could smell the thin one who held her, but could not see him, except for his filthy, elongated hands. The fat one held Sunrise's reins. ''Gor, wot a beastie. I gits 'em if'n ya git first poke at 'er.'' As she struggled ineffectually, the two men began to drag her across the deserted street toward an alley, pulling a nervous, prancing Sunrise after them.

Just as they disappeared into the abyss of the alley, she bit down hard on a carelessly loosened hand and screamed again.

''Ya fuckin' bitch! Oye'll bust ya proper, Oye will.'' She felt the blow and then a sharp stabbing pain to her jaw, followed by great dizziness.

What happened next was so fast that Amanda never took it in. The hands that held her were abruptly loosened and she fell to the ground, dazed. The short, thin duck crumpled in a heap beside her and gasped a strangled sound that ended in a gurgle, with blood foaming out of his mouth. Then he was silent. The obese one put up a loud but losing fight that ended as quickly as it had begun.

Esteban had followed her around the turn in the lane when he heard a scream followed momentarily by a second one. In seconds he found the alley where the two thugs were dragging their victim and her horse. Not daring to use the rifle he had on his saddle for fear of hitting the thrashing girl between the two men, he slipped his knife from its boot sheath. His horse could not be maneuvered in the close confines of the alley, so he dismounted and stalked behind the one dragging Amanda. Before either man was aware of his presence, he dispatched the first with a quick slash across the throat. This freed Amanda. The big one was ahead with Sunrise's reins in his hands. Hearing the commotion, he dropped the reins and whirled like an enraged bull. Was some drunk from the grog shop cutting himself in by dropping poor Alf? He turned and got a full view of Esteban, the bloody knife, and his very dead companion. The "swell" wielding that deadly blade looked ready to use it again. Damn! The horse was blocking his getaway. With the instinct of the streetborn, the duck reached for his knife and charged.

Esteban Santandar had fought Yankees hand-to-hand when the odds were often five to one. This was easy, despite the duck's height, because his weight slowed him down. The leaner, quicker man simply waited for his opponent's lunge and caught him cleanly in the jugular, while sidestepping like a matador. The contest was almost silent and very fast, but it was not neat. Both corpses were quite bloody. Esteban did not want Amanda to see the carnage, and he had to get her out of the area before more of the ducks decided to investigate her screams and the fat man's last roar.

He turned, wiped the blade of his knife on his pants, and resheathed it in his boot in unconscious habit. He had carried it since the war, shrugging aside the laughter of his English drinking companions at his barbarity. One night, in a disreputable section of London, that same knife had saved several blue-blooded hides, including his own. The blood smell was making Sunrise skittish, but the horse was not frenzied. He blessed the careful training his vaqueros had given Sunrise as he guided the big animal by its reins past the two dead ducks. Then he reached down to the dazed girl as she began to stir. Scooping her up in one economical motion, he emerged from the alley before she could see what lay within. She held tightly to him as he whistled for Oro, who was patiently waiting in the street. Esteban lifted her onto the horse and climbed up behind her, tying Sunrise's reins to the pommel of Oro's saddle. Riding double, with her mount trailing, they emerged from the mean streets of the area and headed back toward the main thoroughfare.

Amanda clung to Esteban, shivering from the assault. She could still smell the filthy sweat and sour ale those men had exuded. She knew that if they had gotten away with her, they would have hurt her far worse than even Carver had. The ducks had been a continual problem in

San Francisco since the town began to boom. Though the Committee of Vigilance attempted to clean them out and had hanged a number of them, more continued to filter into the area every year.

Her jaw ached and she had cinders ground into her hands from when she had fallen, but Amanda did not cry. Esteban's presence was immensely comforting. He wrapped his arms tightly around her and stroked her hair, softly speaking endearments in Spanish to her while she calmed her trembling.

"You saved my life. They could have killed us both. I was a fool to cut across Sydneytown. I'm sorry." She gulped out the words in a rasping, whispered voice.

"*Querida, querida,* don't think about it. Put it all out of your mind. I shouldn't have let you ride ahead. Oh, Amanda, if they had hurt you . . ."

Startled, she looked up into his face, hearing the love and concern in his voice. She could see it in his eyes and feel it in his fiercely possessive hold on her. She was holding on to him the same way.

He slowed the horses when they were well away from the danger area and gently touched the bruise on her jaw. She responded and ran her fingers gingerly across his cheek and down to his neck. Suddenly overcome with shyness, she looked down and simply snuggled closer in his arms. Then she saw the blood all over his pants and gasped.

"Esteban, you're hurt!"

He shushed her. "It's their blood, not mine. I'm fine. But we can't ride through your neighborhood looking the way we do. I doubt anyone will miss those two or pursue an investigation into their deaths, but I don't want to take any chances with your being involved. There's an office of the shipping company near the new wharf. I'm going to take you there, where we can get cleaned up before anyone recognizes us. Just hold on. Are you all right? That jaw looks painful."

"No, no, it's all right. I'm just a little dizzy from it, that's all." She paused and then said in a bereft tone, "I wanted to get home before Uncle Paul so I could fix myself up and he wouldn't ask what was wrong. Now, I guess that's impossible." She smiled weakly at him, trying to force humor into her predicament.

He kissed the top of her head and continued stroking her hair. "It was all my fault and I'll explain it to him." At her start of protest, he went on, "I don't mean I'll tell him I attempted to steal your virtue and you fled, only to be attacked by Sydney ducks. That would hardly help either one of us! I'll just say we had a spat, you rode ahead, and took a spill. All right?" He smiled at her with those dazzling white teeth. Suddenly everything seemed better.

She nodded but kept her head down, not daring to look at his face again. Yet, she was desperately hungry to see if that glow of what looked to be love was still visible in his eyes. They rode a bit in silence, and then he pulled the horses up in front of a small frame building, recently constructed with a sign on the front that read, MULCAHEY LTD., SHIPPING.

She could smell the salt air and fishy aromas from the bay as he lifted her off the horse. He carried her into the office, now closed since it was after five in the afternoon. She was grateful for the absence of spectators in the place. When he stood her on her feet, he held on to her shoulders to steady her, then tipped her chin up and looked into her eyes.

"All right? Can you stand?"

"Yes, I think so," was her shaky reply.

He ushered her to a chair and then took a porcelain basin off a dry sink in the corner and went outside to pump some water.

While he was gone the realization that he had killed two men and risked his life, all over her stupidity, sank in! After three years in San Francisco, she knew better than to ride alone anywhere near Sydneytown. What was happening to the calm, cool façade she had held together through that terrible year working in the parlor house? She, who had handled everything from sadistic customers to jealous coworkers, was now coming apart when one man tried to seduce her.

When Esteban came back into the office, he saw Amanda huddled forlornly on a chair, shivering. She looked so small and vulnerable that he wanted to take her in his arms and comfort her, protect her, so that nothing could ever hurt her again. Quietly, he put down the basin full of water and found some clean linens and a bar of soap under the dry sink. He knelt by her side to cleanse her face and hands of the cinders and alley dirt. While he worked, he began to speak.

"Amanda, hear me out, please. I know you're angry, and you have every right to be, but there are some things you need to know."

"I know you plan to leave this country soon and that you're engaged to a countrywoman your family approves of. You don't owe me any explanations. I shouldn't have stayed this afternoon. Let's just chalk that up to my bad judgment." Her firm little chin tilted stubbornly. Then she swallowed hard and continued, "I'm sorry about my stupidity in bolting off like a spoiled child. We could both have been killed. As it is, those two men are dead, aren't they?" She looked at him earnestly.

Esteban had given little thought to the two ducks after all the killing he had done in the war. He nodded affirmatively. "That's not important now. Someone else would have killed them if I hadn't. Don't think of them. We have to talk about you and me. I *want* to explain about Elena Montoya. We're not engaged, yet. Until I return, and a decent period of mourning for my brother is over, nothing can be arranged. Nothing *has* been arranged." He paused, desperately searching for a way to explain how things were when he had left home.

After he had finished tending to her injuries, he touched her bruised jaw softly and then held her chin in his hand, forcing her to look at him. "Amanda, you know there's something special between us—ever since our eyes first met that day at the track. Something I can't explain, just a feeling, like a magnet, drawing us together."

"It was at the wharf." She spoke so low that he could barely hear her. He turned her face in his hands as he listened. She flushed and went on, her eyes downcast, "I saw you that day at the wharf when you unloaded the horses and that awful drunken man almost stampeded them. I was there with Uncle Paul and Doug McElroy." *I saw you first at Lyla's and loved you even as a child*, she wanted to say but could not.

"Then you know what I speak of—you felt it, too?"

"Yes." She looked into his eyes, levelly now, in earnest. "I felt it, Esteban. I felt like a foolish schoolgirl, and Uncle Paul explained to me who you are and why I shouldn't think about you further. I understand about Elena and your family. I have no claim on you or any right . . ."

He put his fingertips on her lips softly to quiet her, shaking his head no. "*Querida*, you don't understand, but now I see why your uncle has been so watchful, tolerating me only for Frank's sake." He smiled ruefully. "I should have known he'd warn you off me and think me a bounder."

"You're not a bounder. It's just that we're from different worlds."

"Amanda, I don't know what will happen. I know we come from different cultures. I also know we haven't had much time to know each other. That's what I meant back on the road. I wasn't telling you I was leaving for good—only that we both need time to think. I have to go away, up the coast on some business for a few weeks. Then I *will* be back." He emphasized that last remark. "But, before I go, I want to leave you with some things to ponder while I'm gone."

Amanda watched him, frozen like a small bird hypnotized by an encroaching cat, unable to tear her eyes from his, yet trembling as if tensed for flight. She was afraid to hear what he would say.

"I'm not exactly a traditional Mexican criollo, as you may have gathered over the past weeks. My cousin Rigo would be quick to point out all my shortcomings—and his finger points—since he seems to want to marry Elena and I don't. Viewing it from the perspective of distance, they probably deserve each other.'' He laughed softly at this revelation as he picked up another of the rickety office chairs and seated himself across from her. He took her hands in his and went on to explain the scene in the ranch courtyard and his suspicions about Elena's duplicity.

"I let it pass even when I was pretty sure she was crying crocodile tears. It all seemed so damn inevitable, so inescapable. I never thought a wife could be other than a shallow, sheltered girl like Elena. Maybe that's why I tried to think so little about it and hoped Miguel would take care of the next generation of Santandars. Then, after he died and she set me up in her girlish scheme, I went along. After all, she was beautiful, she wanted the match, and it would have pleased my family. But now there is you, and you are bright and open and interested in so many things, things I could never talk to Elena about, things she'd never comprehend or want to comprehend.''

"But, Esteban, you've known her all your life. Her family and yours are old friends. Your culture and your religion are the same.'' Amanda was playing the devil's advocate, trying to understand.

"Yes, I have known her all my life. That's part of the problem,'' he said dryly. "She bores me to distraction. And, as for family, I've always been an outsider, spending too much time in the United States and Europe to ever be a real part of it. As for religion,'' he shrugged, "I've always been indifferent. Now, after my university time in Europe, I go through the motions to please my mother when I stay at the house. I'm afraid you're looking at a thoroughgoing heathen, Amanda.'' His smile was both dazzling and disarming. Then he sobered.

"You're right about the different cultures. Sonora is a world away from San Francisco. The life there would be confining, the people honestly hostile. I'm afraid since the war they've formed a considerable dislike for Yankees, even one as beautiful as you, *querida*.''

Amanda listened intently to him, half-afraid of the implications of what he said, half-afraid she was reading it wrong. Did he mean to ask her, Amanda Whittaker, to marry him? If so, could she dare accept?

As if feeling her turmoil and uncertainty, although, of course, not knowing the real cause of her fears, he finished by saying, "I'm not sure what we should do, but I want you to know I didn't plan to seduce you and walk away to marry Elena. You weren't a temporary diversion, Amanda. What happened on that hill—oh, hell, it just happened! That's why I want us to have time to think." He paused and looked at her, waiting for her response.

Tentatively, she nodded in acquiescence. "Yes, we have spent too much time together, too quickly. There are a great many things to think about." As images of Lyla's and even Carver flashed through her mind, she thought to herself, *Oh yes, Esteban, there are so many things to think about.*

He reached over and kissed her softly on the forehead, then stood up. "I must change these clothes before I encounter your butler. I have some clean clothes I keep in the back. After unloading horses I often need to change so as not to smell like them when a buyer comes in." As he rose, they both laughed at the thought of Albert opening the door to admit a bloodstained Esteban escorting Amanda home.

She watched him walk through the door to the back room of the building and found herself staring at the closed door when he was gone, his image still imprinted on her mind.

Oh, Esteban, what will we do?

The question rang through her mind like bells, signaling disaster, or a celebration? She was not sure which. The only thing Amanda was sure of was that she could not forget Esteban Santandar, his voice, his touch, those smoldering sherry eyes, his lean, dark form.

She forced herself to think of practical matters and took advantage of the few moments alone to rebutton her habit, which she had fastened unevenly. Then she peeked in the small mirror on the dry sink in the corner and rubbed her eyes. They looked puffy, but not quite as bad as she had feared. Strange, she had cried when she pulled away from him out there on the hill. Yet, when those horrible men dragged her into the alley and he saved her from a brush with death, she was dry-eyed.

Amanda arranged her hair ribbon and smoothed her cascading, tangled hair as best she could without a brush or comb. Then, hearing the back door open, she turned to see Esteban reenter. He had changed his bloodstained garments and now wore a blue cotton shirt, open at the collar, and a simple pair of black work pants, less elegant than his riding outfit of the morning, but far cleaner. Since no one but the groom had seen him, there would be no questions. Suddenly she remembered Hoot. She hoped he had no eye for clothes and would not notice Esteban's change of outfit.

He walked across the room and looked at her gravely, examining her bruised jaw in the light. "God, you're fortunate, *querida*. It could have been broken." As he lightly put his hand over the already darkening bruise, she laid her hand over his, holding it to her face for a brief moment. The small gesture communicated a great deal between them.

"Ready to go home?"

Amanda nodded and said, "I only hope Hoot doesn't notice your change of clothing. He's awfully sharp about details. It's one thing for me to take a fall and bruise myself, but explaining those bloodstained clothes . . ." She shuddered as he led her to the door and outside to the horses.

"Can you ride Sunrise?"

Amanda walked to her horse's side and patted him affectionately on the nose. "Yes, I'm all right now. The cool compresses and the time spent sitting down stopped the dizziness."

As he moved to help her mount, he looked at her questioningly again. "Now, you're sure? After all, you don't really have to fall off a horse just to make my story convincing." His eyes mirrored concern, but a trace of humor as well.

Amanda remembered little of the return home. Paul and
Hoot were waiting, most concerned over her tardiness. If
Hoot looked closely at Esteban's rough clothing, he said
nothing about the change. Esteban quickly and convincingly
explained the groom's injured horse and the accident.
Amanda was hustled upstairs to a hot tub by her maid,
who called for bathwater immediately.

Paul tried to insist that Dr. Denton be called, but
Amanda convinced him that all she really needed was a
good night's sleep. She fell asleep almost immediately
after her soak in the tub, forgoing even the delicious
supper brought up on a tray. Her dreams were troubled by
a vile-smelling, skinny man and another huge, fierce
attacker. Both were covered with blood. She woke trembling in a cold sweat.

Esteban did not stay for the evening meal with Paul and
Hoot. After all three were assured that Amanda was all
right, he excused himself, saying he thought the two men
had much to talk over and that he felt terrible about the
foolish incident that had led to Amanda's fall. All he
wanted was to go back to his hotel and get some rest.
After Paul and Hoot bade him good evening, Hoot stood at
the door, his pale gray eyes squinted in his grizzled face,
watching him ride down the drive.

As prearranged, Esteban left San Francisco the next day
on a series of stops along the coast to check on some
investments. He sent Amanda a magnificent bouquet of
yellow roses and a note explaining that he would return in
a month. They both had a great deal to ponder.

Esteban felt he could get his bearings on the trip, putting
distance between himself and the golden woman who so
haunted his dreams. He'd left the Mueller place that night
and headed to his room at the International Hotel to bathe
and dress. He wanted to find a woman, a paid woman with
no encumbrances, to ease his aching physical needs. Perversely, when he went out and located a willing partner, all
desire left him. He wanted Amanda, not the pert, pretty
brunette he had picked up. He could still smell the faint,
sweet scent of apricot about Amanda, feel that tawny skin,

so soft and warm, the quick arching movement of her slim young body toward his that afternoon by the coast. He paid the prostitute and sent her off without even touching her.

That uncharacteristic bit of behavior bothered him severely for several days. Then in the hectic weeks that followed, he had so much to attend to on the coastal run up to Port Angeles that he did not dwell on his dilemma during the days. The nights were another matter. Always his dreams were of Amanda, her golden hair spread like a sunrise before him, her green eyes beckoning him, her soft body tantalizing him.

By the time he got back to Los Angeles to report to his uncle Frank, he was sure of only one thing. He had not succeeded in clearing his mind of the Americana. He loved her. Needing to talk the problem over, he quite naturally went to the Mulcaheys. The minute Esteban walked into the office Frank sensed that something was wrong. He waited patiently until after they had discussed the details of livestock and lumber sales. That night at supper with Ursula would be time enough for personal unburdening, if the lad were of a mind to do so. He was.

They talked far into the night at the big round oak table in the Mulcahey dining room. Esteban quickly admitted what his aunt Ursula already suspected. He loved Amanda Whittaker. The problem was, what could he do about that irrevocable fact? He sketched the events that had occurred after they left San Francisco, even confessed his reprehensible behavior that day on the coast and its dangerous aftermath in Sydneytown.

Frank's first impulse was to be furious with Esteban for endangering Amanda, but one look on his nephew's face was enough to calm him. He had seen the effect Esteban had on women. Virtually all women, young or old, beautiful or homely, virtuous or loose, were fascinated by him, but he never became deeply involved. Now, for the first time, here was his arrogant, womanizing nephew brought low by a bright, lovely Yankee lass.

Esteban told Ursula and Frank about Elena's clever ploy

in the courtyard and the informal agreement made with the Montoyas. He knew where his duty should lead him, yet he also knew, now that he had met Amanda, that the prospect of a lifetime with Elena was unbearable.

Ursula was quiet while her nephew and husband talked. *Why, he's seriously considering giving up his family ties for her, marrying a non-Catholic Americana.* She was amazed. Then her own early memories of Frank Mulcahey in that dark, old church in Hermosillo returned. She had felt just as Esteban felt about his golden gringa. Marriage had worked for her and Frank. Perhaps it could work for these young people, too.

She smiled at Frank, who reached across the table and squeezed her hand. "Do you think Amanda would become a Catholic? Your parents will never accept her if you are not married in the Church. Can she speak Spanish?"

At this point in his aunt's consideration of how to handle the family, Esteban interrupted. "I don't care if she's a Buddhist! God knows," he laughed sardonically, "if there *is* a God, that I'm no son of the Church. I'll not ask her to go against her principles to please my family. She's quite good enough as is. As to the Spanish, Amanda already speaks French and German fluently. She's more intelligent and better educated than any woman I've ever met. She has a natural flair for languages. If she wants to, and if they treat her decently, she'll learn Spanish easily enough. The question is if she wants to enter the Santandar family, not if they'll accept her!"

Frank laughed at that point. "Well, lad, for someone so unsure of what to do, you seem pretty set on your course. You're goin' to ask Amanda to marry you, aren't you?"

Startled at first, Esteban realized that what his uncle had said was true. He grinned broadly. "Yes, I guess I am, and the Santandars can accept a daughter-in-law or lose a son. I'm not going to live my life according to their plans. Of course, all this is based on Amanda's acceptance. She might not want to stand inspection in Sonora, or even marry me." That last thought gave him pause.

Frank quickly cut in, "Why is it, me boy, that after

watchin' the two of you together, I feel sure she'll say yes? Can it be the most successful rake on the Pacific coast is no longer sure of his charms over women?''

"Over one woman, no," was the quiet reply. Esteban remembered her painful sobs that day on the coast when she pulled away from his embrace. She had freedom to lead a full life in San Francisco, to work with Dr. Denton, to attend the opera and symphony, to socialize with Paul's interesting friends. Would she give up all that for him? For the first time in his life, Esteban Santandar was unsure of a woman.

Ursula was ever practical. "That is why I asked you about her willingness to please our family. If she loves you—and I agree with Frank that she does—she'll be quite content to make gestures of goodwill such as learning Spanish and even taking instruction in our religion. Amanda is intelligent enough to be aware that marriages work better when in-laws are placated. How do you stand with Paul Mueller?"

That direct question further darkened Esteban's brow. "I don't think he wants the match. Amanda told me he warned her away from me even before we met. Of course, I don't think he ever considered I'd do the honorable thing and marry her. Still, I'm sure he's aware of the differences in lifestyle she'd have to face in Mexico, the hostility of my family. I honestly don't know if he'd forbid her to marry me or how much effect that would have on her decision. They are very close."

Matter-of-factly, Frank stated, "You'll just have to head up there and find out for yourself, won't you, bucko?"

CHAPTER
12

While Esteban was traveling up and down the coast,
Amanda waited in San Francisco. She was not sure what
Esteban would do upon his return. He might conclude that
his family obligations far outweighed any attraction to a
Yankee girl of uncertain pedigree. But what if, oh, what if
he *did* ask her to marry him? The question both tantalized
and tormented her days and nights.

She would tick off all the obvious obstacles like a litany,
all the religious and cultural differences, the opposition of
his family and of Paul. Most of all, however, she was
haunted by her own background. She had been a high-
priced whore. Many in San Francisco knew this. What if
he found out? But the lovely dream of escaping her past in
his faraway land called to her like a siren's song.

Above all, she recalled the physical chemistry between
them. He made her feel wanton, awakened feelings in her
that she had never dreamed she possessed. After her years
in the parlor house, she had been sure she would never be

able to stand a man's touch again. Yet, from that moment when she saw him once again on the wharf, something had drawn her, something shockingly physical. As she got to know him, to talk with him and learn about his life, work, and sense of humor, she realized that the attraction was doubly bonded. He was intelligent and witty, honest and sensitive, not at all the Hispanic stereotype Paul had indicated. Finally, she admitted to herself that she loved Esteban Santandar with all her heart.

A small voice still whispered, *You turned away from him in the midst of passion. You're still afraid of completing that hated act ever again, even with him*. Then another part of her mind countered, *It was only my lack of virginity. He'd know I am not what I pretended to be if I let him* . . . She tossed and turned night after restless night, afraid yet aching to see his face, hear his voice, feel his hands on her body. She wanted what she most feared. There seemed to be no answer.

On a clear, cool morning when the fog had just lifted off the bay, leaving the dark blue water sparkling under the kiss of a dazzling sun, Esteban jumped off the makeshift gangplank that had been tossed between the small steamer on which he'd arrived and the wharf. He hired a hack at the waterfront. While the driver was hoisting his spartan bags onto the back of the carriage, Esteban impatiently reviewed his plans. First he would go to his hotel, clean up and dress, then go straight to Mueller's. He knew he must talk to Amanda before he bearded the formidable Paul on his own ground. The old German would have good and valid reasons for opposing the match.

Amanda was too nervous to eat a morsel of her lunch. She clutched Esteban's message in her hands, folding and unfolding it as she paced across the polished oak floor. He would be here any minute! She moved in front of the full-length mirror, carefully scrutinizing her appearance. She had chosen a pale apricot day dress of fine batiste sprigged with tiny white and orange flowers. It was cut in simple lines, not overly full-skirted, with a modest, round neckline that showed only a hint of bosom. Her hair was artfully piled on her head with a fresh spray of white daisies caught on one side in the profusion of curls. Her eyes looked enormous, luminous pools of darkest green.

She had done a great deal of solitary riding in the past weeks and her skin was an even deeper tawny gold than before. Because Esteban had told her how beautiful he considered the golden glow, she found herself riding more and more without a hat, unconcerned about the strictures of fashion. Now she put her hand to her cheek and then plumped a curl nervously. She ran her hand down the crisp folds of her skirt and eyed her figure critically. Her hair and face were all right, but what of her body? She was slim and slightly tall for a woman. Yet, he found her desirable, she knew that.

The noise of horse's hooves on the hard bricks of the entry road broke the spell of the mirror and she fairly raced to a window. Parting the white lace curtains, she watched him dismount, her eyes devouring him. He was dressed in an elegant buff-colored suit, with high, gleaming cordovan boots and a ruffled white shirt. He swung his long legs down from Oro with negligent grace, then he looked up toward her window, sensing her presence.

Self-consciously she dropped the lace curtain quickly into place as if she'd been burned, and backed away from the window, embarrassed at being caught watching his arrival. It seemed an eternity until Albert climbed the stairs to announce gravely that Mr. Santandar was awaiting her in the downstairs parlor. With trembling steps she left the sanctuary of her sitting room and began to descend the wide curving staircase, to face her future, to find out if she had a future with this man.

She entered the parlor and closed the mahogany doors silently behind her, determined to remain calm and reserved, but she was so hungry to touch him that she forgot herself and dashed toward him.

Esteban had been staring out the huge bay window, trying to marshal his thoughts and arguments. But the quick glimpse he'd caught of Amanda peeking out at him minutes before had unnerved him. She'd seemed so ethereal he almost feared she wouldn't materialize. Then he felt her nearness. As he turned, gold eyes locked with green ones and he reached out to gather her into his arms. He could feel her trembling against him. She was afraid. So was he. He spoke in a hoarse, low voice, "Hello, *querida*." Then he lifted her face, and drawn by the magnet of her lips, he brushed them lightly with his own. Amanda was his again—all the soft, fragrant wonder of her. He deepened the kiss and she returned it, opening her mouth to replay the glorious, startling first kiss he'd given her that picnic day. It seemed an eternity ago. She had missed him so desperately. How thrilling his voice was—deep and gravelly— and the Spanish endearment, *querida*. *Querida*. She loved it! She loved him! With joy she returned the kiss, forgetting fears and families. They were only Esteban and Amanda, now.

As the warm, pliant woman in his arms clung to him, Esteban knew he must end the kiss or move past it into passion. He took her hands in his and led her to a small sofa next to the bay window and they sat down shakily.

Her breathing was uneven and she blushed with embarrassment at her wanton behavior. She cast her eyes down and stared at his dark hands, closed over her lighter ones.

"It's been a long month, Amanda. I've missed you."

Softly she replied, "I've missed you, too, as you may have noticed." Her flush deepened down her neck and spread across the top of her breasts.

He tipped her chin up, forcing her to look him in the eye. "I'm so glad you wanted to see me. I wasn't sure you would, you know. I've done a lot of thinking as I spent the past month traveling, Amanda. First, I thought distance and being away from you would help clear my head. Salt air and attending to business had always put things in perspective before, but not this time, *querida*. The farther I went and the longer I was gone, the more I thought of you."

Amanda's heart turned over and she told him with a shy smile, "I never kept so busy in my life, riding Sunrise, working at the clinic, reading every book in two lending libraries, although I couldn't tell you the name of a single one!''

His eyes were warm as he said, ''Finally, last week I went to Los Angeles to talk to Uncle Frank and Aunt Ursula. I guess I knew what I was going to do already, but sometimes it helps to discuss it. I'm closer to them than my own father and mother.''

''They're very dear people, Esteban.''

''You should think so, since they approve wholeheartedly of you and of my plans. The question is if you approve.'' His eyes had darkened with emotion, piercing her face with a questioning look, almost desperate in intensity.

Before she could say anything he squeezed her hands in his and went on, ''I love you, Amanda. I know that now, and I know I could never marry anyone like Elena. I've been looking for you all my life. I just never knew it, until this past month. Will you marry me, *querida?* I thought about all the differences in customs, the isolation of Sonora, my family. Frank and Ursula will welcome you, but I can't guarantee what the rest of the Santandars will do. But I do promise you this: if they won't accept my wife, they'll lose their son. I have more than enough wealth to care for you even if my father disinherits me.''

At this point she interrupted his impassioned discourse by putting her fingertips gently on his lips. ''Oh, my love, I don't want to break apart your family, but I do want to marry you! I'll try my best to please them, whatever they want. I can speak Spanish, although I'm woefully out of practice.'' At this she blushed, remembering that it was Rita, at the parlor house, who had taught her the language. ''But I'll practice ever so hard, I'll take instruction to become a Catholic—''

Now it was his turn to interrupt her, with a bruising, intense kiss, taking her into his arms and pressing her against the back of the sofa. Then he moved to kiss her eyelids, cheeks, and earlobes, all the while holding her closely. ''Amanda, you don't have to change or prove anything to anyone. I love you as you are and I won't ask you to be anything else. If my parents are too narrow-minded to see your worth, they're the ones who are lacking. But what of your family and your life here in San Francisco? What will your uncle say about my taking the light of his life away? He knows all the reasons for objecting to this marriage, and he's right, from a practical standpoint."

"Yes, I'm sure he'll object, at least at first, but I know I can bring him around." She dimpled and then laughed, "You see, he warned me you'd never propose anything as upright as marriage."

"Then he really believed I'm a bounder, and, come to think of it, he wasn't half-wrong," Esteban said ruefully. "My first thoughts when I saw you at the track were to take you off that horse and . . ." He kissed her deeply, his tongue pillaging her mouth while his hands roamed across her back and breasts. Finally, he brought himself under control and broke off, saying, "Do that, and much more."

Amanda colored at the obvious suggestiveness of his words and actions as he closely pressed her back on the small sofa. "Let me talk to Uncle Paul alone, Esteban. If I discuss it with him first, it will be easier to get him to listen before he makes any pronouncements."

It was obvious that he disliked the idea of leaving her to face her uncle without his support. "He'll have a lot of good arguments to dissuade you, *querida*, beginning with my family. I do feel a responsibility to them—to go home and have you meet them, to give them the chance to accept you. If they do," he paused with a smile warming his eyes and lips, "and I think they will, we will live there part of each year. I'll have to begin overseeing the ranch and mines there when my father gets older. We'll live on my own section of land to the north. There's a smaller house you can fix up. We can take a sailboat from Santa Cruz to Mazatlán frequently, and we'll go to Los Angeles every year. We can visit your uncle and your friends here for a portion of that time, too. But no matter how frequent the trips to California, at least half of the year we must live in Mexico. Your uncle will be aware of how isolated that life can be, Amanda. I'm asking you to give up all the glitter and excitement of this fabulous city—no operas, libraries, philharmonics, elegant restaurants. Also, no Dr. Denton and no clinic. I know how much these things mean to you, *querida*. Paul does, too.''

She shook her head. ''You forget, Esteban, that Uncle Paul made the money in the family. I was a humble Missouri schoolteacher's daughter and I'm used to a far more rustic life than you can imagine. I never had a servant before coming to live with Uncle Paul. I've enjoyed the time here with him, but I won't pine away for want of operas or bay oysters, believe me. I'm used to cooking and gardening and all sorts of domestic things.''

At this his eyes lit with laughter. ''I remember you and your friend Hoot in the kitchen. You were so natural and capable. But it will still be different, away from your friends and family.''

''You will be my family. If we're together, I will be happy, as long as you realize I'm not a blue-blooded lady from a noble family. Esteban, I'm descended from farmers and schoolteachers, no titles, no landed wealth, no . . .''

He kissed her into silence, saying with a growl, ''I think we'll do fine, our families and ancestors be damned! We'll begin a new generation of Santandars, good German, Yankee, and Mexican, all blended together in our children.''

Our children. That thought and all it implied haunted her when he left. She turned the fears over in her mind. After the endless misery of the past month and the sudden burst of joy at her first sight of him that afternoon, she was certain of her love for him. She loved his touch and was eager to return his embrace. However, after a certain point, her mind refused to tread further. With a shiver she forced herself to recall that day on the coast and her sudden cessation of passion. She reassured herself that it was the fear of being taken casually and discarded. But now Esteban wanted to marry her, give her children.

Since Carver's brutal rape, despite all the men at the parlor house, she'd never conceived. Of course, Elizabeth had given her the usual regimen to follow and medication to keep her from becoming pregnant. However, occasionally one of the women at Lyla's did conceive, despite the best "precautions." She feared that she might be barren. Esteban must have children. He was the last of the Santandars. He deserved tall, beautiful sons, like their father. What if she couldn't give him what he was entitled to have?

Another specter was that of her physical state. She was not the virgin he believed her to be. She'd heard of ways to remedy this. The prostitutes at Lyla's talked of things done to "fake the merchandise." The Chinese houses were reputed to be especially good at reselling a "virgin girl" over and over to customers at high prices. She shuddered at such a deception and at the surgical procedure necessary to achieve it.

For many reasons she must talk to Elizabeth before she could face Paul and counter his arguments. Her thoughts scurried back and forth from one thing to another. She changed quickly into a linen day suit and summoned a carriage. She desperately needed the commonsense council of her friend as well as some essential medical advice.

That evening when Paul came down for dinner Amanda joined him, nervous but considerably more confident. She was a bit late and told him she'd been at the clinic visiting Elizabeth. He questioned her no further. Paul had been worried ever since Esteban Santandar left San Francisco. He'd watched Amanda busy herself in a flurry of superficial activities, which he knew signified her agitation over Santandar's absence.

When they were seated and served dinner, he looked at her with his level gaze, commanding no nonsense. "Well, Amanda, why is it I feel you have something to tell me?"

Her flushed face and nervous handling of the silverware convinced him he was right. His heart constricted in fear when she began to speak. "Esteban came back this noon. He was here. He asked me to marry him, Paul." She said the words softly, but the glow in her eyes was rapturous and she was animated with pure joy. His heart ached for her. It couldn't be.

"Amanda, *Liebchen*, you must think long on this. I

confess I did not believe he would ever offer marriage, but still, he can only hurt you. You are not of his nation, his language, his religion. His family will drive a wedge between you, even disinherit him if need be.''

"We've talked of this, of all the differences, the culture, his family. He wants to take me there, to meet his parents. But if they won't accept me, he made it clear where his choice lies. He has earned his own money, Paul. They don't own him, can't hold that over him. But I know I can gain their approval. I can speak Spanish, I'm educated. I've gained acceptance even with your most scrupulous European friends.''

"*Ja, Liebchen*, but they are not as these criollos. Here, we are all immigrants, all newly arrived in America, newly rich. The Santandars are not any of these, Amanda. They are of an ancient lineage, rich and powerful, feudal barons in their own country. Besides, there are more important matters. Even if your Esteban would give up his family, it would be for Amanda, the woman who grew up properly back east and came to live with her uncle in San Francisco when an orphan.''

"You mean my past—Carver, Lyla's?''

"Have you told him of this, of the tragedies that forced you into that life? Does he accept you, knowing that?''

Desperately she cast down her eyes, tearing at the handkerchief in her hands, twisting it as she whispered, "No, I couldn't ever. Oh, Paul, I want so desperately to leave it all behind. I've never felt as I do with Esteban. I love him. I'll never love another man. I don't want to have my husband look at me and know what I've done, what I've been!'' Her voice had risen, then faltered, but she went on, "I don't know whether he'd still love me if I told him, and I don't want to find out.'' She threw up her head defiantly. "I want to go with him to his land, far away from parlor houses and gold miners. Who could ever know in Sonora that I was Mandy, the whore?''

Paul rose and stood by her chair, stooping to put his arms around her shoulders gently. He sighed. "It seems, Amanda, many times before we've had this discussion.

You are no 'whore,' but you are who you are, and you are not being honest with yourself or the man you want to marry. You build for yourself a house of cards in that distant, beautiful Sonora. It may last awhile, but it will crumble just as your gambler friend Mr. McVey's game did. Only this time, everyone will lose."

Adamantly she shook her head, trying to deny his logic. Relentlessly he went on, "You are not a virgin. How can you even think to begin such a marriage?"

She flinched. Paul had never been so indelicate, no matter how close they had been! It was as if her own father had slapped her. Then she looked up at the anguish in his face and knew he was only trying to make her see all the pitfalls. She put out her hand and drew him back into the chair next to her.

"That's why I went to see Elizabeth this afternoon. I—I was confused about a lot of things, uncertain if I had the right to . . ." Amanda swallowed hard and then went on, "to ever marry. I wasn't even sure I could be a normal woman or if I'm barren. She assured me I'm all right and healthy and . . ." Her voice trailed off and she blushed heatedly, lowering her head, but then she faced him and said, "I discussed my rather obvious lack of a maidenhead. It's a simple surgical procedure to put a stitch in. I guess my sordid background was a good source of knowledge, anyway. She agreed to do it."

Paul shook his head and said slowly, almost as if the words were wrenched from him, "Your deceptive web grows more complicated and dangerous, Amanda." He stood up and walked across the dining-room floor to the sideboard. On the ornate marble countertop stood a crystal brandy decanter and a ring of small snifters. He poured two amber shots and brought her one of them, motioning in a way that brooked no argument for her to drink it. She did.

When he finished his, he said, "He's a killer, Amanda."

She froze at this as he went on, "Our friend Hoot has contacts all over San Francisco, including Sydneytown. It seems there was last month a small altercation, the very day of your 'fall' while out riding. Two men quite brutally were murdered by a man skilled with a knife.''

At this she shot up from her chair. ''It wasn't at all that way! It was my fault. I bolted into that awful place and he saved me from those two animals. They'd have done— Oh, it doesn't bear thinking of, what they'd have done if he hadn't killed them.''

''Did you never wonder where he learned to kill so well?''

''He was in the war. My God, Paul, he fought for his country! Of course he learned to kill, every soldier must, or die.''

He waved this aside and went on, ''I do not mean that. Hoot and other friends here have done some careful investigating these past weeks. It seems your Señor Santandar has quite a reputation up and down the coast. The war was not the only place where he shed blood. That can harden some men so they grow to like the killing. He has had numerous fights since returning here from Europe. If rumor is right, also he had quite a few when abroad, mostly over women.'' He looked at her with anguish still written on his face.

A cold chill washed over her as the picture of Esteban returned, calmly wiping a bloodstained knife on his pants and inserting it in his boot. Small, blurred images of that scene in the alley when she was only half-conscious came back to her now. She forced the thoughts from her mind when she recalled his gentleness as he cleansed her face and hands, his fierce protectiveness in getting her home and assuming all the blame for her mistake.

''He loves me, Paul. He won't hurt me. I'm sorry we didn't tell you the truth about that day, but Esteban wanted to spare me, not himself.''

Paul slumped in defeat, realizing that nothing would deter her, that it was useless to go on. All he could do was pray that the future went as she wished and that Esteban Santandar was worthy of such fierce loyalty and love. He knew Amanda was.

A scant two weeks after their reunion, Esteban and

Amanda were married in the Lutheran church to which
Paul and most of his German friends belonged. Since his
Marta died, Paul had not been a faithful parishoner, but it
was the only church in San Francisco he was familiar with.
He made all the arrangements for the small ceremony
uniting a childhood Methodist with a nonpracticing Catholic.

The bride and groom made a striking couple. Amanda
was dressed in pale cream silk that blended with her
sun-tinted skin and glittering masses of hair, while her
green eyes sparkled darkly in her delicate face. Her golden
curls were piled beneath a tiny pearl tiara and covered by a
waist-length veil of sheerest Brussels lace. The gown was
simple with a mandarin collar and fitted sleeves that
hugged her slim wrists. Its soft material was set with seed
pearls, and the design flattered her slim body in elegant
understatement. Esteban was a perfect foil for his bride,
tall and dark next to her willowy goldenness. His pure
white silk shirt, elaborately ruffled at the front and cuffs,
contrasted with a black charro suit so severely molded to
his lean frame. A red sash and the traditional silver trim on
his suit and boots completed the picture of an aristocratic
Californio.

Paul gave Amanda away and Elizabeth was her attendant. Esteban had quickly sent word to his aunt and uncle.
A beaming Frank Mulcahey was Esteban's best man. A
few old friends, including Jebediah Hooter, were present.

Hoot came up to Amanda in the back of the church
before the ceremony and saw her eyes widen in shock at
his scrubbed face, combed hair, and clean new suit. "Wal,
Mandy, I jest want ya ta know this is purely th' first time
since I was a tadpole this ol' carcass had ta face up ta
water, even body up ta it." He flinched with horror at the
memory. "But, I done it ta look right 'n' proper fer yer
weddin'. Ain't ever' day a body gets ta see his own
granddaughter hitched." She kissed him soundly and he
blushed beet red above his gray beard.

After the marriage, they left the church for an elaborate
repast at the Mueller home. Albert had maids and footmen
scurrying about with bottles of the finest French champagne

and trays of raw oysters on the half-shell. The table was set with the household's most elegant crystal and china. Masses of fresh summer flowers filled every room, and the meal was lavish with roasted quail, rare ribs of beef, and, of course, Paul's own ethnic favorite, a huge succulent crown roast of pork with raisin dressing. Luscious fruits, flaky German pastries, and freshly turned ice cream made the table groan under the weight.

As they sat at the feast, Amanda nervously shoved the food about on her plate, too excited and too frightened to eat. Paul proposed the traditional toast to the bride and groom and the small assemblage all raised their glasses in salute. Esteban reached over and whispered in her ear, "To my beautiful wife, Doña Amanda," toasting her and draining his glass, his golden eyes never leaving her face. She smiled as his hand found hers under the table and squeezed it gently. He seemed to understand her nervousness and was trying to reassure her.

If he realized the real reason I'm so terrified . . . she thought forlornly. The next moment she watched him turn and listen to Elizabeth, then throw back his head in that wonderful hearty laugh. Amanda was overwhelmed with love for him. *It will be all right. It must. I'll make it be,* she vowed fiercely to herself as her right hand caressed her heavy gold wedding band. If she felt the weight of it, she also felt the warmth.

The bridal couple said their farewells at the house to all but Paul and Elizabeth, who were to accompany them in the carriage to the Embarcadero. At early morning tide Esteban and Amanda were setting out on a small sailing ship for a leisurely trip down the beautiful California coast, around the Baja and into Mazatlán. From there they would travel overland to Rancho Santandar, camping at night in the exotically beautiful Sinaloa countryside. Esteban was allowing all the time possible for a message to reach his parents and the Montoyas so that they could be ready for his arrival with a Yankee bride.

As they prepared to leave the house, Frank took Esteban aside. Reaching over to clasp him about the shoulders, he gave him a hearty handshake and a level look. "Well, me lad, time to say good-bye. Take good care of the beautiful señora. She'll need all the backin' you can give her when she faces the estimable Santandars. I know from firsthand experience about that!"

Then he broke into a grin, his blue eyes alight. "But, mind you, I'm placin' my bets on Doña Amanda to charm them as if she kissed the Blarney Stone, same as meself. Oh, by the way, the horses are aboard the *Star* and should arrive in Mazatlán in five days."

Esteban nodded. "Good. When I sent word to my parents about the wedding, I asked my groom Pedro to go to the house in Mazatlán and wait for their arrival and then ours." He looked about nervously and said, "Oh, I didn't mention to Papa that you and Aunt Ursula were present at our wedding in a Protestant church. I'll draw enough fire for that without involving you."

Frank threw back his head in a hearty laugh. His Irish brogue took on its thickest intonations. "Bein' the right pious soul that I am, almost as pious as yerself, lad, it tears at me conscience. Now your aunt, God love her, she'll go to Father Rodrigues when we get home. By the time she gets through with him, he'll have her a candidate for beatitude for her efforts to bring the both of you sinners back to 'Mither Church'!"

Shifting uncomfortably, Frank cleared his throat. "You know, lad, we—your aunt and me—we always felt as if you were our son. No way we'd have you married and not be here to see it! Besides, you've married a very special lady, I think. Both you and me, lad, have done right well with our choice of wives."

As Esteban nodded in agreement, his eyes sought out Amanda across the crowded room where she was talking animatedly with Hoot and Elizabeth. Then Ursula came over to the two men dearest to her and put an arm about each. It was an emotional farewell. Esteban knew what it cost his aunt to enter a Lutheran church. The gesture and their support of Amanda touched him deeply.

In the carriage, Amanda seemed to lose a bit of the

tension she had experienced through the afternoon. Understanding the reasons for her upset better than anyone, Elizabeth attempted to lighten the air with a joke. "Your wedding was lovely, but I do think the clergyman would have been happier saying the words in German."

Paul guffawed and Amanda chuckled. "Then Uncle Paul and I would have been the only ones who understood what was said." Looking archly at her husband, she went on, "After all, I wanted this man to know exactly what he's getting into."

Esteban laughed and protested, "That's hardly fair! He could have spoken Spanish, French, or Chinese and I'd have held my own. I haven't had a chance to learn German yet."

Amanda's eyes lit up with curiosity. "Wherever did you have the chance to learn Chinese?"

Even dark as he was, Esteban felt himself blush and answered quickly, "Oh, I trade with a great many Chinese merchants up and down the coast," which was true.

Soon the sharp pungency of salt air was assailing their nostrils and the carriage halted at the foot of the wharf where their ship awaited, a sleek sailing craft, justly named *La Hermosura*, or *Beauty*. This would be their home, beginning tonight and for the next twelve to fifteen days as they skimmed along the coastal waters, visiting small seaports and mission sites, taking in the incredible beauty of Pacific California.

As they alighted from the carriage, Paul looked measuringly at the handsome bridal couple, forcing his misgivings aside and assuming the air of joviality so characteristic of his usual personality. "Now, I want letters often, Amanda. Not right away, you understand, but in a month or two there should be more time for writing."

She colored at that, but Esteban put in, "I promise I'll give her plenty of opportunity to write, and we'll be back for a visit next summer. In the meanwhile, both you, Paul, and the overworked doctor here could use some dry, warm Sonoran air. We would welcome the visit. Who knows, you might decide to stay in our beautiful country permanently."

Paul chuckled disbelievingly and Elizabeth allowed that dry desert air might be more healthful, but a doctor needed to be where people were sick, not well.

Esteban and Amanda boarded the ship after she tearfully hugged and kissed her mentor and her friend. Paul and Elizabeth watched Esteban scoop her up and deftly walk up the narrow planking, depositing her safely on the deck. Paul's last view of her was as she leaned into her husband's embrace and they waved at the retreating carriage.

"Don't look so glum, *mein Herr*," Elizabeth said gently. "Amanda will be fine and happy. You only have to look at them to see they love each other. Even Hoot conceded that to me back at the house."

Paul looked at her through worry-clouded eyes, then sighed and smiled. "*Ja*, they make a beautiful picture together, maybe a beautiful grandchild for an old man by next year?"

PART 4

IDYLL

PART 4

IDYLL

CHAPTER
13

When the dock disappeared over the horizon, Esteban ushered Amanda below deck to their accommodations. The ship was not as large as the smelly power-driven steamers, but had spacious quarters, obviously furnished by a rich businessman for his own traveling comfort. She later learned that Frank had bought it from a New York banker who used it on trips to inspect his various investments up and down the eastern seaboard.

The main cabin was opulently furnished with oriental rugs and elaborately carved walnut furniture. The large bed was covered with a gold velvet spread and the fixtures were of highly polished brass. As Amanda surveyed the room that would be her honeymoon home for the next couple of weeks, Esteban said, "A bit ostentatious for my taste, but it is comfortable and sails quickly and smoothly. Not that we're in a hurry. We'll stop anywhere you wish along the way to enjoy the scenery or sightsee." He stood behind her, puncutating each sentence with soft butterfly kisses to her neck, earlobes, and temples, running his hands lightly up and down her arms.

Then he drew her over to a small sofa in one corner near a porthole. As they sat down, he remarked, "The window is much smaller and the sofa a different color, but it reminds me of the parlor in Paul's house where you agreed to marry me. Any regrets, Señora Santandar?"

Although she was nervous, Amanda was also warmed by his gentleness. She softly replied, "No, never, Señor Santandar. I'll just take a while to get used to my new name. We must begin to speak Spanish if I'm to be intelligible by the time we reach the ranch."

His eyes danced with golden sparks. He replied in that language, "I have an excellent idea about how to 'practice' your Spanish, love." With that he began to whisper soft endearments in her ear and kiss her with gradually increasing ardor. Then he broke off suddenly, shaking himself as he said, "You have such an effect on me I forget everything, darling. You scarcely ate anything at our wedding feast. Would you like a light repast now? The galley is at our disposal and the cook is good at his job."

Amanda shook her head. She wanted to wait no longer to know if what Elizabeth had assured her of was indeed true. Was she really a normal woman who could love? Could she accept a man's attentions, or was there still buried in her that panicky coldness from her past? When he kissed her and held her, she certainly didn't feel cold! Yet, that day on the coast the spell had been broken before the act was completed.

Amanda asked no more for herself than to feel warmed by his caresses, but she wanted desperately to respond sufficiently so that she would please her husband. That she would ever feel the intense satisfaction she heard other women speak of, she did not expect or even allow her mind to dwell upon. After all her sad and brutal experiences with sex, she felt her body incapable of such rapture. No, she asked only that the beautiful, warm glow of love continue through the consummation of their marriage. That would be reward enough. For the first time in her life Amanda truly wanted to please a man. However, her guilt about the deception with the stitch added to her fearfulness. She knew it would hurt, but surely not as much as it had the first time. Somehow, she would get through it. She must, for her love. *Oh, God, please don't let me fail him,* she prayed.

Looking deeply into her eyes, he saw what he believed to be virginal fears and decided there was no use prolonging her initiation into the rites of love. With the passion she had already unconsciously exhibited to him, he was certain he could please her. He rose and took her hands, pulling her into his embrace. "This is a small ship with no room for a lady's maid. So, I'll just have to do the job instead."

He reached up gently and began by taking off her veil and headpiece. Then he continued, pulling the ivory hairpins from her hair, letting the great wealth of gold cascade down her back like burnished metal. He turned her around and took the mass of it, holding it to his face to inhale the sweetness, then laid it over her shoulder so that he could begin the arduous task of unfastening the long row of pearl buttons that ran from her nape to below her waist. As he unbuttoned, he kissed the tawny, silken flesh exposed, warming it with his breath. She shivered but did not pull away. Rather, she pressed herself closer to the man behind her.

When he finished with the dress, he again turned her and began to slowly peel down its whispery folds, baring her shoulders, breasts, and arms. All she had on beneath was her lace-covered camisole. Amanda had always felt acute discomfort in corsets and never wore one. He unfastened the tapes to her heavy petticoats and the dress and underskirts fell to the floor in a soft whoosh.

His eyes raked her from head to foot and he trembled with desire. Forcing himself to go slowly, he paused and said softly in Spanish, "I was right. That day at the track I delighted in your beautiful upper body, but your full riding skirt kept me from seeing the lower half. I had to imagine your hips, legs, the rest. . . ." As he spoke, he lightly ran his hands down from her slim waist over the sweet curves of her hips, down her thighs and back up to caress her buttocks through the sheer silk of her pantalets.

"Now, are you the least bit curious about me, my love?" Slowly, almost hypnotically as he locked gazes with her, he took her hands from where they rested on his forearms and moved them to his chest, where his silk shirt was closed with silver studs. He placed one of her hands over the top fastener. Then he shrugged the suit jacket off in one fluid, careless motion. With trembling hands, Amanda began to take out the heavy silver shirt studs, placing them one at a time in his upraised palm. When she finished, the dense black forest of his chest hair was fully visible through the gaping shirt front. Next, she removed the cufflinks, first the right, then the left. With his eyes he willed her to continue.

She timidly reached up and placed her hands over his shoulders, helping him to peel off the clinging silk, revealing a lean, dark torso with a beautifully symmetrical pattern of black chest hair narrowing into a feathery arrow that disappeared beneath the red sash at his waist. Just above his waist a long, fierce-looking scar ran down his side under the sash. His arms were strong and corded with muscles yet not bulging or bulky. She ran her palms up his arms and across his chest, luxuriating in the hard, warm feel of male, placing her face against his heartbeat and inhaling the pungent, clean smell of him. Her fingers softly traced a pattern on the scar, following it back and then forward again. Although long and thick, it was obviously old.

"A remembrance from the war, beloved. Long ago healed." Esteban kissed her and they locked together in a long, deep embrace, swaying with the slight movement of the ship on the calm waters. He scooped her up and stepped over the pile of clothing. Pulling back the spread and covers in one quick motion, he laid her gently on the bed and knelt to take off her slippers and stockings. With delicate, agonizing slowness he kissed her knees, ankles, and feet before reaching up to unfasten her pantalets and camisole. Smoothly, with the same languorous slowness, he slipped the lacy top over her head, releasing her masses of hair to cascade in a riot of gold against the white pillowcase. Then he bent to kiss and suckle each pale pink nipple to a hard point, before caressing them with gentle hands. Amanda arched against his touch in unconscious abandon, responding to the exquisite sensations he evoked.

"Beautiful, so perfectly beautiful," he whispered and bent again to kiss the peaks. When his hands moved to her waist and began to ease the pantalets down, she stiffened and her eyes flew open, but she forced down her panic and let him continue. Sensing her fear, he slowed his actions, pausing to caress her with butterfly kisses all over her face and body. When he finally slid the pantalets off, he let his hands and mouth warm her all over, using his tongue to trace delicate patterns in the curves and hollows of her body until she was again relaxed and drugged with sensation. By this time Amanda was almost mindless in the heat of pleasure. Her body seemed to have a will of its own when he touched her.

He lifted himself from the feast of her slim, golden body and turned to sit on the side of the bed, quickly pulling off his boots and stockings. Then he stood to unbutton his trousers, now a misery of tightness for him, and whispered, "Look at me, my beautiful Amanda."

Almost unwillingly, she turned her head languorously and gazed up at the tall, lean man looming over her. He pulled off the tight black pants and underwear in one economical movement and then stood like a dark, beautiful god, looking down at her.

Instinctively, as a moth seeks the flame, she reached with her hand and touched his thigh. It felt warm and incredibly hard. Before she could withdraw the small hand, he closed his larger one over it and moved it to his center, to the shaft pulsing with such agonizing life after the protracted wooing. He knelt on the side of the bed and gently guided her hand in one slow stroke up and down, then stopped in a gasp of pleasure and dropped onto the bed beside her.

"Oh, my love, what you do to me, it's beyond all

thought!'' His breathing was erratic as he gathered her in
his arms. Again he kissed her, teasing and enticing her
tongue from her mouth into his, then twining the two
together. Amanda was ablaze with his heat and the incredible, heady feeling of his hard body pressed against hers,
holding her, kissing her even as she clutched him fiercely
and kissed him back. She was responding to instincts she
never knew she possessed. Even the pressure of his engorged penis between them could not stop the intoxicating
sensation now. She writhed and twisted as if—as if she
wanted him to do that which she'd always loathed and
feared with every other man!

Slowly he caressed down her side, over her stomach,
and reached for the golden furry patch between her legs.
She flinched briefly, afraid it would be painfully dry as it
always had been before. She was amazed when his hand
came away wet, brushing her inner thigh with creamy
moisture. He stroked her softly with his hand until she was
desperate with wanting, bucking in an unconscious plea
for release from the exquisite storm of torment he had
evoked. He rolled her back toward the center of the bed
and raised himself over her. Then, parting her legs, he
guided the tip of his shaft to rub on her sensitive, swollen
lips, waiting for her to arch against him involuntarily. With
a whimper she obliged him eagerly. Carefully he eased the
wet, hungry place open and entered. Meeting resistance,
he pushed in one small, fast thrust past the barrier and then
was still a moment, buried deep inside her. She moaned
with the sudden sharp pain after all the delicious pleasure
that had gone before. However, the hurt quickly subsided
as he kissed her and whispered love words in her ears,
supporting his own weight on his elbows.

When he felt assured of her readiness once again, he
began a slow cadence of thrusting. She found it a natural
and unconscious thing to hold on to his shoulders and wrap
her legs around his lower body, arching to meet each
movement hungrily. The heat gradually became unbearable
and a pulsing, driving pleasure infused her where he was
filling her body with his. It was as if they were melting

together. The exquisite sensations grew and grew. Amanda did not understand what was happening to her, but did not ever want it to end!

Suddenly, she gasped as the fierce contractions hit her and she convulsed in an orgasm so intense that she clawed at him, drowning in the pleasure. Unable to hold himself back, he released himself in her at last.

Neither of them moved for several moments after that. Then, tenderly, he held her and rolled onto his side, pulling her with him, their arms and legs still closely entwined, their bodies still joined. Both were breathing erratically, their hearts pounding. When he could speak, Esteban whispered hoarsely, "Amanda, I knew your passion that first day when you felt my gaze and returned it, but I never realized, oh, my love, my wife."

She reached her hand up and stroked his face, reveling in the rough texture of the dark shadow on his jaw. She nuzzled the heavy black beard with her face, loving the maleness of its faint scratch against her soft skin.

He could feel the wetness of tears on her cheek and turned her face to look into her eyes. "Amanda?" His voice held a hint of alarm.

She put her fingertips on his lips and said very softly, "Esteban, I never knew it could be like this. I never dreamed I could feel what you have given me, my darling." Her lips trembled as she smiled and drew closer to him in blissful happiness. It was so much more than she had hoped for, her mind could not take it in. Her tears fell like silent rain.

He reached down and pulled the tossed coverlet from the bottom of the bed over them. Exhausted and sated, Amanda fell asleep in his arms as he gazed in wonder at his small golden wife, then drifted off himself in utter contentment.

Amanda woke to the feel of the ship moving while pink shafts of sunrise shot through the portholes. As she remembered the previous evening, she looked across the empty bed to see her husband gazing out the porthole. He was still naked and she took the chance to drink in the sight of him while he was unaware. His lean, hairy frame was virile and magnetic, the profile of his brow, nose, and jaw finely chiseled. *What a splendid animal*. Her mind jumped as she recalled her words from that day when she had seen him at the track.

Smiling inwardly, she watched him move with fluid, powerful grace across the carpet. He chose a pair of tan cotton trousers from the armoire and slipped them on. As he dressed, she watched, marveling at how beautiful a male body could be. Always before, she had thought of the nude male with revulsion, or at best, in self-protection she had drawn down the icy curtain of forced indifference. But he was nothing like any man she had ever seen in room eleven. Even his scars were exciting, eliciting her fascination and protectiveness. Sensing her eyes on him, he turned, flashing her a dazzling smile and crossing the cabin to sit on the side of the bed. As she sat up to reach for him, the sheets slipped away, exposing her bare breasts. He kissed her softly.

"I was going to get some coffee from the galley and order you hot bathwater for a good soak." He nodded toward the corner where a brass bathtub sat anchored to the floor. "I thought you might be a little sore after last night." She blushed and he grinned. He rose and went over to the armoire, taking a pale green silk robe out and bringing it to her.

As she threw back the covers she saw a few smears of blood on the sheet. She darkened in a red blush and quickly slipped into the robe he held for her. After closing it around her, he wrapped his arms about her waist from behind and nuzzled the side of her neck affectionately. "Amanda, I'll never hurt you again; just that one moment, my love, I had to."

She responded by turning into his embrace and wrapping her arms tightly around his waist. They communicated in silence for several minutes. Then he gently disengaged her arms and said, "I'll be back in a few minutes with some coffee." He kissed her lightly and padded barefoot to the cabin door.

When he was gone she went to the porthole and gazed at

the beginning of what promised to be a glorious California day. Amanda considered the miraculous change in her body last night. The slight twinge from the torn stitch was insignificant, but the incredible beauty of what she had shared with her husband was overpowering. Before, she had found only ugliness in sex. Now it was impossible even to remember any other men or the alien acts they had performed on her unwilling body. She realized, with a sudden surge of joy overshadowing her guilt at her deception, that she had indeed been a virgin. No man had ever taken her in love before, wooed her and given of himself to her as Esteban had. Nor had she ever freely given herself to any man but him. If the physical pleasure was wonderful beyond imagining, the knowledge of shared love was even greater.

The days that followed were an idyll: sailing under azure skies, stopping in picturesque, deserted little coves by golden sand beaches, and visiting small mission villages with beautiful white stucco buildings, red tile roofs, and iron grillwork. Amanda had never seen Spanish architecture before, and the small towns dotting the southern California coast were both exotic and enchanting. The homes had thick walls to hold the sun at bay while the central courtyards were filled with dancing fountain waters and profuse semitropical shrubs and flowers. The cool, spacious comfort of the style, so suited to the climate and topography, made her eager to see Rancho Santandar. She already loved the beauty of the land. If only his family would love her.

They spoke only Spanish, at Amanda's insistence, and Esteban was amazed at how quickly she recalled it. She was naturally facile at languages and had so much at stake that she tried to be letter perfect for the Santandars. Esteban taught her many new Mexican words and phrases of Indian origin not present in the Castilian Spanish Amanda had learned. In order to converse with servants and tradespeople throughout Mexico, a subdialect had to be mastered.

One evening, on a deserted stretch of Baja California beach, well below San Diego, they went ashore to eat supper and spend the night. They had done this on several occasions since they both loved sleeping with the clear stars overhead and the warm Pacific waters nearby. Esteban built a fire while Amanda set out their simple meal. As they sat on a blanket and ate, they watched the crackling flames of the fire and the sun setting in a blaze of orange and purple splendor over the Pacific.

"This is the most beautiful voyage anyone could ever imagine, Esteban. I never dreamed a country could be as lovely as the southern California coast."

Looking at her with deviltry in his eyes, he said, "I know you found Carmel enticing because of our, ah, picnic there. The same for San Luis and Santa Cruz Island . . ."

She sat up and pummeled him, laughingly recalling those afternoons, especially the one at Carmel, high on the bluff overlooking the breakers on a wild stretch of ocean. They had lain on a blanket under the shade of a looming stand of pines, quite naked in the noonday warmth. He gave her a "Spanish lesson," by saying the name of each part of her body as he caressed and kissed it, beginning at her head.

"*La ceja*, eyebrow, *las pestañas*, eyelashes, *la nariz*, nose, *la boca*, mouth, *la garganta*, throat . . ." He kissed as he named each one, moving lower. "*El estómago*, stomach," he went on. At the next point, she had convulsed in shocked giggles.

"Esteban! That's one word I know I'll never have to say in front of anyone in your family!"

He continued, nevertheless.

Remembering that afternoon in Carmel, she slid her body close to his and began to "practice her Spanish" on him. "*Las barbas*, whiskers," she said, flicking her tongue against his jaw. After a bit she paused and said, "When I progress far enough, my love, you may have to help me with vocabulary."

Grinning, he readily agreed. "I'm prepared."

"I can see that . . ."

*　　*　　*

The night before they were to arrive in Mazatlán, they celebrated with a quiet dinner in their cabin. Amanda was preoccupied with the impending landing in Sinaloa. During the voyage they had been suspended in time, joyously getting to know each other, making love and laughing together. But now, the prospect of forsaking the sanctuary of the ship and beginning the passage on land, his land, Mexico, made her apprehensive.

As they sipped brandies after dinner, Esteban lit one of his black cigars and blew a ring of smoke as he watched his wife turning the crystal snifter around and around in her small hands.

"You're worried about our arrival in Mexico." He stated the fact, not asking it as a question. "It will be all right, love. They've had plenty of time to think about all I wrote them, and even my father will have calmed down."

"But what about the Montoyas?" She still dreaded the confrontation with a beautiful Elena awaiting her betrothed and scoffing at a Yankee usurper.

Esteban scowled. "I'll have to talk to Don Diego and tell him why I couldn't go through with the betrothal. I'm honor-bound to make my apologies, although I doubt he'll be very willing to accept them at first. Time will just have to take care of it. With all her suitors, I imagine Elena will choose one and marry quickly. It will all work out. My parents will give us a chance, Amanda, if for no other reason than I'm their only hope for grandchildren."

"But will they accept half-blooded grandchildren? What if one has yellow hair?" She looked forlorn as she considered that.

He let out a low, husky laugh, then said, "Love, my mother's people were from northern Castile. They're blue-eyed and light-haired. My cousin Rigo has very light brown hair and his mother and sisters are redheads. A blond child would hardly dismay them. Anyway, I'm so dark that I've often been suspected of having Indian blood. It's unlikely our children would take after the Whittakers, although I must confess I'd love a little golden-haired, green-eyed minx of a daughter. We'll just have to try our luck.''

She nodded, willing her fears to abate.

He went on, "Let me tell you about Mazatlán. It's the most beautiful city on the Mexican coast, I'd even say on the whole Pacific coast. When we spend a night or two in the house I have there, you'll see. The ocean surrounding it is incredible, with huge breakers coming off the small, rocky chains of islands that jut into the cove both north and south of the city. The beach is pure white sand. The city sits on steep cliffs overlooking the bay, set against purple mountains to the east, the Sierra Madres.'' He went on to describe the landing procedures in such rough water and the shops, markets, and people of the town.

"It sounds so exciting!" she said, then paused a minute. "But are you sure there's no woman waiting for your ship to arrive?" Her eyes held a hint of worry, despite her teasing tone.

He looked startled, then laughed, reaching over to draw her from her chair onto his lap. "I won't pretend I didn't have a past, love. There were women in my life, two in Mazatlán, as a matter of fact.'' When she stiffened, he went on, "One sailed for France before I left here for California. I don't think she'll ever be back. We parted friends with an understanding of no ties. The other is set up in her own establishment. Rigo has kept May Ling for the past three years.''

Her eyes widened in understanding. "So that's where you learned Chinese! I was right that day at the track when I watched you work your charms on all those simpering females. I thought you were an arrogant womanizer. Now I know I was right.'' She was half-jealous, yet also quite amazed at his honesty. There had to be women in his past. She could hardly condemn him for that, but their numbers might well appall her if he confessed more. Just so they were past, not future.

As if sensing her line of thought, he said gravely, "Amanda, if I had married someone like Elena, I'd never have told her about my old mistresses. She'd never have asked. Nor would she ever have questioned my right to keep women after marriage. It's the custom and practiced quite openly. Men and women of our class live by different rules. As I was growing up I was aware Uncle Frank and Aunt Ursula had a marriage different from my parents'. I guess I always rejected the rigid, shallow prescription of an arranged match where I could never really talk to my wife but cosset her and shield her from every reality she knew existed but would never admit to. My mother goes to her prayers and my father goes to his women on the ranch and in Mazatlán. The way they live made me eager to avoid marriage. I assumed what my aunt and uncle had was a fluke, not likely to be repeated. Until I met you." He kissed her temple and stroked her hair. "No other women, Amanda. I don't need anyone else to make love to or talk to as long as I have you."

She turned in his arms and took his face in her hands. Looking into his eyes, she kissed him tenderly, then with deepening passion.

The following evening they were ensconced in Esteban's Mazatlán villa. Amanda was enthralled with the beauty of the city as well as the house itself. She stretched lazily, still full from her first traditional Mexican dinner. The local dishes, tropical fruits, thin corn cakes, and hot spicy beef were superb. The best was the fresh-caught shrimp grilled on skewers with sweet peppers and onions. They washed it down with iced beer from Cerro de la Nevería. Esteban cajoled Amanda to taste the creamy-headed beverage despite her protests that she hated Uncle Paul's dark German beer, which was bitter and evil. She found this to be light, mellow, and clean-tasting and was an enthusiastic convert. Amanda decided that life in Mexico would be very, very good, indeed.

Esteban spent the following day gathering supplies for their trip north into Sonora to Rancho Santandar, while Amanda rested and repacked their clothing for the last leg of the journey. The next day, Esteban took her to the markets to shop and sightsee. She bought a beautiful black lace mantilla, some embroidered white cotton blouses and brightly colored skirts, and several pieces of lovely silver jewelry set with peridots and aquamarines.

Esteban watched her try on the traditional Mexican clothing and felt she looked as natural with a lacy mantilla flowing over her golden hair as she had looked that day in the kitchen with Hoot. *She'll belong here as surely as I ever have*.

The overland trek was another adventure. Sunrise and Oro were saddled and ready to ride the next morning. They had arrived before the honeymoon couple, shipped by Frank before the wedding on a steamship directly from San Francisco to Mazatlán.

Amanda, on her husband's advice, dressed practically for the long ride through rough country in hot temperatures. The traditional Mexican peasant's loose cotton skirts and blouses were far more comfortable than her heavier, stiff riding habits. Nevertheless, she packed one to change into the last day. She would arrive at Rancho Santandar looking every inch a lady.

When she came downstairs, ready to depart, Esteban's eyes lit up in wonder. He let out a low, amazed whistle, pushing his flat-crowned hat back on his head. Then he took her in his arms. The soft white blouse and bright green skirt felt wonderfully loose as he ran his hands up and down her shoulders, back, hips, and buttocks. She broke away and twirled in a pirouette. He put his hands around her waist, so small above the folds of the gathered skirt.

"If feels comfortable. I guess it looks all right, too." She laughed as he nodded in complete agreement.

"My countrywomen's dress becomes you, love. If it weren't for the golden hair and green eyes, you could be the very pretty young bride of a humble farmer. Of course," he added with mock severity, "you'll have to work on your complexion. A bit too gold, not really dark enough."

"I'll do what I can in the next week."

"Ah, but if you weren't so fair, especially here," he ran

his fingers lightly down her breasts and belly, "it would deprive me of such a beautiful sight."

She blushed at his remark, for she knew well what he meant. When she climaxed, the intensity of making love always left a red flush across her torso. He loved to hold her afterward and trace the delicate splotching with his fingertips and lips. He'd never known a fair woman who reacted with such visible passion, and it delighted him greatly.

They mounted their horses in the courtyard and the caravan began the seven- to eight-day trek north from Mazatlán to the Sinaloa-Sonora border and beyond, where Rancho Santandar lay. It was wild country, beautiful but dangerous, with jaguars and snakes as well as rough terrain and more than a minor threat from roving bands of cutthroats. Pedro, an old family employee, had carefully selected six younger men as armed escorts and brought them from the vast estate just to take the new Señora Santandar safely to her home. Esteban approved the old head stableman's choices.

In the days that followed, another world was revealed to Amanda. The wild, exotic countryside around Mazatlán gradually gave way to more arid, desert vegetation and the tropical dampness gradually abated. If Sinaloa was lush, Sonora was stark, although in its own way just as beautiful. Esteban told her to listen to the stillness of the night by the campfire for the sudden, mournful cries of jaguars on the prowl. He picked the huge purple blossoms that wound over the cactus along the trail for her hair. Fireflies danced in a brilliant, flickering blaze each night at dusk.

The vaqueros were at first shy and somewhat uneasy around an Americana, but they soon found the new señora to be a worthy horsewoman and an enthusiastic participant in the journey. She never complained of heat, insects, or the long hours on horseback. When they stopped for lunch or made camp, she helped with simple chores, even as she wore practical, peasant women's clothing. Wanting to master not only the educated Spanish her new family would speak but also the mestizo dialect the servants used, she made every effort to be friendly and converse with the hands. As they traveled, she asked questions about the horses, their jobs at the ranch, and about the countryside and customs. After escorting many highborn Mexican ladies, and putting up with their haughty disdain, the vaqueros were charmed by Doña Amanda. Don Esteban had chosen a fine lady for a wife, even if she was a gringa.

After five days on the road, Esteban drew Amanda to the edge of a cliff. There flowing like a magic fountain out of the side of a sharply jutting rock formation was a natural spring surrounded by scrub pines and a profusion of flowering bushes. The stream meandered back and forth through the jagged rocks alongside the trail. Where the contours of the land formed low dips and hollows, deep, clear pools of water bubbled.

Amanda stood in silent delight as they stopped to admire the sight, and her husband announced that they would make camp for the night by the water. She had endured the long, sweaty ride stoically, occupied with all the new sights and sounds, but now the thought of bathing in a fresh, unlimited supply of water was thrilling. She was eager to find a private spot before sundown when the temperature so near the coast dropped. "Don't worry about cold water," Esteban assured her. "This is a natural hot spring, a mineral bath like the ones so famous in Europe. It will be warm all night." When she tested the water with her hands and exclaimed, "You're right!" he laughed at her skepticism.

They made camp and ate a simple meal. While she gathered a few toilette items, Esteban went in search of a secluded pool where they could be alone. When he returned, she was eagerly awaiting the treat of a heated bathtub the size of a small room.

They walked away from the campfire and followed the stream for a few hundred yards on its tortuous course until a beautiful pool suddenly materialized around the bend in the trail. The water was a deep, clear blue-green. She gasped in delight, then stopped and looked at him.

"You're going in, too?" It was a superfluous question,

since he was already beginning to peel off his shirt and boots.

With a devilish grin, he looked up. "We've bathed together before, love. Why so modest suddenly?" Indeed, on shipboard they had shared the brass tub on more than one occasion.

"But the men, won't they ... mightn't they ... ?"

He laughed. "I told them we would be here awhile and were not to be disturbed. No one will peek, Amanda."

"Oh, then they know what we're ... oh!" She colored as she thought of coming back into camp all flushed from the inevitable consequences of mutual bathing. Everyone would know.

"There's little privacy on the trail, and it's been five days, woman. Come here." His tone brooked no opposition, and she quickly went into his arms, her modesty and the vaqueros forgotten as he began to undress her.

The water was hot and smelled faintly of mineral salts, but not the sulfurous rotten-egg smell of so many European spas. They lathered each other with thick rich soap suds and then plunged into the pool to rinse, laughing and splashing like a pair of young otters. He worked a creamy shampoo through her long masses of hair and playfully held her under to cleanse the trail dust from the shining mass of gold. She spluttered and shrieked at him.

When she finally succeeded in pulling him under with her, they thrashed and laughed until he seized her by the waist and rolled them onto the shallow sandy rim of the pool. As the water caressed their half-submerged bodies, they lay side by side and embraced. He ran one hand up and down the curves of her spine, then over her breast and hip. His other hand held her head, fingers entwined in the wet, dark gold hair. She gloried in the feel of his lips and of his hands, slick with water sliding across her skin.

Amanda stroked the mat of soaked black hair on his chest, following with her palms the patterns of the hair in its arrow descent down his hard, flat belly to the aroused shaft protruding from his submerged pubic hair like Neptune rising from the Aegean. He moaned and rolled her atop him, positioning her hips and pulling her down to sheathe him while her knees sank on each side of him in the soft sand.

Their movement adopted the steamy, languorous pattern of the lapping waters around them, protracting the long-awaited pleasure after days of enforced abstinence on the trail. Whenever he felt they were nearing the brink, Esteban would hold her still by gripping her buttocks firmly in his lean, long-fingered hands, stopping the pace, then would resume slowly all over, until she pleaded for release from the sweet torture. When it finally came, she collapsed on top of him, her hair covering them like a curtain, and sobbed in joy and exhaustion.

Afterward, when they could speak, he caressed her shoulder and throat gently and said, "Love, I think some things are worth waiting for, no?"

She took his hand, lifting it from her neck to her lips, then kissed his palm and fingertips. "Yes, they are. This has been a wonderful trip, in so many ways."

"I wanted you to become familiar with the land before we arrived. If we sailed right into Santa Cruz de Mayo, the transition would have been abrupt, so I chose this overland route."

"Did you also choose these hot springs?"

He laughed. "I knew they were here and I always had a fantasy about, er, bathing in them the way we have, but I never had a suitable partner on my journey home before."

"Then, we christened them?"

"I think we did. Who knows what new mineral benefits might be in these waters now, courtesy of—" She let out a whoop and pounced on him, laughing.

By the time Esteban and Amanda returned to camp, they were clean, dry, and reasonably composed. Even Amanda's shining wealth of hair was almost dry. She let it trail loosely down her back in a profusion of damp, tousled curls. If the vaqueros exchanged knowing grins at the reappearance, hours later, of their boss and his new bride, it was done covertly in a spirit of good humor. It was grand to be young and in love.

The afternoon before they reached Rancho Santandar, one of the sudden torrential rains soaked them, making the rough, treacherous trail even more slippery with mud. It was unseasonably early for the rain to begin, but as quickly as it started it was over and the sun returned. Then, just as they rounded a bend in the road, one of the horses in the lead shied after hearing the sudden snap of a branch behind him. Before the wet, miserable rider could regain his concentration and control his mount, the prancing animal slipped sideways into a patch of slick, red clay and went down, catapulting the horseman onto the rocks below. The horse followed his rider in a frenzy of thrashing hooves. The whole thing took only seconds, and then, just as suddenly as it began, it was over. The drop was not far, fortunately, because the trail was not steep, but it was sufficient to break the hind legs of the animal. Pedro was first on the scene and quickly shot the screaming horse.

The vaquero, Luis Ramiro, was writhing in agony on the ground where he had been thrown clear of the horse. His face was ashen with pain. When they got him onto flat ground and examined him, it was apparent that his upper right leg was broken. The white tip of bone could be seen splintered through the skin and blood on his thigh.

Pedro said, "The bone must be set before we can move him or his leg will heal crookedly." His eyes held a question for Esteban, who nodded grimly.

"All right. I'll do it, but I'll need someone to hold him. Give him some whiskey first." He took Pedro aside and said quietly, "I've never seen a bone penetrate the skin, and it's been years since I set Manolo's arm."

Amanda gently tugged at her husband's sleeve. "I've never done it myself, just assisted Elizabeth, but I've seen her set several compound fractures of the femur."

"Do you think you can do it?" Esteban asked.

She took a deep breath and replied, "Yes, I think I can. I've listened to her explain the technique and the pressures to be applied for leverage to align the bones properly. I'll need disinfectant and two strong men to hold him. And one person must hold the upper thigh still while I work."

Esteban nodded. "I'll do that. Pedro, Mano, you hold him."

The procedure was a grim one. After cutting the pant leg away, she cleansed the break in the skin with whiskey. Then she set to work, pulling the lower half of the jagged bone free and down, aligning it with a strong, twisting motion and gently pushing it up to meet the upper half. Midway, Luis mercifully fainted. It took all her strength to maneuver the broken pieces back together; but, feeling and probing as she remembered Elizabeth doing, Amanda felt she had properly aligned the bones to knit cleanly. In this semitropical heat, infection was another matter. Pale, perspiring, and shaky, she splinted the leg with the pieces of pine the men had hacked down along the trail and bound it tightly with strips of cloth.

After the bone was set, they made camp for the night. Esteban helped Amanda into their bedroll and brought her a bowl of stew. As they sat together, watching the fire send sparks up into the black velvet of the night air, he broke the silence of the meal.

"The men think you're an angel of mercy. That was quite a feat, you know, 'lady doctor.' "

"I only pray I did it properly and that no infection sets in where the skin was opened. Thank God I had that small vial of laudanum in the pack so we can keep him drugged until we reach the ranch and a doctor."

"You were magnificent, my love. The men are right, angel."

As he held her, the half-empty bowl began to slip from her grasp. He took it, set it on the ground, and tenderly tucked her in.

A rider was sent ahead at daybreak to bring word of the accident. With Luis on a sling rigged between two horses, they crept at a snail's pace on the last part of the journey.

Once again, Amanda had time to think about her impending meeting with Esteban's parents. She was apprehensive. Of her ability to get along with the servants at the ranch, she now had no doubts. The vaqueros regarded her with a mixture of reverent awe and genuine liking. But

Don Alfredo and Doña Esperanza were quite another matter. Fiercely, she vowed to win them. She was falling in love with the beautiful land and its warm, generous people as surely as she had with the dark, striking man she had married.

Just before the last miles to the ranch, Esteban gave Pedro a few quick orders and then took one of the pack horses, containing Amanda's baggage, and brought it to where she was riding. Waving the caravan on, he pulled Sunrise and Oro off the trail and led Amanda down a small ravine to where a clear creek gurgled.

"I thought you might want to freshen up and change clothes. My parents are sticklers for dress as I may have mentioned once or twice," he added dryly.

She practically leaped from Sunrise's back and delved into the baggage. She *would* please them, she thought doggedly.

Amanda was fearful and determined to please, but her in-laws were shocked and just as determined not to be pleased. When Esteban's carefully worded letter had arrived two weeks earlier, Don Alfredo had flown into a monumental rage, and Doña Esperanza had immediately taken to her chapel to pray and seek sanctuary until her husband's fury abated.

"What will the Montoyas say! It would serve that damnable young whelp right if Don Diego called him out and shot him dead! Disgrace! I sat there when he all but promised to announce a betrothal as soon as the mourning was over. And now this—this perfidy!" Don Alfredo shook the letter in his hand as if it were a freshly killed rattler. With fury in his black eyes, he read again the words on the page. "Our oldest friends and a finely brought up, beautiful girl. It's insufferable!"

Doña Esperanza let him rave awhile and then softly interjected, "He did not actually agree to a betrothal, only to discuss it when he came back from Alta California. Thank God and Our Lady nothing was made official or public.'' She crossed herself in earnest gratitude. ''He did it only to keep Elena from being forced to marry his cousin Rodrigo. I feared even then, Alfredo, that Esteban did not want the match.''

Furiously Alfredo whirled on Esperanza. ''So, he rejects a lovely young woman of the best blood to marry who knows what! Have you forgotten her countrymen killed our eldest son?''

Esperanza flinched under his cruel attack and he relented immediately, realizing even in his temper that he had wounded her grievously. She still spent hours in their chapel praying for Miguel.

''I'm sorry, my dear. It's just that this woman is a Yankee and one of very uncertain bloodlines at that—her uncle, he says here, is a German butcher! She is descended from German and English immigrants to that accursed land, newly rich. No doubt crass, poorly educated, and vulgar.''

Placing her hand on his arm, Esperanza attempted to placate him. She had lost three children in infancy and her eldest this year. She would not lose her only remaining child. Esteban might be a Ruiz in his finely chiseled features and light eyes, but he was pure Santandar in his temper. He was as willful as his father, from whom he inherited his black hair and blacker scowl. If Alfredo forced the issue, Esteban would take his wife and leave, she was sure. She would never see her son again.

''Alfredo, we have not yet met her. We must give things a chance. Esteban is not a boy. He would not marry a woman of bad breeding. We must extend the hospitality of our home and judge for ourselves after we talk with her. We can do no less.''

Gravely he looked at her, his black eyes piercing her to the very soul. ''It says here they were married outside the Church! My God, she's even made a heretic of him! Do you want to give that a chance, too? Mayhap she can convert half the ranch away from the holy faith!''

At this, Esperanza crossed herself and considered. "That is very serious, but you know as well as I that long before he met her, Esteban had deserted the Church. If we send him away, we risk his never returning. If we welcome them, maybe she will embrace the faith and bring him back with her."

Don Alfredo was amazed at his wife's knowledge of Esteban's religious attitudes. He had long been aware of his son's agnosticism. Indeed, he was no model of piety himself, but it was in form, at least, a matter of cultural heritage and pride to be Catholic. Grudgingly, he nodded. "We shall see. I have played a waiting game this long. I can play a bit more. Of course," he added bitterly, "when he came back from Europe I thought to wait and reel him in. What happened? He went off and made his own fortune. Now I don't even have the hold of money over him, thanks to my estimable brother-in-law Frank Mulcahey. Damn all Yankees to hell!"

The following weeks saw Alfredo vacillate between blind fury and cunning patience. Gradually, Esperanza soothed his ruffled feathers and won him to the cause of civility. They must reserve final judgment until they met the girl. Then would come the reckoning. Nightly she prayed for a miracle.

When in the late afternoon the pack train bearing the injured man came slowly toward the hacienda, Esteban and his Yankee wife were not present. Pedro told Don Alfredo that the two would be there soon and that he had been instructed to leave them a short distance behind.

Esperanza went into a flurry of last-minute preparations. She had been able only to approximate the day of their arrival, trail and weather conditions permitting. While she clucked over the setting of the table and the cook's work, her husband paced furiously in the front *sala*. When the dinner and sleeping arrangements had been taken care of, Esperanza waited with him.

"Where are they? It's almost dark. Fools, they'll be meat for the jaguars!"

Esperanza had to smile at that most unlikely occurrence.

"I imagine they want to make a good appearance. Esteban is probably giving her time to change. After the last day's events on the trail, I'm sure she was exhausted and disheveled." She paused and then went on hopefully, "The men seem to think very highly of her. Her skills in healing are certainly a blessing, Alfredo. We can use help often, since the doctor is a day's ride to the coast."

He stopped pacing long enough to nod at that obvious mark in Amanda's favor. Then he resumed his back-and-forth vigil at the entrance to the *sala*. "Yes, medical skills are useful, if rather unusual in a woman, but as to the hands liking her—if she consorts with servants so freely, she is obviously not of our class. I'm sure she can't speak proper Spanish."

"She spoke to the men," Esperanza volunteered.

He scoffed. "That crude dialect they speak is doubtless all she knows."

Just then, horses were heard approaching in the front. Both Don Alfredo and Doña Esperanza hurried to the door to watch their son and his bride ride up on their huge golden horses.

"She certainly appears to be lovely-looking," Esperanza said.

"Ha, would you expect a womanizer with all Esteban's experience to marry an ugly duckling? Of course, I expect she's beautiful."

Esperanza gave him a reproving look and proceeded out the door and down the front steps. Alfredo came more slowly, the better to survey the young couple. Quite dramatic, he so dark and she so golden. Amanda was dressed in her best russet silk riding habit. Its highlights brought out the pale reddish glints in the masses of gold hair caught up in a pile of curls with a few small locks artfully coiled down over her shoulder. The huge, dark green eyes and clear, tawny skin were superb, the old man admitted grudgingly. Her delicately arched brows, high cheekbones, fine nose, and firmly sculpted mouth and chin all bespoke good breeding. She was a bit slim for Alfredo's taste in women, yet well proportioned and graceful.

Esteban lifted her gently off Sunrise and then, placing his arm around her waist, led her forward to meet his parents. Amanda gave her warmest smile as she walked toward them. She could see where her husband got his dark coloring and tall, lean frame as well as his formidable scowl. The golden eyes and finely sculpted features, however, came from the woman standing next to her fierce-looking husband.

"Father, Mother, this is Amanda, my wife. Amanda, my parents, Alfredo and Esperanza Santandar."

Esperanza came to clasp the younger woman in a warm embrace, attempting to make up for Alfredo's standoffish manner as he looked his new daughter-in-law over. He waited for her to speak. When she did, he was as taken aback as Esteban was amused. Amanda's responses to her mother-in-law's questions were in beautiful Castilian Spanish. She spoke fluently with a soft, well-modulated voice.

His gold eyes glinting with deviltry, Esteban addressed his father. "Aren't you going to extend traditional hospitality to your new daughter-in-law, Father? She will be able to, ah, understand you, I believe."

Coloring beneath his swarthy complexion, Don Alfredo came over and took Amanda's hand, bestowing a gracious kiss on it. His piercing jet eyes seemed to penetrate her skin, and his smile, although white and dazzling like his son's, lacked Esteban's warmth.

"My son, with his impeccable taste in beauty, has chosen well. You are most beautiful, Amanda, as is your Spanish. How, in so brief a courtship, did you master our tongue?"

She dimpled. Two could play the game. "I had a dear friend in San Francisco who was from Madrid. Long before I met my husband, she tutored me in this beautiful language." It was as if she were back at Lyla's, posing and playing a masquerade with the older men who were customers. She had learned to excel at it.

Esteban watched his wife work her wiles on his unwilling but weakening father as they entered the house.

"Actually, Father, my wife is too modest. She speaks

German and French as well as English and Spanish."
Although Don Alfredo was impressed by education, he did
not think it appropriate in women. However, it put him on
guard. He might be a bit intimidated by so bright a
woman. That, his son thought, might keep him off balance
long enough for Amanda to charm the rest of the household. She had made a good beginning.

Dinner went well. Amanda, in an elegant cream silk
gown, carried her end of the conversation brilliantly.
Esteban fed her questions and made comments to smooth
her explanations about her background and family. Although it was new, Paul Mueller's wealth was certainly not
to be sniffed at, even by Santandar standards.

When father and son excused themselves for their traditional cigars and brandy, Esperanza guided Amanda on a
tour of the magnificent hacienda. The size of the huge,
two-story building with its parallel wings and central
courtyard awed the younger woman. Of particular delight
was the courtyard itself with its ornamental shrubs, trees,
and sparkling fountain.

Touring the kitchens, Amanda looked at all the ovens,
tables, and utensils and talked at length with the head cook
in her mestizo dialect. When they departed, Esperanza
could not help but ask where a wealthy young woman had
acquired an interest in cooking.

"I was raised in a small household in Missouri." She
went on to explain about her schoolteacher father and her
recent trek west to live with her uncle Paul. She concluded
forthrightly, "I've loved cooking over campfires since my
trip across the Rocky Mountains. I'm really very domestic
at heart."

Esperanza smiled with real warmth. "I'm sure you will
love it here. There is much to be done on Esteban's house.
He has used it as bachelor quarters for the past three years
when he has been here working with the stock, but it is
quite primitive. Nonetheless, the structure is lovely and in
a beautiful setting. If you wish to begin redecorating, I can
obtain all the servants you wish for the work."

The two women talked at length about the house and

what could be done to give it a woman's touch. Amanda
was very excited about having a home all her own with
Esteban. He had mentioned it to her but never really
described it. Now she was bursting to see it and begin to
make it their own private sanctuary.

In the study, father and son were far less congenial as
they sat facing each other. Waiting for the volcanic eruption he knew must come, Esteban lit a cigar and leaned
back in a wing chair, stretching his long legs in front of
him indolently. He sipped at the brandy and thought
fleetingly how much he's rather be sharing it with his wife
than his father.

Seated behind his oak desk like a king on a throne, Don
Alfredo glared over the rim of his crystal snifter for a
minute. Damn, he'd never been able to bring Esteban to
heel as he had Miguel. There he sat, as if he hadn't a care
in the world, blowing smoke rings!

"What exactly do you plan to tell Don Diego Montoya?"
Alfredo kept his voice low but couldn't keep all the growl
out of it.

Esteban locked gazes with his father, sherry gold with
jet black. "I know it will be unpleasant, to say the least,"
he stated dryly. "I also realize it's my obligation to face
the man, not yours. Don't worry. I'll go over tomorrow,
early in the morning."

"Just as simple as a few words, eh? I can see it now,
telling Diego how sorry you are to desert his only daughter
for a Yankee. After all, your 'wife,' " and he emphasized
the word with a sneer, "is highly educated, traveled, a
veritable wonder of medical skills, and has a fine family
tree." He threw up his hands. "She will not fit in,
Esteban. You're not even officially married in Mexico, and
you know it!"

Esteban's eyes darkened in anger. He took his cigar
from his mouth and struggled to maintain his composure.
Biting off each word carefully, he replied, "I'm as married
as I'll ever be. There will be no one else but Amanda. Do
I make myself clear? If she wants to take instruction, and I
stress *if*, I'll go through with the marriage again in the

Church, here. I plan to give her time to learn about her new home. Then we'll talk about what *she* wants to do." He let his eyes rest steadily on his father's face until the message was clear.

"What about your mother? She is most distressed about the matter of religion. You have grievously hurt her, Esteban."

"I think Amanda will please Mother well enough. If she's hurt, it will be because of you and your stubbornness, not because of my wife, be she Catholic or not." He stood up and ground out his cigar.

His father, realizing the futility of all his arguments, particularly in light of Esperanza's unexpected affinity for the girl, decided it was useless to argue further. Resignedly, he stood up and then came around the desk to put his arm around his son's shoulders. "All right, let's call a truce, Esteban. I can't fight against both you and your mother. She's become amazingly strong-willed after all these years. You," he paused gravely, "always were."

Softening, Esteban looked at his father and said, "Give Amanda a chance, Father. Let me take care of the Montoyas. It will all work out. Now I realize that I could never have married Elena. She'll select a husband in no time. We'll both be happier this way."

Although Esteban was happy, the Montoyas decidedly were not. His interview with Don Diego was brief and quite strained. To Esteban's relief, Elena had accompanied her mother on a visit to a neighboring ranch, so he did not have to face her hysterical recriminations. He sighed in gratitude and sadness as he rode home after politely declining a gracious invitation from Diego for a noonday meal. In time, after Elena's future was secure, the Santandars and Montoyas might again resume their ancient friendship. He hoped so.

The weeks that followed were busy for Amanda. Never, even when she first went to Lyla's, had there been so much to do, so many new things to learn. The servants, as was customary on a large estate, had their own grapevine. Word of the new señora's kindness spread to the rest of the help from the vaqueros who had been with them on the trail.

Her setting of Luis's leg was talked of across the ranch and in neighboring areas. Since the only physician in the region lived in Santa Cruz de Mayo, a day's ride away, anyone possessing healing skills was an invaluable help. When the doctor arrived at the ranch and checked Luis, he complimented her on a job he could not have done better himself, then departed, leaving the vaquero in Doña Amanda's capable care.

From near and far, peons and villagers treked in with broken limbs, coughing babies, fevers, and all other manner of illness and injury. If Amanda was thankful for what she had learned from Dr. Denton, she was also panicked at its inadequacy in the face of the awestruck trust of so many people. She dispatched letters to Paul and Elizabeth on the first sail from Santa Cruz, assuring Paul she was happy and pleading with Elizabeth for any medical books she could spare.

Among Amanda's many converts was the older servant, Lupe Valdez, who had worked for the Santandar family all her life. Lupe was assigned to Amanda that first evening by Doña Esperanza. Amanda now had a personal maid, even though she had always preferred to dress herself even when surrounded by servants at Paul's.

Sensing that it was a custom she should accept graciously lest she hurt the proud old woman's feelings, Amanda allowed Lupe to assist her in dressing and bathing, as well as keeping her wardrobe in order and tidying their quarters in the hacienda.

Lupe was surprised that Don Esteban was adamant about using one bedroom for his wife and himself. There were, as custom dictated, a master bedroom and a smaller bedroom, as well as a sitting room and bath, in the wing reserved for the newlyweds. However, if this was one place where both the young patrón and his Americana wife broke tradition, Lupe quickly adjusted. After all, there was one less bed to make up in the mornings, and *quién sabe?* The arrangement also increased the likelihood that there would be Santandar grandchildren for her to love. She had been nurse to Miguel and Esteban in their childhood years and was eager to have that work once more.

Curious about Esteban as a boy, Amanda asked Lupe all sorts of questions as they spent the mornings together after he left for his own duties outside. Lupe's leathery old face creased in a wide smile, revealing an uneven array of teeth and gums. She was as generous with words as she was spare in body. Her small, wizened frame was thin and sinewy and her back slightly hunched as if she bore the troubles of the world, but when she smiled and her dark brown eyes gleamed, any indication of sadness or defeat vanished.

"What kind of games did Esteban and his brother play as children?" Amanda asked one morning while Lupe was brushing her mistress's hair.

Pausing to push a wayward strand of her own iron-gray hair back into its severe knot, Lupe replied, "Oh, mostly wild deviltry, I can tell you. The three of them, Don Esteban, Don Miguel, and their cousin, Don Rodrigo, were always together, wrestling, climbing trees, sneaking off from their tutors to hide in the horse corrals and try to ride Don Alfredo's biggest and wildest stallions. It's a wonder any of them lived to grow up! Don Rigo was the mean one." Her eyes darkened in remembrance. "I recall once when a horse threw him. He'd been forbidden to ride it—a half-trained filly. Your husband caught him beating her with a heavy whip, like the ones hands use to herd cattle! Don Esteban used the whip on Don Rigo until Don Miguel had to pull his younger brother off. Don Miguel was always the gentle one, the peacemaker, like his mama. Your Don Esteban was wild. Oh, not mean wild like Don Rigo, but still full of life and pranks. He used to love to sneak away from the others and go down to where the hands were working cattle or breaking horses. As he grew older, he spent a lot of time with the blacksmith's son, Manuel. Since Manuel was mestizo, Don Rigo and Don Miguel didn't approve, but Don Esteban, he never cared.

Of course, that one, Manuel, he was a bad one, too, even worse than Don Rigo.''

So, Lupe's monologues provided Amanda with a wealth of information about her husband's childhood and forged a bond between servant and mistress. As Lupe discovered Amanda's adoration of her husband, she realized that, gringa or not, her lady was the right wife for him. No other woman could hold his interest as she did. Amanda's openness, like her husband's, banished the class-conscious barriers that most criollos put between themselves and their help. Lupe became devoted to Amanda, and she did not give her devotion lightly.

One afternoon, as Amanda was tending the cook's feverish baby in a small cabin adjacent to the main hacienda, Esteban came home early to search out his wife. She was bending over a small boy in a crib beside the fireplace. Her hair hung like à golden curtain, falling over her back and hiding her face. Dressed in the simple, loose clothes they had selected in the Mazatlán market weeks ago, she looked like a golden incarnation of the dark Virgin of Guadalupe. Feeling the warmth of his eyes, Amanda looked up, a spoon of greenish medicine in her hand poised at the infant's mouth. She neatly inserted it. The baby made a face, then settled back in his crib to sleep evenly. Smiling, she rose and came into Esteban's arms.

"*Querida*, Luis said you'd be here. I have a surprise for you. I've tended to the mines and my father's stock, and the paperwork is done too. Tomorrow let's go look at our own hacienda." He spoke English, which had now become a special language reserved only for the two of them when they wished no one else to understand.

At last! The chance to see her very own home and begin to refurbish it! She smiled in delight and kissed him quickly. Then, relishing the taste of male sweat and hard, warm, whiskered flesh beneath her lips, she prolonged the kiss until he reacted as he always did.

"If we are very quiet, we can go up the back stairs unnoticed and get to our room before dinner. Then I can . . ." He whispered his plans into her ear, while emphasizing his point skillfully with his body. She agreed.

The following day they set out for the smaller place Esteban had used as his private retreat when working stock at the ranch. About 14 miles north of Rancho Santandar, it was convenient without being close enough for intrusion. Although Amanda had developed a warm relationship with her mother-in-law, Amanda was not certain the old don would ever accept her. She forced the worry from her mind and concentrated on the ride.

It was a beautiful day, crisp, dry, and golden. As they rounded the final twist in the trail, Amanda saw the low building shaded by cottonwood trees and flanked by a small curling stream in the shallow, narrow valley. The house was a one-story, tan stucco structure with the traditional black wrought-iron grillwork on the windows and doors. Cool and inviting, it seemed to beckon them. Its long, low wings stretched off into the deepening shadows of the tall, gleaming stand of trees. The stream, not a hundred yards downhill from the house, burbled its own enchanting welcome, then vanished around the curve of a hillock in the distance.

Amanda was awestruck. Her very own home, her first ever. Not even her parents' modest, comfortable cottage in Saint Joseph had truly been hers. Now she would be the lady of the house. The lady, Doña Amanda. She felt a sudden rush of emotion, a lump in her throat and a misting of her eyes. "Oh, Esteban, it's so beautiful!" She kicked a startled Sunrise in the flank, sending him galloping toward the cottonwoods.

Esteban followed her in delight, watching her leap agilely from horseback and stand gazing up at the towering trees around the house. Before she could enter, he was behind her, scooping her up in his arms and kicking the door open. He carried her in saying gruffly, "Surely you're not forgetting all your best Yankee traditions, *querida?* You are my bride and this is our first home."

In reply, she tightened her arms around his neck and

kissed him soundly. Very slowly he let her down, molding her against him, deepening the kiss. The wind banged the door shut, finally ending the spell. They broke apart reluctantly to look at the interior. Today all Amanda planned to do was make a list of supplies needed and then return to the main ranch house for a complement of servants to help with the renovation. Any new furnishings she desired were to be ordered from Mulcahey, Ltd., in Los Angeles.

With equal parts of glee and efficiency, Amanda set out to inventory the low, open rooms, beginning with the lovely *sala*. The house was far less formal than the Rancho Santandar hacienda, but still spacious with a dining room and four airy bedrooms in one wing. The beautiful *sala* and a charming library were in the center. A sitting room and servants' rooms were in the other wing. The kitchen, surprisingly well equipped, was behind the dining room.

They moved in the next day. For the next several weeks Amanda joined Lupe, Nita, and Juan to clean, scrub, polish, and thoroughly rearrange the lovely old house. She learned from Lupe, the wellspring of family information, that this outlying, smaller house had originally belonged to Don Alfredo's bachelor uncle, Don Carlos. Like his young great-nephew, he bred fine horses. He had lived in seclusion here until his death, whereupon it stood vacant for many years, almost forgotten until Esteban returned from Europe and sought out his own private bachelor domain. Miguel and Inez then resided at the main house, in the quarters she and Esteban had just vacated. Esteban had needed distance from his family even before he had married her, Amanda realized.

The work on the house delighted her and the servants had become her loyal coterie. Yet, there was a nagging sense of insecurity that occasionally plagued Amanda. Esteban had never mentioned taking instructions in the Catholic religion since the day he proposed, but Doña Esperanza, in her own gentle way, managed to bring the issue up obliquely several times. Amanda knew that her father-in-law did not consider Esteban validly married to her. If it would make peace and settle the issue, she vowed to go through the process of instruction and become a Catholic so that she could be married in their church.

One hot afternoon she was in the library deep in thought about that problem as she methodically took down one book after another from the shelf to dust, catalog, and replace. With the volumes Esteban had accumulated since childhood, his acquisitions while in Europe, and her own books still arriving sporadically from Paul and Elizabeth, they had a formidable array of reading material. She heard horse's hooves coming rapidly up the front trail. It was too early for Esteban to be home from the range where he was checking colts. She pushed her hair back from her eyes and rose. Who could it be? Brushing off her wrinkled red cotton skirt and pulling back her white blouse, Amanda walked to the front *sala*.

A strikingly beautiful, immaculately groomed young woman was dismounting from a small white mare with help from a most respectful Juan. Amanda took in her appearance from the *sala* windows. The girl was about her age; maybe a bit younger, and expensively dressed in an elegant black riding habit that set off her glossy black hair, dark eyes, and ivory complexion. She was tiny yet voluptuous and walked, riding quirt in hand, with the imperious air of a criolla, born to command and be obeyed unquestioningly. Juan obviously knew this as he stood back holding her horse's reins.

With a sinking sensation, Amanda realized who the beautiful, cold-eyed woman was. Glancing down at her disheveled appearance in simple peasant work clothes, sandaled feet, and tangled masses of hair tied back carelessly with a ribbon, Amanda was aware she was no match for the beautifully groomed Elena Montoya. Amanda sighed. There was simply no help for it. She had to face the girl, although she surely would have chosen more favorable circumstances.

If Amanda had even a fleeting hope that the jilted fiancée would show good manners, she was immediately set straight when she walked out to the front porch to greet

Elena. The black eyes were icy and venomous when they met those of her American rival. Involuntarily, Amanda shivered, remembering another pair of fierce, black eyes that pierced her with instantaneous dislike—Don Alfredo's.

Amanda smiled politely, forcing aside her misgivings, and extended her hand to the young woman. In her best Spanish she said, "Good afternoon and welcome. I'm Amanda Santandar. You must be a neighbor."

Elena smirked as if they were playing a game and she alone knew the rules. She ignored the hand. Drawing herself up to her full five feet, she tapped the quirt against her thigh in a typical Latin gesture of agitation and said, "I am Elena Maria Dolores Juana Montoya y Sandoval. My family owns the adjoining lands." She made a sweeping gesture toward all the eastern landscape with one hand while she coolly surveyed Amanda from head to toe.

Her disdainful look was unmistakable as she took in the loose, brightly colored, and now, alas, quite wrinkled peasant clothes and the tangled masses of golden hair. When she glanced at the simple leather sandals, Elena had seen quite enough. A slow smile showed her even, small, white teeth. Amanda was reminded of a shrew when she looked at the set of the incisors, as if they could shred her up in seconds.

"For a 'lady,'" and Elena emphasized the word to make clear her thoughts on that subject, "you certainly do not set the example a Santandar should, when you dress like a peasant. I would not have known who you were if it were not for your unmistakable American accent and mannerisms."

"Oh, that's rather astute of you, *Miss* Montoya." Amanda stressed the unmarried title with a vengeance. "I would have known you anywhere."

"Esteban has spoken of me, then?"

"Not at all. No one had to describe you physically to me. Your mannerisms give you away also. I am rather shocked to see you out without a chaperon, however. I am learning the customs of your country, you see, and know unmarried ladies should not go out unattended."

At this thrust the girl's aggressive stance slipped a notch and she colored, mortified at being caught in such a faux pas. She raised her head and gave a quick, vicious slap of the quirt against the side of her heavy riding skirt. "I wanted to see the Yankee woman Esteban brought home. My dueña would not have permitted me to ride here without invitation, so I simply slipped out while she was taking an afternoon nap."

Amanda noticed how Elena avoided using the word *wife*, as if by ignoring it she could make her rival vanish with a slap of her quirt.

"Do you often give your dueña the slip? My husband told me you did it at least once before in the Santandar courtyard, quite late at night." Recalling Esteban's recounting of that carefully orchestrated incident, Amanda had to laugh to herself, but kept a grave face as if rebuking the girl for her scandalous behavior.

Elena was livid by this time, fighting down the urge to fly at her enemy with quirt and fingernails. "Esteban is *not* your husband! You were not married in the Church. You are a cheap American slut, and when he realizes what his family already knows, he'll discard you as he does his mistresses in Mazatlán. He's merely amused by your unusual coloring and foreign ways. His family will never allow you to bear the next generation of Santandar heirs."

"Get out." Amanda's voice was steely and controlled. "I extended my hospitality to you as any lady would to a guest. You've shamefully abused it like a spoiled child. You may return, properly chaperoned by your family, when you grow up."

With that curt dismissal, Amanda turned to go back into the house. However, before she could take two steps, the furious Elena stamped her foot, then lunged and raised her quirt, bringing it down across the thick mane of golden hair on Amanda's back. Luckily, her hair absorbed the cutting force of the blow, but, unluckily for Elena, it also served to infuriate the señora. Amanda was about four inches taller, but slimmer than the curvacious Mexican woman. They were evenly matched in weight, but Amanda had grown up on a hardscrabble farm. She was used to extreme physical exertion and exhausting chores. She'd also seen more than one fight in Willow Valley and in San Francisco. One golden tanned hand snatched the riding quirt and tossed it across the porch. The other slim hand grabbed a hunk of black hair from beneath the smart, flat-crowned riding hat and loosened it unceremoniously in one determined yank.

Elena shrieked and kicked, boots a distinct advantage over Amanda's soft sandals, but the Americana dodged adroitly while keeping her death grip on the ebony hair. Elena lurched forward and lost her balance. Both women fell to the flagstones in a tangle of skirts, black and golden hair, and clawing hands. Amanda quickly rolled on top and pinned her squirming, shrieking opponent to the ground.

Suddenly the melee was broken up as a pair of strong hands and arms lifted Amanda off the girl. Elena scrambled up instantly, still flailing furiously, only to have a tall, dark man interpose himself between the two combatants. Esteban gripped his wife closely about her waist at his right side while he held Elena at arm's length on his opposite side. Amanda instantly froze in mortification. His arm around her was flexed hard as iron and crushed the breath from her lungs. Elena was hysterical and infuriated, but not so much that she forgot the ploy that had worked with such splendid results since childhood. She began to sob desperately and loudly, forcing the tears to roll down her now smudged and flushed cheeks.

"Oh, Esteban, she—she was trying to kill me! Thank the Holy Mother you came to save me. I only came to welcome a new neighbor and this is the way—"

Before Elena could go any further, he cut her off with a short bark of laughter. "Save it for your papa, Elena. He's a fool for your tears. I'm not. I overheard the end of the conversation and saw you leap at Amanda." Turning to Juan, who was cowering near the corner of the house still holding the reins to Elena's white mare, Esteban commanded, "Juan, escort this young woman back to her dueña before she injures herself further."

"Esteban, you cannot take her side against me! She's a foreigner, a Yankee murderer. They invaded our country, stole our land!"

Coldly, with a clipped, impatient voice, Esteban spoke as he released Elena and continued to hold Amanda tightly to him. "Amanda is my wife and no one will speak ill of her in my presence."

Seeing that Esteban was not to be so easily handled as her father, Elena stamped a booted foot with rage and gulped out an inarticulate cry. Then she whirled on the other foot and fairly flew toward a terrified Juan. He was so nervous in assisting her to mount that he let her foot slip through his hands, so that she fell against the horse most ungracefully. The mare shied, but once she was in the saddle, Elena took command with a vicious kick into the horse's flank and sped down the road, minus hat and quirt and rather the worse for her encounter with the gringa.

Her parting words, flung over her shoulder, filtered through her flying black hair to haunt Amanda's dreams: "Someday you'll be sorry you brought her here, Esteban! You'll see."

As Amanda stood watching Elena thunder away with a distraught Juan trailing behind her, Esteban loosened his hold around her waist. When she remained motionless, he turned her toward him, taking her chin in his hand and tipping her face up to look at her.

"Amanda? You *are* all right? I'd hardly expect the winner to be so subdued and the loser so vocal." There was more than a hint of a smile tugging at the corner of that beautifully sculpted mouth. The obvious amusement glinting in his eyes suddenly turned her mood from one of mortification over her hoydenish behavior to fury over his arrogant pleasure in finding two women fighting over him. He loved it! And here she was ashamed of looking like a tramp instead of a lady!

Angrily she jerked her chin out of his grasp and tried to free herself from his encircling arm. "You—you insufferable, vain, womanizing . . . *male*, you!" She seethed in a rage, unable to think of anything vile enough to account for how miserable the whole incident made her feel. Then, just as suddenly, she sobbed, surprising and humiliating herself even more.

He drew her back into his arms, all the amusement of the earlier moment fled. "*Querida*, what is it? What's wrong? Elena's gone and I'm sure won't be back. Whatever gave her the nerve to come here I'll never know." As he spoke, he stroked her hair and held her securely. She returned his embrace, holding onto his waist fiercely, pressing her head against his chest. As her tears stopped Amanda whispered, "Oh, Esteban, I'm sorry," then drew herself up again. "No, I'm not either. I'm just confused and . . ."

"And?" he prompted her to continue her muffled discourse from the tight embrace.

"And afraid. She's so beautiful. The minute I saw her ride up I knew who she was." She looked up into his face, her eyes wide and dark green with fright. "She belongs, don't you see? I don't. Your parents wanted you to marry her in their church, here, not me in a foreign land. She said our marriage isn't even legal in Mexico. It's true, isn't it?"

Esteban looked down at his wife's impassioned face and placed his fingertips gently on her lips to silence her, then stroked her temple and cheek as he spoke. "I don't care what my parents wanted. I married you. We've been over that before, *querida*. You are my wife, the only one I'll ever have. Elena is a jealous, willful child. Forget her."

"But what if we aren't really married in this country? I know we are in California, but we live here."

"I told my father, and you earlier, if you recall, that you could make your own choice. If you want to become a Catholic, you decide, but you don't ever have to do it for me or to placate my father. You certainly don't have to do it out of fear of Elena."

"I know, I know you don't care about churches, but we do live here, Esteban. I think one church is as good as another. My parents were Methodists, but I'm not bothered by what denomination I am, I just want to belong. This is my land now and your family is my family. I'd like to do it for that reason, truly I would." She paused and looked earnestly at him, waiting for his answer.

Sensing her insecurity, he realized that his own perverse pride and rejection of his father's narrow prejudices had led him to assume she could live as he did. It was easy for him to flout religious convention. He had been born here. For the woman in his arms, it was a far more difficult problem. She was in an alien land, and instead of helping her assimilate, he had unwittingly added to her burden. He kissed her eyelids, cheeks, and forehead gently. Then he replied, "Of course, whatever you want. Here I am, wanting to keep my father's bias from hurting you, and I force my own beliefs on you instead. *Querida*, I'll talk to Mama's priest at the rancho tomorrow. Father Dominic will be delighted to instruct you. I know he and my mother have made you the object of many prayers in the past month." He chuckled. "As for me, they've probably burned up a shipload of candles and said uncounted thousands of prayers over the years. I've been a lost cause since I was twelve years old!"

That night before supper, Esteban sat and watched Amanda work in the kitchen. Here in her own small domestic kingdom she fitted in perfectly, as if born to live in this place. With effortless grace she broke eggs and beat them, chopped fresh vegetables, sliced veal tenderloin, all the while laughing and talking with her husband. *She worries about belonging*, he mused to himself. No one ever belonged more completely or adapted so naturally to a land and its customs than did his wife.

The meal of sauteed medallions of veal in a light egg batter with crisp greens and rice with tomato sauce was marvelous. The candle flames at the small dining-room table reflected on both their faces in warm golden flashes. Although she could have the table extended with leaves to seat twenty people, Amanda preferred the intimate proportion that now accommodated only the two of them.

Vibrations surged between them in the dim light. As she sipped the last of her wine, he gazed at her with desire in his sherry eyes. She wore a white blouse, sheer and low cut with beautiful embroidery on it, handmade by Lupe. The simple lines of the peasant costume accented her high, pointed breasts and the smooth expanse of skin across her collarbones. The full, bright green skirt was fitted at the waist, emphasizing her slenderness, yet also stressing an easy freedom of movement that more formal clothing could never achieve. Her only jewelry was a pair of big gold loops in her ears. She wore her hair loose down her back.

He smiled. "You look like a golden gypsy, free and wild and so very desirable. No woman ever belonged here as you do, *querida*. No one could ever take your place. Come here." He stood up and stretched out his hands to her. Mesmerized, she set the glass on the table and rose, eyes locked with his, to move into his embrace. He quickly reached down and picked her up with a whirl of her bright green skirt and carried her from the dining room down the hallway to their bedroom.

Kicking the door shut, he slowly let her slide her feet to the floor while her arms were still locked about his neck. He ran his hands up and down her back. She arched her lower body to his and he grasped her buttocks and held her tightly in position. Swept by a wild frenzy of kisses, they managed quickly and roughly to undress each other and moved amid the welter of thrown clothing and shoes toward the big bed.

Taking her hands in his, Esteban kissed one palm, then the other. They stood facing each other, naked in the flickering candlelight of the bedroom. Slowly he knelt before her, gripping her hips in his hands, kissing her breasts, her belly, and then that mound of golden fur. As his lips and tongue continued their caressing probe, she gasped and held on to his shoulders, reeling in a shocked dizziness of raw pleasure. Never in all the encounters at the parlor house had this been done to her! It was electrifying! Gently he nuzzled her until the backs of her knees touched the edge of the bed and she half-fell across it. Her feet were still on the floor; he was still kneeling between her legs. Esteban continued the exquisite probe as she spread wider for him and felt her hands tangling in the dense, black hair of his head, urging him on.

Just when she thought she'd go mad with the pleasure, he lifted his head, swung her legs up and rolled her onto the middle of the bed where he lay down beside her. Then, as she lay flat on her back, he spread her legs, held them wide apart with his hands and once again buried his dark head against the small golden mound. She arched and writhed in pleasure, coming to a sharp, sudden climax. He continued to hold her thus for a minute and then again began to slowly lick and stroke, ever so gently on the tender tissue until it responded. Through the haze of exquisite new sensations he was evoking, she turned her head and gazed at his lean, beautiful male body. His pulsing, engorged shaft looked as if it ached for her touch. Through a shudder of pleasure, she reached her hand across and gently grasped it, wrapping her fingers around it and stroking up and down. It was velvety, hot, and hard. He stopped caressing her for a brief moment, as if sensing what she might do, then resumed loving her in the strangely wonderful way, groaning in pleasure at her hands on him.

Almost without her conscious volition, Amanda felt drawn to reciprocate the incredible way he was making love to her. She slowly turned her upper body toward him and guided his shaft into her mouth, gingerly at first. He gave a sharp intake of breath to indicate how good it felt, then resumed his ministrations to her. They lay side by side, locked in an intensity of unsurpassed pleasure as each moved in unison, loving the other, slowly, gently, then with increasing ardor. She reveled in the exotic new sensations, loving the taste of his hot, hard manflesh in her mouth. What had been a loathsome demand at Lyla's was now a beautiful act, joyously done, freely given. As she felt herself again nearing the pinnacle, she intensified the pressure of her lips, sucking on his thrusting length until they both exploded in climax. Amanda eagerly drank the warm, sweet semen, a thing she never had done in the parlor house. This was Esteban, her love, her husband, and it was right.

Slowly, kissing her from inner thighs to belly and breasts, he raised up over her as they disentangled. Then he kissed her face softly, his eyes aglow with wonder.

"Amanda, *querida*, my sweet, sweet love." He kissed her with velvety softness across her throat and temples, eyelids, then her lips again.

She smiled, feeling suddenly shy after this wonderful new kind of intimacy, and nestled in his arms, against his chest. She blushed as he tipped her chin up to kiss her again. She said softly after the kiss, "So that's how I taste?"

He nodded. "Sweet, as I said, *querida*."

Boldly, she looked into his golden gaze, brushing his beard with her fingertips lightly, saying, "So are you, my darling, hot and sweet."

He nuzzled her neck and chuckled. "Oh, *querida*, only a fool would keep a mistress if he had a wife like you to love him! Temptress and guardian of the home fires all rolled into one perfect . . . small . . . golden . . . woman." He punctuated each adjective with a kiss.

Then his countenance grew serious. He held her face between his hands and looked earnestly into her deep green eyes. "I love you, only you, no one else. Not Elena Montoya, not any criolla. Never doubt it, Amanda, never doubt it."

"Oh, no, no, Esteban, I never will." Holding him tightly, she realized he had reaffirmed their love, calming her fears about the Mexicana with his beautiful homage to her body. Together, nothing would ever defeat them.

True to his word, Esteban rode to the main hacienda the next morning and returned with an old man in a black robe following uncomfortably on a small, wiry mule. Father Dominic's mule moved at a snail's pace, and the journey took far longer than it should have. Amanda could see by the exasperated look on her husband's face that it had been a grueling ride holding Oro back to accommodate the unhurried pace of the elderly man and his mount. She decided that for all future lessons she would ride to the ranch.

Father Dominic was a wizened, slight man of indeterminate age, probably in his sixties, but possibly far older. His dark eyes were level and honest yet quite gentle in such a lined, thin face. He was most happy, as Esteban had surmised, to have at least one of the younger generation of Santandars interested in salvation. She vowed to be a diligent pupil.

In the weeks that followed, Amanda found the lessons with the padre a pleasure, but what was even more important was the open joy she saw in Doña Esperanza. Amanda's baptism was a private family affair with only Esteban and his parents present. Even the sour, old Don Alfredo was won over. One more obstacle out of the way, she thought. Nevertheless, she was always apprehensive about her father-in-law and fearful of any comparisons he might make between her and Elena.

Often while at the ranch for instruction with the padre, she took extra time in the afternoon to visit the small cottages of the various peons who worked for Rancho Santandar. Illnesses and injuries were fairly frequent, and her medical skills, although limited, were far better than any other remedies available.

CHAPTER
15

One bright, cool morning in late fall, several hours after Esteban had set out for a far corralling area to begin the saddle training of several young stallions, Amanda prepared to ride to the main hacienda to meet with the padre and have lunch with Doña Esperanza. She and her mother-in-law had begun to grow close and they could communicate warmly, especially, Amanda thought, on the one obvious love they shared, Esteban.

Amanda enjoyed the view from the trail, marveling at how slight the seasonal changes were by her Midwestern standards or even those of northern California. Here, the spring cactus flowers and seasonal rains were the only ways winter and summer were truly distinct. Day and night, however, were far more significant in the desert, since the sun could be baking hot and the sudden nightfall frightfully cold under clear, dazzling stars. It was wild and magnificent country. Amanda could see the reason why, despite all his conflicts with family and tradition, Esteban chose to live here.

As she looked across the jagged expanse of a rocky ridge, she saw a rider and squinted in the brilliant light to make out his appearance in more detail. She recalled uneasily that she'd seen him on several other occasions in the past months. He was quite large, dwarfing the big, rangy bay he sat upon, and he had a beefy, almost fat body with a thick shock of straight black hair that hung down beneath a battered sombrero of a size to match his physique. His face was shadowed by the large hat, but she felt the malevolence of his eyes set in the flat planes of his face. His clothes and gear were dusty and old, of poor quality. Despite the fact that she had seen him three or four times inside the vast expanse of Santandar land, she was sure the unkempt, menacing man was not an employee in any capacity.

Her impulse when she saw him the first time was to tell Esteban, but then the man merely watched her return from one of the cabins where she'd tended a sick boy. He was there and gone so quickly that she almost felt foolish. The next two times he had been at a farther distance, as now, watching from a ridge when she was coming and going between the main house and her own home. Once when she had seen the man she had started to ask one of the hands who always rode with her about him, but by the time she had asked and pointed, the ridge was clear and the rider gone like a wraith. It was eerie, especially since she felt he watched only her, not the hands or the other peons who were always around her.

And now, weeks later, here he was, back like a sentinal on the ridge. As she pulled closer to Juan to ask him who the rider might be, the figure turned and vanished behind a large stand of scrub pine. Amanda sighed. The rest of the trip was uneventful.

Then one rainy winter morning she awoke to sudden cold when Esteban left the bed and walked silently across the room to dress for the day. He had to go quite a distance to one of the farthest quartering areas. With the intermittent winter rain, it would be slow traveling. Therefore, he intended to leave early without awakening Amanda. Remembering the night before, he smiled. She needed the rest.

She watched him turn and smile at her as he pulled on a heavy, dark blue wool shirt. "You are up so early, I almost overslept and didn't get your breakfast," she said, her hands outstretched. "I missed your heat and the chill always wakes me. How did I ever keep warm before I married you?"

He came into her embrace and sat on the side of the bed, wrapping his arms about her and nuzzling her neck. "Mmm, you smell so good and feel so soft and warm. Stay in bed and sleep, *querida*. Lupe is always up and she can fix me something."

"Nope, I won't either. I alone send you off into the cold."

It had quickly become a scandal, even when they lived at the main rancho, that Amanda loved to cook and was frequently seen puttering around the kitchens. She could not persuade the cooks there to relinquish their power, but here in her own domain she often shooed Lupe and Nita from the kitchen to prepare particular dinner favorites for her husband. Their special time together, however, was morning, and the breakfast ritual was unbroken in their small household. Smiling, Esteban followed the small determined form of his wife toward the kitchen.

After breakfast, Esteban left and Amanda returned to their bedroom to dress. She planned, considering the evil weather, to stay in and do some long-overdue correspondence as well as some sewing and mending. By midmorning she was deep in thought over her letter to Elizabeth, telling her friend about the accidents and illnesses that had lately befallen the people about the ranch.

Suddenly, Nita burst in to tell her a rider was out front asking for her. Amanda could tell this was an urgent matter. Nita, who was usually exceptionally polite, had come into the library without even knocking.

"Did he say what was so important?" Amanda asked.

The girl, pale and frantic, could say only, "Hurry, please, señora."

Amanda felt the damp chill of winter air hit her as she opened the main door and stepped out into the rain. The man on horseback was unfamiliar to her, young, overly thin, and rather shabby. But then, that could describe a great many of the vaqueros on a place the size of Rancho Santandar. He whipped off his hat despite the inclement weather and, crushing it in his hands, said haltingly, "Doña Amanda, please come very quick! Don Esteban's been hurt. He was up on one of the new stallions, a half-trained one, and the mud, it was slippery, the horse fell . . ."

Amanda blanched and grabbed the rough wooden hitching post, not feeling its splinters bite into her hand. She quickly caught her breath and whirled, commands flying behind her, "Send Juan to bring the doctor from Santa Cruz! Nita, you must ride to the ranch and tell Don Alfredo to come at once. I'll bring Esteban back here."

With that, she pulled an old poncho from the closet in the *sala* entry and flung it over herself, then dashed into the kitchen for the medicines and instruments Elizabeth had sent her. As she raced to the corral for Sunrise, she found Juan already saddling the big horse for her. Her full cotton skirt flew as she gripped the saddle with her knees. Thank God she'd learned to ride astride. It was imperative that every woman know how, should an emergency arise. Esteban had taught her. Oh, Esteban!

Juan was still questioning the wisdom of her riding out over the wet, muddy trails with only one boy for escort when she raced away, the thin vaquero in the lead. There was no stopping her. Juan saddled his own mount and went off toward Santa Cruz and the doctor, worrying all the way.

Amanda and the boy rode for about an hour, and in that time the day began to clear and warm a bit. She had no time to question where they went. Now, finally able to look about without wind and rain in her eyes, she could see they were riding in an area different from the one

where Esteban and his men worked. She'd never been to
the camp but was certain that this was not the way. Just as
she was about to pull up with him and question their mad
ride's destination, they rounded a bend in the trail and a
group of riders quickly surrounded them.

One man blocked Sunrise's path and the boy suddenly
reached over and grabbed the great palomino's reins as the
horse reared. Amanda struggled to keep her seat, wildly
looking at the surly bunch of pistoleros who converged on
her from all sides. She gasped as the boy, who was
obviously with these men, began to pull sharply on Sunrise's reins. The nervous horse was no happier than she.

She marshaled her courage and spoke in the dialect the
ranch peons used. "Why have you led me on this false
chase? My husband is Don Esteban. You cannot dare think
to harm me!"

A sly, low laugh from behind caused her to whirl in the
saddle. The mysterious, big rider who'd watched her for
those weeks past was sitting ominously close, still mounted on his rangy bay.

"Who are you?" She made her tone as peremptory and
brave as possible.

"I see I have you confused. I know who you are,
beautiful Yankee wife of Esteban, but you do not know
Manuel Escobar, eh?"

Manuel. Where had she heard that name before? Suddenly it came back to her from Lupe's stories about the
families on the ranch. Manuel was a childhood companion
of Esteban. Gaining some confidence from that, she asked,
"If you are a friend of my husband's, why are you
waylaying me like this? Didn't you play together as boys?"

His laughter was surprisingly silky and low for one so
coarse and big. "Ah, we grew up together, yes, but,
señora, whatever makes you think we are friends?"

An icy chill slowly climbed the back of her neck as the
man surveyed her from head to toe and then smiled. The
thick lips parted to reveal yellow, large, square teeth. His
fat cheeks, blotched with half-trimmed beard, pushed the

pockets of flesh up beneath his eyes, slitting them into razor-edged malice.

"As we escort you to our humble camp, beautiful Amanda, I will tell you all about Esteban and me, yes, all of it." His huge, meaty hand brushed hers as he took the reins the boy had given back to her when Sunrise quieted. She shivered in revulsion at the contact and again he laughed in that soft, strange way.

Amanda tried desperately to remember what Lupe had told her about Manuel, the blacksmith's son. That he was a bad one was all she could recall. The man filled in the rest of the information for her as they rode, surrounded by three heavily armed, hard-looking men. The boy rode behind.

"Esteban and I were raised at Rancho Santandar from birth. The only difference was that his papa was patrón, mine a blacksmith. Some difference!"

"But he played with you, he wasn't like Miguel and Rodrigo, Lupe told me."

At her protest, his face darkened in sudden rage, causing her to draw back across Sunrise's saddle, expecting he would strike her a blow. Then, just as suddenly, his mood calmed and he went on.

"Yes, we played together. Esteban wasn't like the other criollos who were always cold, better than the people who worked for them. At least, I thought he wasn't, but I learned different. We grew up stealing horses from the corrals and riding them before they were trained for sale. Of course, we'd return them after our larks. Then the old don caught us one time. We couldn't have been more than thirteen or fourteen. Don Esteban, the patrón's son, was sent to spend the summer in Alta California with his aunt. I was whipped and put to work at the bellows in the forge that hellish summer!" He spat and let loose a volley of Spanish epithets.

"But you can't blame my husband for what Don Alfredo did. Esteban was only a boy!"

Almost patiently he continued as they rode, "That was only when I learned the difference between being master and being slave. No, I did not blame my 'friend' then. But when I took my rightful vengeance, he showed his true blood, the blood of a criollo, by God and all His saints! I took all I could from my father and Don Alfredo. When I couldn't stand another minute, I did what a man does.'' He raised his head and glared ahead fiercely. "I took a herd of good breeding horses and ran them into Sinaloa where I got a high price for them. My men and me, we finally got a taste of the good life, eh?'' He glanced around, and the two evil-looking, burly men at his left grinned and nodded in agreement.

"I still don't see why you want to hurt my husband or me.'' By this time Amanda was exerting iron will to keep her terror from showing. She must stall and keep Manuel rationalizing his thievery until help arrived. God only knew what horrors he had planned for her!

"I will tell you, little one. I stole from every ranch. I took the best horses from Montoya, Ruiz, Rodrigues, Sanchez, Obregon. During a roundup on Santandar land, my old companion Esteban and his men from the ranch ambushed us and he took me prisoner, back to Santa Cruz, to face certain hanging. What were a lousy handful of horses from a ranch with thousands? They'd never even be missed! For that my childhood friend would have let me die. I swore the old don would pay, and the young don who betrayed me would be the price!''

"You can't mean to kill him?'' Even as the words were wrenched from her, Manuel laughed again.

"Ah, but I was in prison when the war came. It almost cheated me of Esteban. But he's a survivor, that man of yours, lovely.'' He gloated in triumph. "The old don did lose his firstborn, that mewling, holier-than-thou Miguel. Then Esteban went away. And I was still in prison. By luck I escaped, just in time to hear some very good news. The rich young patrón had taken a Yankee wife and brought her right to me.'' He saluted her by touching his hat in a mocking gesture.

Now stark terror gripped her. She could anticipate the form his vengeance would take. *If only Esteban is left alive, if only,* she repeated to herself like a litany to block out the rest. She rode with her back straight and did not look at her captor.

"Ah, I see you are quick. You know my plans, eh? You know your man has the pride of a criollo. My men and me, we take you to a special place nearby. It is clean and dry, nice for . . ." He made an obscene gesture she would not allow her eyes to follow.

"Then, when we are done, we send you back to him. He'll follow us—away from this ranch, away from all the places where we're hunted, to where we can move free. Then, in my own place, my own time, I will have him just where I want him."

Amanda couldn't stop herself at this juncture. She whirled in the saddle to face her antagonist. "I'll never tell him who you are, I'll not return, he'll never know! I'll kill myself!"

Before she could say any more he cut off her protest: "Yes, you will return, lovely. We will tie you to that beautiful horse and send you back with a special message. He will know, anyway. Such a pity. You are quite brave, yes, a brave little Yankee. How much more I would enjoy using that Montoya bitch. She was the one everyone thought he would marry. Now, that one," he shook his head in grim remembrance, "she would cut your heart out for a prize. Too good to even spit on me. She would ride after Esteban every time she could sneak off from her dueña, even when she was a small girl. Never look at me, ride right past me like I was not there, and beg him to come away from the peasant's son. Hah!" He snorted in disgust. Then his eyes slitted. "If I had her here now, she would beg, offer to sell that lily-white body to me, do anything I want, if only I would spare her!" Abruptly he turned to face Amanda. "Would you sell your body, Doña Amanda?" He looked at her with half a sneer, half something else she could not read on his face.

"To save my husband, I'd do anything you want. Anything." She looked levelly at him, sensing the animal cunning in the man. He was uneducated and deranged, yet he was far from stupid. It would do no good to cajole or feign attraction to him. He would know. A hopeless fear for herself, but more so for her husband, welled up in her.

"You, I am sorry for, that it had to be you he married, not Elena. You have courage, like your man. A pair of eagles, eh? Yes, he will follow me after I finish with you. Whatever else he is, Esteban is no coward. We will fight on my terms this time." On that grim note, he let her ride in silence for several minutes. Then he reached over and ran a huge, gnarled hand with dirty, broken nails down her side, over her breast, and across her hip. She shuddered, but held herself stiffly on the horse and looked straight ahead, attempting to show no fear.

"Ah, you shiver with such dislike, little golden lioness. You do not find me as pretty as your man, your fancy blue-blooded husband? From him you don't shrink away, I know."

At his suggestive tone, she felt herself shiver anew and glanced out of the corner of her eye toward him. He sounded as if he'd seen them together. As if reading her thoughts, he went on, "I have been watching you for several months, ever since I got here and found Esteban had a new wife. I have waited for my chance to get you away—not an easy thing, Doña Amanda, not on Santandar land. I watch you bid him farewell in the mornings, greet him at the corral at noon, welcome him home at night."

Abruptly he reached over, snatched her off Sunrise, and held her close to the length of his huge, unwashed body. She gasped in outrage and revulsion, flailing wildly in an attempt to throw herself under the horse's hooves. She would kill herself before allowing Manuel to use her to hurt Esteban. Manuel laughed that evil, silky laugh again.

"You do not pull away from him, all prissy, cold, and stiff. Ah, I watched you, little golden one, watched you press yourself against him, kiss him." He chuckled mirthlessly. "Very fiery for a northern woman. And we always believe our women are hot-blooded and Yankees are cold." As if appreciating his own joke, he continued to chuckle in a low rumble as he fondled her body.

They had been traveling upland into foothills for a while and crested a ridge to come upon a camp at the mouth of a cave. It was at the base of a steep hill and well hidden in the ripples of hundreds of ridges that corrugated the area. No one could ever track them over the rocky ground, Amanda thought dismally.

"First we build a fire and make everything nice and warm, get out of the damn wet. Then maybe we try to warm you up, eh, little lioness?" Gazing at her stoic face as she stood stiffly beside him, Manuel said almost sadly, "You are brave, I admire that, but what I will do, I will do."

Esteban was in a foul humor as Oro cantered through the sticky mud, cutting across from the holding corrals on his land toward the main rancho. It was too wet to work horses today, so he would finish the paperwork in the office and settle things with his father about their business contracts in Los Angeles and the upcoming trip in the spring. At least, he chuckled to himself, Amanda had mollified the old devil by her diligence in instruction with Father Dominic. At this point Don Alfredo was more pleased with his gringa daughter-in-law than with his son.

His reverie was suddenly interrupted by a shrieked, "Don Esteban! You're here! You're not injured, but—but the rider! Doña Amanda?" At the question and the mention of his wife's name, Esteban pulled the reins from Nita's hands.

"What about Amanda? Where is she, Nita?"

The story of the rider and his wife's flight to the north with him was quickly related. God! If he hadn't left the corrals and headed toward the main ranch, Nita would have ridden all the way there and back before the ruse was discovered! Quickly Esteban dispatched her to Don Alfredo with instructions to send a large party of armed men after him. As he set out in the direction in which the boy had led Amanda, he was grateful for the mud, which might enable him to pick up some tracks.

As he rode, he tried to figure out who might want to

harm his wife. He or his father were far more likely targets. Someone must be using her to lure him. But who? He had a fairly long list of enemies accumulated over the years of traveling, business dealings, and fighting over women. For that matter, so did Don Alfredo.

After nearly an hour of riding he picked up Sunrise's trail. He followed it in a direction that gave the information he sought, even as it formed a sick knot in the pit of his stomach. Four men had taken Amanda and the boy toward the caves. The caves! The place where he and Manuel had played and hidden when they stole his father's horses as children. It was the only logical destination in this wild back country. Manuel had Amanda! And, if Esteban hadn't chanced on Nita, Manuel would have had her all day before she was even missed! By the time Esteban lost the trail on rocky ground, he no longer had to follow tracks, but was spurring Oro on furiously. He had only the rifle on his saddle with minimal ammunition and, of course, his knife. As he rode at breakneck speed, he left the clearest trail he could for his father's men, but knew he couldn't wait for them. He might already be too late. Deliberately he forced that thought from his consciousness and settled into a deadly, killing calm, his mind separate from the wild, jarring of his body as he raced Oro over the rocky earth.

When he reached the ridges surrounding the caves, he slowed the horse and then circled as quietly as possible. If a sentry killed or captured him, he would do Amanda no good. He encountered the first man just to the south in the most obvious place to post watch, on a high ridge that overlooked the open ground where riders would enter the foothills. Sweat pouring off him, despite the damp cold, Esteban crawled silently from rock to rock. The man on watch was sitting indolently against a boulder, his legs dangling over the sharp edge of the hillock. Even if he heard the one small noise Esteban made as he jumped down and struck, the man had no chance for any action. The knife sliced cleanly across his jugular, spurting a fountain of blood to the wet earth as he fell. Esteban rolled him over on his side and hid him behind the big rock, then turned to search for more sentries.

The other lookout was a boy stationed on the hilltop just above the mouth of the cave to guard the entrance. He was nervous and paced noisily back and forth. Esteban crushed the boy's skull with his rifle butt.

It would probably be safe to try for the entrance. Esteban knew how Manuel thought. More sentries were unlikely. He had to chance it. *She could be screaming for help and I couldn't even hear,* the tortured thought wrenched him. Silently he eased down the hill and into the entrance. When he got inside, he had to pause and let his eyes adjust to the darkness. The main room he and Manuel had used as boys was down and to the right. It had ventilation, so a fire could be lit. That was the place they'd probably take her. As he neared the widening part of the cavern, he heard voices. There must be three of them. Poor odds with Amanda in the line of fire. How could he stall for time? Improve his chances? First, he must get close enough. The voice became more distinct as he inched nearer.

"Now you have your fire, little lioness. Come, warm yourself." Manuel's tone was oily, almost solicitous.

"Only if I can push you in it first," came the low, steady reply. Amanda had been goaded beyond endurance by Manuel's crude, smelly pawings. As he ordered the men about, he held her and rubbed his hands over her disgustingly, ripping off her blouse after a bit and then even running his hands up under her loose skirts. Now, as she shivered in a thin camisole, he mocked her with false hospitality.

"We don't have all day and I want to get started. We must, um, do our work here, and then send you back to your husband by the time he returns from a long, hard day at the corrals. Then, lovely, we move very fast to the south with him in pursuit."

Realizing the uselessness of protest or pleas, Amanda stood by the fire, ramrod straight. She faced him. God, he was like a darker version of Carver Cain, but now she was no sixteen-year-old girl. Never again would any man

humble her or cause her to cringe. Amanda Whittaker had
paid her dues.

The fire in the cavern was beginning to take the damp
chill from the air, but in her thin camisole Amanda felt
deathly cold; her mouth was dry and her limbs were almost
numb. Slowly, Manuel moved his fat girth toward her,
tossing his huge sombrero on the ground next to a carelessly
spread, filthy horse blanket. With a low, guttural command, he told the two men to go into an outer cave so that
he would have privacy with the woman. With a few
leering, jocular comments about his needing help, the two
big men shuffled toward the entry. Perhaps they would get
their turn at her later.

She forced herself to swallow the dry, hard lump in her
throat. As he neared her, the flickering firelight bounced
off the greenish-gray walls, making Manuel's face even
more malevolent as the shadows distorted it. He reached
for her and tore the strap on her camisole. When instinctively
she tried to hold the fragile fabric covering her breasts, he
reached again and pulled her small hand free, touching the
pink-tipped breast with his filthy paw.

From his position outside, Esteban heard Manuel send
the two men from his presence. His Patterson Revolving
Rifle had five shots. He must kill them quickly and
cleanly. He crouched in a dark corner of the small outer
cavern, shadowed by an outcropping of rock, waiting. The
second both men were in clear view, he acted. The noise
of the blast reverberated across the high ceiling of the
caves, from room to room, deafening Esteban as he
watched one pistolero thrown to the right, his huge frame
crumpled like a rag doll. The second man, silhouetted in
the opening, freed a handgun from his holster but neither
cocked nor raised it before he, too, was catapulted into
eternity. The second body flew into the larger cavern with
the impact of the slug, and Esteban jumped over it,
confronting a dazed Manuel, who still held one hand on
Amanda's shoulder. They were frozen in tableau. She
stood covering herself and mouthed her husband's name as
he broke into the entry of the big cave. Manuel began to

smile a slow, hate-filled grin, silent and terrible, as he watched his adversary advance.

Esteban looked like a dark angel of death, the firelight illuminating eyes darkened with fury, as he waited, deceptively still.

Amanda's gaze went from her husband, whose fierce, hate-consumed countenance was that of a stranger, to Manuel, who still smiled that awful smile. Both seemed so calm, as if the whole confrontation had been rehearsed.

Manuel broke the silence. "Always I underestimate you, 'Don' Esteban. I won't ask how you got here so fast or if my lookouts are alive. So, now it is time." He gestured around with his free hand. "Not the time or place I would choose, but it will do; it will have to do."

"You put your hands on my wife. For nothing else than that I'll kill you, Manuel." Esteban's voice was low and emotionless.

Releasing Amanda, Manuel turned to face his adversary directly. She hurriedly backed away from his looming presence toward a far corner of the big cavern. Despite Manuel's greater height and girth and his oily, menacing manner, she could not take her eyes off Esteban's taut, slim frame.

"This time we end it, friend of my youth." As he spoke with low, cutting force, he slipped the long, wicked-looking blade from its boot sheath in one lightning-smooth motion.

Manuel's big, yellow teeth gleamed dully in the eerie light. Moving slowly and carefully, he slid his own blade from its sheath at the back of his waist. "Let's see, my pretty criollo, what your gentlemen's education taught you. Not enough, I bet. Me, I got lots of practice that time in jail. How do you think I got out, eh?"

As he talked Manuel circled away from the fire. Esteban followed him as if in a ballet, an arm's length between them.

"You bet your life, Manuel."

"Ah, so do you, 'Don' Esteban." He spat the title like a curse, then made a quick feint, low toward the leaner man's right side; but with amazing speed for one of such bulk, he switched to cut in a high arch toward Esteban's throat. With calm ease, Esteban blocked each move, despite Manuel's deadly agility.

Amanda crouched in her corner, watching the silent, deadly dance being played before her eyes. She dared not move and risk distracting Esteban, but she desperately wanted to reach the handgun lying on the floor near the entrance where the dead bandit had dropped it. She could not let Manuel kill her husband! Yet, as she watched, she knew the outcome, knew Manuel would die. It was almost as if the sheer force of will in Esteban's implacable, beautiful face would make Manuel lose the contest. Swiftly the men lunged and feinted left and right, low, high, and then again low, each carefully parrying the other's attacks. Both began to sweat, the droplets running in their eyes, plastering their shirts to their bodies, making their dark beards glisten in the firelight. She was not sure how long it went on or who drew first blood, but soon both men had small cuts that bled freely, Esteban on his forearm and chest and Manuel across his collarbone and left thigh. Their moves were too fast for her untrained eye to follow. She held her breath as they danced near the fire in the pit at the cavern's center. Suddenly, Esteban's foot hit a loose stone and he went down on one knee. The huge body of his foe came crashing on top of him and they rolled dangerously close to the leaping flames, each holding the other's knife hand immobilized, even as they thrashed to gain advantage.

Just when she was ready to risk a desperate lunge around them toward the entry and the gun, she heard the unmistakable crack of human bone splintering against stone. In mid-step she looked up to see Esteban now on top, holding his knife at Manuel's throat with his right hand, while his left held Manuel's shattered forearm against a jagged outcropping of rock on the cave's uneven floor. Esteban had smashed the arm in one lunge, rendering his foe's knife useless. It dropped from Manuel's big hand and clattered on the stones.

Involuntarily, a low, jagged gasp of agony was torn from the bandit, who lay still, looking up into the face of certain death and, once again, waiting.

"You should have stayed in Sinaloa, Manuel." With that, Esteban made one quick, clean slash with the blade in his right hand. Amanda watched the coldblooded, incredible efficiency of the killing. It was an execution, one part of her mind registered.

Wearily, Esteban got up. His body was drenched in perspiration and blood from several superficial cuts and abrasions, his shirt almost torn off. The lifetime ritual of cleaning the blade was unconsciously observed again. He wiped it on Manuel's pants, then replaced it in his boot. Amanda had not moved from where she stood when she heard Manuel's arm break.

As if coming out of a trance, Esteban turned toward the pale, trembling form of his wife, so still against the wall of the cave. He moved stiffly now, limping from when he'd crushed his knee on the stone floor. As he walked toward her, she searched his face. His cold, terrible mask was off now and he grimaced in pain as he took her in his arms. He was soaking wet with perspiration and more than a little of his own blood. Gently he enfolded her in his arms. Amanda still clutched the torn remnants of her camisole to her breasts, not moving. He kissed her brow and neck softly and stroked her. She was trembling, but dry-eyed, unnaturally stiff in his embrace.

"*Querida?* Amanda, it's all right. He didn't hurt you. No one will ever hurt you. I'll kill any man who touches you. You're safe now."

He stopped his low murmurings, aware of her frozen state, and grasped her by her shoulders firmly, willing her to look at his face. Now it was Esteban's face again, her husband, his eyes full of concern. Still, that cold deadly mask of the dispassionate fighter was engraved in her mind. Which man was Esteban, her lover or the killer?

Desperately she searched his face as he returned her gaze with a fiercely possessive stare. He continued to hold her tightly, demanding that she understand.

"You are my wife. I'll never let anyone touch you or harm you. I love you, Amanda; whatever else I am, whatever I've done or will do, I love you. You belong to me!"

The impassioned plea in his voice drew her from her entranced state. He was her love, her life, and if he had killed, he had done it for her. She let the torn camisole fall, baring her breasts as she wrapped her arms tightly around his waist, kissing his bare, blood-smeared chest where the shirt hung in tatters, more off than on his body.

With a low, exultant cry of triumph, he kissed her, hard and deeply on the mouth as if branding her his for all time. She returned the kiss, grateful that they were both alive in the midst of so much death.

When they made their way from the cave, he took a poncho from Oro's saddle roll and wrapped her securely in it. He tied all the outlaws' horses together and put them on a lead rope. Then, when she insisted that she was well and could ride Sunrise, he helped her mount. He rode Oro and the five riderless horses followed. Both the big golden palomino and his master were exhausted, Oro from the hard, furious ride to the caves and Esteban from the fighting.

The slow, steady drizzle came down again as they rode. After about half an hour they came upon Don Alfredo and a dozen heavily armed men from the ranch. Laconically Esteban informed them of what had happened. Four men and a boy dead. Simple narration. Her father-in-law's black eyes pierced her through the heavy wool poncho. A mixture of relief that she had not been raped and genuine concern for her safety were woven together in his expression. One of the vaqueros took the extra horses and rode toward home with Esteban and Amanda. The rest went with Don Alfredo toward the caves to dispose of the dead.

On the long ride back to their own house, Esteban's words kept ringing through Amanda's mind: *I'll kill any man who touches you. You belong to me!* And Paul's admonition: *He's a killer, Amanda.* In her exhausted, fearful state, she forced herself to huddle on Sunrise, thinking about all the men Esteban would have to kill, beginning with Carver Cain. A small, hysterical hiccup of laughter almost surfaced. Her husband's possessiveness and violence still terrified her, and every time she closed her eyes, she would relive the scene of slaughter in the cave and then a more blurred one in a Sydneytown back alley.

Only when she felt his hands, warm and gentle, lifting her off the horse did she begin to think of anything else. He moved to pick her up to carry her inside, but one look at his bruised, bleeding state convinced her that he was far worse off than she. Shaking her head, she wrapped her arm about his waist and they trudged together into the house. A nearly hysterical Lupe greeted their bedraggled appearance with a barrage of questions. After explaining as briefly as possible, Amanda ordered hot baths for both of them, insisting that Esteban go first in the tub. She had to check the severity of all the cuts and abrasions and see if any bones were broken. Only then would she rest and bathe.

After she had tended his wounds, Esteban came over to sit by the bedside table where she quietly sorted out her medical supplies. Ever since the cave she'd been unnaturally reticent. On the ride home, he had assumed that the same sort of exhaustion he felt made her so still. Now, he was not so sure.

"What's wrong, *querida?* You aren't afraid of me, are you?" The words were spoken softly, in English. He gazed directly at her face. Trembling at his perception of her mood, she almost dropped a bottle of disinfectant.

She looked up, locking eyes with him, needing to relieve the tension between them. "No, not exactly . . . I mean, not of you. I know if you hadn't done what you did, they'd have raped me." Her voice lowered to a bare whisper. "But, the way you killed Manuel—I know you had no choice with the two men in the outer cave, but Manuel was crippled, at your mercy." She stopped and then felt horribly guilty. That was only part of the truth and she knew it. Her own guilty secrets crouched in the back of her mind.

He sighed and took the bottle from her hands. "Let me tell you about two boys growing up at Rancho Santandar."

It all stemmed from the caste system in Mexican society and the gulf between a Santandar and a blacksmith's son, he told her. After living for months on the ranch, she understood in a general sense the injustices of the system, but the particular details of this case were different, just as Esteban was different from Miguel, Rodrigo, and Elena. Despite the disapproval of his parents and of Manuel's own father, who didn't want his son overstepping the bounds of class, the boys frequently had gone on larks together.

Gradually, however, the inequity between their stations in life began to rankle Manuel. He stole small items from the blacksmith shop and other ranch buildings. Ironically, his worst punishments came not from Don Alfredo, but from his own father, who whipped him unmercifully. When Manuel and Esteban were fourteen, they took the half-trained horses for a ride to the caves, and the wrath of both fathers came down on them. After that summer's separation, the breach was irreparable.

"I couldn't be his friend anymore. He began addressing me as 'Don' Esteban, making the title an insult. I gave up and decided there was nothing I could do. Then, when we were about eighteen, I caught him one summer with two of my father's best studs, the finest breeding stock on the ranch. He was obviously going to sell them in Sinaloa and slip back before anyone connected him with the theft. He was alone then and so was I. I persuaded him to return them before they were missed from the corral, even helped him sneak them back that night. Then he fell in with some older men, bandits, drifters, and cutthroats from northern Sonora. They took him with them on a rampage of killing and stealing horses. They even raped a young girl from one of our families here at the ranch. When they came back for a large herd of prize stock, it was my patrol that caught them. By that time Manuel was a leader. Several men were shot, two killed, but I took Manuel alive. Since one of the dead men was an old vaquero from our ranch, all the men in my party wanted to lynch the whole bandit group. I persuaded them to take the prisoners to the magistrate in Santa Cruz de Mayo. I never found out what happened to Manuel until after the war. He'd escaped prison and fled to the south. I never thought our paths would cross again, but I knew he had sworn vengeance.''

Esteban stopped speaking and Amanda looked up into his eyes, reading the hurt he felt for the death of a friend, a friend who had died long ago, not that afternoon.

He shrugged, then winced as he stood on his bad knee. "I don't know whom to blame. Maybe his own father was too harsh. The system's wrong, Amanda, I'm sure of that, but not every man born poor turns into a ravening animal because of it. I let him go once and a girl was raped and men killed because of my decision. Taking him off to prison again wouldn't stop him. I wouldn't ever take the chance. If that's hard, that's the way I am, the way this place is. I can't change either one.''

He searched her face, gently reaching out to stroke her cheek and push back a wayward golden curl from her eyes as she stood up. He seemed to wait for her response. Her eyes locked with his and she came into his embrace, molding her body to his, letting it speak for her all the words and feelings she couldn't express. She loved him, beyond fear, beyond all reason.

They held each other very tightly for a long while, their bodies communicating what words could not. Then he took her by the shoulders and said, "Now, my lovely nurse, it's your turn for the tub. I'm sure Lupe has it filled and waiting. You smell of horse blankets and cave mold!''

Later that evening as they ate supper, he told her about the war. He'd mentioned it only briefly when she had asked him about the terrible saber scar. Now the release in talking about his childhood with Manuel let him loose all the horrors he had suppressed with iron will for so long. He told her of things he'd never shared with anyone before: the senseless killing, the stench and gore of the battlefield, the retreats and routs because of inept or dishonest generals, Santa Anna's perfidy. The waste of all the young lives like his brother's was the worst part. His own injuries and months of feverish recuperation were the least of his tale of horror. Learning what he'd lived through brought Amanda closer to her husband. She understood his pain.

After dinner they collapsed in an exhausted sleep. In the predawn hours, Amanda stirred in a restless nightmare, crying out his name and awakening Esteban. He reached for her and began to croon soft Spanish love words, consoling her at first, then as his hands slid over her thin silk nightrail he began to kiss and caress her with more ardor. It was as if she floated into a beautiful dream after the horrors of the preceding day. She responded, drowsily at first, then with heated passion as she came fully awake. The room was warm and her gown far too cumbersome. With his help, she slipped out of it, kneeling up in the middle of the bed and pulling it over her head. He quickly brushed the covers to the bottom of the large bed and also knelt up, oblivious of his wrapped knee as they embraced hip to hip. Softly she caressed the small nicks on his chest and his bandaged arm, then kissed each one as he ran his open palms up and down her back and hips.

Pressing against the hardness of his erection, she entrapped it between her slim flanks and then moved sensuously until he groaned with passion, kissing her neck and tangling her long golden hair in his hands. He pulled the hair downward, tipping her head back, then devoured her opened mouth. Breathlessly, he left her lips and moved again to the open expanse of her throat to trail rough bites and kisses along its slender golden column.

Gasping and writhing, she moaned in urgency, "Now, my love, please now," and arched her hips toward his thrust between her legs, making it clear what she wanted, even as her hand reached down to grasp him and guide his entrance. As they strained together in fierce, joyous rhythm he held her up against him and they exulted in the joining pleasure.

When his injured knee could no longer bear their weight, he rolled them onto their sides, still locked together. Then he pulled her on top of him. Greedily Amanda moved her hips up and down to meet his thrusts. It was as if they were sealing the pact of their love anew. There was so much she wanted to tell him, so much she now understood about him. This was their most intimate, immediate, and wondrous communion. They loved as the sun broke over the eastern horizon and filtered across their large, warm bed, bestowing a blessing.

PART 5

VOID

CHAPTER
16

The following month, Father Dominic decided that Amanda was ready for the sacramental reenactment of her marriage. The padre, true to his word, approached Esteban about the ceremony. Happy to do anything that pleased his wife, he agreed. His parents decided to honor Esteban and Amanda's wishes for a small, very private ceremony since the young couple already felt, as Esteban said, "as married as we'll ever be." But there would be a fiesta, a large, public celebration to honor the new Santandar daughter-in-law. The actual ceremony was to take place the week following the fiesta in Esperanza's chapel in the hacienda. At last Amanda had the full blessing of her husband's parents. She would face their society, even the redoubtable Montoyas, secure in her role.

After nearly six months of marriage, Amanda's only worry was that she had not yet conceived. The old fears about barrenness, which Elizabeth had assured her were groundless, surfaced anew. Each month since her wedding

night on the boat, she had greeted her periods with
increasing anxiety. Esteban seemed unconcerned, assuring
her that they had the rest of their lives, not to fear. Yet,
remembering the brutality of and possible injury from
Carver's assault, she still worried.

For his part, Esteban played down her fears about not
getting pregnant while his own fears grew that she would.
His mother had suffered agonizing, protracted labors to
produce two stillborn daughters and another son who lived
only a year. He viewed his young wife's concern over
Santandar heirs with mixed feelings. That Amanda was
young and strong did not console him. That anything
might happen to her was unthinkable territory where he
could not let his mind trespass.

The evening of the big fiesta, Amanda modeled her
dress in front of the giant mirror in their bedroom. They
had returned to the big hacienda two days earlier to help
with preparations. It had been months since they had left
these quarters for their own home. Now Amanda was
happy to return for a visit. Both her mother-in-law and
even old Don Alfredo looked on her in a new light. They
were now advocates instead of adversaries.

As she looked into the mirror, she saw her husband walk
up behind her. He was resplendent in his tight, perfectly
tailored black charro suit, with elaborate snowy white shirt
and red sash. It was a costume almost identical to the one
he wore that day at the track when he had first melted her
with his bold, smoldering gaze. Now as he held her from
behind, they posed together, a dazzling couple reflected in
silver and framed by gilt wood edging.

Tonight Amanda was dressed in a singularly beautiful
gown that fairly lit up the mirror. It was of the sheerest,
softest silk, cut as she preferred in straight, simple lines
with a minimum of petticoats. It was designed to cling to
her arms and waist and came to a deep vee between her
breasts, just low enough "to tantalize but not scandalize"
as her dressmaker liked to say. The most stunning thing
was the color. It was a deep, vibrant orange-red that
glowed with iridescent light at her slightest movement.

The unusual color highlighted the gold of her hair piled high on her head, covered with a gossamer-thin, delicately worked black lace mantilla. Her complexion was a tawny, rich hue and her eyes were darkest brilliant green. She was as radiant as her beaten-gold necklace and heavy gold wedding band, the only jewelry she wore.

As he put his arms around her waist, Esteban bent his dark head to plant a kiss just above the necklace, carelessly nuzzling the lace out of his way to allow his lips access to her throat. She closed her eyes and leaned back into his embrace, never so happy to be alive in all her life.

"I can see you're quite ready to make the grand entrance." He turned her and held her at arm's length to drink in the vision she made, all golden warmth and scorching red fire. "God, but you're lovely!"

Languorously she surveyed him from the crown of his black curly head to his gleaming black boots, then up again to his smoldering gaze. "I might say you're quite magnificent yourself, Don Esteban." A hint of a secret smile curved about her lips. "Yes, a very splendid animal, indeed."

He grinned wickedly and offered her his arm with a mock bow. "We'll see, my lady, how well you can ride a splendid animal later tonight."

They walked onto the balcony and looked down on the scene below them, a kaleidoscope of color and babel of music and laughter. Braziers were strewn across the courtyard. The light of the glowing coals and the brilliant costumes of the guests created the illusion of a summer day in the midst of a winter night. Tables lighted by candles were placed around the courtyard, and a strolling band of mariachis stopped to play favorite melodies at each one.

As they surveyed the scene below, Esteban identified numerous illustrious visitors from important families of the area. When he pointed out Diego and Maria Montoya, Amanda's eyes widened and she turned to him with a question unspoken.

"Elena has not deigned to grace our gathering with her

presence." He added mischievously, "I guess she's not grown up yet."

Amanda, remembering her dismissal of her rival that long-ago day, met his gaze with undisguised amusement. She let out a small, low laugh as Esteban squeezed her waist and guided her toward the stairs.

"Tonight you'll even get a chance to meet my mother's family for the first time." His rather subdued tone—or was it a hint of disgust?—caused her to look up at his face as they descended the curving wrought-iron stairs to the courtyard below.

"You don't like them?"

He shrugged. "My aunt Dolores is a vapid, pleasant woman, I guess, but Uncle José is a man who lives far beyond his means, and his means are considerable. He's my mother's brother, yet so unlike her. And, of course, my cousin Rodrigo will be here. He's an insufferable provincial who dislikes all foreigners."

"Especially Yankees?" she supplied, already sensing that he was warning her about his boyhood companion.

He smiled his dazzling white smile to put her at ease. "I don't think he really dislikes Americans any more than he dislikes the French or English. I'm surprised he's not been around before this. He always had an eye for women, and I know he's heard about my incredibly beautiful wife." With that he leaned over to give her a quick, reassuring nuzzle on the neck.

"Flatterer," she said, but pressed herself into his soft, swift caress.

"Of course, he's been spending time in Mexico City with his political cronies. I heard last night from my father he's even been to California a few times with some playboy friends. He brought one companion with him, an older, wealthy banker, an exile who left Alta California when you won the war." His jesting reference to the outcome of the war and her native land's role in the disposition of California always made Amanda defensive, even though she knew he was teasing.

"I'm a Mexican citizen now, thank you, Don Esteban, and I can't help who claims California as its state!"

They both laughed, but were interrupted by Don Alfredo as they reached the bottom of the stairs.

"Finally, you two arrive. I have two bands playing, one in the *sala*, one out here, yet no one can dance until I make the announcement and introduce you, Amanda." He surveyed his beautiful daughter-in-law with approval.

Doña Esperanza came up with her brother José Ruiz and his wife, Dolores, in tow. After the introductions, Esteban inquired about his cousin Rodrigo.

"Ah, that young rascal will be along shortly. He is bringing an old acquaintance who has spent a great deal of time in your country, Amanda." Don José's eyes, pale and piercing, were almost lascivious in a veiled way. Amanda had know men like him at Lyla's and she shivered in remembrance. He looked vaguely familiar, although she knew she'd never seen him before. She knew now why her husband did not like his uncle José. Doña Dolores was, as Esteban had said, a vapid, simpering woman who stayed in the shadow of her husband.

As more people filtered near the guests of honor, Don Alfredo gave a signal to the band, and after a fanfare to get everyone's attention, he made the formal announcement regarding his son's marriage, presented Amanda, and commanded all to enjoy the music, dancing, and food. Both the newlyweds were glad to have that ritual over.

A rather portly, kind-looking man with a small, strikingly handsome woman approached Esteban and Amanda. When he bowed before Amanda, Esteban introduced his father's oldest friend, Diego Montoya. His eyes smiled benignly and he was the epitome of Hispanic gallantry. His wife, however, was another matter. As they spoke of trivial things and the old man went to lengths making Amanda feel at ease, the small, dark woman, an older version of her daughter, looked daggers at the gringa who had stolen Elena's property.

Why, she still hasn't given up hope for her daughter, Amanda thought as she noted the venomous look behind the artificial smile on Doña Maria's face. Amanda was glad her marriage would be sealed in the family chapel the following week. The sooner, the better.

When the music started up again in a wild folk rhythm, Esteban made their excuses and led Amanda onto the dance area cleared in the central courtyard. As they went through the sensuous, intricate movements of the dance she had learned to love so well, she felt hypnotized by its primitive beauty. Esteban, feeling her flow in and out of his arms, sensing her mood, responded with a smoldering gaze that locked them in intense concentration. They were oblivious to the crowd of onlookers who stood by admiring the striking couple.

Two latecomers to the fiesta stopped on the balcony stairs after changing into more formal attire in upstairs guest quarters. They looked down at Esteban and Amanda dancing. Rodrigo Ruiz's companion, Alesandro Mercero, an older man, fiftyish with thinning gray hair and the beginnings of a paunch, suddenly grasped his friend's arm.

"God's blood, Rigo," he exclaimed. "Isn't that supposed to be your cousin's American wife?"

Straining to see through the flickering light from the braziers and lanterns, Rodrigo followed Amanda's movements. "I've never met her, but yes. Leave it to Esteban to pick one who's beautiful and rich, even if she is a filthy Yankee."

Glancing at his friend, then pulling him farther down the stairs, Alesandro said silkily, "Look closely at her, Rigo. Didn't you say you'd heard she was from San Francisco? Doesn't she look a bit familiar? I realize I had cause to, er, see her in slightly closer quarters than you, but . . ."

As he let the suggestion trail off, Rodrigo gasped in stunned recognition. "It's Mandy! That fancy yellow-haired piece you had at Lyla's. Damned if it isn't, or her exact double!"

Alesandro nodded. "I doubt two such incredibly beauti-ful green-eyed blonds with those, ah, physical assets could both come out of San Francisco in the past few years. Too much coincidence, eh, Rigo?"

"Still, I must be sure." He moved closer. "Yes, it's Mandy! If we'd only had another evening in San Francisco that trip, I'd have paid a fortune to have her."

"Well, I had her and she was worth the price, ice maiden notwithstanding."

Rodrigo's laugh was low and ugly. "Well, my friend, I'll have her now. By the saint's balls, this is too good! My proud Santandar cousin, so rich, so independent, he could have any woman on earth, but he marries a gold-rush whore! I'm sure he doesn't know. I wonder where they met? My father told me Esteban's bride was wealthy in her own right."

"It's not uncommon for a woman of beauty in her business to gain a rich, old protector. Who knows?" Alesandro was beginning to enjoy the possibilities of the situation.

Rodrigo's eyes were ablaze with excitement now. "Just look at him! He's besotted with her! That arrogant son of a bitch who had every woman from Santa Cruz to Mazatlán falling at his feet is in love with a high-class prostitute. It's too good to be true! Oh, 'Sandro, you can't imagine how long I've waited for a chance like this, and here it drops in my lap! He even broke a family agreement with the Montoyas and threw over their daughter Elena for his soiled dove." His eyes hardened, going from laughter to icy calculation. "Now, I'll marry the rejected Creole belle. If I have to take Esteban's castoffs, at least that one will be a virgin, and I'll have my revenge in the meanwhile."

As the two men spoke, the music ended with a resounding round of applause for the young dancers, who melted into the crowd of well-wishers. Doña Esperanza whisked Amanda off to be introduced to a group of elderly women, the matriarchs of the best and oldest families of Sonora and Sinaloa. Regretfully, Amanda followed her excited mother-in-law into the *sala*, leaving her husband in the clutches of a group of old friends, some of whom were most attractive young matrons.

As she made polite conversation with the four older women, Amanda's eyes strayed in search of Esteban. Then

she saw someone else. As Rodrigo stood in the far doorway to the *sala*, entering from the courtyard, he tipped his
head in a mock salute to Amanda. His eyes and facial
expression spoke volumes. She froze. It was as if her heart
had stopped beating. Then, years of self-discipline and
practiced façade took control.

She ignored him and leaned toward the ancient Doña
Margarita, who was sure to know everyone present, and
inquired who the man in the doorway was. Even before
she received the reply, she knew. That was why José Ruiz
looked so familiar. Rigo, Esteban's cousin, his constant
companion in childhood, was the one Lupe had said was
so mean! Oh, God! She could hope he would hold his
peace, but she felt instantly upon looking across the room
again into those cold, blue eyes that he would not.

All she could do was brazen it out, pretend she'd never
seen him before. Thank God he'd only looked her over at
Lyla's, not taken her upstairs! Then he began to move
slowly, almost languorously, across the long expanse of the
sala toward where she was seated in her fortress of staid,
old dueñas.

Rodrigo made a courtly bow before Amanda and introduced himself, while the admiring glances of the old
women confirmed his position in their society. "I am
Rodrigo Ruiz, Doña Amanda, Esteban's cousin, your Mama
Esperanza's favorite nephew." He rolled his eyes slightly
as he said the last, amid the titters of the matriarchs. "I've
been told my cousin married a beautiful, golden-haired
woman. I did not realize how lovely she was."

Amanda inclined her head stiffly toward him and forced
a smile as false as his own. Glacial green eyes clashed
with icy blue ones. She would not give him the satisfaction
of flinching. Taking her hand, he kissed it gallantly in front
of the assemblage and said, "Your husband is in the
library and needs to discuss something urgent with you,
dear cousin. Might I have the privilege of escorting you?"

She could not deny his request without being obviously
rude. Perhaps it was better to face him immediately. She
rose and made polite excuses to the women, then went

with her adversary into the huge oak-paneled room off the main hallway.

Once inside the door, what she suspected was confirmed. Esteban was not there. The room was empty. When he followed her inside, she slammed the massive oak door behind them and stood with her back against it, confronting him boldly.

"Obviously my husband is not here, Don Rodrigo. What do you want?" She looked at him, practicing the level gaze Paul Mueller used to shrink bluffing business adversaries down to size.

His smile was a nasty, slow thing, revealing even white teeth. If it weren't for his sadistic, icy manner and dissipated air, he would have been quite handsome, she thought. He looked nothing like the Santandars with their piercing direct gaze. He was Don José's son, cold and leering.

"Ah, Mandy, you know what I want—what I was unable to stay long enough to purchase at Lyla's. Pity I had to sail the next morning, but then I never dreamed I'd see you here, so conveniently."

He reached for her shoulder. She knocked his hand off with considerable force and stood her ground, daring him to try again.

"Don't play the grand lady with me, Mandy. I know who you are, a very high-priced courtesan, shall we say, from the very best brothel on all the west coast of your big United States. So stop the airs and listen. You cooperate, come to Mazatlán to my place for, er, shopping trips, what you will. We'll have a very pleasant time, you and I. Esteban need never know."

When he again moved to touch her, she pushed him back and said furiously, "Esteban would never believe you! If you think I'd ever come to you, you're insane, you cur, you filth!" She began to whirl away, to flee the room and the ugly proposition, but he stopped her with three words.

"Alex Mercer's here. Ring a bell, dear cousin? Rich, middle-aged, graying banker and land speculator. He was with me that night at Lyla's. I believe he was your, ah, companion for the evening?

"Ah, you thought he was a Yankee, I see. A common error. Like my cousin, my friend Alesandro Mercero was raised in California. He learned to speak English as fluently as his native tongue. When California was stolen by the Americans, he moved to Mexico. His business interests often lead him to give the impression he's a Yankee." He spat the last word like a vile epithet.

"Well, Mandy?" He turned her cold, still form around to face his lopsided smile.

"Go to hell!" She bit off each word and again moved to leave, but the door swung open and Alex Mercer entered, followed by Esteban.

Once inside, Esteban looked at his cousin and then glanced to Amanda. He smiled. "What's all the secrecy, Rigo? What was so urgent you and your friend had to drag us away from our guests?"

Rodrigo assumed a very aggrieved air as he turned and paced in the library, compelling Esteban to follow him curiously toward Don Alfredo's oak desk.

"What's wrong, Rigo? You look as if you've been poisoned."

Without preamble, Rodrigo launched into his attack with an anguished-looking face. "Esteban, I don't know how to say this any other way than directly. That's why I brought Alesandro here to confirm it. We both knew your wife, Amanda, in San Francisco over two years ago. She worked at a place called Lyla's. Perhaps you've heard of it?"

Esteban stiffened in recognition of the name. He'd seldom frequented the place, but its name was such a byword that every rich man from Oregon to Sonora was familiar with it.

"Rigo, for even suggesting such a thing, I should kill you, slowly." He moved menacingly toward his cousin, but before he could take two steps, Alesandro put a hand on his shoulder.

"Don Esteban, I was there also. Surely you can see we'd have no reason to lie. What he says can be easily verified, can't it, Mandy?" Alesandro turned toward Amanda with an indolent tilt of his head, awaiting her reply.

The eyes of all three men were riveted upon her. All the tension between Esteban and Rigo evaporated and was directed toward Amanda, slim, pale, standing in the middle of the high-ceilinged room, very small and vulnerable.

One look at her face, riven with anguish, guilt, and terror, was enough to hit Esteban with sledgehammer force. It was like a booted kick to the solar plexis, knocking all the breath from his body. He stood very still, hands clenched at his sides, staring at his wife, waiting for her to speak. His jaw was clenched as tightly as his fists, and his gold eyes darkened in hurt and fury, like some magnificent wild animal tormented beyond endurance.

"Amanda?" The voice sounded like Esteban's. It was low and gravelly, the beautiful voice that had caressed her with love words in the night. But now, instead of sensuality and tenderness, it carried a note of desperation, almost a plea.

Amanda stood facing the three men. Both Rodrigo and Alesandro were off to the side, behind her husband. Alex Mercer smiled indifferently, almost benignly. Rigo's triumphant hate radiated across the room, striking his cousin's back and Amanda's face. She looked only at Esteban.

"Please, tell them to leave so we can talk, Esteban. There are things I want no one but you to hear."

He stiffened at her low, seemingly calm voice. "After all they've seen, *querida*, what can't they hear? Have you lain with both of them or perhaps only one?" It was as if he couldn't stop himself once he'd begun. Esteban moved in one lithe, long-legged stride toward the proud, slim woman, chalk white in the vivid dress, but she did not back away or flinch. "How many others? You even had me believing you were a virgin. A friend of mine from Canton told me about a way her 'uncle' used to reinstate a woman's innocence, again and again, and again! I guess the Chinese aren't the only ones who know the trick." He stood before her, shaking with anger.

"Was your 'Uncle Paul' one of your best customers? Did you—"

Before he could finish she slapped him with all her

strength, surprising even herself with the impact. She
gasped. "Call me whatever you will, but don't you ever
drag that dear old man into the filth!"

"*Puta!*" He fairly growled the epithet at her. *Whore.*
She flinched then, from the word much more than the
stinging blow he delivered along with it. Her hair flew
from its pins with the impact and the lace mantilla floated
to the floor silently in the ringing aftermath. He struggled
to control his uneven breathing.

Amanda's green eyes were flecked with amber fury now
as she looked from Esteban to the icy hate of Rodrigo and
the careless amusement of Alesandro, three prize males,
all righteous in their double standard.

"How dare you!" she ground out. "How dare you
condemn me for what you all do! You frequent Lyla's
Place and a hundred others like it. Did you ever think what
sends a woman to a place like that? Did you ever care? My
stepfather raped me when I was sixteen. I was lucky to be
alive when Paul Mueller saved my life and took me out of
that hell." She stopped suddenly, beaten in the realization
that nothing she could say would change anything. "Now I
find I'm right back where I started."

She turned and quietly walked out the big oak door,
closing it softly behind her on the three silent men. A faint
trace of her jasmine perfume and a sprinkled trail of ivory
hairpins remained in the room. That, and the black lace
mantilla. Slowly, Esteban knelt and picked it up, holding it
in his hands and gazing at it as if he'd never seen it before.
It was the one he had bought her in the Mazatlán market.

With grim solicitude, Rodrigo came and put his arms
about his cousin's shoulders.

"Man, I'm sorry. I never wanted to tell you, but you
had to find out, better now in private then in public
someday."

Esteban stood, seeming to ignore his cousin's gesture,
then murmured in a voice so low that Rodrigo had to bend
closer to hear, "All right, Rigo. I'm sorry you had to be
the one. Just leave me alone now, please. Don't tell
anyone. I'll talk to my parents tomorrow."

With that he walked over to the big, carved sideboard where Don Alfredo kept brandy. Ignoring the half-filled crystal decanter and the glasses on top, he opened the bottom door and pulled out a full bottle. Using the mantilla as a towel for leverage, he twisted off the tight cork and threw it and the lace scarf onto the floor behind him. He took a long drink.

Amanda, hair trailing down her back and the red mark from Esteban's blow still stinging the left side of her face, fled silently down the back hallway from the library. Mercifully, she encountered no guests. She quickly climbed the servants' stairs to the second floor and went to their bedroom quarters where she began to rip the red silk dress from her body, while inside her head a voice taunted, "red for a whore, red for a whore." She would never wear red again.

As she furiously flew through the closet, searching for a riding skirt, heavy blouse, and jacket, she remained dry-eyed. Only her dilated pupils attested to the shock her system had sustained. She was jerkily putting on a skirt and blouse when Lupe came in and stopped short, seeing her mistress engaged in such strange behavior.

"I thought I heard someone in your room, señora. What are you doing?" She came closer and gasped when she saw the tangled mass of Amanda's hair, pins still askew, caught in its length, then the red, rapidly discoloring side of her face. She put a sinewy old arm around the younger woman's shoulders and guided her to the edge of the bed, where they both sat down.

Gently she examined the bruised face and then went to the adjacent bathroom, where a dry sink sat with a porcelain bowl of clean water. She quickly returned with a cold cloth and put the compress on Amanda's face. The patrona's unnatural, dry-eyed silence, almost shock, frightened the older woman, who would much rather have dealt with hysteria or rage. The young woman just sat mute.

"Where are you going, Doña Amanda?" Lupe spoke softly, hoping to elicit some response.

As if shaking herself out of a brief trance, Amanda

pushed the cloth away and rose, walking over to the
armoire to begin selecting a few simple traveling clothes.
As she moved, she began to speak. "I must leave Rancho
Santandar forever, Lupe. I'm not Don Esteban's wife
anymore. Since we haven't yet been married in the Church,
the family won't even need to arrange an annulment."

"He did this, then." She looked at Amanda's face, not
inflecting it as a question, but pronouncing it as a statement of fact. Whatever could cause such a sudden breach
between two young people who seemed so much in love?
She did not ask, but simply stated, "I'm going with you,
Doña Amanda."

Amanda jerked her head up from the small pile of
clothing. "Oh, Lupe, I love you for saying that, but I'm
going back to California, to San Francisco, far from your
homeland. I can't ask that of you."

A look of determination brooking no opposition was
etched in every line of the wizened, brown face. "You
can't go alone. It's a long, dangerous trip to your uncle's
home. I will come."

Amanda sighed and came over, sitting them both back
on the bed. "Paul Mueller's not my uncle, although he is
as dear as my own father to me. I had better explain why I
have to go. Then you'll understand why you must stay."
As simply and briefly as possible, sparing herself in no
way, Amanda explained her deception of Esteban and her
background from the farm to Lyla's to Paul's. When she
finished, she looked up from her tightly clasped hands.
"So, you see, I'm not who I said I was. This family has
disowned me and I've disgraced them. I'm sorry."

Lupe's strong, old hands closed over the slim, young
ones, soothing them into stillness on her lap. "You had
great wealth and freedom in California. You did not marry
Don Esteban for his money or his title. You loved him.
You are a good woman, loyal and loving, and if he cannot
tell this is so, the patrón is a young fool! I go with you. I
will not stay here."

"Oh, Lupe, you must think of how hard it will be to

leave your home and friends, to journey so far. Are you sure?''

One look said it all. The two women embraced like mother and child. Still dry-eyed and calm, Amanda stood and unfastened the gold necklace, placing it in the jewel case on the dressing table. She began to take off the heavy gold wedding band, but it would not come off. With a ragged sigh, she gave up.

"We'll need money for passage from Santa Cruz to Mazatlán. Then more for our fares to San Francisco. I'll take nothing from here that belongs to the Santandars. I do have some money of my own at our . . ." she had started to say "home," but shifted, "at the smaller house. We'll have to borrow a horse for you to ride to Santa Cruz. Gather your things and these few items I have here into bags and wait for me behind the kitchen. I should be back in a few hours if I ride hard.''

While Lupe protested the danger of a fast ride in the dark, Amanda slipped on her boots, braided her hair in a long, loose pigtail down her back, and hurried from the room. Lupe shrugged in resignation. At least her mistress was decisive; the mute apathy of shock had worn off.

When it was announced to the guests that Doña Amanda was suddenly taken ill and her husband was attending her, the festivities broke up almost immediately. An unctuous Rodrigo made the explanations about a fight of an unspecified nature to his uncle and aunt. Doña Esperanza then became ill and took to her bed. A livid Alfredo hid his fury and got the guests to leave as gracefully as possible, even hinting that it might be a dangerous disease such as cholera, so that any well-meaning or lazy souls who might attempt to stay over would be sure to flee.

After helping his uncle attend to the multitude of farewells, Rodrigo went back to the library, where he found Esteban dead drunk, passed out on a sofa. Beside him lay one empty bottle and another, three-quarters consumed, seeping its last amber droplets slowly on the thick carpet where it had slipped from Esteban's nerveless fingers as his arm dangled off the sofa. With luck, he'd be drunk for a week, Rodrigo surmised with grim joy. He closed the door and headed upstairs to the end of the wing where Amanda should be. He felt like collecting his first installment.

She was gone, and evidence of packing indicated that she planned to leave permanently. Damn! Not before he sampled what Alesandro had assured him was so good. How long had it been since that scene in the library—two, maybe three hours? Where would she go? The logical place to begin a search was at the stables.

Just as he reached the stable door and began to open it, he heard rapid hoofbeats coming from the north, the trail to Esteban's house. Of course! She had gone back for something and now was here to collect her bags and leave. He watched from the shadows as Amanda entered the barn, tied Sunrise by a stall, and then began to walk toward another stall where one of the gentler mares was standing patiently.

She crooned low to the horse as she reached in and looped a bridle over its head. "You'll do just fine for Lupe, yes, you will. Now be a good girl and let me saddle you."

Moving from the shadows now, Rodrigo grasped her from behind roughly and said, "Forget about saddling horses, Mandy. You're the one whose going to be ridden." He shoved her to the stall floor into a pile of hay and quickly followed her down. As he attempted to pinion her flailing hips and legs beneath him by laying his body weight across her, he grabbed for her clawing hands. She let out a loud, fierce shriek, and then he hit her jaw, stunning her into semiconsciousness.

"Now, I'll just sample what my dear cousin has had all to himself lately."

Even dazed, she ground out through a cut lip, "You filthy bastard, whoreson!"

His long, low laugh cut off her string of curses as he finally succeeded in capturing her hands and holding her small wrists together over her head in one slim, strong hand. The other he placed over her mouth. Then he spoke in a harsh, guttural whisper. "Now, my pretty little tart, you be a good girl and maybe I won't kill you. Your 'loving' husband is quite out of hearing, about two bottles of brandy worth. No one, least of all he, will save you, so why make an ugly scene and cause me to have to mark you up? Eh? I want what he had and I mean to get it!'' As he saw her cease her struggles, he took his hand from her mouth.

"You really hate Esteban, don't you?" she said in dawning realization. It wasn't her he wanted, nor to avenge the family honor. He wanted *Esteban's wife*.

The hate that she'd first glimpsed in the library, but had ignored to concentrate on Esteban, now loomed over her in Rodrigo Ruiz's face, twisting the pale, handsome visage into an ugly caricature. "Why?" The question seemed almost wrung out of her as the force of his venom hit her.

He laughed. "Why, indeed? Sometime when we have all night, I'll tell you."

With that, he began to unfasten his trousers. Before he could do more than move one hand to his belt, there was a deep growl of rage behind him and Luis Ramiro flung his considerable bulk onto Rodrigo, pulling him off Amanda. The two men rolled across the stable floor, dangerously near the nervous, shying horses.

As they kicked and punched furiously at each other, Amanda scooted away and stood up, looking around frantically for a weapon to help Luis. She spied a wicked-looking pitchfork, but it was on the other side of the thrashing men. Then, in the stall behind her, she saw the heavy wooden bar that served to block the stall door. She grabbed it and edged nearer. Luis, seeing her out of the corner of his eye, backed Rodrigo toward her and ducked as she sent the heavy club splintering down across the back of Rodrigo's head. He crumpled to the floor as Luis neatly extricated himself. Except for a few minor cuts and bruises, Luis's flat face and brawny body were not hurt.

When he came toward her, she saw that he had even lost his limp as his broken thigh had healed. He really was as good as before the accident, as he had often informed her over the past months. He stood before her, shocked at what he had just seen and what Don Rodrigo had tried to do to a rich, powerful nobleman's wife. "Are you all right, Doña Amanda? He didn't hurt you?"

"Thanks to you, Luis, no, he didn't have the chance."

"I heard a scream as I was leaving the corral. I was out late checking on one of my favorite colts. I'm so glad I was here, señora." He shuffled nervously.

Realizing that she must explain to the vaquero and that she needed his acquiescence to ride out with Lupe, she began, "Luis, Lupe and I are leaving. I'm getting a boat for us in Santa Cruz. We have to hurry. I'm taking Sunrise, but we're only borrowing the mare for Lupe to ride to the coast."

"But, señora, you cannot leave your husband!"

Amanda forced a weak smile with her cut lip and said sadly, "Luis, Don Esteban does not want me. I must leave. It's best for everyone if I go now and avoid any more hurt for the whole family."

He looked at her, not comprehending, but sensing the desperation and honesty in her plea. He nodded abruptly. "Yes, Doña Amanda, I'll saddle the mare and my own horse also. It is not safe for two women to ride to the coast all alone. I must ride with you and see you safe aboard."

Amanda put her hand over Luis's big, bloodied fist, deeply touched by his offer. "Thank you, Luis."

"It is only right that I ride with you now, Doña Amanda, for without your help I would never have ridden again." With that he bowed and turned to pick up the bridle from the stall floor. Amanda rushed to get Lupe while Luis readied their horses.

The ride to the coast was a headlong rush through darkness. Exhausted from her devastating scenes with Esteban and then Rodrigo, Amanda held the saddle pommel in a semiconscious state. The country was rough and the trail unfamiliar. She had never traversed it, and Lupe had gone only by day in years past. Without Luis, they might never have made it.

As the rosy, faint fingers of dawn gripped the Sierra Madre Occidental and climbed the jagged peaks, the three

riders arrived at the small seaside village of Santa Cruz de
Mayo. Luis left them at a spartan but clean inn and went in
search of a sailboat to charter for the day's journey down
to Mazatlán. If they were lucky, this time of year there
might be one free. If not, they would have to take a room
at the inn and wait. Amanda's eagerness to be away from
Sonora left her desperate in the hope of a charter.

Her prayers were answered when Luis returned with
news of a sailboat that could take them. Her horse would
be in dangerously close quarters on deck, but if Amanda
was willing to pay extra to compensate the owner for the
load of dried beef in barrels that he'd have to leave behind,
she could take her beloved Sunrise along. Weary beyond
all thought, she agreed to an exorbitant price and they
boarded within the hour. Her last memory of Sonora was
of the small cove of Santa Cruz with a fiery orange sunrise
blazing over the purple mountains far beyond it, and of
Luis, hat in hand, patiently bidding her and Lupe goodbye.

Amanda waved farewell to Luis and this harsh and
beautiful land, and farewell to her love, as harsh and
beautiful as the mountains and deserts that had bred him.
He belonged here. She never would again. Her house of
cards had crumpled around her just as Paul had warned.
She set her eyes toward the Pacific and thought of San
Francisco.

CHAPTER
17

Amanda sat in the soft, late December sunlight feeling the gentle swing of the rocking chair as she held her infant son, watching the yellow light play across his tiny, dark features as he nursed. His hair was black and curly and his huge eyes were already turning golden below thick black lashes and brows. Paul Steven Mueller was three months old today. Soon it would be 1857, a brand new year.

It seemed almost like last week instead of almost eight months ago that she had returned, exhausted and heartsick, to San Francisco, to the big stone house with the circular driveway, to Paul Mueller and his unquestioning love.

The voyage from Mazatlán to San Francisco had taken longer than usual because of terrible late-winter storms. By the time the boat arrived, Amanda had attained a calm numbness. The reunion with Paul had been a bittersweet distraction.

He had arrived home from work that night to find her sitting stiffly in the front parlor, unwilling to go to her old

room before she faced him to admit the accuracy of his
prediction and confess her folly. She looked so vulnerable
that it hurt him terribly. She sat straight on the edge of the
gold velvet chair, her dark blue traveling suit still damp
from the ocean salt spray. Paul knew that she needed to tell
him all that had happened from beginning to end, but he
insisted she have a bath and a night's rest first. Her new
companion and maid, Lupe, accompanied her upstairs.

In the morning Amanda was less shaky, yet still hollow-
eyed and pale at the breakfast table. As had been his habit
in days past, he leaned over and kissed the top of her head,
then sat down across from her. He would allow her all the
time she needed to collect her thoughts and tell him what
she wanted to tell. Her last letter, arriving only a few
weeks before she returned, had been so brimming with joy.
The reversal was sudden, but he knew she would explain
in her own good time. He buttered a roll as he watched her
play with her food, pushing a crepe about on her plate.
Her first words, delivered in a resigned voice, shocked
him.

"It's over, as you predicted, crumpled to dust." Amanda
sounded as calm as death. "I was a fool to think I could
ever escape what I was. I know that now. I'll learn to
accept it, but there is one thing. . . ."

When her voice trailed off, he reached over and took the
fork from her icy-cold but steady hand. "One thing, *ja?*"
he prompted gently.

Looking into those kindly eyes, so full of concern and
patience, something inside her snapped. She had schooled
herself in cold anger and controlled desolation on the
whole voyage home. She would accept and survive. Now,
suddenly, confronting this man whom she loved as a
father, she broke. Much to her horror, once the tears
finally began, she couldn't stop them. She had not cried
since—quickly she blocked from her mind the thought of
those tears of joy that night on *La Hermosura*.

"Oh, Paul, I wasn't going to come apart. I've tried so
hard to hold myself together. I didn't cry the night of the
fiesta or on the ship coming back. I swore I'd never cry

again. I don't know what's wrong with me. I feel, I feel, oh, I don't know!" She sobbed in low, desperate wrenches, as if forcing the tears from her eyes.

He held her gently as a father soothes a child after a nightmare, waiting for her to get past some of the pain. Finally, she calmed.

"What I was saying before, I have to face my life for what it is, and I'm so grateful to have you—you are my whole family, Paul. You warned me and I didn't listen."

"Ach, I have no joy that my prediction has come true, Amanda," he said softly. "I wanted to be wrong."

"I know that, but I needed you to understand that I'm out of my dream world now. I'll face reality, but I never will marry again. If I've lost what I gained by deception, then that's an end to it. But I won't ever be open to that pain again, and I can't settle for less than what I had, even though it was for such a little while."

Paul nodded. The wound was so raw and fresh that to attempt to cheer her with new suitors was obviously absurd. It was even too soon to arrange a divorce. He knew better than to move in that direction now. For now, she needed to talk, to tell him what had happened, and to purge herself of all the bottled-up agony he saw in her eyes.

She talked haltingly, pausing for long periods of time to gather her strength to go on. He waited patiently. She told him of the beauty of the voyage to Mazatlán, of learning about new people and customs on the long overland trek, about her mother-in-law's patient love and her father-in-law's fierce resistance, but most of all she spoke of Esteban, his love, his frightening violence, his humor and tolerance, all the contradictory things that made him what he was. After describing the terrible confrontation in the library and the fight in the stable with Rodrigo, she concluded simply.

"We will never see each other again. There's nothing left. Esteban will marry a proper, virginal girl with *pureza de sangre*. I'm back where I began. Yesterday when I stepped onto the Embarcadero, just a few piers up from where I first saw him, it was like reliving it all over again.'' She stood up and with a rigidly set jaw said, "But that was yesterday, all yesterday. And this is today. I'll go on from here, on my terms, making my own life, with your love, Paul.'' She turned back to the old man, who suddenly seemed her only anchor in a storm-tossed world, but she would not be a millstone. She had needed to tell him all of it. Now it was over and done.

"Tonight we go to Saddlers and eat oysters and terrapin, just for old times, *ja?* Just the two of us.'' It was a favorite restaurant that Paul had taken her to when he first met her at Lyla's. Esteban had never taken her there during their courtship. Now the reweaving of the threads of her old life would begin. She nodded.

Her attempts at resettling her life were rudely interrupted two weeks later. Amanda had been visiting regularly at Elizabeth Denton's clinic, renewing their friendship and helping with patients. One day she suddenly became very dizzy and slumped into an old chair in the supply closet, almost dropping the porcelain bowl and instruments she was taking to the doctor. All morning she'd been tired, even more than usual, but she had decided it was simply her forced pace of continuous activities over the weeks since she had come home. She was keeping very busy in an effort to hold memories at bay. If she dropped into bed each night in exhaustion, she dreamed less, also. The lightheadedness passed, and she began to rise, when Elizabeth came through the open door into the small room in search of her.

"There you are. I was wondering what . . ." Dr. Denton stopped short and looked at Amanda. "You're white as chalk and your pupils are dilated. Come here.'' The tone was the doctor's most professional and peremptory. She ushered the unprotesting, slightly disoriented Amanda into her back office and sat her down facing the light from a large, unshaded window.

"I'm all right, really. It was just that I missed breakfast this morning and I guess I'm a little dizzy. That's all.''

"Amanda, you never miss a meal unless you're sick.

You should have had an egg at least." She took Amanda's hand in hers. "Your joints are so swollen I can't take your ring off."

At the mention of food, Amanda had begun to turn from white to pea green.

"Were you nauseated this morning?"

"And last night, and all week, I guess. I must have some strange sort of influenza I picked up on the boat from Mazatlán. Maybe I should stay away from the clinic so I don't spread it to sick people here. I'm sure it'll go away if I rest."

"I'm sure it will too, the question is when," the doctor said dryly. Over Amanda's protests, she did a thorough physical examination and asked numerous questions. In the middle of the routine procedure, Amanda realized what her friend suspected and knew the origin of her sickness.

Paul greeted the news of Amanda's pregnancy that evening with mixed emotions. His instinctive reaction was joy. At last he would have that long-awaited grandchild. But then, perhaps, after all she'd been through at Esteban's hands, Amanda might not want his child. Her announcement was simple and straight to the point, but he wasn't sure of her emotions.

"Is this good news, *Liebchen,* or not so good for you?"

She looked at his gentle face. "I should hate him, not want anything from then to remind me of him, but, oh, Paul! As soon as I realized what Elizabeth was telling me, I felt, oh, I don't know how to explain it, as if I had something no one could take away from me. This child will be mine. It will love me as I love it, with no recriminations, no prerequisites. I guess you'll get to be a grandfather after all." She smiled at him, a bit sadly, but still with a quiet sort of happiness. He hugged her in relief. It would be all right.

And it was. Young Master Paul burped contentedly and opened his sherry eyes to gaze up with the half-vacant fascination babies have for those who hold them. He was beautiful, good-natured, and healthy. She loved him to distraction. The pregnancy had been uneventful under

Elizabeth's watchful eye. The spells of exhaustion and nausea passed in a few weeks. The delivery, in her own room in the Mueller mansion, was safe and relatively easy for a first time.

As she rocked little Paul, Amanda thought sadly that for all her ease in bearing him, she would never be able to give him any brothers or sisters. Yet, a fierce joy surpassed her sorrow as she looked into the little face, so like that other one. She had a part of her love here safely with her.

Ruefully, she thought of what her life in Willow Valley would have been. That horrible Wellsley boy had been right. It she had stayed there, she would have married and borne child after child, but none in love, none like this one. "Lots of brothers and sisters aren't necessarily a good thing, Pablito. You'll not lack for attention or playmates. I'll see to that." As if he understood his mother, the baby settled back comfortably and dozed.

Lupe tiptoed into the room and efficiently took the young patrón, as she insisted on calling him. She placed him in his crib as Amanda rose from the chair, lacing up her blouse.

"Every day he grows bigger and stronger, and such a love, so good-natured," Lupe said. "You are blessed, Doña Amanda."

Smiling, Amanda agreed, even though the use of her old title still hurt. It was the only way Lupe knew to address her mistress. Amanda had decided upon leaving Mexico that she would not use her married name. Paul insisted upon legally adopting her, so she used his name now. If Esteban didn't want her besmirching the illustrious Santandar name, she would never impose. She was simply Amanda Mueller, Paul Mueller's daughter.

The birth certificate listed her son as Paul Steven Mueller, although she did record his father's name when the attorney asked for it on the legal papers that were signed when Paul changed his will to leave everything to Amanda and her son. The difference in names brought a few strange looks from Attorney Warner and the witnesses in his law offices, but all were too discreet to inquire further.

In the year that followed, another legal matter was continually being brought to Amanda's attention—a divorce. Paul had waited until after his grandson was born to broach the subject to Amanda. It was for her own protection and her son's to get the divorce, which he could easily arrange with his money and influence. If she did not, her husband had a claim on the boy, might even be able to take him away from her. Paul argued to no avail. Amanda insisted that Esteban would surely be remarried by now since their American ceremony was not valid in Mexico. He was certainly free from any legal ties or obligations to her. Besides, she pursued the subject with the relentless logic born of desperate hurt, since he considered her a whore, Esteban would never acknowledge the boy as his. One look at the child at sixteen months dispelled that argument for Paul, if not for Amanda. The boy was growing to resemble his father more with each passing day.

Paul worried that if Esteban ever found out about his son and took him from Amanda, she would die. She had sustained so many blows already in her short life. The old man wanted to shield her from more yet was powerless in this matter.

He feared that her unwillingness to do anything about the divorce was deeper than her dislike of notoriety and her sad assurances that Esteban would never admit the child was his. As time passed, she never took off the heavy gold wedding ring. She said she couldn't get it off before she left Mexico. Then, she needed a ring while pregnant if she was going to be at all conventional. Then, she forgot about it. Even two years later, she always found an excuse to keep her ring. Both Paul and Elizabeth were sure of the true reason.

The two discussed this over tea one day, while Amanda was upstairs dressing Pablito for an outing. To distinguish young Master Paul from his grandfather, the Spanish diminutive of his first name was used.

"Elizabeth, I know she still grieves, but it is not safe to wait. In California, at least, the marriage is still recorded.

He would have every right under our law to take his son from a wife who deserted him."

"That means you're sure, too, Paul, that he hasn't dissolved the marriage?"

In his characteristic gesture of Teutonic exasperation he threw up his hands and made a guffaw of disgust. "How do I know what that one will do or think? Only my Amanda I want to save from more hurt. And never should he have a right to raise that boy!"

Dr. Denton prodded more. "What would his position be if she's right and he remarried in Mexico?" Paul made a dismissing gesture. "See? You don't think he did, and neither do I."

"Then, all the more the danger!"

"Or," Elizabeth paused for emphasis, "all the more reason to believe neither of them wants it to be over." She stopped Paul's indignant protest and continued. "I'm not saying he has any rights after what he did to her or even that it could ever be worked out, just that we can't interfere."

Paul sighed a long, slow breath of resignation. "I do not know, Elizabeth. I know I cannot force her to change her life, but after all her brave words when she came home, that she was going to start over and put his memory behind her, even now after all this time the ring stays."

Elizabeth's face reflected an old pain, one she had not shared with anyone since Amanda has come to her confessing her fascination for Esteban that day in summer nearly three years before. She felt the need to tell Paul about her own past and a lover long dead but never forgotten.

"I never had a ring, Paul. I lost the man I loved in a different way, but I can understand her need to hold on to the ring as a talisman, a symbol, perhaps, of the good part. I'll always remember the happiness I shared, even through the pain of losing. The man I was going to marry died, Paul. It happened back east, long ago, but I still hold on. I've never been able to find a substitute even after the finality of death, so I guess I can see how it is with her.

And she has the blessing of a beautiful child, the embodiment of all the good things they shared.''

"All the worse, dear Elizabeth, if he should take the boy away. I know she needs time, but she must accept the fact that he will only hurt her. For her I want more than a life of only memories. You have made for yourself a life in a new land, in a career few women would ever dream of, but what of Amanda? I want her to have more than raising Pablito only to have him grow up and leave. She could marry again.''

Sadly, Elizabeth shook her head. "I don't know if we can ever hope for that, Paul, any more than we can hope for a reconciliation between the two of them. We must let it rest for now.''

"*Ja*, time, I know, only time it takes."

"Time you don't have, my friend?" Elizabeth looked levelly at Paul with a probing question in her facial expression.

"How did you guess?"

"Since when did you start going to other doctors? Don't you trust my professional advice because I'm female?" Her gentle levity was tinged with infinite sadness and renewed understanding of his desperate haste in recent months to get Amanda and Pablito safe from all harm. Paul Mueller was dying.

She had observed the signs gradually over the past months: decreasing appetite, weight loss, sallow complexion, a whole series of symptoms indicating illness. She had treated him in the past years for minor ailments but now realized the seriousness. Amanda, so preoccupied with Pablito and her shattered love, was not yet aware of her old friend's failing health. However, to a trained eye such as Elizabeth Denton's, it was sadly clear.

"I knew something was wrong, and I have this feeling about it. That is why I go to old Dr. Staltzman. I do not want to have you give me bad news." He smiled ruefully. "It is a tumor, nothing even you, my good friend, with all your latest medical training, can help.''

"So, you want to get Pablito free of Esteban's claim on him before you are gone? How long, Paul?"

He shrugged his shoulders, his jacket looser on his big frame than it used to be. "A few months, maybe a bit more. As the time goes on, I am not so sure she will ever want to make the break. She still loves him, doesn't she, Elizabeth?" He switched the conversation from his own plight back to his paramount concern, Amanda.

"Yes, Paul, I think she does. And it is hard, as you say, to forget the father when the son is his image. Time may never help, but only bring more memories as the boy grows."

Upstairs, Amanda was unaware of the conversation concerning her future and that of young Paul, who was sitting up, giggling and pulling on his mother's long hair as she struggled to put shoes on his wildly wiggling feet. As she worked she marveled at his perfection—this tiny bit of humanity who was her son. He was growing so fast, the barely defined baby features sharpening into those of a little boy already. He had walked at only nine months and had enough teeth to chew voraciously when scarcely a year old. She watched him toddle across the room, shoes finally fitted, and pick up his favorite toy, a stuffed golden horse, a gift from Hoot, who said he had had it made to look like Sunrise. She knew Pablito would be a splendid rider. How could he not be?

The thoughts always turn around, don't they, she thought grimly. How could it be otherwise when everything about the child spoke of the father? Pablito's clear sherry eyes darkened to brown when he had a temper tantrum, the brows were already well pronounced, and the nose showed promise of being a straight Santandar one.

Paul, hugging his toy horse, was ready to go for a ride on the real article. Now that he was approaching a year and a half, she took him riding with her, securely held in front of her as she trotted Sunrise across the park near the house. It was a pretty sedate ride for Amanda, but for the child, the motion on horseback was a pure thrill. He would

squeal in delight when he saw Sunrise at the stables and
loved the bounce of natural rhythm in riding.

They went downstairs where a subdued Elizabeth and
Paul awaited. Elizabeth came to ride with Amanda and her
son when she could get free of her busy practice for an
hour or so. It was good exercise and relaxation for her.
She enjoyed the antics of the child so much that his mother
often remarked that between Grandpa Mueller and Aunt
Elizabeth, the boy would be hopelessly spoiled, but certainly much loved.

Although Paul was never a horseman, he encouraged
Amanda to get out as much as possible, taking young
Pablito with her for park rides. Secretly he hoped that
some of the young men in the park might notice his
beautiful ward and her pretty child and take an interest. If
any did, Amanda never told him. Even Elizabeth seemed
to support Amanda's tendency to avoid social contacts.
When they left, he sighed and went into his study to work
on some correspondence. Elizabeth was probably right.
He'd have to let the situation take care of itself.

He said quietly to himself, "It's time to let go, old man,
time to let go."

That evening at supper Amanda was agitated but didn't
want Paul to know it. When he finally got her to confide,
she admitted to an encounter in the park that afternoon
with Doug McElroy and his new bride.

"It was really pretty awful. Being an established resi-
dent millionaire hasn't improved his disposition. Quite the
contrary, it seems to me. He's even more egocentric and
spoiled since he can buy whatever he wants. He no longer
even travels to his mines in the gold camps. I was riding
Sunrise, of course, and had Pablito with me. We stayed for
one more turn around the park after Elizabeth had to leave
for her afternoon calls. That's when he saw me."

"And did what?" Paul tilted his head in interest. Lately
he'd been hearing stories about the young Scot that disturbed him. Money had, indeed, seemed to go to his head.

Amanda flushed and took a sip of her wine, then
continued, "Well, he was riding a new black, treating it

not much better than he handled Sunrise the day he was thrown. He came over to say hello, and then asked me whose baby I had with me! I know damn well he's aware I've been married!'' Her face flamed at her own use of profanity, something she tried hard to avoid. ''He hinted that he didn't think Pablito could be any relation to me since he's so dark! The nerve of that boor! Then, while I was humiliated enough and ready to use a horsewhip on him, his wife rode up, looking daggers at me. As if I'd ever wanted that sickly, pale-skinned, overgrown lout! She's from a fine, old eastern family and really let me know how she looked down her nose at a woman with a baby and no husband. I imagine Doug told her all about my sordid past, but, of course, never that he'd asked me to marry him despite it and been turned down!''

Paul smiled, ''Amanda, now I'm glad you turned him down. You agree, *Liebchen?*''

She chuckled, her mood shifting to see the possibilities. ''Oh, yes, that's for sure. Can you imagine Pablito with buttermilk-white skin and fire orange hair! Ugh!'' They laughed.

However, that night when she lay in her lonely bed, tossing fitfully, the afternoon's incident returned with all its ugly implications. Everyone in San Francisco must know her marriage was over and she was alone with a small child to raise. Well, damn them, she'd not flinch from that or any of the rest of her failed past. She had a beautiful son and a future with him and her dear friends here.

But an inner voice nagged: *You're alone. You'll always be alone. You'll never settle for anyone like Doug McElroy. Or any other man, no matter who.* ''Oh, Esteban, why couldn't I have been the woman you believed I was?'' She sobbed into the pillow, then pounded it in helpless anger, aching with the unfairness of it all.

She thought of him constantly. The nights were the worst, when she was alone in the big, empty bed with silence surrounding her like a shroud. The physical needs he'd awakened in her were most terrible then. Before he

loved her, she'd never needed or wanted a man, felt
nothing. Now she ached for his hands, his lips, his lean
body next to her, caressing her, whispering Spanish love
words in that low, gravelly voice. She wanted to feel him,
run her palms and lips over the muscles and dense hair of
his chest and arms, rub against the abrasive, wonderful
scratch of the beard that was never shaved completely
smooth. She wanted Esteban. She loved him, still, despite
everything. After being away from him for over two years,
the hunger only grew, never abated. During the latter
stages of her pregnancy, her need had lessened and she'd
hoped this physical side of her nature would disappear
with motherhood. However, despite her joy with young
Paul, within a month of his birth she found her dreams
invaded again.

Seeing McElroy only made clear to her what she'd
known all along. No one else would ever take her husband's place. She'd wanted no man before she saw him.
She'd never want anyone else again. He was her love.
There was nothing before, nothing afterward. But she
hugged the memory of those golden moments to herself
and thought of him.

My dark love, where are you? Do you ever think of me?

CHAPTER
18

Esteban felt the sweat trickling down his back as the sun beat mercilessly on him. He'd been in the corral all morning working the new palomino stallion. With his spirit and size, the horse reminded Esteban of Oro. Small wonder, since the great beast was one of Oro's get. The breeding had gone well. The line was well established and he had more requests from buyers than he had horses to train. The price he could get for one of the supurb saddle mounts was astronomical. That's why he'd come to live in the back country of Rancho Santandar in the spring and train mounts with the vaqueros. At least, that's what he had told himself and his father.

After that terrible night in February when Amanda fled during the fiesta, he had stayed drunk for weeks until his father threatened to have him tied to his bed and dried out. When he began to sober up and face life, he decided that the best thing to do would be to remove all temptation by going out to his north section and working stock. He

321

would sleep outdoors and live in the wilderness, away
from liquor, women, gambling, anything that would cloud
his thinking. Good hard work would clear his head and
cleanse her from his thoughts and his body.

Now as he felt the bruised ache where a new colt had
kicked him in the leg and flexed his aching right hand, he
winced. Good hard work all right. The sweat flew off his
face as he shook his head, then wiped his brow and ran his
gloved fingers through his thick black hair, pushing it off
his forehead.

Juan watched the young patrón. Don Esteban had been
working that new stallion since sunup. He was pushing
himself to exhaustion, taking wild chances, even breaking
mustangs. The small, mean, wild ponies were periodically
rounded up, broken to saddle, and sold cheaply. It was a
task for itinerant hands, one that called for no particular
skill, only the willingness to risk broken bones for meager
pay. Yet, almost as if he wished to tempt the fates, the
highly skilled trainer risked his neck on such menial tasks.
Juan shook his head. It was the señora, gone now these
past six months, who made the young patrón so wild and
mean.

Juan had heard rumors of a quarrel and the lady's flight
in the night, taking with her only her maid and her
palomino, leaving behind her clothes, jewelry, all else of
value. What had caused the quarrel? Some said jealousy of
Doña Elena. Some said Don Rodrigo, the patrón's cousin,
had paid too much attention to the patrón's wife. No one
knew for sure. After months of observing the young
couple together, Juan didn't believe it was petty jealousy
or that the señora would do anything improper or disloyal.
Don Esteban was like a man driven by demons. If he was
short-tempered and took unnecessary chances, it was grief
that caused it. That Juan knew for sure.

Juan had seen both Miguel and Esteban grow up under
the hawkeye of their father, the old don. Now, with only
the young patrón left to carry on the family name, Juan felt
a fierce loyalty to that cause and to the young man on
whom such a heavy burden fell.

He had spent months at the smaller hacienda of Don
Esteban and his new bride, observing them together and
getting to know the kindly, hardworking young Americana
who spoke their language as if born to it. She was as good
and loyal as she was beautiful. Small wonder the patrón had
been so bad-tempered and unhappy since she left.

Juan remembered the incident only last night around
the campfire. Don Esteban had kept to himself since he
returned to the work camp in March, no longer indulging
in camaraderie with the vaqueros. As was now his custom,
he rode in after dusk, exhausted from taking one last turn
around the track with a new horse. The men were already
gathered around the fire, laughing and talking about the
day's work, awaiting supper and drinking coffee laced with
tequila. The latter was a luxury reserved for the charro
trainers who were paid more than regular hands.

Two of the newer men, one hired from the Montoya
place and the other a drifter who worked mustangs, were
talking a distance away from the campfire. Perhaps they
were a bit drunk on pulque, a cheap fermented brew, or
perhaps they were simply stupid.

"I heard that Doña Elena's going to Mexico City.
Maybe she'll marry his cousin if he doesn't get shut of the
Yankee woman. Old Don Alfredo is fit to be tied and
branded because his son won't apply for a divorce in
California."

"Yeah, man, I been wondering why that fancy yellow-
haired piece left him in such a hurry. The boss is sure a
bastard to work for ever since. She must have been
something. God, what I'd give to fuck her!"

"Aw, I don't know. Maybe I'd take the Montoya daughter, but then, I never had me a blond woman. I'd like to
spread her out—agh!"

Esteban came up so quietly behind the two men sprawled
on the ground that neither heard him. He grabbed the one
talking, a big, rangy fellow with shoulders like a grizzly
bear's, and literally lifted him by his heavy leather vest,
viciously twisting his neckerchief until the man's eyes
bulged. In a lightning-swift move he kneed the man in the

groin with wicked impact, then whirled to face his companion, who was backing away on all fours, terrified.

"Do you have any more opinions about how it might be to fuck my wife? Any more comparisons between her and Elena Montoya?" His voice was low and deadly.

Before the supplicant could get off his hands and knees, Esteban caught him by the shirtfront and lifted him up. Then, with his right hand, he struck the man a sharp blow to the jaw while still holding him with his left. Bones cracked. The thick, squat body crashed unconscious to the ground. Esteban's other adversary was still grunting in extreme pain, but he undoubled his sizable bulk, took a deep breath, and lunged in a rage for his enemy's back. Both men crashed to the ground where they rolled over and over in a blur of motion toward the campfire. With a catlike twist, Esteban finally came up on top astride his victim's chest. He landed a quick punch to the other's throat, then continued to rain blows to his face, another and yet another, until the big vaquero was unconscious and sprawled out on the rocky ground like a broken toy. Seeing the helplessness of the unconscious man and the patrón's blind fury being released, Juan and several other men had pulled Esteban off the inert form.

Recalling the two broken bodies that were sent to the doctor in Santa Cruz, Juan sighed sadly. They'd probably never work horses again, certainly not for the Santandars, at any rate. But Juan was even more sorry for Don Esteban's pain. The young patrón had been deathly quiet last night after the incident, as if daring anyone else even to mention his wife or why she had left him. He sat before a very subdued campfire group and drank tequila until he passed out. That was the first time Juan had seen the patrón drunk since he'd come to the camp in March. It was not good. This morning Esteban had risen early, skipped breakfast, and gone to the training track.

Esteban let the hot sun bake some of the stiffness from his aching body. That stupid fight last night had left him without an unbruised place on his body, and his head ached with a miserable hangover. *God keep me from tequila,* he vowed. *A man needs cold beer or good brandy.* He dismounted and felt the pull of the reins on his right hand. Damn, the glove was tight! He pulled it off and the pain lanced through him.

Juan came up, took the horse's reins, and led the beast to the post. Then, looking at the hand, he casually commented, "It's broken, patrón, but not as bad as that bastard's jaw. You need to have it set and stop using it for a few weeks so that it can knit."

Esteban moved his fingers, then shrugged off the pain. "It'll heal!"

"Heal, yes, but well enough for you to use that if you need to?" He gestured toward the knife he knew was always in Esteban's boot.

Esteban sighed. "I guess you're right. I'm trying too hard to prove something out here in the back of nowhere, and it isn't working."

"Let me wrap your hand up tight for now and you ride into Santa Cruz and let the doctor look at it." Juan had a tentative expression on his face, as he chose each word with care. No one spoke carelessly around the boss these days.

Sensing his old companion's unease, Esteban managed a grin. "Think you can get the boys to finish training six for sale by fall without me? I'd like those two fillies ready, too."

Juan nodded, also grinning now. "Yes, boss, we can have them all ready. You just take care of that hand."

It was sunset on Mazatlán's cove and the usual artist's palate of vivid colors filled the western sky on the Pacific. Esteban had been at his villa for a month, restlessly recuperating from broken knuckles. Now that the splint was off, he was eager for travel and activity more than the simple paperwork and dull transactions he could conduct from Mazatlán. He needed to go to Los Angeles, where Frank had been covering his end of the business for months.

Esteban swore absently as the crystal snifter slipped

from his bandaged hand onto the stone floor of the villa porch. His hand was still too weak to grasp a heavy object firmly.

"Oh, Esteban, wait, I'll get a broom. Don't cut your hand!" May Ling hurried inside.

Strange, he thought, *having her here with me after all this time.* When he had arrived in Mazatlán to reopen his villa he had not even thought of May Ling. Yet, she was here. After Rodrigo had deserted her, shutting down the small house he'd kept her in, she'd gone back to her uncle's, taking no other protector, although she could have done so. Life with Rigo had not been so good. She preferred to be free. Then Esteban had arrived. That changed everything.

One evening an acquaintance took him to the Canton Royal and he saw May Ling carrying a tray of drinks. She was serving tables at the restaurant just as she had years earlier when he'd returned from Europe. She came across the space that separated them with that calm dignity he'd always admired. She bowed formally. "Welcome back, Don Esteban." Then, seeing his right hand, she exclaimed, "You're injured! What has happened?"

He smiled at her worry and said, "Just a few small fractures over a minor matter. It's almost healed. I heard you were back here, China Doll. You shouldn't be, you know. You could've found someone better than Rigo."

She looked up at him, reading the expression in his golden eyes, then ventured, "I did, long ago. Perhaps again?"

That night he'd taken her and her belongings to his villa. In the ensuing month, he'd spent days and nights with her. After the long period of enforced abstinence at the camp in Sonora, he felt a fierce physical need that May Ling was more than willing to satisfy. He used her. Gradually it dawned on him that she loved him and perhaps she always had, ever since he had first frequented the Canton Royal before the war. Thinking back on it now, he realized how blind he'd been and how thoughtlessly cruel, when he'd left her to Rigo nearly five years ago.

He had not spoken to May Ling of his marriage or its end, but he knew she must have heard that Amanda had sailed from Mazatlán to San Francisco over eight months ago. Yet, May Ling never pried or assumed any rights in his life. She just listened to him, laughed with him, and loved him.

Stepping around the broken glass, he went inside and carefully poured another brandy, carrying it in his left hand. When she returned with the broom, he took it from her and set it outside on the porch.

"Leave it for the maid. It's not your job to clean up."

Smiling, she came to his embrace. He bent to kiss her then carried her to the big bed where he began to undress her slowly, marveling at the perfection of her small body. Eagerly she reached for him, helping him quickly shed his clothing. He covered her small white body with his big, lean, dark one, caressing in unison with her, feeling their passions build together. If it were not for her eager response, he would always have been afraid of breaking her. Far from breaking, however, she cried out in joy as he entered her and raked her long, lacquered nails down his back.

Later, as the moon rose and filled the room with silvery light, he woke, gently disentangled himself from her waist-length black hair, and silently got out of bed. He threw on a robe and padded over to the bar to retrieve the snifter of brandy he'd poured and forgotten earlier. Sipping it slowly, he sat down in a high-backed cane chair beside the bed. As he drank, he watched the sleeping woman while the moonlight played over her.

A whore loves me and I love a whore, but not the same one.

The bitter irony of his thoughts caused him to choke on the fiery brandy as his throat contracted in anguish. Silently he swallowed hard against the liquor's burn. There, he'd admitted it! What had been eating at him like a cancer all those months. He still loved the treacherous, conniving bitch! Damn her. She'd deceived him, made him love her more than life itself, then humiliated him and vanished.

She was no better than May Ling. He reconsidered: No, she was worse. Much worse. At least May Ling was always honest about what she was.

He studied the sleeping woman sadly. He must go soon and shouldn't give her the hope of a permanent liaison. Not that she'd ever asked or even intimated that she expected such, but now he knew that she loved him and he didn't want to hurt her more.

Just as he took the last sip of brandy and set the glass down silently, May Ling woke and sat up in bed, the thin covers falling around her slim hips. He smiled and slid across the bed toward her, then kissed her lightly.

"I didn't mean to wake you."

"I do not mind, Esteban. I often rise early." She gestured toward the pale streaks of sun filtering in the window. "You could not sleep because you are worried about something," she stated simply, not questioning or expecting an answer unless he desired.

"I have to leave, China Doll, for Los Angeles to work with my uncle. From there, I don't know." He shrugged. "I want you to stay here at the villa and do as you like. I'll leave enough money. I just can't tell you when I'll be back, or how frequently."

She put her lacquered nails on his lips softly. "You owe me no explanations. I always knew you must go. I will stay here. I am honored to have shared a portion of your life. I will be here as long as you wish. When you do not, you need only say."

"You are so good and lovely, China Doll. I'm taking advantage of you." She shook her head, but he quieted her and went on, "No, it's true. I can't make any commitments to any woman. I never will again. I'm through with any illusions about lasting relationships." He took a cigar from the box on the bedside table, lit the cigar, and inhaled deeply.

She watched his agitated movements, then said very quietly, "Is this because of Amanda?"

He clenched the cigar between his teeth. "What stories have you heard about my wife?"

She returned his angry gaze with a calm, sad strength. "Nothing, Esteban, nothing at all. I only heard you had married."

"Then how do you know her name?"

"You often cry it out in your sleep, and sometimes . . ." she paused, "sometimes when you are making love to me."

The dreams, God, the dreams! At the camp in Sonora, he'd slept far away from the rest of the men because he often awakened with Amanda's name on his lips. Gradually the dreams had become less frequent. He had thought they were gone. Now, to find he even called her name in the throes of passion!

Through clenched teeth he rasped, "She left me. She's gone. There are no more commitments. I will be free." It was as if he were talking to himself.

May Ling answered enigmatically, "Perhaps you will be, Esteban, perhaps you will not."

Ursula Mulcahey crumpled the letter she held in her hands and tossed it onto the big desk in the library of their Los Angeles house. Then she began to pace, tearing the lace handkerchief in her hands to shreds before she realized it. What to do? Her brother's letter, the third she'd received in the past month, again implored her help and that of Frank to get Esteban to apply for a divorce. In the eight months since Amanda had fled Sonora, Alfredo had grown increasingly impatient. Esteban must clear the Santandar name by getting a divorce in California.

She could not believe Esteban's terse, shattering letter when she first read it last February. Yet, the pain between the lines of the brief narrative was real. Amanda, a prostitute from a San Francisco bordello! Ursula recalled Frank's reaction: "No matter what she did or where she came from, I'll never believe she was Paul Mueller's mistress. I've known the man for twenty years. Sure, and he's not capable of such a thing. If he took Amanda out of a brothel, he did it because she reminded him of his dead wife. He loved her like a daughter, plain and simple."

Despite his anguish at his nephew's unhappiness, Frank would not condemn Amanda. "She loved the lad, dammit, I know she did, Ursula! Paul Mueller is rich as Croesus and has no family. With all his money, why would she need to marry Esteban and go to live in his land if not because she loved him? No, I tell you, it makes no sense, but I'll get to the bottom of it all. I swear it!"

He sent investigators to San Francisco to keep track of Amanda. The report in September precipitated a major breach between Frank and Ursula. Unknown to Esteban, he was a father. Amanda had given birth to a son during the first part of the month. Ursula felt that her nephew had a right to know at once, but Frank had insisted upon caution and wanted no word sent to Esteban.

"My God, Frank, this is the only Santandar heir, Esteban's only son. He has a right to know!"

"So he can charge up there and take the boy away from his mother? No, Amanda has a right to her son, too. Give him time to cool off, to realize that he still loves her; and mind, I think he does. I think they still love each other. They just need time to find it out. I'm sure about it. I made me livin' readin' people, darlin', and I've not done too bad. Amanda loved him and he loved her. I think they still do, if only the young fools realize it."

His insistence on keeping the news of Paul's birth from Esteban never wavered over the next weeks. Now it was late October and they had received another letter from Esteban. He was leaving Mazatlán and would be arriving tomorrow in Los Angeles. Today Ursula received this last plea from her brother. Don Alfredo had begged his son repeatedly over the past months to sign divorce papers. It was only a matter of time until the formalities of dissolving the disastrous marriage were completed. However, there was one obstacle: the obstinate refusal of Esteban to sign. He would not discuss it, nor would he budge. Alfredo implored his sister to use her influence and to enlist Frank in the cause. The old don knew his brother-in-law had far more influence on Esteban than he.

Ursula stared down at the crumpled letter. Frank might

have influence with Esteban, but these days Ursula had little influence with Frank! And, to be honest, she was not sure she wanted him to persuade their nephew to sign the papers. She, too, had been struck with Amanda's integrity and love for Esteban. Perhaps Frank was right. Yet, Alfredo's desperate plea accused her through the crushed paper on the desk. And what about Alfredo's grandson, a child he did not even know existed? How could she face Esteban and not give it all away? As she agonized, Frank came home.

When he entered the room, even his heavy tread across the *sala* did not break her concentration.

"Well, me darlin', what is so distressin' that you've no welcome for your tired, old husband?"

Almost guiltily, she started, then forced a weak smile, the strain showing through. "I was thinking . . . Frank, oh, Frank!" Very uncharacteristically, Doña Ursula, who was a most serene and unemotional woman, sobbed bitterly against her husband's vast frame.

If she was upset, he was even more so, for Ursula Santandar Mulcahey did not break down and cry. "Love, love, what is it?" He glanced over her thin shoulder and saw the crumpled letter on the desk. "Might it be another letter from your estimable brother in Sonora?"

She nodded, fighting to reconcile her conflicting loyalties. "Esteban must know he has a son and Alfredo that he has a grandson. Oh, Frank it isn't fair! He pleads that we try to persuade Esteban to divorce Amanda—maybe we should perhaps try. I don't know, anymore. I do know that I can't see him and not tell him about the child. How can we pretend ignorance while he's here?"

He stroked her back soothingly. "I know, love, I know. I don't know meself on that one. It'll be the divil's own time not to tell him, but, Ursula, I still think it's best. Don't you see, darlin', my agent in Sacramento just found out—the marriage is still on record in the capital. Amanda has taken no steps to dissolve the marriage. With his power, Paul Mueller could have quietly gotten Amanda a divorce anytime. Yet he didn't. Esteban won't dissolve the marriage either. It must mean something! Give 'em a chance. Don't let it end in a bitter fight over the boy. All three of them'll lose. I feel it in me bones, love, I do!'' Frank Mulcahey was not a praying man, but he fervently prayed that his instinct was right.

With a resigned sigh, Ursula agreed, ''You will have to lend me strength, but I'll manage to face Esteban and not tell him.''

When Esteban arrived, neither Frank nor Ursula was reassured by his appearance. His face had a grim, hollow-eyed set, as it had when he first returned from the war. Though his body wasn't as ravaged, his soul was. The hearty jesting between uncle and nephew was a thing of the past. Frank couldn't cajole him.

Esteban never spoke of Amanda. The effort of writing the letter to the Mulcaheys the previous February had taken all he had. There was nothing he wanted to add, nor was there anything they felt they could ask. The raw pain evident in his manner made them feel that time was the only answer. Time and, perhaps, a miracle.

The morning after he arrived Esteban went to the office with Frank. He was adamant that he would make up to his uncle all the work he had neglected when he withdrew into the wilderness of Sonora. And work he did. For several weeks he toiled over papers and accounts. Then, with those in order, he turned his attention to making contacts up and down the coast, from Port Angeles, in Oregon Territory, south to Oaxaca, in Mexico. He set up a grueling itinerary to meet prospective buyers for horses and timber, dry goods, beef, and even silver. There was one place where he sent an agent instead of going himself: San Francisco.

With a sad smile, Frank noted this arrangement and hoped the aversion to crossing paths with his estranged wife might work to some advantage.

The next year, however, did little to bolster the fading hopes of the Mulcaheys. Esteban grew increasingly irritable, subject to outbursts of anger and sarcasm. His close and cordial relationships with the men who worked on the docks and in the office suffered as he distanced himself from them.

While in Los Angeles, he sought release from his misery with various women from the town, sometimes discreet widows from good families, occasionally whores. He kept late hours, often not coming back to the Mulcahey residence at night. The rumors of his gambling, as well, became legend in the small, quiet town. Although he won more often than lost, he derived no more joy from that than from his business profits.

It was during that year in Los Angeles that Esteban's hours of carousing began to take their toll. One afternoon, Esteban returned from the office after staying out all night the preceding evening. Frank had been on the docks all day and arrived home immediately after his nephew, who was in the study, pouring a before-dinner brandy.

He stepped through the door of the low-ceilinged, comfortable room and surveyed Esteban. "Make that two of those, lad. Jasus, do you look like you need it!" Frank looked at Esteban's red-rimmed, smoke-irritated eyes and generally hungover stance.

Esteban smiled thinly and handed Frank his drink. "I missed some sleep, but I'm used to it. I'll live."

"Yes, you'll live, right enough, but a hell of a way *to* live you've chosen."

"I won two thousand at monte last night. That's not all bad."

"That why you're enjoyin' it so much, then?" Frank assessed Esteban's appearance with a level gaze. "Aw, lad, you're foolin' no one but yourself. You're so deep down the well in misery you're drownin'."

"And you've come, I suppose, to throw me a rope. Well, don't do me any favors, Frank." Abruptly, he turned his back on his uncle and tossed down the fiery liquid as he walked over to a sofa and indolently sprawled across it.

"When's the last time you heard from 'himself'?" Frank's Irish brogue always thickened when he discussed his brother-in-law.

"Do you mean really talked to him, or just read his

threats in letters? Oh, I went to the ranch last month when I had to check on the training of the last bunch of palominos. They're ready to be shipped in June. He talked, I listened. Nothing's changed. Some things never change." With a sigh he upended the snifter.

"Aye, some things don't change. Your pa has no monopoly on stubbornness, and that's the Lord's own truth! You still won't sign his papers. It's been, let's see, nearly two years now since Amanda left."

At the mention of her name, Esteban's hand tightened on the glass and his jaw clenched. The bitterness in his voice was overshadowed by a plea. "Let it alone, Frank, let it alone, for God's sake."

"And what about *your* sake, lad? You'll not dissolve the marriage. There's no one you'll be wantin' to marry, ever again?"

"After the luck of the draw the first time, I don't feel inclined to gamble again."

"Strange it is, your holdin' on to a scrap of paper, then. Why not at least please your father and apply for the divorce? It'll buy you peace while it goes through the courts." Frank fixed Esteban with a penetrating gaze, but Esteban just studied the bottom of the brandy snifter as if it had some answers to life's riddles.

Finally he replied softly, almost wearily, "Let her go to the trouble of getting a divorce if she wants it. I don't give a damn, but I'm not jumping through paper hoops for anyone, not the Santandars, not her."

"What if she feels the same way? What if she doesn't want to divorce you, either?"

"Then it really doesn't make any difference at all. I'll never marry again. In her business she hardly needs to," he scoffed bitterly. "Anyway, I'm sure both you and my father are wasting energy over a settled issue. Paul Mueller could get her a quiet divorce in Sacramento with a snap of his fingers. I'm sure he's taken care of everything."

"Aye, that he could, easy enough, lad, that he could." Frank paused, then added, "If she were of a mind to let him." He looked at Esteban, who shifted uneasily on the sofa. "The pain never goes away, does it, son?" He asked the question softly, feeling the anguish in the young man he loved as a father loves his son.

Esteban's eyes were dulled with hurt as he looked up. "Why are you doing this? Why now, after all this time? You let it lie when I first came, and I was grateful. Nothing's to be gained by raking it up now."

Frank strode across the room and sat down in a big wicker chair across from the sofa. "Maybe nothin', maybe everythin'. Look at yourself, Esteban. It's been two years and you're still in love with your wife! You're right—some things never change. Maybe, just maybe, she's still in love with you, too. Someday, you have to face it, to face her again. It won't be finished until you do. All the whorin', drinkin', and gamblin', all the drivin' yourself to death at work—none of it'll do any good."

During Frank's impassioned speech, Esteban flinched at the truth of his uncle's intuition regarding his love for Amanda, that accursed love he couldn't kill. He walked over to open the liquor cabinet and gripped the brass handle until his knuckles were white. "All right, you win, if you want me to admit it. Yes, I still love the bitch, but it changes nothing."

"If you knew why she deceived you, why she did what she did back in San Francisco, it might change things, son. Just think on it." Putting his arm around the younger man's shoulders, Frank repeated gently, "Just think on it, Esteban."

PART 6
THE ODYSSEY

CHAPTER
19

Amanda stood alone on the windswept hill. A late spring rain was threatening with occasional mists, and the breeze coming off the bay was unseasonably cold for the end of May. She looked down at the stone engraved with the date, newly chiseled with its edges sharp and angry, almost like the raw wound in her heart.

Paul Frederich Mueller
Born August 15, 1790
Died May 20, 1858

How little that said of a man's whole life, all the joys and sorrows, the exuberant, hearty laugh punctuated with upraised hands, the clear, level gaze that made business opponents squirm and friends confess their troubles to him. The stone had been set that morning, eight days after his funeral. Elizabeth had wanted to accompany her but Amanda had been adamant: "You'll be here to tend the

339

grave after I'm gone. This is my last chance to be alone with him. It's something I have to do, Elizabeth. Please.''

Now she knelt and placed an early yellow rose on the raw earth in front of the tombstone and thought back over the past months. With a terrible pang she realized how her hurt and self-pity had kept her from realizing how ill Paul was until so late. Elizabeth had known for much longer, but the two of them had kept it from Amanda. She should have been comforting him, caring for him. He had been more than just a father; he had been her whole family.

"That's something I owe to you, Esteban," she said low and bitterly. "I grieved so for your lost love that I neglected someone who truly loved me unselfishly. I'll never forgive you for that."

All the months Paul had pleaded and cajoled, trying every tack to get her to agree to a divorce, she'd put him off. When he had tried to get her to go out and meet people and become active in the outside world again, she had balked, retreating to a small circle of their friends, her work at Elizabeth's clinic, and, of course, to Paul's young namesake.

At the thought of her son, she smiled. Paul Steven Mueller had indeed brightened his grandfather's last years. He was increasingly active and had been especially fond of the times he could spend with his 'Mpa. Paul had found joy with the child. For that Amanda was grateful.

How could she have been so unobservant, though, not noticing Paul's thinness, paleness, tiredness? When she had finally confronted Elizabeth to ask about his failing health, the doctor was blunt.

"I can't put off telling you any longer, no matter what Paul wishes, Amanda. He is dying of a tumor. Nothing can be done. He didn't want to add to your other griefs, but you should know."

It explained Paul's insistence that he legally adopt her as his daughter and claim both her and Pablito as his heirs. Amanda had argued that he had cousins in Prussia who should share, but he was concerned only with securing her future. The future when he would not be there.

After that, his illness had progressed swiftly and dreadfully. Elizabeth told Amanda after he died that it had been a mercifully quick and painless death for that kind of disease, but deep in her heart Amanda knew that the strength and stoicism of Paul Mueller would have enabled him to hide an ocean of pain. She had sat by his bedside these last few weeks, nursing him as she had so many people in the clinic. But the old man was no unknown patient. He was Paul, her only link to love and security. He had saved her life at the parlor house, restored her sanity and dignity. And all she had been able to do was sit and watch him die.

Without Elizabeth Denton, Amanda knew that she would have not survived the funeral and all its attendant social complications. It seemed she and Elizabeth greeted mourners by the thousands. Paul indeed had many friends. The whole international community of San Francisco grieved at his passing. The funeral was simple and dignified, and he was interred next to his beloved Marta. Elizabeth made many of the arrangements and stood by Amanda as she decided on the most essential things.

The final sorrow came at the reading of the will. The letter that Paul had enclosed with the will was heartrending. Written in his precise, bold script, the essence of his legacy of love was evident in each carefully composed line:

Amanda, Liebchen,

When Herr Warner gives this to you, please consider very carefully my wishes. Ever since you came home to me so full of hurt, I have thought on how to protect you. Legally, you still are married to Esteban Santandar. As long as I was alive you could live in peace in San Francisco, where my political friends were strong.

Now, you must be sole protector of young Pablito. Your husband can take him from you if he wishes. Herr Warner will explain all this to you. My money alone, I fear, cannot keep him from his son if he desires to take the boy away from you.

You must leave San Francisco and go somewhere that will be safe, somewhere the Santandar wealth and vengeance cannot follow. Find a place your heart chooses, but cover your trail carefully. This is not an easy thing I ask you, I know, to give up all your friends and the security of home. But, Liebchen, you set out once before bravely across a whole continent and overcame many trials. Above all, you must keep young Pablito with you to raise and love. I know you can make a new life for yourself.

Herr Warner will explain ways of transferring money that cannot be easily traced so you can settle where you want and then have all your financial assets at your command.

Hold your head up proudly, Liebchen, and remember all the joy you and my grandson gave me in my last years. I will be watching over you both.

With all my love, daughter,
Paul

Find a place my heart chooses. Amanda remembered the words as she stood before the grave. The misty drizzle had dampened her clothes and kinked her hair into windblown ringlets, but she didn't notice. It was a melancholy day of good-byes, first to Lyla, buried over in the far side of this same cemetery, now to Paul, two people who had never met, yet who were nearer to her as parents than Mollie and Randolph Whittaker ever had been. Now that Lyla and Paul were gone, where would she go?

As she stood looking toward the bay, Amanda saw a spring storm brewing. She was about to retrace her steps down to the waiting landau when the crunch of footfalls took her from her sad reverie. She thought the driver must have come to fetch her before the storm broke, and was surprised to see Jebediah Hooter limping up the path.

"Mandy, gal, the doc said ya'd be here. I been lookin' ta find ya fer nigh on a hour. Too many good folks dyin'. I went to Lyla's grave, then had me a fierce time findin' my way over ta Mr. Mueller's." He doffed his battered hat respectfully at the gravesite.

Pausing in front of her, Hoot noticed her pallor and her disheveled hair and clothing. "You all right, gal? Doc said I was ta leave ya be, but after all this time, what with the storm brewin' out there an' all, I bethunk myself ta come anyways."

Amanda smiled at the concern in the seamed old face. He had been a staunch visitor at Paul's bedside, livening up the sick man's last days with ribald tales of adventures in the American River gold camps, as well as a great consolation to Amanda after the funeral. Just his kindly presence was reassuring. She had been blessed with a multitude of friends.

"I'm fine, Hoot. I just needed to think about where we'll go, and I had to say good-bye to Paul and Lyla." She reached out and took his grizzled and none too clean hand as they walked toward the landau.

"When ya figger ta head out, you and the boy?"

"Soon, I guess. It would be foolish to wait too long. Attorney Warner has taken care of all the financial transfers for me, so I'll have ample funds when we arrive. I can buy a home for Pablito and me. Lupe is coming with us, too. After I'm settled, I'll have the lawyer there contact Attorney Warner and tell Elizabeth where I am, so you'll both know how to reach me. The two attorneys will forward all our correspondence. I don't like this secrecy, but all Paul's friends and his attorney insist it's the best way." She sighed. She could not risk losing her son to the vengeful Santandars, yet it was hard to leave her friends here. "You know, the attorney is going to find out if he—Esteban—is married now. If he is, once he has children, I'll come back here. Pablito should be safe then."

"Wall, I'm glad it's all settled and ya got a place fixed on, but there be a thing I got ta tell ya, Mandy."

"Oh, yes?" She grinned ruefully, knowing what was bothering him.

Hoot fidgeted as they neared the elegant landau and its aloof driver. The ragtag drummer's wagon with Bitsy and Baker, as scraggly as ever, stood across from the carriage.

"Let's ride back in your wagon and we can talk. I'll send the driver home with the landau."

He grinned at her as she gave instructions and the driver took off with a disbelieving but obedient nod. Hoot then helped her climb aboard his rickety wagon and they began the slow ride back to the Mueller mansion.

"Mandy, gal, I knowed ya might try an' do somethin' fer an old coot like me, but, damnation, er, pardon, shucks, I can't accept it, I purely can't!"

Amanda had made arrangements with Attorney Warner about the disposition of her considerable wealth. The bulk was being held in trust for young Paul. Amanda had bequeathed a sizable amount to her mother, who was again a widow, struggling to keep two small sons on that hard-scrabble farm in Willow Valley. Dr. Denton's clinic was amply endowed. All of the people at Lyla's who had befriended her as a young, frightened girl were also remembered, as was the kindly old wayfarer who had brought her to Stockton Street. Amanda felt Hoot would refuse the money set aside for him but was adamant. He was old and barely scratched a living out of his peddling. Someday he would be unable to work and would need care.

"Yes, you can, Hoot. You listen to me." Amanda fixed him with a stern schoolmarm gaze and went on, "Pablito and I have a great deal of wealth, more than we could spend in a dozen lifetimes. I've put most of it in trust for his future. But I've provided for all those who helped me, too. Without you and Rita, Kano, Mina, Sophie—all my friends at Lyla's—I'd never have survived until Paul Mueller found me. Of everyone, I owe you most, Jebediah Hooter, and I pay my debts! Oh, Hoot, don't go and get all uppity on me now. It would make me happy to know that you have a nest egg for your old age—whenever that comes. Lord knows, you're spry enough to bounce Pablito on your knee for years to come! Just let it sit in the bank, and *if* you ever need it, it'll be there. Is that too much to ask?" She concluded with her most winsome smile, and he weakened.

"Wall, bein' as how ya put it that way, how can I say no? I'll jest hang on ta it, and when I cash in, the doc'll take care a me an' I'll leave it ta her. That's a real grand thing ya did, Mandy, helpin' the doc with her work. She's already plannin' how to begin to add more beds, even hire more nurses. Yep, we'll have us a real, honest-ta-goodness hospital in San Fran."

"It was all Paul's idea. He had discussed it with Elizabeth before he died. He knew how important it was for the city to have more trained medical people and facilities. I just followed the plans he'd made. Oh, Hoot, I miss him so! I'll miss you all so much."

As the mules plodded along through the spring dampness, Hoot put his arm around Amanda. If a grizzled old man with stringy hair and ragged clothes and a sobbing, beautiful young woman in an expensive black suit made an odd-looking couple, neither cared.

Saying good-bye to Elizabeth was even harder for Amanda than parting from Hoot. The two women stood on the Embarcadero that bright June morning, hugging each other and fighting back tears. The boat which would carry Amanda, Lupe, and Pablito far away was bobbing gently on the morning tide.

Amanda memorized Elizabeth Denton's dear face. How she would miss her friend over the long months of separation! "I'll write often and you reply whenever you can spare the time from your work," she said, forcing down the lump in her throat.

Elizabeth's gentle brown eyes were misty as she replied, "I'll always have time to answer your letters and I expect full reports on this young man—every new word he says, tooth he cuts—everything." She pinched Pablito's cheek playfully as she spoke and was rewarded with a gurgle of musical baby laughter.

"As soon as we arrive, I'll send my first letter to you about our temporary home. Oh, Elizabeth, I pray it's only a temporary home," Amanda said with fright in her voice.

The doctor replied positively, "Soon I'll be at this wharf to welcome you all home—that's a promise."

Travis Mitchell was very pleased with himself. Without turning a finger, he'd fallen into a veritable gold mine—a rich widow from San Francisco moving to the isolated seacoast village of San Bernal. He had settled here almost three years ago to begin a law career. Now, as the only attorney in miles, he had established a flourishing practice. Travis had a reputation as being fair, willing to wait for payment, and astute in legal matters.

When the prestigious San Francisco firm of Clive Warner referred a wealthy widow's affairs to him for discreet handling, he realized that the fees would be substantial. But why all the secrecy? Warner's explicit instructions stated that no one was to know where Mrs. Amanda White hailed from. He was to meet her at the dockside on June 4 and install her in a boardinghouse. Later, he was to assist her in buying a home and setting up a business. She would provide more specific instructions after her arrival.

As Mitchell paced back and forth on the small pier, he imagined what Amanda White would look like. Not much, he was sure. Why else would a fabulously wealthy young widow, even if encumbered with an infant son, want to bury herself in San Bernal? She must be dowdy, shy, and withdrawing from people after the shock and grief of her husband's death.

Of course, he had come to San Bernal as a young man and had never found the town unpleasant. It was picturesque and the people were friendly. The scenery was breathtaking with steep rocky cliffs overlooking a white sand beach and clear blue-green waters. The small cove was calm, lined with spruce trees. The inland soil was fertile, suited to cattle growing and produce farming. Despite its lack of excitement, Travis Mitchell liked it.

The climate was splendid. Back east he'd always been sickly, pale, and gaunt, with a perpetual cough. He pushed himself to graduate with honors from law school and then was told by his doctors that he must move to a warmer place or face the distinct possibility of consumption. Even

Travis was frightened by the specter of that dread disease. He had worked himself to exhaustion in university. What good were honors when one faced eternity? In the three years he'd been living in this wonderful climate, he'd grown tan and hard-muscled and his cough had gone.

Mitchell brushed a piece of lint from his elegant suit. He was careful of his appearance: first impressions were important in his business. He was slightly above middle height, with a thick shock of pale blond hair and piercing blue eyes. He wore a neatly trimmed pencil-thin mustache. The women of San Bernal and adjacent areas considered him the best catch around. Travis Mitchell, once shy and stuttering around women, was now charming and self-assured. At twenty-six he was in no hurry to marry. Yes, he had come into his own in many ways.

Now he wondered what this latest piece of luck would mean. He was eager to meet Mrs. Amanda White and her small son.

As the ship pulled into the cove and put out her longboats to ferry passengers ashore, Amanda took Paul from Lupe's arms. The deck was abustle with sailors carrying luggage and other cargo to be loaded onto the pitching boats. Shouts, curses, confusion, and a riot of colors and smells surrounded them. The sunlight was unusually brilliant, even for the southern California coast, and the breeze was warm and brisk. Paul, rather than being cowed by all the activity around him, was fascinated into a solemn observation of it. His bright golden gaze was intent under the thick fringe of black lashes as he followed sailors, bales, and boxes as they vanished overside to the boats. The wind tousled his curly black hair, and Amanda lovingly ran her fingers through it as he turned in her arms to follow the movement of a huge, bright red trunk hoisted on the shoulders of a tiny seaman.

Mitchell scanned the boat for his first glimpse of the widow White. At first he thought she wasn't on board. Then he was amazed, not believing his luck. The young woman being helped ashore must be Amanda White. God! She was a real beauty, with golden hair glinting fire in the brilliant sun, clear, dark green eyes, and the most provocatively proportioned slim frame. She was dressed in a cool, light cotton frock of pale gray. Utterly enchanting. Only when she reached to take a squealing child from the Mexican servant did he notice her son. Quite a contrast! The little boy was much darker than his mother. Mitchell wondered what his father had looked like. The plain English name of White suddenly seemed suspect. The boy's coloring, if not his features, was far closer to the servant woman's than the mother's. Interesting. Most interesting, indeed. Mitchell's first explanation of Mrs. White's coming to San Bernal was obviously false. He smiled. Here was a mystery to investigate.

With a flourish he doffed his cream-colored, high-crowned hat and approached her, so that the wind blew his thick, straight wealth of silvery blond hair away from his face. He wanted to make a good impression and knew he would.

"Mrs. White? Please allow me to introduce myself. I'm Travis Mitchell, your attorney here in San Bernal. May I welcome you to our fair city." He kissed Amanda's hand and gave her a dazzling smile, boyish and earnest, most appealing.

"I'm very glad to meet you, Mr. Mitchell. This is my companion, Mrs. Valdez, and this is my son, Paul." Amanda was pleasantly surprised with this handsome young man who seemed so open and friendly.

Lupe sized the man up with her dark, slitted gaze, immediately sensing his curiosity about Paul. She nodded to him as he smiled at the introduction. Paul stared wide-eyed, but no smile broke his solemn reverie at first.

They chatted about inconsequential things as Travis arranged for Amanda's luggage to be taken to the small boardinghouse in town where she, Lupe, and Paul would reside at first. "I'm sure you'll like Mrs. Jordan's place. It's clean and quiet and really rather pretty. She will put you up for as long as you need while you decide where you want to live."

"What is available, Mr. Mitchell? Are there very many

houses for sale, or might I have to wait and build on a piece of land after I purchase a lot?''

Travis smiled. ''Actually, I think you may have a piece of good fortune. Last month Roberta Rameriz put her house up for sale. It's very well kept and quite a good buy. Of course,'' he added, glancing at Lupe, ''it's Spanish in design, with an open central courtyard and fountain, a great white stucco and red tile place. If you'd prefer a more traditionally American structure, there is—''

Amanda interrupted. ''I'd love to see the Rameriz place! I've grown quite used to Spanish architecture. It suits California's climate far better than those ugly multistoried frame monstrosities lined up along that street.'' As she spoke, she gestured toward the section of town they were approaching, where a series of recently constructed wooden buildings stood in stark relief against the skyline.

Nodding in grudging agreement, Mitchell wondered where Mrs. White had spent the past years of her life.

After settling in at the boardinghouse, Amanda left Paul with Lupe and went with Attorney Mitchell to see the Rameriz hacienda. Amanda was enthralled. It was a sprawling one-story house, whitewashed brilliantly with a gleaming red tile roof. It seemed to recline amid the gently rolling hills and clusters of trees that surrounded it. The central courtyard was elaborately landscaped and the fountain was in working order.

The house was about a half-mile outside San Bernal, off a gently winding road that served as the main thoroughfare between the town and several inland agricultural villages. Several acres of wooded estate went with the property. The barn and corral were in poor repair, but Travis told her there were many willing laborers in town. There would be room for Sunrise and the numerous other horses which Amanda had kept from Paul's fine stable. By the time she could have the animals shipped from San Francisco, the facilities would be ready.

A large section of good grazing land adjacent to the estate was also up for sale. Amanda pondered starting a small ranch, raising some beef cattle and saddle horses, but decided to wait until she could secure competent advice about the local business community. As things stood, the funds Paul had left her were well invested; she had far more income than she needed. Nevertheless, the prospect of establishing a business in this lovely community appealed to her. If only she could consult Frank Mulcahey about the wisdom of such an enterprise. Sadly she reflected that he, like the rest of the Santandar family, was lost to her forever.

That evening when Mitchell dined with Amanda, she was bubbling over with questions and plans about the house. Travis was more than happy to oversee the sale for her. He was professional and quite competent and did not pry into her past or her personal life. At the same time, he was charming and witty, making her first social venture in over two years enjoyable. She laughed and felt young again. It seemed as if there would be a future for her and her son in this beautiful little town.

Within two weeks of her arrival, the widow White had bought the old Rameriz place and hired a cook, a maid, a yard man, and a stable man. A bevy of carpenters and their skilled craftsmen were brought in to make minor repairs in the interior of the house and to rebuild the barn and the corral. The shipload of fine horses that arrived soon after astonished the local populace, especially the great golden beast called Sunrise, which the slim woman rode with such consummate ease. The woman, with the small boy held securely in front of her, could be seen early almost every morning out for a ride along the soft, sandy trail near the beach.

While the widow was generous and gracious to her employees, she was also very quiet and private. She mixed little with the townspeople, whom Travis described as being from diverse backgrounds. The basic substratum was Mexican, since San Bernal had been established as a mission over fifty years earlier. Even before 1849, overland settlers had poured across the prairie to farm California's rich soil, wagon trains of Yankees coming from New England, the South, and the Midwest. The most recent were argonauts who came to California in search of gold but who had either given up before reaching the camps or had left in disgust when they hadn't struck it rich. A few were educated people like Travis Mitchell, but most were simple farmers and merchants. It was a quiet, prosperous community, overlooked by the larger commercial centers. This sleepy atmosphere appealed to Amanda. She was unlikely to be noticed and did little to attract attention after the initial flurry of her settling in.

Throughout that summer, Amanda became increasingly reliant on her attorney. He handled all legal matters, but he was also her only real friend besides Lupe. Amanda tentatively made a few women acquaintances, but when they began to ask about her husband and to question Paul's physical appearance, obliquely referring to his Mexican heritage, she retreated. Some were avid gossips and others were simply curious and concerned as are small-town folks anywhere. Amanda's past was so painful—and the danger of exposure so great—that she could not risk confiding in anyone. Not even Travis.

When Travis saw how withdrawn she remained, he tried to persuade her to mix with other people. "Amanda, you must go to the dance at Shafers' on Saturday. It'll be a quiet affair, just a few really nice families. You'd enjoy it. Please?"

"I don't think so, Travis. Thank you anyway. I'm still in mourning for my father and I don't think I should."

Amanda was aware that Travis's attitude toward her had subtly changed in the past few weeks. He was an entertaining friend and godsend when it came to legal and business advice, yet she had begun to fear he wanted more from their relationship.

Lupe also was aware of this and frequently brought it up. This morning she had made one of her penetrating observations. "Señora, you know you should not lead Señor Mitchell on. You are a married woman and he has no right to spend time with you. It is not fitting."

Amanda had been fretting over that very thing since the night before when Travis had kissed her good-night. Lupe had interrupted them in the courtyard, loudly clanging the iron gate as she opened it for her mistress to enter.

Although she loves me and Paul, a part of her is still loyal to Esteban, Amanda thought to herself, feeling too guilty to chastise her servant for overstepping her place. She was uncomfortable with the charade she played as a widow. Yet, she was trapped.

"What can I do, Lupe? I need Travis to handle my affairs. He's the only lawyer in the area. Besides, he's a good and decent man and I like him as a friend." Amanda brushed her hair furiously. She had fought this battle inwardly before, trying to balance her feelings.

Lupe looked sternly at the young woman. "He is in love with you and thinks you are free to marry him, no?"

Amanda put down the brush and looked up. "I'm afraid he does, but I've told him I'll never marry again."

"Humph!" Lupe threw back her head in a gesture of disgust. "Did you tell him why you can't marry again? That you already have a husband?"

Amanda became angry at this last unfair thrust. "As to my having a husband, I sleep alone, which I'm sure is more than Esteban can say! He will remarry. I'm not his wife. It's just that I can't bear to tell Travis I have a failed marriage, to explain all the sordid reasons why I'll not marry again. I will handle this myself, Lupe. Travis will understand my feelings and choose someone else as his wife. I just need his help and friendship. That's all I'll ever ask of any man as long as I live." The proud tilt of her head and hard glint in her eyes informed Lupe that the discussion was closed.

Unlike Lupe, Travis Mitchell would not let Amanda end their disagreement. He finally cajoled her into accepting his invitation to the dance on Saturday evening. He assured her she would like the Shafers since she had so much in common with them. They had arrived in the area only a year before from Missouri where they had run a general store. Now they operated one in San Bernal. George and Phyllis Shafer were quiet and well read. Both enjoyed music, books, and plays, things Travis knew Amanda loved.

George was a small, boyish man with wispy brown hair and a serious yet warm, homely look. Phyllis was taller than her husband, rawboned, with a wide, earnest face. She knotted her coarse yellow hair in a huge bun at the back of her neck. They had made friends with Travis when he helped them purchase their store. Phyllis was always arranging parties and dinners to introduce him to the prettiest young women in San Bernal, despite the fact that he was well able to meet them without help. Now that he seemed so taken with Amanda, Phyllis was interested in befriending her. She wanted the best for the most eligible bachelor in town.

The gathering that night was small, as Travis had promised, with only the Shafers and their friends the Wilcoxes and the Mortons. Both couples were somewhat older, with teenaged children. Grandpa Schultz, Mrs. Wilcox's father, was a fine fiddler and Phyllis played the piano. George only half-joked that shipping it all the way around the Horn to California had cost as much as establishing the store, but since his wife loved it so much and everyone enjoyed her music immensely, he considered it worth the price.

Phyllis introduced Amanda to the other guests. She already had a nodding acquaintance with Mr. and Mrs. Morton and their fifteen-year-old son, Thad. The Wilcoxes were farmers who lived a few miles out of town with their three pretty daughters. Amanda charmed them all. Everyone was curious about the beautiful, wealthy young widow whom Travis Mitchell squired around town. All speculated that his bachelor days would shortly end.

After an hour of lively dancing, Phyllis excused herself to arrange the simple buffet dinner she had prepared. Amanda, eager to become friends with the kindly woman, followed her into the kitchen. "Please, let me help you with the serving."

Phyllis looked at Amanda, still flushed breathless from a rollicking reel danced with Travis. "You do suit, you know, you and Travis, that is. You're both so fine-looking, bright, and lively. I hope you don't mind my forthrightness, Amanda. George says I always speak before considering enough, but after I consider, I always seem to say the same thing. So, I just speak out.'' She smiled and her luminous brown eyes and generous grin made her broad face almost pretty.

Impulsively, Amanda took Phyllis's large, callused hand and gave it a squeeze. "I appreciate your forthrightness and I would so value your friendship, but I think you should understand about Travis and me.'' She groped for a way to explain, then burst out, "I don't ever plan to marry again. As much as I enjoy his company, friendship, I've explained my feelings to him and I am doing the same for you because I know how you and George have adopted him into your family.''

Before Amanda could go further, Phyllis looked into her eyes. "Does Travis agree with what you told me?''

Amanda sighed and her shoulders slumped in dejection. "No. Honestly, I'm asking for your help. He'll listen to you. Would you try to persuade him to court one of the young girls in town? Lord knows, he could have his pick.''

"Why not wait and see. How long since your man died?''

Amanda flinched at this straightforward sally. Yet, Esteban *was* dead—dead to her, to Paul, out of their life forever. She looked Phyllis in the eye and answered, "Two years last February.'' It was the truth, in a way.

"That's a mighty long time for someone as young as you to mourn, Amanda. Have you ever considered your son? He's never known a father. Doesn't he deserve one? I know Travis is fond of the boy. He speaks of him often, and he'd raise him like his own.''

Amanda wanted to cry out her hopeless protest, yet she stood mute and miserable, a bread knife in one hand and a big loaf of rye in the other. Trembling, she put down the knife on the table. Before she could reply, Phyllis put her arm around the shaking shoulders. "Here you ask me to be on your side and I turn the tables on you without giving you a fair chance. I'm sorry, honey. I guess I do let my mouth run ahead of my wits at times. You have all the time in the world, and no one's pushing you. I won't let Travis do that, I promise. Now, just take a deep breath, and let's get this food out before those young people start peeling off my new wallpaper and eating it.''

The rest of the party was pleasant for Amanda. She played a few of Paul's favorite Beethoven compositions on the piano, which pleased the music-loving Shafers. The Wilcox and Morton clans were appreciative but obviously preferred Grandpa's lively fiddle. When the gathering finally broke up, Amanda realized that she did need the stimulation of company besides her son and Lupe. She must stop burying herself and make friends. Phyllis was a wonderful person. Even if Amanda couldn't make her understand her real feelings, she could still have her as a friend. Perhaps, in time, after she was sure that Esteban was remarried and she was legally free, she might consider Phyllis's advice.

"You're quiet, Amanda. Didn't you enjoy the party? They all loved you, you know.''

"Oh, yes! Truly I did. You are right about my getting out, Travis. I was just thinking about it, about all the really nice people around here. I'll just have to make more of an effort.''

"Does that include me, ma'am?'' He gave her a mock leer with a theatrical twist of his mustache.

Despite herself, Amanda laughed. She felt good. The evening had been all right. Perhaps, as Phyllis had said, in time her whole life would be all right. She hoped. "I'll certainly consider including you on my list of people to befriend, Mr. Mitchell,'' she replied primly.

Now it was his turn to laugh. "If that's the most encouragement I can get, I'll just have to settle for it.''

When they pulled up in front of the house, it was quiet and dark. Lupe, for once, was not lurking in the shadows with lights ablaze in the *sala* and gates clanking in welcome. Travis seemed as aware as Amanda that they were alone. He stopped the team but made no move to jump down from the landau and assist her to alight. Instead, he turned slowly to her with a soft smile.

"Befriend me now, Amanda. Oh, my darling, how I need you to befriend me." Slowly as he spoke he caressed her face lingeringly, hungrily, yet with great delicacy and tenderness. The moonlight glinted in his silver blond hair and it fell across his forehead as he bent over to kiss her gently, his hand just grazing her cheek. He was a skillful seducer, but never before had he wanted a woman this badly. He wanted to marry her, love her and care for her forever. Amanda was no easy conquest to be taken and then forgotten.

With no Lupe to rescue her, Amanda was not sure how to react. Perhaps she should take Phyllis's advice now and try. She did not resist and he took that to mean he could proceed. As she sat still in the close confines of the landau on the soft leather seat, he moved closer, wrapping one arm about her waist while the other caressed her neck, shoulder, and face. She let him draw her pliant body nearer as he began a trail of warm, tender kisses down her throat, across her shoulder, and back up to her face, brushing her eyelids, temples, and the edge of her mouth with his lips. Then hungrily he kissed her lips, deeply, while his hand moved deftly from her shoulder, down to cup and fondle her breast through her thin summer gown. She felt warm and languorous. It was pleasant. She almost hoped for more.

"Amanda, I knew you had passion the first time I saw you. Oh, my love." He kissed her again. His words, however, shattered the tenuous stirrings of passion as she recalled another's words, spoken the first time they'd made love:

Amanda, I knew your passion that first day you felt my gaze and returned it, but I never realized, oh, my love, my wife.

With a tortured sob she broke free of Travis's embrace and pushed him away, feeling cruelly cheated and at the same time terribly angry with herself for putting him through her hopeless attempt to get free of Esteban.

"I'm sorry, Travis. I just can't. I should never have let you start. It's all my fault." She sat there, saddened beyond measure, knowing that any attempt to forget Esteban was hopeless.

"It's the memory of your husband, isn't it?" His face was bleak.

She nodded, unable to speak, tears streaming down her face.

"Amanda, he's dead, you're alive! You can't go through the rest of your life denying yourself, your emotions, your passion. You're a warm, loving woman, I know it!"

She shook her head forlornly, softly choking out, "Only with him, Travis. Only with him. I'll never be free, never."

His eyes were like shards of blue ice now and his jaw worked, clenching and unclenching. He bit off each word. "I'll set you free, Amanda. If it's the last thing I ever do, I'll set you free. I love you and I want to marry you. Someday, not right away, perhaps, but someday, you'll see, his memory will fade. He'll be gone and I'll be here. You will be free!"

He climbed out of the landau and gently helped her down, making no further attempt to kiss her, just gallantly taking her arm and escorting her to the gate. The moonlight made his face all planes and angles, the elegant blond hair in a glittering curtain across his brow, shadowing his piercing blue eyes. With a boyish, impatient gesture he shook it back across his head, running his fingers through it to comb it out of his way. Then he smiled and the corners of his thin mustache tilted up. That made him seem younger, and very dear.

Amanda stood ready to open the gate, uncertain how to end the evening. He was in love with her and he deserved far better than the shell of a woman she was. Yet, she could not bear to see the scorn in his eyes if she told him of her sordid past or that she was still married to a man who was very much alive. Her conscience warred over this. The hurt and contempt he would doubtless feel toward her kept her silent.

She put her hand on his arm gently and said, "It's no use, Travis. Someday you'll meet someone who will love you the way you deserve, but it won't be me, not ever me." With that she flung open the gate with her other hand and vanished inside like a wraith, leaving him standing there alone in the moonlight.

Travis was hurt and frustrated, but beyond that he was exceedingly perplexed. How, after more than two years, could a dead man have such a hold on her? She was young and alive, meant to be loved, to love. He was no novice at seducing women, and he knew his own attractiveness. Any unmarried woman in the three-county area would fall into his arms if he proposed marriage; most would do so even if he proposed something less honorable. And he had to go and fall in love with the only woman he'd yet encountered who was impervious to his charms!

Travis swore as he slowly climbed back into the landau. No, there was more here than met the eye. As he had repeatedly done in the past, he puzzled over the mystery of Amanda White and her son. Even if that dark child's father possessed an English surname, he certainly was not of English ancestry. On that Travis Mitchell would bet a year's legal fees! If the boy was not Mexican, like his nurse, Lupe, then he was of some Mediterranean ancestry on his paternal side. Who was Paul White's father?

Why the false name and, indeed, why all the elaborate precautions about transferring funds from San Francisco to San Bernal? Why was no one here to know that Amanda came from San Francisco? And there was the mystery of the correspondence. Letters for Amanda were often delivered in Clive Warner's legal pouch to Travis, and Amanda sent letters with the courier to San Francisco. Why did he and Warner have to act as intermediaries? What was in these letters?

Now that he was desperately in love with Amanda, Travis wanted to solve the mystery all the more. Could she be a criminal, wanted by the law? Was the dead husband a criminal whose disgrace she and Paul were trying to flee? Both possibilities seemed remote to him.

He considered the letters. He could easily open them and find some answers that way. However, the thought of prying into Amanda's personal correspondence offended his sense of propriety, and even contemplating such a petty act made him wince.

He urged the horses to a brisker pace. As a successful student of the law, he was a patient and methodical man. There had never before been a puzzle he could not solve. He laughed ruefully to himself. *There was never before a woman you couldn't seduce, either.*

Travis had never intended to fall in love. He had planned his life carefully since his lower-middle-class childhood in a drab section of Boston. Securing a scholarship to the university had been the first step to a successful career. He had worked hard in law school and made advantageous contacts in the profession. His goal was to escape the poverty in which his parents were trapped. He had done admirably by sticking to his own timetable.

He'd even turned the severe illness that threatened him in graduate school to a positive end. To have just left Boston, a town built on the family connections he lacked, would have been a retreat. Here in California, no one worried about family name. He'd made money and not only recovered his health but gained a robust physique he'd only dreamed of in the east. Travis Mitchell had become used to getting his own way. *But I sure as hell get nowhere with my lovely little green eyes*, he thought with a sigh.

This compulsive desire for Amanda, even to the point of wanting to marry her and accept the child of another man, this madness was not in the master plan, yet here he was, vowing to wed the beautiful widow, no matter what. It frightened him that in a few short months she had laid such a strong hold on his mind and body.

However, he had never felt so alive or enjoyed life so much as he did when with her. It was more than beauty, although she was quite the most striking female he'd ever seen. Her bright, inquisitive mind was both flexible and logical, qualities he had thought never to find in a woman.

She had read widely, possessed a wonderfully sharp wit, and was genuinely kind. Perhaps, he mused, he'd never planned to fall in love only because he'd never imagined a woman like Amanda existed. How to get the lady to agree to all his plans? That was the question.

Travis reached a decision. As soon as his hectic schedule permitted, he would take a quick trip to San Francisco. It would be better to visit Clive Warner in person than to write an inquiry. It would be harder for him to evade his questions face to face. If he handled it just right, earnestly appealing to the old friend of his law-school mentor, he'd have Warner eating out of his hand. And law offices have greedy clerks who are sources of information. One way or another, he'd find out what imprisoned his love and he'd free her. Resolving that, he began to whistle the jaunty reel he'd danced with Amanda. Once again, his plans would come together.

As the summer drew to a close, Amanda became more and more restless. In a few weeks it would be time to celebrate Paul's second birthday. Every time she gazed at her son, she could see his father. And, try as she might to free herself, Amanda still ached for the touch of her dark lover. Travis could never take his place.

Travis had left yesterday on some mysterious business trip he would not discuss with her. He only smiled and said he'd be away for about two weeks or so and to plan a big celebration when he returned from his errand. She knew he had numerous legal contacts in San Francisco and Sacramento and always worried that he might stumble on her real history. Amanda did not relish having to explain her sordid past or failed marriage to anyone. She'd done penance enough on both counts and never wanted him to know the truth. She prayed he would meet someone to capture his love soon.

Amanda tossed, kicking the covers off, letting the moonlight bathe her slim body's curves and hollows in its cool, silvery glow. Her skin gleamed through the thin nightrail. She always wore a gown to sleep in now, and woke in it in the morning. This night it was unbearable. With one swift, tearing motion she pulled it over her head and threw it to the floor, then rolled in misery across the wide, empty bed.

When she closed her eyes, hot golden ones burned into her. She could feel the heat of his smoldering stare, insolent and enticing at the same time, as he had been that day at the track. She could still remember his hands on her, undressing her ever so slowly, kissing each inch of exposed flesh as he gently removed her wedding dress. She could feel the hot mineral waters lap about their entwined bodies as they loved wildly in the sand at the campsite in Sinaloa. She buried her head in the pillow, squeezing her eyes shut tight until she saw red stars, blotting out the visions of their loving. Yet still, like traitors, her palms rubbed across the cool, smooth expanse of the sheets, craving the hard, hairy feel of his skin. Finally, near dawn, she fell into an exhausted sleep.

CHAPTER
20

Esteban came into Frank's crowded office on a hot June afternoon, sweat soaking his thin linen shirt, his hat pushed back on his head. He slung himself into a waiting chair, tossed his flat-crowned hat onto the desk, and put up his booted feet.

"The damn handlers on those steamers need to be fired, Frank. I just unloaded two more horses with bruises on their legs. One prize gold is limping, for Christ's sake! I'm going back to the ranch next week and get a crew of our own hands to travel with the horses. Seamen don't know how to calm a frightened animal. Hell, they don't even like horses!"

"Can't argue there, lad. Can you spare enough trainers from the ranch to shuttle sale horses up the coast? Each trip back is a dead run for 'em, time they could be spendin' workin' new stock."

Esteban sighed and shrugged. "It's that or lose a valuable animal or two each voyage. I'll have to spare them.

Anyway, if I go to Mexico City, I can recruit more trained handlers in León and Auguascalientes along the way. I know the Lorca family and a couple of others who might be willing to move to Sonora.''

"Me boy, I got to hand it to you." Frank saluted his nephew. "This business has done better than even I dreamed.''

"The whole idea for promotion goes to Aunt Ursula. She got it all started."

Frank waved his hand in dismissal, grinning. "Mayhap, but I recall, about five years ago it was, an earnest young man just off the boat from Europe with his head full of wild ideas about specialized horse breedin' and all the grand fortunes to be made."

Esteban laughed. "It's all been quite an education, but without your ships and other contacts I'd never have done so much so fast.''

"Not bein' of modest inclination meself, I'll accept that as bald fact and congratulate us both on gettin' rich. Ah, lad, money's a grand and lovely thing! If you'd been born in County Cork and grown up with the smell of rotten potatoes still wrinklin' your nose, you'd be more impressed with your own accomplishments!" Frank turned serious and asked suddenly, "How's himself? Any more letters of ultimatum lately?''

"No. That's what worries me. As long as he keeps up a steady correspondence of threats and pleas, I'm sure he's fine. But I haven't heard from him in about two months. No word from Mama, either. Oh, I don't imagine they're ill, or I'd have heard that, but I haven't been back in a while. I should check in with the ramrod at my ranch and see to the paperwork in Mazatlán. I'll spend a few days with my parents and then head toward Mexico City.''

"You goin' to visit your cousin and his new bride while you're there?" Frank watched Esteban's lean body unfold from the chair and stretch indolently as he rose. The older man was keenly aware that Elena Montoya's marriage to Rodrigo Ruiz had displeased Don Alfredo, but he wasn't certain of Esteban's feelings.

"I'm sure they'll insist on my being their guest. I understand Rigo has some sort of fancy cabinet post in the government, all window dressing and bribes, no doubt," he scoffed.

Although Esteban realized that he was off the hook as far as marrying Elena went, he felt sad and unreasonably guilty. "Rigo will go through her income in a year or two," he told Frank. "She could have made a better match."

Elena had turned down suitors for over a year and then had gone to the capital to visit friends and participate in the gala social life. When it became clear that Esteban was not going to cooperate and free himself to marry her, she favored his wastrel cousin, Rodrigo, who had a glamorous diplomatic job and spent money like water. If she could keep Rigo in Mexico City and not be buried in the backwaters of Sinaloa, life might not be so bad as his wife.

For Rigo's part, he had set his mind on having her long before but played a waiting game until Elena realized that Esteban was fully out of the picture. He had, with some considerable help from his irresponsible father, gone through most of the Ruiz family wealth. At the age of twenty-nine, he considered it essential that he marry the Montoya girl for a variety of reasons, the most immediate being her dowry. His position in the shaky dictatorship of General Zuloaga yielded a few paltry bribes, and he still had a small income from the family estates back in Sinaloa, but that was dwindling because of absentee ownership. Also, how long the unstable, usurper regime of General Zuloaga would hold Mexico City was uncertain at best. When it toppled, his social position and political appointment would fall with it. Rodrigo found the cosmopolitan delights of Mexico City enticing and wanted to say.

By the time he'd finished talking with Frank, Esteban had decided he'd visit them while in Mexico City, and he hoped he would be able to reassure his parents of their domestic felicity. Maybe Rigo's government job would work out. God knows there was enough corruption to get rich on if one were inclined to make the effort!

The party was loud. Esteban heard a mariachi band playing in the courtyard. Champagne, tequila, and iced beer were available. Dressed formally in black silk evening clothes, he leaned against the dark mahogany bar. In its gleaming varnish were reflected the sparkling lights from two enormous crystal chandeliers. As he sipped his beer, he watched the glittering scene around him. The Lopez family could always be depended on to stage the most lavish balls in Mexico City. As he surveyed the women clad in satins and velvets, dripping with diamonds and men whose clothing had accents of gold and silver everywhere, he realized it rivaled even the best galas of Paris.

The ballroom was of European design and vast proportions. Double-tiered balconies of elaborate wrought iron encircled it. People danced to the music of a full string orchestra on the polished marble floor in the center of the room. From the balconies above, more guests looked down on the festivities as waiters carrying silver trays of drinks and canapes worked their way through the throng.

"You look bored, darling. And still drinking that terrible beer when real French champagne is at your fingertips." Collette's husky tone indicated that the champagne wasn't all that was available at his fingertips.

Esteban smiled at the tall sable-haired wife of the French ambassador. "French crystal light fixtures, French champagne, pretty soon your countrymen will own all Mexico, or try to." He downed the last of his drink in one quick swallow, then paused and quirked one thick black eyebrow at the beautiful woman who laughed so insinuatingly. Collette's silk dress revealed her ample cleavage; in fact, the bodice looked as if it might slip from her shoulders at any moment.

He touched her arm. As if making the next movement in a rehearsed dance, she moved closer and leaned against him, pressing her almost bare breasts against him. She was a big woman, almost as tall as Esteban in her high-heeled slippers, and she knew how to use her body to advantage.

"I could help with your boredom, you know, love. We could leave this tiresome affair. Andre would be happy to have you escort me home."

Esteban chuckled. "I can imagine how happy he'd be, Collette." He looked across the press of people to see a tall, portly man, with thinning blond hair and an immense mustache, engrossed in conversation with a leading Mexican banker and a Prussian cabinet minister. Andre would be tied up with diplomacy all night. He never paid any attention to his wife anyway, unless he needed her sensual skills to help win some politician or diplomat to his cause. Tonight she was free. So was Esteban. He shrugged and guided her from the bar, his hand proprietarily around her waist.

During the carriage ride from the French embassy, he realized that the night had been a replay of countless others since he had arrived six weeks ago. As he had suspected all along, bribing the appropriate people got him some concessions in landing cargoes from the east coast of the United States. Once that was taken care of, he could have gone home. But it was cool and dry in Mexico City, and the steamy trek across the mountains to Mazatlán held no appeal. Besides, the warring political factions fought in skirmishes throughout central Mexico. Travel was uncertain. God, he was sick of war and politics! Even business. He had decided to take a vacation and set out on a round of parties, horse races, bullfights, and other amusements, liberally interspersed with drinking bouts and all-night stands at the card tables in the most exclusive gambling establishments the city had to offer.

The city also had women to offer, a satiation of women, not only expensive, elegant courtesans, but the wives and daughters of the best families in Mexico. In Paris and London in his schooldays he'd seen his share of women of the upper classes who carried on affairs outside their marriages, but it had seemed a world removed from his own country. Now the realization of immorality in good, convent-raised Mexican women shocked and disillusioned him. He concluded that corruption, especially in the flesh-pots of capital cities, was a universal constant.

The second night after he had arrived, Señora Maria del Flores, the handsome wife of one of the wealthiest bankers in the country, had practically thrown herself into bed with him following a reception at her palatial mansion. Her husband was upstairs with two young girls. Esteban declined the offer only to receive and make a number of other ones in the ensuing weeks.

He'd tried to discuss this with Rigo, who still held to his provincial opinions about the virtues of good women from old criollo families, especially his Elena. Rigo had no objection to *other* men's wives being unfaithful and turned the conversation to censure of foreign women and, by extension, Amanda. Rigo was very careful not to mention his cousin's absent wife by name, nor to discuss what both men knew Don Alfredo wanted—the divorce. He did mention how much fun was available to an attractive man in Mexico City, married or not.

As he reflected on all of it, Esteban felt disgust with the women and the husbands who used them for political or economic gains, disgust for the whole debauched system. Small wonder the Prussians, the English, and the French were piling up assets all over Mexico while the nation became increasingly impoverished and in debt to foreign bankers. He'd always been cynical and embittered about his country's political chaos. Now he questioned its very moral fiber.

Then, being honest, he forced himself to consider that what he really was most uneasy about was his own moral fiber. He had cast out his wife for being a harlot, yet whom did he consort with here in the most rarefied circles? What was he doing with his life but washing it down the sewer with expensive French brandy?

Jesus, I'm getting maudlin because I'm drunk! He pulled out two black onyx studs from his shirtfront and stuffed them into his jacket pocket. Collette hadn't done a very good job refastening them. He hoped he hadn't left any in her bedroom. They each bore the carved Santandar crest. Even the most tolerant husband might not like such a blatant remembrance stabbing him in his bare foot. Esteban had enough enemies already.

He was tired, half-drunk, and entirely unhappy when the carriage stopped in front of the Ruiz residence. He slowly descended and began to walk up the front stairs, only to be greeted by music at the entry. He groaned. Another party. Rigo was politically ambitious, always hoping for another, more lucrative government position.

Entertaining was the usual route to make contacts— contacts like Alesandro Mercero. When the thought flashed unbidden into his mind, he realized he'd not seen Rigo's friend since that terrible night at Rancho Santandar. Esteban assumed Rigo feared he would kill Mercero just for having been with Amanda at the bordello and was keeping them apart. Rigo feared rightly; he probably would kill the bastard. He shoved the thought away and entered the house.

It was late and the party was breaking up. Several revelers were leaving and passed him in the hallway. Good. He was half-dressed, needed a shave, and was not in the mood to be polite to Rigo's political cronies. He began to quietly ascend the winding marble staircase to the second floor and his room when the big door to the main *sala* opened and more people emerged. Elena was with them and escorted them to the door like a dutiful hostess. They must be politically influential.

Elena had become quite a social climber. Back in Sonora, he'd thought her shallow and vapid. She was that, but there was a ferretlike cleverness about her he'd only glimpsed in that scene she contrived in the courtyard at Rancho Santandar. Now she was the sophisticated wife of a politician. In the few short years since he'd last seen her, Elena had changed. Gone was the hysterical, vindictive girl Amanda had so soundly thrashed. Peculiar, he mused, that the memory of Amanda should come into his head as he listened to the honeyed tones of Elena's farewell to those guests.

He was almost up the steps, his tread catlike and silent, but she caught the movement from the corner of her eye and called up to him.

"Esteban, is that you, naughty fellow! Sneaking off to bed when I've been waiting to introduce you to our friends all night. Now they've all left. Rigo's gone out, too. Some foolish crisis at the minister's house. He'll be away all night." As she spoke, she climbed the stairs to where he stood gazing down at her. Her gown of deep burgundy velvet clung like a second skin to her upper body. In the deep cleavage between her ample breasts a huge pigeon's-egg ruby nestled. Great coils of black hair were elaborately coifed high atop her head. When she reached the top step, she stopped next to him and looked up at his face. Elena was tiny, only a bit over five feet tall, yet voluptuous. Looking at her large bust, pinched waist, and full hips, he wondered why he'd ever been attracted by her overblown curves.

"Look, I'm tired, Elena. It's been a long night and I need some rest. Tell Rigo—"

Before he could say anything more she gasped. Elena raised one beringed little hand, slipped it through his unfastened shirtfront, and buried it in his thick, black chest hair, raking her long nails against his skin. As she leaned into him and buried her face against him, his heart started to pound.

"Ooh, I knew you'd feel this way, so warm and hard. I've always wanted to do this, you know, ever since we were young, at your father's ranch."

Caught off guard, he put his arms around her small body as she burrowed closer to him, rubbing insinuatingly against his hips. One greedy hand snaked up and pulled his head down and he found himself kissing her opened lips. Pure instinct and years of practice took over as he replied in kind, feeling her buttocks through the heavy folds of the dress, then pulling down the low bodice of her gown to fondle a heavy, brown-nippled breast in one hand. She eagerly helped him ease the rest of the dress from her upper body, then slid her arms inside his shirt and began to work it free from his pants.

"Esteban, oh, Esteban, don't stop, please!"

Perhaps it was something in the panting, lustful tone of her voice, perhaps the practiced way she worked their clothing off, or perhaps it was simply the fact that she had set him up by intimating that Rigo would be away all night; but some shred of conscience stopped him abruptly, and he pulled away. This was his cousin's wife and he was about to rut with her in Rigo's own house!

"Holy Mary! Stop it, Elena, this is insane!" He held her hands in his, trying to calm them both.

Elena, her nipples hardened in anticipation, let out a low, wicked laugh. "After all this time, let's not get religion, Esteban. After all the women you've bedded since coming to Mexico City, surely you won't deny me the pleasure, lover? After all, I'm safely married and deflowered now, so what difference can it make?" She looked at him measuringly, confident of her ability to overcome his scruples.

He stared at Elena as if seeing her for the first time. *What difference can it make?* The words hit him like a bucket of cold water. Innocent, convent-raised, chaperoned every waking minute of her life until the day she married, Elena was of the best family, old aristocracy, the *pureza de sangre*. Montoya, Santandar, Ruiz. And here they stood, betraying each other, Rodrigo, the honor of their heritage. He felt ill.

"I think we'd better forget this ever happened, all of it." His voice was flat, ice-cold.

Once again the vengeful child with a temper emerged in Elena and she shrieked at him, "You bastard! You holy stinking relic! You think you're so damn righteous, you who married a paid whore. Turn from me, will you? I wasn't good enough for you, not educated enough, not traveled enough. I don't speak English and French. Well, let me tell you something—I do what I want to do because I enjoy it!"

"Somehow I never thought offering yourself to any

available man for free was a greater virtue than doing it for money, Elena.'' She raised her hand in a claw to rake at his face, but he grabbed her wrist and twisted it aside.

She hissed, "Why don't you go back to your Yankee trash? Maybe if you pay her enough she'll take you back!''

"Yes, why not, cousin, go back and leave my wife alone?'' Rodrigo's clear, staccato words carried up the stairs like bullets. He stood taking in their half-dressed state from the open front door.

Elena's eyes widened in terror and she frantically pulled the inadequate bodice of her velvet gown over her heaving breasts. "Rodrigo! You don't understand . . .''

"I think my cousin understands all too well,'' Esteban said in a low growl of disgust. "How much of our enchanting little conversation did you overhear, Rigo?''

She began to descend toward her husband, her hands out in supplication. "Oh, Rigo, it isn't as he says. He attacked me, pulled my clothes off, I swear it.''

Rodrigo stood stone still in the doorway; Esteban stood at the top of the stairs.

"Give it up, Elena.'' Esteban looked down at his cousin. "She came after me, Rigo, but I didn't move too quickly to turn her down. We're both guilty, just as you are.'' He sighed, bone-weary. "Just what 'minister' in the cabinet had your attention tonight?'' Rigo had been involved with a striking redhead for the past week or two and had probably been with her that night.

"He lies! I am innocent and so are you, my love, I know. He's as bad as that Yankee slut he married. Why, he's half Yankee himself!'' She flung herself against Rigo's chest, sobbing piteously.

"Your lady wife, cousin! Gracious and courageous to the end in the true Creole tradition.'' Esteban made a sweeping gesture of disgust with his arm. "I'm sick of the hypocrisy of this whole charade. If you overheard what I said, you heard what she replied and you know the truth. What's your pleasure, Rigo?'' He waited, too tired even to care if one of them killed the other.

Rigo took Elena by the shoulder slowly and held her at

arm's length, then struck her a stinging blow across the face with his right hand while still holding her with his left. Her head snapped back and she began to whimper. He dropped his grip and said, "Go to your room. We'll discuss this in the morning." He paused, then added, "*After* Esteban has left Mexico City." He turned and looked up at the dark, bare-chested figure at the top of the stairs. "I could hardly kill my only Santandar cousin, since our family line is already dying out." He looked down at the crying Elena. "Small wonder, too. We choose such splendid wives!"

Rigo followed his wife upstairs, soundly thrashed her, and locked her in their suite. Then he went out for the rest of the night to seek the gaming tables. He would return and deal further with his wife when he was sure his damnable cousin was on his way.

Esteban turned and headed for his room, glad to see it end, gladder yet to take his leave of the decadent beauty of the capital. After a restless night, he rose before daybreak and silently left the Ruiz house.

At nine o'clock in the morning Rigo slowly climbed the stairs, pulling off his jacket and cufflinks, preparing to sleep for a few hours. Time enough for Elena then. Rigo's bedroom was adjacent to hers in the large front wing of the house. His high-heeled boots clicked across the tiles of the hallway to the bedroom, then sank into the soft, thick carpet inside. He threw his jacket on the bed and cursed, "Dammit, where is Raoul? You pay a servant handsomely and get no service when you most need it." He yanked furiously on the bell pull and got no response for several minutes. Then, a youngish, thin man, dressed in severely cut dark trousers and a hastily tucked-in shirt, appeared in the doorway. He was out of breath, obviously having run from below stairs to respond to his master's summons.

"Don Rodrigo?" He bowed and moved to assist Rigo as he undressed. The boy was a poor excuse for a valet, and Rigo sighed; he had to make do since he'd not been able to secure a highly trained man for the unenviable position of his personal bodyservant.

After he was comfortable in a robe and had a tray of fresh fruit and tequila brought up in lieu of breakfast, he dismissed Raoul and prepared to sleep, now thoroughly exhausted after the scene last night and the ensuing hours of gambling and drinking. He had tried to erase from his mind the humiliating vision of Esteban and Elena.

Just as he dozed off, the door between his room and his wife's opened and Elena stood there, hair falling to her waist in wild tangles, one eye blackened shut and an ugly bruise beginning to run its purple course from her jawline down her slender throat and across her right shoulder. Her red silk negligee hung open, revealing the extent of damage done to her lush body last evening.

Never in her young, spoiled life had she been quite so filled with loathing. No, hate. Open, fierce hate. She stood silently in the door watching Rigo sleep, recalling his words to her last night as he struck her blow after ugly blow.

"You fucking, whoring bitch, slut! When I finish with you, my 'dear wife,' you'll never have a shred of hope my cousin will look at you again, unless it's with pity! I have plans to reward you, my love!" He caught her by the bruised shoulder, pulling her roughly to face him again. In a hoarse whisper, he went on, "I'll take you with me tomorrow. We leave for my father's estates in Sinaloa. I'm keeping you away from all the temptations of this glitter! No more Mexico City for you, my darling. No more balls, bullfights, fiestas. In short, you do nothing, go nowhere, unless I decree.

"And I decree you breed for me! Yes, I need an heir, a blue-blooded heir. First, I'll keep you locked up long enough to be sure any get on you is mine, not some Mexico City stablehand's! Then, you'll carry my children, many of them, Elena."

At this she flinched. Such a future, a prisoner of his family and servants on that crumbling ranch, continually pregnant, growing haggard and old! God! The very existence she'd seen so many Creole women fall victim to was a fate she'd sworn to avoid.

Last night she had had only enough strength to crawl into bed, too humiliated even to ring for a maid to undress her. Rigo had probably ordered the servants not to attend her anyway.

This morning she rose with dawn's gray light to see her broken face in the mirror. Mother of God! If he'd done this once, here in Mexico City, what would he be capable of on Rancho Ruiz, in his own little kingdom? She knew what she must do.

Now, standing in the doorway between their bedrooms, she looked across the large room at Rigo's sleeping form, her eyes shooting venom. He snored softly in drunken sleep. She held a heavy brass candlestick in her right hand, but a sweeping glance across his room took in the bedside table and the fruit platter sitting on it. Beside a large half-eaten peach, spilling its juices onto the earthenware bowl, lay a long, slim, very sharp paring knife.

Silently she set the candlestick down on the thick, red carpet and moved toward the table. Rigo never broke his even snoring. She picked up the knife, its smooth handle sticky with fruit juice, its blade gleaming dully in the dimly filtered light of the bedroom. It felt good in her hand, an extension of her hate. Standing over the still body under the thin sheet, she raised the knife in one swift, final motion.

The overland trek from Mexico City's high mountains toward the coast and his villa at Mazatlán took ten days. Esteban paid little attention to the discomforts of the tropical heat and insects. As he rode down, up, and again down steep mountainous trails, he hardly spoke to the other men in the group. Despite the rigors of the trail, sleep alluded him and he took the night watch. Even the constant danger from bands of marauding soldiers did not concern him. Most of the skirmishes were to the east and south. The journey was uneventful.

His thoughts were concentrated on that last ugly night in Mexico City. What a fool he'd been! What fools they all were, all the men like his father and Rigo, men everywhere. They believed that just because a woman was from good bloodlines, raised in a sheltered environment, kept in purity until her marriage, it somehow conferred honor and loyalty on her. Elena had been raised with every advantage, yet she behaved more deceitfully than Solange who had no such advantages.

He remembered his feelings when he'd first considered a conventional marriage to please his father. He'd made the usual assumptions about a virgin wife who would be faithful. Solange had countered by asking tolerantly, *Just like* you *will be faithful to her?*

Yet, he reflected now, when he'd been secure in Amanda's love he had no interest in other women. God, he'd wanted her insatiably, only her! Then, with a rush of sudden realization, he *knew*, truly *knew*, that in all the time they were together she had felt the same. She had loved only him, desired only him. Amanda would never have betrayed him as Elena had betrayed Rigo.

Did her past really matter? Frank's defenses of Amanda surfaced once more. Perhaps she did have good reasons for what she'd done. God knows, he'd never given her a chance to explain anything. The servants at the ranch had instinctively trusted her and had been angry at him when she fled. She had taken nothing of value with her except her own horse and a little money for her passage home. She had left all her clothes and jewelry and never asked anything of him in material terms. Amanda certainly hadn't married him for his money or to escape boredom. When he'd met her, she was rich and lived in an exciting city. Why would she have given all that up and moved to the back country of Sonora?

And what of Mueller? Frank swore that the man was above keeping as a mistress a girl young enough to be his daughter. As Esteban considered this and Amanda's blazing reaction to his vile insinuation that night in the library, he realized sadly that Frank was a better judge of character than he was.

By the time he arrived in Mazatlán, Esteban knew what

he had to do. It was long past time to go in search of his wife.

On the final leg of the long ride into Sonora, he wondered what his parents' reaction to his decision would be. His mother might just retire to the chapel and pray, but Don Alfredo might be intractable. If so, he'd simply tell his father good-bye. He remembered explaining to Amanda long ago that if his family made him choose between her and them, he would choose her. He had not changed his mind.

When he arrived unannounced at Rancho Santandar, Pedro greeted him in front of the main barn where he stopped first to stable Oro.

"Don Esteban, we did not expect you back so soon! Your mama will be happy."

Esteban nodded in greeting. The obvious lack of enthusiasm on the part of his papa was not mentioned. Pedro watched the young patrón walk wearily toward the house.

Esteban went to his father's study and knocked. Don Alfredo gave perfunctory permission to enter and looked up to see his son standing silently inside the door, dusty from the long ride, hat still in hand. Noticing the quiet way Esteban stood, measuring his father, the older man suddenly knew what his son had come to tell him. Perhaps he'd known all along.

He went to the cabinet by the window where he kept brandy. Efficiently he poured two drinks as he spoke. "You look as if you could use this. So could I. Sit down, Esteban. Your mama is resting before dinner. I think we should talk before we awaken her, eh?"

Esteban smiled grimly, took the proffered glass, and, raising it in a salute, downed a significant portion of its contents. His father followed suit, then walked over to the window and stood waiting.

"I've been doing a lot of thinking since I left Mexico city, Papa. I guess you could tell that. I'm going to San Francisco to find Amanda." There, it was out. He braced his legs, waiting for the eruption. None came.

Don Alfredo looked intently at Esteban with that piercing jet gaze that had cowed many men but had never moved his son. He nodded and said not one word.

"You already knew!" Esteban's voice registered bewilderment. "I only decided this past week; how the hell could you?"

"Maybe I always did. At least," he waved one hand disparagingly, "since you went to the back country for all those months. Juan told me about those two men you almost killed." The old don sighed and turned to look at the sunset sky and its blaze of colored light. "You would not ever be free of her even if you signed those divorce papers, would you?"

Esteban listened in amazement. After a lifetime of confrontation, this was a mystifying reversal.

"No. It's taken me a long time to realize what should've been plain. I've lied to myself for the last time. I don't know what will come of this. She may refuse to see me, may already have divorced me in California. But, maybe not. I judged her without giving her a chance. Lately a lot of things I've seen and done, well, they've convinced me I had no right to judge her at all. Frank once told me there must've been reasons for what she did. I didn't listen then. Now I see it differently. I'm going to find out. There is no peace for me unless I do." He stopped and waited, looking at the gray-haired man standing by the window.

Don Alfredo turned, walked over to the desk, and stood next to Esteban. "Go with God, my son."

This blessing was the last thing he expected. Esteban was stunned.

"You've been a stranger these past two years. We've always argued and you flouted my authority, but now there's such bottomless grief in you. It is so turned inward, so self-destructive, I've feared you seek death. If she can heal you, so be it. I want my son back! Alive!"

It was a difficult admission for his father. Esteban embraced the old man. They were closer than they had ever been before. No more words were necessary.

That evening Esteban went down to the barn to check on Oro. When he opened the stable door, he was surprised to see Luis Ramiro currying the palomino. Ever since Amanda had fled and Luis had helped her and Lupe, Esteban had sensed the man avoided him. Luis was fiercely loyal to the young patrona who had set his broken leg. Esteban had thought little of it and ignored the man. Now he wondered what had happened that night when Amanda fled. He was grateful to this man who had helped her. He owed Luis an expression of thanks.

"Hello, Luis."

The older man turned, startled that the young patrón would speak to him after all this time. He was uncertain how to respond. "Welcome home, Don Esteban. Pedro asked me to groom your beautiful mount. I'll be finished soon." He turned to continue the task.

Esteban moved over to Oro and stroked his muzzle gently. "Yes, he is beautiful. Only one other I know of that's his match. Sunrise. I raised them both."

Luis stopped his grooming and looked expectantly at his boss.

"I'm going after her, Luis. I was a fool to let her go. I just wanted to thank you for helping her that night. It was a long, dangerous ride to the coast."

Luis looked at him with a keenly assessing gaze. "The worst danger did not lie on the road to Santa Cruz, Don Esteban. It took place right here." He gestured to the horse stalls behind him.

"What do you mean?"

Luis told how he had heard Amanda's screams and rushed into the barn to find Don Rodrigo assaulting the patrona. He described the fight and how Amanda had helped him with the wooden latch.

Esteban was horrified, then blindly furious. Damn Rigo! Just because he thought she wasn't worthy of their fine Creole name, he had tried to punish her in the most degrading way a man can hurt a woman.

I should have taken what Elena offered! He deserved that dishonor and more. The next time I see him, he'll pay dearly, he vowed to himself, rigid with rage. Now finding Amanda was more important. But Esteban Santandar always paid his debts.

"Luis, I owe you much more than I ever knew.

Thank you. You have my gratitude even if I've taken so
long to express it.''

The seamed face of the older man broke into a smile as
he shook the patrón's proffered hand. ''Go with God, Don
Esteban, and bring her back home where she belongs.''

The salt air was invigorating. Esteban stood at the rail of
the ship, feet braced against the roll from long years of
practice. He watched the sunset as he lit a cigar. A week
ago he'd left Rancho Santandar with tearful admonitions
from his mother to be very sure of what he was doing.
Amazing. His father, a proud old Creole don, was willing
to accept his quest, while his gentle mother was reserved
and fearful. He was not at all sure that even if Amanda agreed
to return to him, he would ask her to live in Sonora again.

He was getting ahead of himself, he realized impatiently. It would be nine days before he reached San Francisco,
before he even knew if she would see him. God, it was
like the summer of 1855, when he returned from Los Angeles
nervously wondering whether Amanda would marry him.

He had sailed straight from Santa Cruz de Mayo to
Mazatlán. Like Don Alfredo, May Ling had immediately
recognized his purpose and understood the desperation that
drove him. He remembered their parting sadly. If he were
fortunate enough to get Amanda to return with him, they'd
probably live in the villa in Mazatlán. May Ling knew this
without being told. Esteban had no wish to simply abandon
her as Rigo had, and was relieved when she told him that
she planned to move to Acapulco. For several years she
had known an older rancher from there, a man of some
means. Many times he had asked her to marry him, but she
had always refused then, even though she liked the man and
knew the arrangement she had with Esteban would not be
permanent. Now she would accept the rancher's offer.

As he paced the deck, he felt sure that his feelings for
Amanda were not one-sided. She had loved him, he knew.
If he couldn't kill that love, neither could she. He would
not allow himself to consider otherwise at this point. He
set his face to the north toward San Francisco and the
golden lady who haunted his every dream.

CHAPTER
21

Elizabeth Denton had just finished one hell of a day, delivering two babies, splinting three broken limbs, and stitching up an ugly gash in a miner's arm received in a bar fight down the street from her Portsmouth Square clinic. As a result of Amanda and Paul's generous bequest she had several new nurses, but getting another physician to practice under the supervision of a female doctor was more difficult. She was not completely discouraged, however. A letter from Philadelphia, written by a man who would graduate in the spring, held promise. He was neither shocked nor discouraged by her being female but was genuinely interested in the kind of work to be done in a boom town where injuries were numerous and physicians scarce. She sat at her desk reading his letter once again, trying desperately to squeeze from the dry pages some impression of what this idealist might be like.

"Hello, Elizabeth."

The voice that interrupted her reverie was unmistakable,

the low, gravelly baritone of Esteban Santandar. Elizabeth whirled as if she'd been burned, rising from her chair to confront the tall, dark man standing in the door. At first glance he looked as he had three years ago, still hard, lean, faintly dangerous, and startlingly handsome, yet there was something else. A few faint traces of gray were visible at his temples, the beginning of lines about the mouth and forehead, but most noticeable of all was the change in his golden eyes. They looked dark and haunted, like Amanda's green ones, she thought in sudden shock. Then her instinctive caution for her friend asserted itself.

"Why are you here, Esteban?"

"I've come looking for Amanda, but the people who live in Paul's house say he died this spring and they bought it from his attorney. Where is she, Elizabeth?"

The directness of his question made her wary. How much did he know?

"It's been two years last February since Amanda arrived back here, heartbroken and alone. You threw her out. Why come after her now, my fine Creole lord?" Her words were level, but bitterness lanced through Elizabeth.

Esteban seemed to share her pain. He sighed as he pushed her office door closed, then said, "I don't claim to be anything but a fool. It's taken me a long time to realize I still love her. I want a chance to tell her, to ask her to come back to me." His gaze was straightforward. He stood, waiting for the small, plain woman to reply.

"Just like that." She snapped her fingers. " 'Come home, Amanda, all's forgiven.' After two and a half years, you suddenly reappear. Do you have any idea what you did to her? How you wounded her? She loved you more than life! She's gone through hell because of you!"

He slowly walked over to Elizabeth's desk, tossed his hat onto its cluttered top, and sat down in the old leather chair next to it.

He managed a small, rueful smile, then laughed ironically. "I guess, Doctor, we're even. I've gone through hell for her! Oh, I tried not to. Started by staying drunk for weeks, then nearly broke my neck working horses, traveled for Frank. Gambled.'' He stopped and looked straight at her. "Yes, I also went after women, all kinds, in all places. None of it was any good. Last month when I nearly took my cousin's wife, I realized what I'd become." He ran his fingers agitatedly through his unruly black hair, then rubbed his hand over his face and went on. "I realized a lot of other things, too. Things I need to tell Amanda, not anyone else."

As he spoke in a low, tortured voice, hoarse with remorse, Elizabeth sat down across from him, gauging his words, watching him. He did hurt, just like Amanda! Surely no one could act that well. But how could she be sure? Had he found out about Pablito and come to take him from his mother? Elizabeth shuddered at the possibility. Esteban missed his wife, but did he really accept her? Elizabeth feared that his disgust with Amanda's past might surface again. He needed to know, to understand what had shaped his wife's life so cruelly long before he had met her.

He sat slumped back in the chair, watching the play of various emotions over her usually calm, friendly features.

"I don't want her hurt ever again, Esteban."

A hint of the old arrogance surfaced as he rose from the chair and fixed her with his intent gaze. "Give me a chance with her. I won't hurt her again. I'll spend my life making her happy. I intend to find her, with or without your help, Elizabeth!" He leaned over the desk, his hands resting on the paper-strewn top. "Please, tell me." It was a plea tinged with desperation.

She measured her words carefully before she spoke. "I believe you, Esteban, but I also think there are some things you should know about Amanda, things she never told you. They might help you understand why she deceived you and why I helped her. Will you trust me and go for a couple of days' ride south of town, to a small farming valley? There's someone there you should meet. . . ."

Two days later, Esteban rode up to the dilapidated farm in Willow Valley. God. It was a hardscrabble place! The land across the valley was well tended, but this plot was rocky, covered with wild blackberry brambles and weed-infested, as if the owner had no interest whatever in seeing a crop harvested.

Esteban noticed that the house had been newly painted, although the barn was gray and falling apart. There was no sign of livestock. He dismounted and tied Oro to the post by the rickety barn, then went toward the small house. Suddenly the door flew open and two small boys clad only in canvas pants and plaid shirts raced barefooted down the path, nearly colliding with him. The two red-haired urchins yelled as they ran, apparently oblivious to Esteban until he stopped them by kneeling down and grabbing one with each hand. Their lapse into silence was just as sudden. They regarded him gravely with big yellow eyes, instantly suspicious.

Esteban flashed his most disarming smile and spoke. "Hello, Abe and Hank. You must be Abe, you Hank—am I right?" He turned, pinching one chubby nose, then the other. They giggled and then the twin he'd guessed was Hank spoke.

"How'd ya know our names, mister? Who be ya?" He stood, hands in his belt, legs spread apart, while his twin brother stood back almost shyly, looking at the stranger.

"Someone who once came to visit your mother told me about you. Do you remember Dr. Denton?"

"Aw, that lady doctor?" Abe said disparagingly.

"She ain't no doctor, not a real one, anyways. No female's a fer-real doctor!" Hank asserted.

Esteban chuckled. "My word of honor," he put up his hand, "she's a real, honest-to-goodness doctor in San Francisco."

Hank wiggled from Esteban's grasp. "What ya doin' here, mister?"

Before Esteban could answer, Mollie Cain emerged from the cabin. The years had not been kind to Amanda's mother. Although only forty-five, she looked at least a decade older. Her slight, fine-boned frame was thin to the point of emaciation, and her once silvery blond hair was grayed and lank, and drawn severely into a braided bun.

Her face was pale and her eyes were a translucent blue,
almost as colorless as the thin lashes and brows around
them. However, she was neatly dressed in a clean blue
calico frock. She smiled uncertainly as she regarded the
stranger, shifting her gaze to his obviously expensive
mount by the barn, then back to him.

"Hello. I'm Widow Cain and these are my boys."

"He already knowed our names. Knowed 'em when he
come, outtin' our tellin' 'em," Hank ventured.

Mollie looked questioningly at the man who now stood
up and took off his flat-crowned tan hat. He bowed
formally. "I am honored to meet you, Mrs. Cain. I am
Esteban Santandar, a friend of Elizabeth Denton."

Her lips moved in a silent "oh," then she turned to the
curious boys. "You boys go play by the creek, but mind,
don't get wet or muddy."

"But, Ma—" Hank protested.

"Do as you're told!"

With one last curious glance at the mysterious stranger
they ran in a gallop to the nearby creek.

"Please, I forget my manners, Mr.—Santandar." She
hesitated ever so slightly over the Spanish name. As he
nodded in assent to her pronunciation, she smiled and
continued. "Come inside and set a spell. Tell me how that
nice lady is. I'll make some coffee, or tea if you prefer?"

When Esteban's eyes adjusted to the dim interior of the
house, he looked about. It was spare, but clean. A new
yellow checkered cloth covered the table, and a gleaming
copper kettle sat on the stove. Mollie motioned him to a
chair by the long table in the center of the room and then
bustled over to the stove and began to stir up the coals
beneath the iron top, adding more wood to stoke up
sufficient fire for her granite ware coffeepot. She poured in
some ground coffee and placed the pot on the hot surface
to boil, then came over and sat down across from Esteban.

"You're a friend of that lady doctor from San Francisco?"

"More to the point, Mrs. Cain, I'm Amanda's husband."

At that she started, her pale eyes widening in pain and
guilt. "She—the doctor—didn't say Amanda was mar-

ried." She looked down at her lap, nervously twisting her hands, then went on in a low voice, "She only told me my daughter had come into some money and wanted to help me, with my man dead and all. You must be the one who sends the money?"

Esteban shook his head. Elizabeth had told him little about Amanda's childhood, only that her mother was alive and that she had seven-year-old sons by a second marriage. He wondered what was worrying Mrs. Cain.

"No, Amanda had her own money before she met me. She was adopted by a very wealthy older man in San Francisco who treated her like a daughter. He left her his whole estate when he died last spring, and she arranged this for you herself. That's why Dr. Denton handled it for her. I wasn't here.

"Mrs. Cain, your daughter never told me about her childhood. We hadn't known each other very long when we married. I'm Mexican. My family has large holdings on the west coast of our country. I took Amanda there to live." At this point he stopped, unsure how to continue, then decided to plunge headlong into it. "Why did she leave here and never come back? She sent Elizabeth here, but wouldn't come herself."

Again Mollie Cain stared down at her hands laced in her lap. She paused for a moment, then began to shudder. After a moment she regained a tenuous control of herself and looked into his face with haunted, guilt-stricken eyes.

"Why should she, after what he did to her? What I—oh, God, I let him!" She began to sob brokenly, putting her head on the table, resting it in the cradle of her arms.

Hearing the coffee boiling, Esteban got up and took two cups from pegs on the wall next to the stove and poured each of them a mugful. When he put the coffee down next to the distraught woman, she raised her head and looked at him.

"You didn't know, did you? She never told you. She told that doctor. Oh, the lady didn't say so, but I could tell she knew when she came to tell me about the bank and the allowance. Why do you want to know from me? Why now?'' She was reluctant to dredge up the painful past.

With horrible clarity Esteban recalled Amanda's scathing words in the library: "I was raped by my stepfather when I was sixteen!" He'd been so full of self-righteousness, so shocked and hurt, he'd not let her words register then. With a sickening lurch, they did now. He looked intensely at Mollie Cain.

"My wife left me. I love her and I want her back. I need to know what happened to her. Please, Mrs. Cain, will you help me?"

She looked at him for a moment, seeing the earnestness in the handsome face, as anguished as her own.

"Yes." She spoke so softly he could scarcely hear her. Then, resolutely, she took a sip of the coffee and began in a stronger voice. She told him of the wagon crossing, Randolph Whittaker's death, the plight she and her young daughter faced, Carver Cain's offer of marriage, and the life in Willow Valley. Her voice broke when she reached the point of her overnight stay at the Wellsleys' with the twins while Carver returned home.

"I knew it wasn't right between him and Amanda. For over a year, I'd seen him looking at her, but I was sick after the boys were born, worked to death. I guess I just gave up and let it be. He beat me and when he said I was to sit with Kate Wellsley and he'd see to Amanda, I was afraid to speak up." She stopped and drew a ragged breath.

"When I came home the next afternoon—he never did come to fetch me—I, oh Lord! He was passed out with his corn jug at the kitchen table and . . ." She put her hands up over her face, then went on. "He was undressed, and the door to her room was closed." She motioned to the lean-to adjacent to the stove. "Amanda was gone and the window was open. She must have climbed out. There was blood all over the bed—her clothes . . . her clothes were on the floor, part of them, what was left. She must've changed into her good dress. The chest was open and the dress was gone.''

Esteban thought he was going to be sick as the bitter taste of bile backed up in his throat, choking him, squeezing the breath from his lungs.

His voice was incredulous. "And you never saw her again, not since she was sixteen?" Visions of Amanda as an injured, terrified child fleeing the brutality of Carver Cain flashed before his eyes.

Mollie shook her head, then again covered her face with her hands and slumped down sobbing in the chair.

"How did Carver Cain die?" The question was icy and flat.

She looked at the man who was her daughter's husband. His expression was no longer anguished. She shivered at the hardness in his face as he waited for her answer.

"He was killed last year in a fight. A stranger staying at the Wellsleys' accused him of cheating at cards, and when Carver stood up to fight, the man shot him with a pistol, right in the head. He died instantly." She measured her son-in-law, knowing that if Carver Cain were alive, this man would not grant him so easy a death. She was glad when Carver died. Now she almost wished he were still alive to receive what he deserved.

"I was a poor excuse for a mother. I never was strong like Randolph or Amanda. She was so like her father. I always prayed she'd be happy someday. I failed her. Was she happy . . . ?" she trailed off, leaving the question unfinished.

"I failed her, too. I won't, ever again."

It was dusk when Esteban rode back into town. He'd covered the distance between Willow Valley and San Francisco in a hard day and a half of riding, stopping in a dingy wayside inn late last night. Despite her offer he could not bring himself to stay overnight with Mollie Cain and her sons. She was so guilt-stricken and distraught that he did not want to impose any further, and his own inner turmoil demanded the solitude of the trail.

He had tossed and turned in the narrow bed at a roadside inn, remembering the past. No wonder Amanda talked only of her schoolteacher father, never of her mother! He could well imagine the drudgery and back-breaking toil she had endured on that obscene excuse for a farm. A dream about a huge, brutish man with yellow eyes tearing at Amanda's small, adolescent body made him awaken in a cold sweat. God! How fervently he wished the man were still alive so he could kill him, like he'd seen the Mayo Indians dispose of their enemies in the wilds of Sonora, slowly, an inch at a time. Then his own guilt stabbed at him. What her stepfather had done to her didn't mitigate what Esteban himself had done. No, it only made it more painful!

Esteban arrived at the International Hotel dust-covered, unshaven, and exhausted. Before he went to see Elizabeth, he would rest a bit and clean up. They had a lot to talk about.

Refreshed by a long soak in a steaming tub, a shave, and a change of clothes, Esteban stood outside the inn considering whether the good doctor would be working late at her clinic or be at home in her small quarters next door. It was late and she did not expect him until tomorrow. He decided to walk to the clinic. If Elizabeth had gone home, he'd go back in the morning.

As he strolled down the busy night streets, Esteban was unaware of the eyes fixed on him. Two unremarkable men followed him from a distance, weaving and blending into the late-evening shadows between the gaslights. Esteban was absorbed in his thoughts as he headed in the direction of Elizabeth's office, cutting across side streets, oblivious of the late hour and the darkness. He had a great many questions to ask the doctor and he turned them over and over in his mind like a tongue worrying a sore tooth.

Any man who had grown up in Indian country, lived through the carnage of a no-quarter war, and frequented backstreet gambling houses developed instincts for survival that were deeply ingrained, no matter how great his preoccupation. Even before he heard the gravel crunch behind him, Esteban knew someone was there. He whirled just as a small, thin man came at him with lightning speed ready to stab him with a wicked-looking knife. As Esteban pivoted and raised his left arm to deflect the blow, he bent over in one fluid movement to extract his own weapon from its resting place in his boot. His attacker's stiletto slashed across Esteban's forearm, cutting his expensive jacket and silk shirt from elbow to cuff and raising a red line of blood.

The cutthroat was not alone. A taller, gangly man stood behind the first attacker, also holding a knife. Otherwise the street was deserted and dimly lit—an excellent place for a robbery. With a practiced eye, Esteban glanced at his surroundings, searching for any advantage. To his left stood an old storage barrel. If he could roll it toward one man, perhaps he could finish with the other before the first man could kick it out of his way.

Both men closed in, the smaller still a pace or two in front, his stiletto gleaming evilly in the semilight. Esteban feinted toward the rear attacker with his knife, then side-stepped with one blurred motion to kick the empty barrel and send it rolling toward the taller man, who kept his eyes glued on his victim. It worked better than Esteban expected. The tall man fell over the hurling cask with a crash as Esteban parried the attack of the leader. The man was good with his weapon, fast and unpatterned in his attack as small men often were. Esteban knew he had to finish with this man before the backup man regained his footing. He feinted low and lunged high, slashing the assassin in the soft space just below his solar plexis. He ripped upward with all his strength, literally raising his attacker off the ground as the blade drove toward his heart. With his last wheezing breath, the man cursed "that damned swell...not worth the money," and dropped his knife. Esteban heard the gravel spray as the other attacker half-scrambled and half-ran into the darkness.

Pursuit was pointless. Thugs were commonplace, even in better areas. He would just disappear into one of the nearby bars. If one was well dressed and out alone late at night, one invited this kind of thief. Esteban winced as he cleaned his blade and replaced it in his boot. Damn stupid!

He should have taken a hack and saved his good clothes, not to mention his left arm. He shrugged. At least he was going to see the right person to repair the damage to his arm, if not his wardrobe.

Elizabeth was still in her office working on some correspondence. Her graduating doctor from Philadelphia was indeed coming in the spring and she tried to concentrate on her letter to him describing the practice and her plans for it. But her thoughts kept turning to Amanda's last letter. Amanda said she was happy and that her new house was lovely. Pablito and Lupe were fine. Yet, the doctor read loneliness between the lines.

What would she tell Amanda's husband upon his return from Willow Valley? She was reasonably sure that Esteban sought a reconciliation and did not know of Paul's existence. Yet, the same instinct that had urged her to send him to see Mollie Cain now urged further caution.

''I'll tell him all about Lyla and what Amanda did for her and see how he takes it on top of just finding out about Carver Cain. Then I can decide whether to send him to her,'' she said to herself. ''Oh, God, if only it works out!''

Forcing her attention back to the overloaded desk, Elizabeth pushed a strand of her pale brown hair back from her forehead and turned to the clutter of notes before her.

A sharp tap on the door caught her attention and she stood up quickly. *Don't tell me it's Mrs. Eatham in labor—or God forbid, another accursed bar fight.* When she opened the front door in the outer waiting room, she gasped and reached toward Esteban, who stood calmly dripping blood onto the wooden planking of the stairs.

He walked into the office with his left arm elevated, the remnants of his jacket wrapped around it to stanch the worst of the flow.

''What happened? How did you get back so soon?'' As she questioned him she half-pushed, half-led him into the treatment room.

''I rode in this afternoon late, took a bath, and headed here. Being a jackass, I walked through a slightly less than desirable section of your fair city and got waylaid by two ducks, from the looks of them. It's not serious, just messy."

"I'm sure you've had worse," she said dryly as she unwrapped the jacket and peeled the blood-soaked silk from the nasty-looking gash. "Well, no major muscles or tendons severed. You'll keep the use of your hand. How'd your opponents fare?"

"One not so good. The other . . ." He shrugged without interest, then changed the subject. "How did Amanda get from that place to San Francisco? She must have been hurt, really hurt by that bastard." His voice was gray with anguish.

"Someone found her on the road the second day, bedraggled and hungry. He took her with him on his semiannual trip to town for supplies."

He looked at her. "Hoot?"

"Yes." She cleansed the wound with disinfectant and said briskly, "I have to suture the widest place or it'll take much longer to heal and be pretty ugly."

"It's hardly my first or worst scar," he said indifferently. "If you'd permit me first?" He pulled a cigar from his jacket and held it up, asking her permission to smoke. He needed to calm his nerves, not because of the suturing but because of what he was afraid she might tell him.

She nodded and helped him light up, saying, "They're your lungs."

Esteban waited until Elizabeth prepared her instruments, then asked, "Why the hell did he take her to a brothel? God! That's the last place a girl like her should have been!"

"Put yourself in Hoot's place, Esteban. How many good families do you think he knew who'd take in a raped farm girl? Besides, you have the wrong idea about Lyla Deveroux. She was my friend. She didn't take advantage of Amanda. I was there that first night. Lyla called me to examine Amanda. She gave her a decent job and took care of her."

As she stitched up his arm and bandaged it, Elizabeth related the whole story, going step by step through the past, telling him about the terrified girl with her dreams of being a lady, the woman who wanted a daughter, and how Lyla formed and polished Amanda into that very lady of her girlhood dreams. Elizabeth then described the grisly night of the stroke and the shattering aftermath. By the time she reached Amanda's sacrifice to protect her friend, Esteban was deathly still, his fists clenched in a pain that far exceeded the ache in his left arm. She was twice punished for her loyalty, not only by that terrible time in the brothel, but also that night in Sonora.

"God, how she must have hated it, hated all those men mauling her, paying for what Carver Cain took by force!" He ground out the words in a long, low, agonized breath as he remembered her furious words: *"Did you ever think what sends a woman to a place like that? Did you ever care?"*

Elizabeth answered him, interrupting his reverie. "No, Amanda didn't like men. Oh, she loved her dead father and old Hoot. She tolerated a few young men whom Lyla introduced her to in the hopes she might come out of her shell and eventually marry. But deep inside she was always afraid. The horror of the rape and later the degrading experiences in the parlor house left her," Elizabeth groped for a word, "frozen, I guess. She had to accept the life until Lyla died, but she still feared men, at least the sexual side of them, even after Paul Mueller met her and treated her like his own child."

Wanly, Esteban looked up at her, flinching in remembrance of what he'd said about Paul and recalling her furious response that night. "Even Frank Mulcahey told me Mueller was a fine man and acted honorably toward Amanda. I didn't believe him, or her."

Elizabeth watched him closely. He was on the edge of breaking, but she had to be sure. "Paul warned her not to marry you, told her to tell you all about her background. He was sure that if you ever found out, you'd divorce her or even kill her."

At that his head shot up. "Kill her? Look, Elizabeth, I confess to being a fool and a rotten bastard, but kill her!

Dios mio!" He ran his fingers through his hair as he sat slumped in the leather chair.

"Paul and Hoot looked into your background in Amanda's interest. You must admit, Esteban, there's more than a little blood on your hands."

He shrugged. "I grew up in a violent land, fought in a war, lived a life where things happened and I did what I had to, but to kill Amanda . . ."

"Paul wanted only her happiness. He knew about your past, your heritage, all the obvious reasons that assured him the marriage wouldn't work. But, for the first time in her young life, from the moment she saw you, I think, she loved you. Strange that it should happen that way after all she'd been through." Elizabeth sat down next to Esteban in the other well-battered chair in her private office. Looking him in the face, she continued her exposition.

"Amanda never talked much about the customers at Lyla's. I did get her to talk about Cain. I knew she had to get that out of her system, but later on, well, I guess it was impossible for her even to talk about it. Oh, a few times she'd tell me that a night was bad or long. That's about all. Once a young girl's been traumatized like Amanda was, the distinctions between rape, purchased sex in a whorehouse, and the intimacies of marriage aren't very clear. She was repelled by any physical contact with men. Once, when a perfectly harmless young man simply tried to steal an innocent kiss, she was so upset she ordered him never to come to the Mueller household again!"

She paused. "But one day she came to me to make what she saw as a shocking, unladylike confession. She'd seen this man at the wharf unloading a shipment of horses. She was mesmerized by him and asked Paul if he knew him."

"And Paul told her to forget about it," Esteban interjected, recalling Amanda's confession about seeing him that day.

"Just so. But she came to me for advice, scandalized at her own feelings. After the years of frozen emotions and physical denial, here was the first breakthrough. I encouraged her to go to your exhibition at the track, to go out with you for dinner. Your courtship was against Paul's better judgment. But I was sure you and only you could reach her. No one else ever had. No one else since she returned here has, either. Esteban, she gave you something a hell of a lot more precious than virginity."

Elizabeth had finished. Esteban stood, turned his back to her, and leaned against the window. All the revelations interspersed with Amanda's own actions and words, whirled in his mind. It all came together now. So much was explained—her initial eagerness and then terrible fear that day on the coast, her nervousness the afternoon of their wedding and her stiffening in his arms when he moved to consummate the marriage, her tears afterward: *"Esteban, I never knew it could be like this, never dreamed I could feel what you have given me. . . ."*

The words haunted him now. Fool! Blind, ignorant fool! He'd taken her words for the simple fears of an inexperienced girl. Now he realized their true meaning.

He'd been privileged to give her something very precious and then had been the one to take it all away, shattering her life in one final, cruel blow: *"Puta!"* His own accusations hit him anew with sickening force as he saw himself strike her, saw that shimmering mass of golden hair fly loose from the pins, saw her turn and leave the room, leave his life, take his soul.

He didn't realize the anguished cry he let out, or that he was sobbing, holding on to the window sash with splintering force, but Elizabeth did. She also knew when a proud Creole don needed to be left alone to compose himself. Silently she went into the outer office where she kept a pint of good whiskey. They could both use a drink.

Well, Elizabeth, I guess you have your answer. Damn you for the way you got it, though, she thought. Amanda's pain had been just as intense. Now she must help heal the breach and reunite them. First, she would tell him he had a son. Then, they would have to wait for Clive Warner to give them Amanda's address. Pray God it wouldn't be long!

Finally, realizing that he was alone, Esteban straightened up from the window. The pain lanced through his arm in waves when he released his rigid grip on the sash. Absently he touched the stitches and walked across the cluttered office, collecting himself, forcing his emotions under control. He had so much to atone for. He'd find her, convince her, somehow. If he had reached her once when no one else could, he would do so again.

Then he saw it, half-buried in the pile of papers on the desk. The edge of a small portrait of Amanda. He could see only her head. He reached over and picked it out from under the clutter. Esteban stared as if hypnotized, unable to take his eyes away. All the breath left his body. There was his beautiful Amanda, seated, and on her lap a baby—no, a little boy. The wide dark eyes stared back at him from under dark brows and a mop of curly black hair, the nose and mouth already unmistakably Santandar.

"You really didn't know you had a son, did you." Elizabeth stood in the doorway, speaking the words softly, a statement, not a question in the inflection of her voice. "That's why I had to be sure you understood Amanda's past and really wanted her back. If you had just come to take your heir, I wouldn't help you. I was going to tell you. I didn't mean to leave the picture out."

He tore his gaze from the picture of his son and looked up at her, dazed. "Did she know, when she left Mexico?"

"No, but it was only a few weeks later that I diagnosed her pregnancy."

"How—how old is he?"

"Paul will be two in a few weeks, September fifteenth. Amanda named him for his grandpa. He gave great joy to the old man's last days, Esteban."

"I'm grateful for that. I know how much I must have hurt him, too." He looked down at the picture again. "She looks as beautiful as ever. It must've been hard on her, that long, terrible trip with only Lupe to help her. Then, enduring a pregnancy alone. She wanted children so much, but I wasn't in a hurry. To tell the truth, I was afraid for her. She's so slim and delicate. Was it very bad?" His face was ravaged by all the revelations of the past twenty-four hours.

Elizabeth smiled gently. "No, Esteban, it wasn't hard at all. She was so happy about the baby. I never performed an easier first delivery. She's quite strong and healthy. Little Paul can have many more brothers and sisters, as many as the two of you want to give him."

Elizabeth handed him the whiskey she had held forgotten in her hand. Gratefully, he accepted it and they both sat down again. He tossed down the shot in one gulp while still holding the picture in one hand, gazing at it. She sipped at hers more sedately, observing Esteban over the rim of the glass, waiting for him to speak.

"Where are they, Elizabeth?"

This was the question she dreaded. After all he'd been through, she scarcely had the heart to tell him that she did not know. Indeed, she feared he might not believe it, and she could hardly blame him. Choosing her words carefully, she began.

"Within a few weeks, certainly by the end of September, I'll know, Esteban. Since they left San Francisco the first of June, I haven't known. Paul and his attorney, Clive Warner, arranged things before Paul died. When Amanda left, Warner employed a personal contact of his in her new home town, another attorney, to handle the transfer of funds. All correspondence between Amanda and me has been handled through these two law firms. Only Clive Warner and the other lawyer know where she is until the end of summer. It was agreed that once she was safely settled in and felt that you or your family weren't pursuing her, Warner could tell me her location. Then, I could discreetly visit. We presumed that after about four months, if anyone were making inquiries, we'd know. Within as little as two or three weeks, he should inform me. I know it all seems Byzantine and cumbersome, but mail is so easily traced."

"If you don't know now, Warner does. I'll go see him in the morning." Esteban accepted her explanation. "I'm not going to sit here and wait for weeks, not after all this time. I've wasted enough of our lives."

Gently Elizabeth put her hand out to him. "Oh, Esteban,

I fear you may have to wait. You see, Clive Warner was an old friend of Paul Mueller. He wrote the will, handled the adoptions of Amanda and young Paul. He understood all the enmity between your family and his clients. Even if I try to assure him, he's a stubborn old German just like Paul. I don't think he'll trust you, and I don't think we can sway him. In fact, he might even have heard you're here now and decided not to trust me if I go alone and ask.''

''In other words, even if you trust me, you're positive he won't.''

''Paul's instructions were emphatic, and Attorney Warner is incredibly conscientious. If you just keep out of sight so he's unaware of your presence, when I'm told where Amanda is, we can go together.'' She looked at his face and saw the fierce light in his eyes. Even though she didn't know Esteban well, the set of his jaw was a clear indication that he'd not lie low and wait. She could read the signs. It was useless to ask him to comply.

''I can only tell you this much: I think she went somewhere south, along the coast. I'm not sure why, but she wanted to be by the sea.''

Before Elizabeth could say more, Esteban's eyes lit in remembrance of those warm, golden days of sailing and nights of loving. He smiled. ''I'm sure I know why. The question is only one of pinpointing the exact town. I have a few pretty good guesses. Before your Mr. Warner decides to impart his information to you, I should be sending you word I've found her!''

When Esteban set out the next morning in search of his love, he was watched by a pair of calculating blue eyes. *So, a boat for Carmel. I'll be right on your heels, never fear, Esteban. Right behind you, on the next boat.*

As the small craft sailed down to Carmel with Oro stowed safely below deck, Esteban considered where to begin his search after he reached the first site he remembered so fondly from their honeymoon. He decided to make inquiries in Carmel, but he felt sure it would be too obvious for her to have moved there. However, it was a center from which to begin combing the smaller ports and country towns that dotted the California coast.

Esteban stayed the night at an inn in Carmel. Early the next morning, he made inquiries about a beautiful, golden-haired woman with a small, dark-haired son and their Mexican maid. No one had seen or heard of them. Expecting this, but disappointed nonetheless, he set out south along the twisting, winding coast trail with its spectacular view of the angry ocean tossing itself against the sharp rocks below.

He rode uneventfully all day, stopping on occasion to rest Oro and eat a bit of the simple food he had purchased at the inn. By late afternoon, the autumn sun was hot and dry. A searing wind was raising dust, for it had been a rainless summer this far south of San Francisco's perpetual damp.

Just as he reached up and doffed his hat, wiping the trickling sweat out of his eyes, a rifle slug whizzed by his head, missing him by inches. Esteban rolled from the saddle and clung to Oro's left side, placing solid horseflesh between himself and the source of the shot. He urged Oro into a fast gallop off the hilly trail into a brushy, boulder-strewn ravine where he threw himself to the ground. No more shots. No wasting of ammunition. He crouched in the deep, prickly grass of the ravine, listening for any sound to give away the whereabouts of his assailant or assailants, while he assessed what a near thing he had just escaped. If he had not moved his head down and wiped his brow just as the killer fired, he'd be a dead man!

Whoever was out there was a professional, no backstreet cutthroat. That gave him pause. He'd assumed the attack in San Francisco by the ducks was just a random attempt of clumsy thieves. Was it? Out here in the middle of nowhere, the likelihood of a second robbery by chance seemed remote.

Someone wants me dead, but who? He considered this while he listened for any tiny noise that would betray his attacker. As he scanned the rough, hilly terrain, rocks and patches of brush and tall grass, he made a quick list of enemies, then abandoned it. There were just too many of them.

It was nearing dusk and the long gray fingers of night were stretching from the east to grasp and envelop the blazing western sky. Oro was well trained and would wait quietly among the huge boulders near the opening of the ravine shielded from rifle fire. If he delayed until full dark, Esteban could get to the horse and chance a fast run. To catch him, his assailant would have to have an incredibly good mount. He'd just have to gamble. In the close quarters where he was boxed in, there could be one man or a dozen around him. The safest course was to stay alive till dark and make a run for it.

Instincts honed over years in Sonoran Indian country stood him in good stead now. He had his Paterson Revolving Rifle and his two handguns, specially made ivory handled .44 caliber Dragoon Colts. He'd pulled the rifle from its scabbard when he rolled off Oro. The Colts he had on his belt. At least he had ample fire power if they rushed him, although Esteban surmised they were far more likely attempt to creep up for a shot.

The wind had died down, and that was to Esteban's advantage. A twig cracking could be heard for a hundred yards. Mosquitoes buzzed in the first cool of evening. In the distance the low murmur of the tide coming in made a monotonous sound. The waiting was nerve-racking, but Esteban was a patient man when he had to be. That was why he won so often when gambling, and this was the game of his life. The stakes *were* his life.

When Esteban heard a rustle in the grass, he crouched low and waited silently behind a cluster of jagged rocks, the Colt in his hand cocked and ready. Dead silence. Another five or ten minutes elapsed. Suddenly a pistol was cocked, snapping loudly in the still evening air. A man rolled out of the grass less than twelve feet away, blurred from the speed of his movement, raising his gun to fire as he got Esteban in his sight. Esteban was waiting. As the killer raised his head, he looked into the face of death. Esteban placed a bullet cleanly in the center of his fore-

head. There was silence once more. After a few minutes he
heard horses on the other side of the hill, heading up the
trail. There might be other men in wait. He hid among the
rocks until full dark, then moved silently to Oro, swung
up, and fled the hellish place at a speed that was perilous
on the dark, uneven ground.

After an hour of riding, carefully skirting any possible
ambush sites, Esteban saw the winking lights of a small
seaside village. He left the trail, now lighted by a clear,
bright moon, and circled around the town, entering it from
the southeast. No more chances.

The village was tiny and poor. He found a small cantina
and got a room, cramped and none too clean. He paid the
squint-eyed bartender for the lodging and a simple meal of
beans, tortillas, and beer, which he took to his room to eat.
The food was greasy and stale and the beer warm and flat
but he was starved and thirsty. Even the gray sheets looked
inviting after he shook them free of a few roaches. He
moved the bed to a corner, where it was out of the range of
fire through the small window. The frame squeaked loudly
when he attempted to move the sash. Good. He braced the
room's one rickety chair in front of the door and decided
to sleep dressed, with his gun and knife in easy reach.

As he lay, almost ready to doze off, he reviewed the
attempts on his life. The first had been just after he saw
Mollie Cain. Was there any possibility Cain was still
alive and trying to have him killed out of fear? Unlikely
he decided. He had made enemies up and down the Pacific
coast, even had enemies left over from his college days in
Paris and London. Again, it was unlikely that anyone from
Europe had followed him so far after so long. Business
enemies or men he'd taken women from, that was a more
likely area, yet no one person came to mind immediately.

Lurking like a nagging ache in the deepest recesses of
his mind was another possibility. Finally, he consciously
considered that Amanda and Elizabeth might want him
dead to free Paul from any threat of his father reclaiming
him. For the life of him, he couldn't believe it. As he
thought about Elizabeth's pained reaction during their last

conversation and her words about how Amanda loved him, he did not believe the doctor was dissembling. Amanda could never wish him dead either, no matter what.

That left him back at square one, with no answers at all. It could be any one of a long list of people he'd crossed one way or another over the years. He thought of the pistolero he'd shot that evening. *Pity I didn't have time to examine him more closely. He was probably just a hired gun, a Mexican mercenary, the kind for sale in any waterfront cantina from Mazatlán to San Francisco.* All he could do, Esteban resolved as he drifted off into a light sleep, was be very wary of possible ambush sites and never turn his back on anyone.

Upon waking in the morning, he sat up stiffly in the rickety bed, gingerly testing his sore muscles, aching from the roll onto the rocks and the hours of tense waiting. Suddenly another possible danger struck him after considering all his enemies last night. What if he was leading someone to Amanda and Paul? Might they be in danger? That froze him with terror. Then, yet another insidious idea: If he stayed away and his foe somehow found them alone and unprotected, how much worse?

He cursed as he got up and strapped on his guns, then padded across the room to a cracked washbasin filled with marginally clean water. Glancing through the window to make sure no one was out there, he lowered his head and splashed his face. Little could be said for the sanitary facilities in this hole, he thought as he used a rather peculiar-smelling towel to dry himself. He considered cleaning his teeth but decided that a gargle of the brandy in his saddlebags was far safer.

By the time he got his gear together and went cautiously down the creaking wooden stairs to the back alley, he had decided it was best to find his family as soon as possible. Safer to risk ambush or even leading a killer to them than to take a chance that the killer might find them by himself.

Over the following days he employed every trick of covering his trail: camping nights without leaving a sign, entering towns and buildings without presenting a target, every skill that a childhood in Sonora, a year in war, and a life of survival in urban cesspools had taught him. It seemed he was not followed, but Esteban feared he was leading skilled assassins to Amanda and Paul.

Grimly, he made careful inquiries in three more small coastal villages. The same answer: no such people lived there. *Perhaps Elizabeth and I are both wrong*, he considered. Had Amanda gone back east, to some unknown, distant kin in Missouri, or even abroad? No; if that were true, she would not have given Elizabeth the hope of visiting her so soon. She loved this beautiful coast and the picturesque little villages it sheltered. She must be here. Every instinct told him she was near. A born gambler, Esteban trusted his intuition.

San Bernal was just another sleepy fishing port and agricultural village on the southern California coast. The scenery, Esteban admitted as he crested the ridge and looked down on the cove, was quite spectacular. This was true of most of the coastal towns from Santa Clara to Carmel, and on down. Yet, this cove was especially striking with the Pacific waves rolling in blue-green splendor on the golden sand, then foaming back to sea. Tall spruce trees stood majestically on the high ridge around it.

He stopped just below the crest of the trail, warily surveying the terrain for followers. Satisfied that he was alone, he dismounted to drink from his canteen and rest Oro. It was midday and hot after a long morning's ride. He considered eating the cold lunch he had packed in his saddlebags, then rejected the idea. Something drew him toward the lovely little cove. He'd eat there. He mounted Oro and quickly rode down into the village, skirting it and entering from another direction, as had become his precautionary method.

When he rode up to the small cantina, he heard the sounds of noonday customers yelling for beer, boiled eggs, tortillas, and beans. It was a saloon like a dozen others he'd been through in the past week. The compelling urgency of that feeling on the ridge was gone, replaced by a sinking hollow of desperation.

I'll never find her this way. Where has she gone? His thoughts were in a turmoil of frustration, exacerbated by his constant watchfulness against ambush on the trail and his fear that the enemy might find her before he did.

He stood outside the small saloon and sized it up, then slowly walked inside. Strangers were not rare in San Bernal. It was on the coast trail, which saw some traffic in drummers, disillusioned gold seekers, and the riffraff who drifted across the West. However, quite a few locals noticed the tall, dark Mexican as he walked in and ordered a cold beer at the bar. He was trail-dusty, yet expensively dressed with quality leather hand-tooled boots and gunbelt. His ivory-inlaid Colts were deadly and carried only by those who could afford the best and needed to use them. The linen shirt, leather brush vest, and cord pants were the garb any affluent traveler might choose, but this one stood out. Perhaps it was because he looked arrogant, even dangerous. A dozen or so pairs of eyes sized Esteban up as he leaned indolently against the end of the bar, sipping a beer with his back to a wall. Certainly he was no run-of-the-mill pistolero. He, in turn, looked over the noonday crowd.

He finished, flipping a coin on the scarred pine bartop. The bartender picked it up with a nod, looking him in the eye curiously.

"There a newspaper office here?"

"Naw, used ta be, but it burnt down last year. Damn wood's dry in summer. Whole street caught fire. That's why we got us a whole new row of buildin's on Lucas Street. Editor up and left, though. No paper since." He looked at the stranger, waiting to see what else he fancied to know. *Real peculiar,* the barkeep thought to himself, *he talks like a Yankee, but looks like one of them high-tone greaser rancheros.*

"You have a mayor or sheriff, who's in charge?"

As he wiped glasses, the fat man behind the bar nodded toward a silver-haired man dressed in a dapper, pale gray suit who sat at a table in the corner. "That's him, Mayor Turbin. He's the judge, too. Him 'an Travis Mitchell, they do all the record keepin' hereabouts, if that's what ya want."

With a nod of thanks, Esteban strolled over toward the little man, once again expectant, once again braced for disappointment. As he approached the table, the mayor shifted and a pair of keen gray eyes under pencil-thin silver brows peered up at him. The little man cocked his head and said, "What can I do for you, Mister . . . ?" He waited for Esteban to fill in a name as he motioned him to sit down in an empty chair across the table.

"Santandar, Esteban Santandar, Mayor Turbin. I understand you're the judge and all-around chief civil authority here." As he spoke, Esteban eased himself into the chair and shoved his flat-crowned hat back on his head. "I need some information."

The shrewd gray eyes sized him up, noting the cut of his clothes, the expensive guns, and, most particularly, the unaccented, educated tone of voice.

"You look as Mexican as your name. You sound American. Which is it?"

Esteban smiled at the older man. He was smart and missed little. Perhaps the oblique approach was best. Amanda might well have made some friends who were protective of her, although he doubted very much that she had told anyone about him.

"I'm Mexican, from Sonora, but I have a Yankee uncle in Los Angeles who practically raised me. That's why I'm here. One of his wife's cousins, a woman named Lupe Valdez, left them a little over three months ago. I'm looking for her. Mrs. Valdez took a job as a nurse and companion for a family whose name, alas, I don't know. She didn't confide in my aunt before she left."

He had used the story before on his quest. What was more natural than a Mexican man searching for his aunt's distant cousin, a Mexican woman?

With the mayor keenly watching, Esteban described Lupe, Amanda, and Paul in some detail, saying he'd seen them from a distance the day they left Los Angeles. For some reason, as he unfolded his tale, Esteban had a hunch that he was on the right track this time.

"Sounds familiar, all right. About that time Mrs. White and her boy and a Mexican nurse moved here. I don't know where they hailed from. The widow keeps to herself, except for Travis Mitchell, of course, ah—her attorney. Now I think the young devil's become—a bit more." Mayor Turbin chuckled, not noticing Esteban stiffen. "Yes, you'll find your Lupe Valdez at the old Rameriz place the widow bought, about half-mile due east of town."

Esteban thanked the older man and left the cantina with its curious onlookers. As he rode out of town, he was less cautious than he had been since the ambush. Amanda was here, at last! She was also seeing a great deal of the young lawyer Warner had hired to handle her financial affairs. Jealousy ate at him, but he forced himself to consider it from her point of view. He had cast her out over two years ago, left her alone with an infant son to raise. She had every right to be legally and morally free of him, to make a new life for herself and Paul. If that included a new marriage to this gringo lawyer, was it unreasonable? Damn, yes, it was! Esteban couldn't believe she had stopped loving him, whatever her provocation, however much of a bastard he had been, but there was only one way to find out how she felt. As he pulled Oro up in front of the beautiful Spanish house and dismounted, he knew with a tightening around his heart that the answers to all his questions lay behind the big oak doors. He walked slowly up the front steps.

PART 7

THE
RECKONING

CHAPTER
22

Lupe warmed up a late-afternoon snack for Pablito because the cook was off sitting with an ill sister. She had just begun to call for her young charge, who was helping his mother with the gardening, when she heard a rap on the front door. Most people came to the side door. Only strangers knocked on the front door. The maid was out on her day off and the gardener was out in the back acreage digging up ferns. Alone in the house with her mistress and the boy, Lupe moved quickly to answer the summons, opening the heavy wooden door wide.

"Good afternoon, Lupe," Esteban said in Spanish, smiling gravely at her.

She looked at him intently, not knowing what to do. He looked weary and travel-stained, yet the same bold commanding man he had always been. She was torn. He was the patrón, but she was loyal to Doña Amanda.

Sensing her mixed emotions, Esteban continued gently, "I've come to see my wife and my son, Lupe, please."

Old habits die hard. Lupe gave a small nod of acquiescence. "Yes, Don Esteban, they are in the garden."

His stride was firm and purposeful, but inside he was shaky and confused. What would he say to Amanda? How could he explain the reasons for his long, painful odyssey of over two and a half years? How could he reach her? He didn't know, but somehow he must do it.

Silently Lupe led him through the beautiful house and toward the dazzling sunlight of the courtyard garden. She stopped at the door, nodding at the golden-haired woman who knelt with her back to them, pruning a yellow rose bush. Next to her a small, black-haired child sat playing with a collection of toy soldiers.

"Hello, Amanda," Esteban said in English, switching automatically to the language they had used when they wanted no one to share in their conversation.

She gasped at that low, gravelly voice, so familiar, so painfully remembered. Clutching her pruning knife, she rose to face him. He stood silently just outside the courtyard, only a few yards from her. Her eyes drank in the sight of him, tall and lean in dusty trail gear. His hair was cut a little shorter now, curling more around his face. Was it lightened with a faint touch of gray? She resisted the impulse to reach out and stroke the silvery strands at his temples. His eyes, golden and compelling, were dark with emotion. His beard was already shadowing his jawline as it always had by afternoon. The same Esteban who nightly haunted her dreams was standing in front of her now, a little older. Perhaps, a little sadder.

She took a step back, then thrust her chin up and hid her clenched hands in the folds of her brown cotton work dress. Her ramrod-straight back belied the trembling she felt as emotions warred within her.

He could read her. God, how it made him ache to see the fear, the hurt, the mistrust mixed in those dark green eyes. And, could he hope, just a touch of longing was present as well? He had wounded her so grievously. Could she welcome him now?

"What do you want Esteban?" Her voice was controlled as she casually placed the knife on a small iron table. Then, remembering Pablito, Amanda scooped her son up in one quick, protective gesture and thrust him into Lupe's arms and told her to take him to his room.

As Lupe scuttled by carrying her charge, Esteban looked hungrily at his son and the boy looked back. Two pairs of gold eyes locked for one brief moment as the child was whisked away. Esteban moved slowly a few steps closer to Amanda, who stood her ground, warily facing him.

"You can't have him, Esteban. He's mine!" The wail of anguish surfaced despite her attempts to be calm.

Forcing himself not to take her in his arms and have her resist, he stopped in front of her, hands at his sides. "That's not why I came. I honestly didn't know I had a son until I returned to San Francisco, Amanda. If I hadn't gone to Elizabeth's, I still wouldn't know. I came looking for you. My life's no good without you, Amanda. Elizabeth thought you'd come south, and I remembered—"

She cut him off indignantly, "You even enlisted her to your cause! How? How did you accomplish that, Esteban? Oh, I can't believe she'd tell you!" She put a white-knuckled fist to her mouth in agitation.

"I learned a lot of things back in Mexico, even more from Elizabeth in San Francisco, things that sent me in search of you. Oh, Amanda," his voice was hoarse with longing, and, despite his resolution to go slowly, he instinctively reached out and enveloped her in a fierce, possessive embrace. "Oh, *querida*, I love you! I need you! Please forgive me!"

She said nothing, but he sensed a sudden weakening in her resolution. She didn't fight him, but stood still in the circle of his arms, her hands trembling against his chest. Unable to stop himself, he bent his head and kissed her deeply, drinking in her soft, pliant mouth, then burying his face in the thick golden hair, brushing his lips along her neck, murmuring soft Spanish love words. He held her to him and prayed the spell wouldn't be broken.

Amanda felt hot and dizzy in the brilliant sunlight, but she knew it was not the heat but Esteban who caused her breathless flush. Feverishly she clung to him, abandoning reason, pride, self-restraint. If he lied, if it were all a sham, she was beyond caring, beyond control. *Querida, querida!* When he spoke the beautiful Spanish endearment in that low voice, Amanda knew she was lost.

Sobbing, she returned his caresses with ardor, choking out between kisses, "Oh, Esteban, I still love you! Damn you, I love you!" The tears streamed down her cheeks.

Gently, almost reverently, he took her face in one hand, cupping her chin in his fingers and tipping it up to gaze into the fathomless green eyes shining with tears. He took his thumb and traced the path of one silvery droplet down her tanned cheekbone.

"Still golden from the sun, *querida*. So beautiful." He kissed away the tears, first from one cheek, then from the other. "I love you, my wife." Softly he brushed her lips again, then asked, "But, are you still my wife, Amanda, or have you divorced me as I deserved?"

"No, I couldn't." She spoke so softly he could scarcely hear her. Her eyes strayed to her left hand, which curved around his shoulder. She still wore his heavy gold wedding ring. Following her gaze, he looked at it, then reached up and took the hand in his to kiss each finger, lingering on the ring finger.

She asked, hardly daring, yet so eager to know, "But you, you must have, I mean—your family . . ."

Vehemently he shook his head. "No," then almost joyously he went on, "not that my father didn't try his damnedest." He looked deep into her eyes. "I couldn't, either."

If she had any doubts, any lingering hurts, they were swallowed up in the moment's joyous revelation. They were still married! Reaching up, she put her arms around his neck and tiptoed up to begin a kiss. Fiercely he ground his mouth down on hers and they swayed together, lost in time and space, in their own world.

A cool, sardonic voice speaking in Spanish shattered the spell. "How touching. So loyal. So besotted with each other after all this time. Still legally man and wife, at least in California. Pity.'' Rodrigo lounged carelessly against the iron gate at the courtyard entrance, his icy blue eyes riveted on the lovers.

Amanda gasped as she looked into those hard blue eyes with the naked, obsessive hate shining out even more viciously than it had that night in the stable.

Esteban put her behind him protectively as he faced his adversary at long last, cursing himself for a fool. In a flat voice, he said, "It was you, wasn't it, Rigo, in San Francisco, on the trail." He knew, although he didn't know why.

"He's always hated you, Esteban. The night I left the ranch, he—''

He interrupted her harshly, "I know. I found out when I left Mexico to come for you." He looked levelly at his cousin. "I always figured to pay you back for that, Rigo. Luis told me what you tried to do. Is that why you decided to have me killed on the trail?''

Amanda gasped, but Rodrigo only laughed. "And in San Francisco. Bunglers, those pathetic foreigners. I had hoped my pistoleros might fare better, but you always did have the devil's own luck, cousin.''

Three armed men emerged from behind the shadows of the courtyard arch. Negligently Rodrigo motioned with his hand toward the men, whose guns were trained on Esteban and Amanda. Like poisonous snakes they spread out into the bright light of the garden. Amanda stared at them. They wore dusty trail clothes and were weighed down heavily with guns and knives. They were hired gunmen, who would kill anyone without compunction, even a child! Amanda shuddered as they eased over toward Esteban, who stood deceptively calmly, measuring the situation. Amanda moved from behind him to stand by his side.

Rodrigo sent one of the hirelings inside with instructions to lock up Paul and Lupe and search the house for any other servants, then to keep watch at the front. With a brief nod, the smallest of the three strode into the house after his quarry.

"At least that madman only told him to lock them in a closet, not kill them," Amanda whispered to her husband.

Esteban was not deceived. If Rigo killed him and his wife, he would leave no witnesses. No, Rigo was playing some kind of macabre game. Esteban knew he must stall for time, find out what his cousin's plans were, and maneuver for a chance to attack. If he didn't fight, no matter how poor the odds, he knew the outcome was certain death for them all.

"Take his guns and—oh yes, I seem to recall your fondness for knives, cousin. The right boot, I believe?" While the tall, gaunt gunman leveled his piece at Esteban, his heavyset companion pulled the wicked-looking blade from its hidden sheath. The tall and fat duo took their positions, one on each side of their disarmed victim, ignoring Amanda. Rodrigo now turned his attention toward her.

His handsome face was distorted with malevolent glee as he raked her from head to toe. "So disheveled, my dear. But then, my cousin always did have such a devastating effect on women, even my wife. Ah, yes, my dear Elena." His eyes went from feverish brightness to flat opaqueness as he recalled her attempt on his life that morning in Mexico City.

"Is that why, Rigo, because of Elena and me? I wasn't the first one she tried to seduce, you know that," Esteban said to distract his crazed cousin from Amanda.

Rodrigo turned his attention to Esteban. "I know what Elena Montoya is, cousin. I've known for a long time. She is, however, a pure-blooded criolla and my legal wife. I'll just have to keep her under lock and key. She can prove dangerous." He stroked the scar on his arm, where he'd deflected her blow. A very near thing, that!

"Is that why you wanted to punish my wife, Rigo, because she's loyal, not a tramp like Elena?"

Rigo barked a harsh laugh. "Oh, at the time, dear cousin, I didn't care at all *what* your wife was, only that she was *yours*." His eyes again grew feverish with hate as he glared at Esteban.

For the first time Esteban saw Rodrigo as he was, not the provincial, petty wastrel, petulant and spoiled, but a truly twisted, dangerous enemy.

"Why, Rigo?"

"Why, indeed, cousin? You ask in all innocence. I'll tell you, you who was always first. Your family had all the money, you won all the races because you had the best horses, drew the women who always turned from me to you. I've lived my whole goddamn life on your leavings! From the cheap whores in the villages to that Chinese bitch in Mazatlán! Then, of course, there was our dear Elena. Everyone knew she waited for you, her rich, traveled, 'half Yankee'! But, you jilted her for a gringa. Only when she was sure you'd never marry her did she consent to my suit. But she had to have you, even if it meant rutting with you in my own house in Mexico City!"

Amanda clenched her fists in rage at the cousins and their rivalry that now endangered her child.

"So, it does come back to Elena, Rigo," Esteban taunted, his pose deceptively indolent.

"Ha!" Rodrigo threw his head back at that, dismissing it. "Elena is only an insignificant part of it. I never even loved the bitch. You and your 'holier than thou' brother, you were the ones! You half beat me to death when I whipped a brute of a horse, and Miguel nobly saved me—but that was only half as galling as your father's charity! Always the rich Santandars."

Esteban looked amazed. He well remembered the incident at the horse corral when they were children, but charity from his father?

"Ah, I see you didn't know," Rodrigo sneered. "My papa was always a poor manager. I'm afraid we're meant to live the good life, but unfortunately weren't blessed with enough money. After Papa used all of Mama's dowry, he begged—actually *begged* his sister to get her rich husband to make him a loan!" He shuddered with loathing at the remembrance.

Esteban had heard rumors only in recent years of the Ruiz's

decline in fortune. Apparently it went back to his cousin's childhood.

"So, it's our wealth you envy, Rigo, is that it?" Perhaps if he could taunt his distracted cousin enough, he'd find a way to turn it to his advantage, perhaps jump the two calm killers if their boss went berserk.

However, even as Esteban struck verbally at Rodrigo, the latter suddenly became very still, a crafty, eerie light in his eyes. "Oh, yes, I do indeed covet your money, cousin. At least, your father's money. Of course, when you're all dead, you and your family, I'll inherit it all!"

At this Esteban stiffened and Amanda went chalk white. Rodrigo continued, "You see, Esteban, you really played into my hands, jilting Elena and marrying your little whore." When Esteban lunged at him, Rodrigo stepped back to let the two pistoleros seize their victim. "You left the field free for me to marry Elena and get her dowry. It kept me well for a while, but," he shrugged in careless abandon, "now it's gone." His laugh was an ugly chuckle. "Oh, how I commiserated with you, my cousin, when I had to tell you the sad truth about your lady wife. You cooperated, as I knew you would. I sat back to wait until you drank yourself to death or broke your neck or got killed in a senseless fight over your wife.

"After our little scene in Mexico City when I played the noble, aggrieved husband, I took my sluttish wife back to Sinaloa. All I had to do, I thought, was lock her up under my mother's watchful eyes, breed her, and provide my own heir. You would conveniently kill yourself, and I, as the only male member in our whole family line, would inherit my dear Uncle Alfredo's whole estate But then, then, just when I was sure you would destroy yourself, I found you'd gone in search of her!"

He wagged his finger teasingly in front of Esteban. "Your dear distraught mama was visiting our ranch when I arrived with Elena. Aunt Esperanza told me you had just left for Mazatlán, intent on finding your wife! That meant you might not kill yourself. Worse yet, you might even provide the Santandar line with a legal heir and cut me out of the inheritance! So, I followed you to San Francisco. The rest, you know. Now I find you are ahead of yourself—a son you didn't even know of, eh, cousin?'' Rodrigo's crazed laugh made the hair rise on Esteban's neck.

''My father won't leave you a peso, Rigo. He always said you were a wastrel. He'd sooner give his estate to the Church!''

Rodrigo snickered. ''Oh, I've softened the old man up, with some help from your mama. When you're killed so tragically along with your wife and son, well, who else will there be?

''But first,'' he became almost businesslike, ''I will see you pay for every indignity, every slight, every time I took second place to you.'' He turned to the two men. ''Hold him.'' They tightened their grips.

''Now . . .'' He unbuckled his gunbelt and then took off his shirt as he talked almost conversationally. When he'd bared his pale, muscular chest, casting the gun and shirt aside, he continued, ''I get my final revenge, cousin. You must watch while I take what she denied me at the ranch. I'll fuck your fancy piece, your whore wife, and you'll be powerless to stop me! That's why I reconsidered killing you on the trail after that botched attempt. Why not let you lead me to her? I'll have her and then kill her. And then there's the boy; the boy complicates things—a Santandar heir. No, no I couldn't allow that, Esteban. I'll have to kill your son, and then, at last, you. By that time you'll wish to be dead, eh?''

As he moved to unbutton his pants, Amanda lunged. While he had been talking she had quietly and slowly edged to the small wrought-iron table to her left, where the forgotten pruning knife lay. She picked it up and hid it in her skirt. Nearest to her was the man holding Esteban's left arm. Rodrigo was farther to her right, eyes still riveted on his cousin, who strained in the grasp of the two gunmen. She struck with all her strength, burying the knife deeply in the back of the closest gunman. Thanks to Elizabeth's anatomy classes, her aim was perfect. He gasped one loud, harsh sigh, then fell forward onto Esteban.

Both Esteban and the man holding his right arm were knocked off balance, but Esteban righted himself more quickly and grabbed a gun from the holster of the dead man at his left. He smashed the face of the other man with the barrel. The crunch of broken bones was accompanied by a wild spray of blood. The gunman's face exploded.

After a few blurred seconds, Rodrigo turned toward his discarded gun behind him. Before he could grab it, Esteban tackled him, preventing him from reaching the weapon.

"No, Rigo, not that easy." Steel fingers gripped his shoulder and neck, whirling him around to face the hoarse yet icy voice of Esteban Santandar. "No guns, no knives. I'm going to kill you with my bare hands, cousin."

As the two men circled each other, like two predatory beasts, all Amanda could think of was Paul and that third killer. If only she could reach a gun! To hell with Esteban and Rigo and their accursed vendetta! She backed toward the door to the house, avoiding the men locked in combat. Rigo's fair limbs entangled with Esteban's dark ones as they twisted.

The gunman with the smashed skull lay against the side of the house where Esteban's blow had sent him. She darted to him and pulled the gun from his holster. He had never even had a chance to use it on his lightning-quick opponent. Armed, she fled into the house toward Paul's room, praying the third man had not heard the struggle. Holding the cocked weapon, she cautiously slipped down the hall toward the last bedroom on the east side of the corridor, praying all the while.

In the courtyard the cousins battled. Rigo was a duelist, but this was no duel. Esteban was a born streetfighter, hardened in war. There were no rules, and Esteban meant to kill him. Knowing this, Rigo fought with the cunning and strength of a cornered wildcat.

They rolled off the path and into the dirt, both bruised and bloodied. Esteban's shirt was in tatters, affording him little more protection than his shirtless cousin had. Finally, Rodrigo rolled free of Esteban's punching fists and lunged again for his gun. Before his hand closed over it, Esteban was on him again, pulling him to the ground, plastering his back to the hard patio tiles, raining punishing blows onto his face.

"Touch my woman—threaten my son—you filthy whoreson—you'll never put your hands on anyone again!" Each phrase was punctuated by the hard crack of Rodrigo's skull as Esteban bashed it again and again against the patio.

Esteban never knew how long Rodrigo lay dead before he felt the shot. Suddenly, there was a hot, searing pain in his right side.

Amanda opened the door to Paul's room, her heart beating in trip-hammer terror. No one was inside. She tore the covers off the beautiful walnut bed. No child lay within. The red and blue curtains flew freely on the open window and toys were randomly littered across the floor, just as they had been left that morning.

She took a deep breath and whispered, "Lupe, Pablito, where are you?"

At once, she heard a tapping noise and a child's suppressed wail from behind the closet door in the small alcove. Amanda rushed over and threw the bolt on the door. Lupe tumbled out with a sobbing Paul in her arms.

"Are you all right?" Amanda uncocked the weapon and put it on the armoire, gathering her son in her arms as she looked at the pale, wizened Lupe.

"Yes, señora, we are all right. He laughed about what Don Rodrigo was going to do to you and the patrón. Then he pushed us in here and went to search the house for other servants. I told him there were none—" Lupe stopped short as a shot rang out from the courtyard.

"Esteban!" Amanda dropped Paul into his bed, grabbed the gun from the dresser, and rushed out of the room. Lupe gave one glance at the sobbing but uninjured child and ran after the patrona.

Just as she reached the blinding brilliance of the courtyard, Amanda saw the third gunman, his back to her, standing over the prone form of her husband. As he raised his gun for another shot, Amanda cocked her gun. The man heard the telltale click and whirled, but not in time. She was less than six feet from him. The impact from the pistol ball blasted a hole in his chest, sending him sprawling backward. She moved closer to his body and fired a second time, point blank, after he hit the ground. He lay in a grotesque heap on top of the mangled remains of Rodrigo Ruiz. Satisfied that they both were dead, she dropped the gun and moved to where Esteban lay, very still.

Forcing herself to be calm, she felt for a pulse. It was there, but very faint. She turned to Lupe, standing behind her.

"Run for help, take the gray mare from the corral! He needs a doctor, Lupe. Hurry while I try to stop the bleeding!"

The old woman was gone in a blur of red skirts and padding sandals.

Amanda ripped her skirt and underslip, tearing off cloth to wad against Esteban's freely bleeding right side. Desperately, she tried to remember what Elizabeth had taught her about gunshot wounds and vital organs. In the clinic Elizabeth had been there, calmly telling her what to do. She had always prided herself on her nerves, but men shot in barroom brawls in San Francisco weren't Esteban.

"Oh, my love, don't die! Please God, don't let him die," she prayed aloud as she tied off the binding, then looked for something flat to use as a stretcher to carry him inside when help arrived. The table in the dining room had big, wide leaves in it. One of them would serve.

With a knife from the body of one of the pistoleros, she began to cut away the tatters of the torn shirt. Then, tearing another strip from the remnants of her dress, she dipped it in the courtyard fountain and began to bathe his face and upper body, bending over him to shade him from the fierce sun. If only they'd hurry!

After what seemed an eternity, Amanda heard furious hoofbeats. The sheriff, his deputy, and Dr. Murray ran into the garden through the side gate. As the doctor knelt and opened his bag, Amanda ordered the two lawmen to fetch the leaf from the dining-room table. In a minute they returned and slid the polished oak board underneath the wounded man. The bleeding began again as they gently pulled his inert body onto the center of the makeshift stretcher and he moaned softly. Amanda let out a small cry of anguish, then stifled it.

"Where do you want him, Mrs. White?" the deputy asked.

"This way. Follow me." Amanda led them into the master bedroom at the end of the passage. She pulled back the covers and motioned for them to place him in the bed.

"But, ma'am, that's your bed." The sheriff seemed taken aback.

"What better place. He's my husband," Amanda snapped, almost hysterical in her impatience. "And my name's not White, it's Santandar, Mrs. Esteban Santandar."

Amanda found Lupe in the kitchen, firing up the stove to boil water, when she ran there to do so herself. Lupe had ridden back from town as quickly as she could after the men. She took one look at her mistress and put her strong, sinewy arms about the young woman.

"He will be all right, Doña Amanda. I'll bring the water. I know doctors always need it. Go to him."

"After you bring it, Lupe, please see to Paul. I'm sure he's frightened." With that she was gone, flying down the hall to her husband's side.

The doctor, a middle-aged, sensible, competent man, was stripping Esteban's boots and pants. The lawmen had departed.

"Here, I'll do that. What else do you need? I've been trained as a nurse."

"I can see that. You may have saved his life by applying pressure to stop the bleeding at once." He issued a series of crisp instructions and Amanda forced herself to be calm and efficient. They disinfected the area and probed for the bullet in Esteban's side, then carefully cleansed and sutured the wound. As she helped, Amanda was grateful that this doctor was as knowledgeable and skilled as Dr. Denton.

When they had finished, Dr. Murray gave instructions for treating and dressing the wound and attempting to get fluids into the patient. He promised to return later that evening to check on Esteban.

"Will he live, Doctor?" Amanda steeled herself. She had seen many gunshot wounds and this was a bad one.

"He's young and strong. You stopped the blood loss from being worse than it could have been. He's got a chance. That's small comfort, but it's all I can tell you, ah, Mrs. Santandar." He added the unfamiliar name awkwardly. "I'll tell the sheriff to come back in a few days. Neither of you are going anywhere!" He smiled and left the room.

Following the doctor's orders, Amanda carefully sponged Esteban's face and neck with cool cloths and attempted to force a few drops of water between his lips every hour or so.

"Oh, my love, my life, you must not die, not now, after so long. I won't let you." Her voice was fierce, and as she ministered to her unconscious husband, willing life back into him.

The next seventy-two hours of vigil were a nightmare for Amanda. Neither Lupe nor Dr. Murray could get her to abandon her post by Esteban's side. She slept for only a few minutes at a time sitting by the bed in a wicker chair. His fever raged and she sponged him. Oh, but he was so pale! That swarthy body she loved so well was chalky. By contrast his hair seemed blacker than ever.

She feared he might reopen the wound with his feverish tossing, but he had not. He had thrashed and raved over the past days, cursing Rigo, arguing with his father, calling for her, and speaking of Mollie and Carver Cain, of Lyla and the parlor house, of Elizabeth. Amanda realized that the doctor must have told him everything about her background. She was unsure how to cope with that.

Elizabeth obviously trusted him. Amanda was not sure why her friend had done so, but she herself had readily confessed to him that they were still married. How ready she was to do his bidding once again! He had only to look, to touch, and she fell into his arms, lost. Damn him, but she loved him! Yet, did she trust him? Was he only after his son? Bitter as bile, memories of Rigo and Esteban's exchange about Elena surfaced in her mind. Elena had married Rigo and then betrayed him, with *her* husband! Maybe Esteban still wanted Elena. Amanda had never been able to forget her own insecurities. She was a foreigner from a family of farmers, possessed of a shameful past, while Elena was a Montoya, of a fine aristocratic bloodline, approved of by the Santandars. And now Elena was conveniently a widow as well.

In her exhausted state Amanda fretted over these speculations, her emotions in turmoil. She was very tired that third night. She sponged Esteban's face and got a bit more water past the parched lips. His beard, not shaved in four days, was dense now, making him look fierce, almost like a Spanish buccaneer. Settling into her accustomed chair by the bedside, she fell sound asleep.

Amanda woke to bright morning sunlight. She rubbed her eyes and stood up, then ran her fingers through her tangled hair. She looked down at her wrinkled skirt and began to smooth it, and when she looked up again, Esteban's sherry-gold eyes were staring at her dazedly. Amanda's heart was suddenly in her throat. He rose slightly on the pile of pillows to face her, grimacing in pain with the movement.

"You're awake," she said, able to think of nothing else to say.

Esteban smiled. "You tell me. I think I may still be dreaming. The last thing I remember was feeling a bullet in my side and looking up at that pistolero. He should've finished me."

"He almost did," she finished dryly. "Now you have matching scars, one on your right side and one on your left."

"What about Paul and Lupe?" He was starting to become fully alert.

"They're fine. He locked them in a closet but didn't hurt them."

"But, then how—"

"I killed him!"

"And Rigo?" He was pretty sure about that one.

"He's dead. So is the one I stabbed and the one whose skull you cracked with the gun butt. The sheriff said it looked like the Mexican war. He disposed of the bodies. I didn't know what you wanted to tell your aunt and uncle about Rigo, so I told the sheriff they were all bandits who followed you and tried to attack us. There were 'man wanted' posters out on two of them, so he didn't question me further. It's over."

"You saved our lives, Amanda. If you hadn't used that knife, I'd never have been able to break free." He paused, then went on, "Thank you for not sending word to my family."

"What will you tell them? It's so awful." She shuddered, remembering Rodrigo's twisted hate.

"My aunt and mother don't need to be hurt any more than they will be by knowing he's dead. I'll make up some story about his helping me defend us all from bandits. They'll believe it, the women, at least. Somehow I doubt my father will. I'm beginning to find depths of perception in him I never appreciated before." He paused, lost in thought. Then he looked at her, noting her exhausted and disheveled appearance for the first time. *Why, she must not have left my side for days,* he thought.

Gingerly he reached up and rubbed a rather luxuriant growth of bristly black beard. "How long have I been out?" Already, he was getting sleepy again.

"Almost four days now. The fever broke yesterday. Dr. Murray is good, or else you'd have awakened to Elizabeth. If I hadn't trusted him, I'd have sent for her."

He reached toward her with his left arm and caught one small hand in his, drawing her to sit on the edge of the bed.

She looked at the healing scar that ran down his forearm. "I think I recognized the fine stitch of our San Francisco friend."

"The ducks Rigo hired. It's only a scratch." His fingers lightly caressed the inside of her wrist, holding her fast as he looked into her eyes, willing her to come nearer. She swayed toward him.

Just then the door creaked open and Lupe looked in. She entered, grinning and rubbing her hands in excitement. "See, didn't I say he'd be all right! And you so fearful he might die. I've watched this one live through many things since he was a boy!"

She turned to the patrón with a twinkle in her old brown eyes. "Hungry? I have good, hot chicken garlic soup simmering, waiting for you to wake up."

Suddenly Amanda felt painfully shy and self-conscious. She was filthy and disheveled, with tangled hair, wrinkled clothes, bleary eyes. She must look awful! She rose from the bed, retreating to the door.

"You bring the soup, Lupe, and see that he eats it, then let him rest. I'll send for Dr. Murray to check on our patient this afternoon." She needed time to think, to sort out all her conflicting emotions, and just to sleep!

Lupe did as she was asked, insisting on carefully feeding the patrón as if he were a child. He was weak and did not protest as much as Lupe thought he might. As he ate she told him of Amanda's vigil. He already suspected as much, but his heart felt lighter, with this tangible proof of her devotion. The doctor came, checked his patient, and declared he was on the road to recovery. Esteban fell into a deep, healing sleep that afternoon and night, awakening only to take small amounts of nourishment and drop off again.

As for Amanda, once she was sure he would live, she allowed herself to be exhausted. She barely had the energy to take off her dress before she fell across the bed in the spare bedroom and slept for twenty-four hours.

Lupe awakened her the following morning with a huge breakfast tray of steaming tortillas, huevos rancheros, fruit, and black coffee. While Amanda ate, the maid filled a tub with hot water. Amanda soaked, washed her hair, and called Lupe to brush it free of tangles.

Over the following week, Esteban's strength returned gradually. Dr. Murray concluded that he was amazingly resilient. He still slept much of each day but was up by the end of the week for brief walks around the room, building his strength.

Amanda left Lupe and the yard man, Manolo, to see to his needs. She visited him only briefly during the following days as he mended. Each of them seemed restrained, as if waiting for some signal from the other: he afraid to confront her reticence too quickly, she uncertain whether to trust him.

At night Esteban lay abed, feeling the nagging ache of his healing side fade from sharp agony to dull discomfort. As he tossed fitfully, he considered how to approach his wife. First he must be stronger, recovered physically, mentally alert. He'd moved too fast that first afternoon before Rigo interrupted. He needed to explain so much to her, a painful, draining confession that he knew must be made, but handled very carefully. He bided his time.

Amanda was increasingly restless as the days wore on. He was so near in that room at the end of the hall, her room. Yet, perversely, even though she knew he was confined and couldn't come to her, her pride kept her from going to him. The matter of Elena still stood between them, as well as her fear about Paul. She had given him the very weapon he needed to take the boy away. They were still legally married. Perhaps when Travis returned he might be able to clarify her legal rights. Of course, he'd learn about her marriage, but the whole town knew anyway. The widow was not a widow after all!

Lupe watched her patrón and patrona caught up in a torture of longing, uncertainty, and pride. She must do something, but what? Don Esteban was getting stronger each day. Doña Amanda worked in the kitchen and garden, even rode Sunrise like a demon. It was a wonder she had time to play with Pablito. Of course, Pablito! He was the answer! Don Esteban, eager to see the boy, had asked about his son numerous times in the past week. He watched from the bedroom window as Pablito played with Lupe in the courtyard. She resolved to act.

The next morning, after Amanda went into town to learn when she could expect Attorney Mitchell to return, Lupe took the little boy into the big master bedroom!

Esteban was up and about. Clad only in simple cotton pants, he stood at the dressing table, shaving off two weeks' growth of beard. When Lupe came in with her giggling, delighted charge, he turned to see what the commotion was. That dazzling smile, all white teeth in the dark visage, lit up the room. To Lupe, he was once again a boy, just like his son.

"Patrón, I've brought Pablito. I thought you might want to get acquainted."

As the gold eyes of the father gazed into the gold eyes of the son, the boy grew suddenly quiet, fascinated with the magnetic, mysterious stranger. Thumb in his mouth, his big eyes luminous with curiosity, he stared up at Esteban.

"What does Amanda think of your idea, Lupe?" he asked, not taking his gaze off his son.

She shrugged, as if the matter were long ago decided. "You are his father. It is your right." Then she grinned slyly. Speaking in a conspiratorial whisper, she said, "Besides, Don Esteban, what she does not know, she cannot prevent, eh?"

He threw back his head in that old careless laugh. "Lupe, you are a treasure!" He reached out tentatively to Paul, testing to see if the boy would come to him, completely forgetting that he was half-shaven. The boy responded by reaching his tanned little arms out to the stranger.

Careful of his right side, which was still tender, Esteban took the boy on his left side, holding him while the enraptured child reached up into the sudsy side of his father's face, giving a fierce tug on the strange hair growing there.

"Ouch!" Esteban remembered his unfinished task suddenly.

Lupe smothered a laugh and quietly slipped from the room, deciding it was best to leave the pair to make friends on their own. Neither one noticed her leave.

Esteban sat Paul on the high-backed chair next to the washstand and talked conversationally to him, explaining what he was doing as he finished the shave. Paul watched gravely as the last vestiges of the beard disappeared. Magically, the stranger now had one smooth, whole face, just like his own. He rubbed his own silky cheek and let out a burble of laughter. Esteban followed suit, and the day was theirs.

Travis was not back yet and the judge didn't know when he might be, perhaps in a day or two. Amanda was worried. He'd already been gone for three weeks, longer than he'd said he might be. She needed to talk to someone about what to do. Increasingly, she felt she could no longer expect unbiased advice from Lupe. The patrón was here and in charge as far as his old nurse was concerned. Amanda felt alienated as her son watched the stranger from a distance, interested in his every movement. She had to make some decision soon, confront her husband and know, once and for all, whether he truly wanted her back. Yet, she feared the answer.

Everything was fine until he turned up, she thought petulantly as she drove the wagon back from town. She gave the team a harsher than necessary jerk of the reins as she stopped by the side gate, then forced herself to face the truth. *No, nothing was fine before he came. I wasn't fine. Oh, damn, I'm miserable without him, miserable with him.*

She went inside, toward the kitchen to see what the cook was preparing for the midday meal. Then she heard a blend of laughter and clattering noise coming from the other end of the long hall in the bedroom wing.

She walked quickly down the hall to the door of the master bedroom. Two black, curly heads were bent together in concentration, the man and boy sitting on the woven rug in the center of the room. They were constructing a huge tower of Paul's wooden blocks. Each time Esteban placed the last block on top of the tower, Paul would pull a bottom block out, sending the rest flying. Then they would begin the fun all over again. They did not see her enter, so intent were they on the game.

Amanda stood very still, struck with the pair they made, so startlingly alike, dense, curly black hair, thick brows, long lashes, arresting golden eyes, prominent noses, sculptured mouths, even long, slim fingers and toes. The dark skin tone was the same, tanned without benefit of sun, darkened even more where its rays had touched. As they sat facing each other, she could see the father's childhood in the son and the son's future likeness reflected in the father. She swallowed hard, her throat suddenly tightening inexplicably.

Esteban looked up, catching her unawares as she spied on them. Covering her own start at being caught so bemused, she decided it was time to get some things settled.

"Pablito, it's time for lunch. Come with Mama." She reached her hand down.

With the instinctive perversity inherent in all small boys, he stuck out his lower lip and refused to give her his hand. "No, Mama, play with Papa." He turned around and began to consider the blocks, one in each hand.

At this juncture, Lupe whisked past Amanda toward the small figure on the floor. "Pablito, I have fresh, hot tortillas with cheese melted on them. Come." Cautiously, looking first at his father for approval, the boy considered. He *was* hungry. . . .

"We'll rebuild it later, I promise." Esteban took the blocks from the smaller hands and lifted the boy up to Lupe.

"*Papa!*" Amanda fairly spat out the word. "Who told him to call you that?" She already knew the answer.

"I did, Doña Amanda. You know it is only right." With that Lupe picked up her small charge and left the two antagonists facing each other.

Gingerly, for sitting on the hard floor so long had hurt his side, Esteban rose to stand before her. He was bare-chested and barefooted, still wearing only light cotton pants. He had shaved off his pirate's beard, she realized suddenly. Her heart gave a small lurch as she faced him, trying not to let the tall, lean, almost bare body affect her.

"He's a wonderful boy, Amanda. I'm happy you named him for Paul. I hope he grows up to be like his grandpa. What is his full name?"

She turned, suddenly drawn to contemplate the washbasin. "Paul Steven Mueller," she replied, barely audibly.

He smiled at the anglicized version of his name. "No, legally he is Paul Steven Santandar, and you are Amanda Santandar, 'Widow White,' " he addressed her with a hint of amusement in his voice.

Something inside her snapped after all the pent-up emotion held at bay over the past weeks. All the fright, jealousy, and uncertainty bubbled to the surface.

"You can't walk in here and become his father, just like that, in a trice!"

"I don't intend to leave him, Amanda. He's my son."

"And I'm his mother—a rather inconvenient fact, isn't it, considering your Mexican enamorata is free now!"

"I suppose you planned to let that Yankee lawyer become his father in a trice," he shot back jealously before he could control his rising temper.

"What if I did? What right do you have to stop me? To come back into our lives? Oh, go the hell back to your Creole belle and take up where you left off in Mexico City, but leave me my son!" Furiously she stood her ground, eyes blazing green fire as she clenched her fists, placing them on her hips, bracing her booted feet resolutely apart.

Suddenly he realized what had triggered the hostility, the mistrust of the past weeks—that damnable exchange with Rigo about Elena. His anger evaporated as suddenly as it had come. God! She looked so frightened and fierce at the same time. He had hurt her again when he meant only to love her.

"Amanda, please." He reached out one long brown arm, placing his fingers over her small fist, loosening it from its rest on her hip, drawing her to walk toward the cushioned sofa with him. As he took her hand, his eyes compelled her to follow and sit beside him. She did so, sitting warily on the edge of the seat and holding herself stiffly.

He leaned forward, elbows on his knees, running his fingers through his hair as he cradled his head in his hands, tense and afraid of how to proceed.

"You're still my legal wife, Amanda. I could take Paul . . . but I won't. I have no moral right, if that's what you want. I gave up all my rights that night in the library. But I still love you, Amanda. I know I have no right to be jealous, but I can't bear to think of you being with another man."

"I've already 'been with other men,' remember, Esteban." Her voice was cold, as she recalled that terrible night of accusation. She stared straight ahead.

"No, no you haven't, Amanda. You gave to me what you gave no one else, never before or since. Now I realize that, maybe too late. Is it too late, *querida*? Do you love this Mitchell?"

Anguished, she looked at him. "No, I tried to—to feel something, but I couldn't. I couldn't even respond to a kiss." She gave a sad, bitter laugh, looking down at her lap, twisting her hands around each other as she always did when agitated.

He reached over gently, covering them with his own, drawing them together, holding her small fingers interlaced with his larger ones.

"Let me tell you a long, sordid story, *querida*, a story about a vain, stupid man. . . ."

CHAPTER
23

Slowly Esteban recounted his life since that night in the library at Rancho Santandar: all his misery, his self-destructive acts, all the compulsive, driven behavior. He told her of Frank's faith in her and repeated encouragement to go in search of her. When he got to that last, ugly scene with Elena and Rigo in Mexico City, he spared himself not at all.

"I was sick of her, sick of myself, sick of the whole sham of our lives. I was faithless, just as Elena was. But on that long, dreary ride back home, I knew, Amanda, that you would never have betrayed me. Whatever was in your past was in the past. I didn't care about any of it anymore. I only wanted to find you, to see if you'd give me another chance. My father knew the minute I came home. He gave me his blessing, *querida*. He knew my life, my salvation was you, you alone."

"Not Elena—or some suitable Creole virgin?" She looked into his eyes and had her answer. He did not want

Elena! He had been willing to forsake his family, everything, just to find her!

"Oh, I've been a fool, too, Esteban." She reached up slowly to stroke his temple, to touch the sprinkle of gray hair as had been her impulse that first day in the courtyard. "I lied to you, deceived you, lied to myself, really. Paul told me it couldn't work, that a love built on deception would fall, like Tom McVea's house of cards. I didn't listen. I never wanted you to know about my past. I wanted to be a lady, like the women of your family, not a reformed whore."

Unable to bear her pain, he took her in his arms, silencing her sobs with gentle kisses, shushing her. "Amanda, oh, *querida*, you *are* a lady. Elizabeth explained so many things to me. She sent me to see your mother, to understand what happened to you when you were only a child."

She looked up in wonder. "You went to see her? I was a coward, I guess. I never went back to Willow Valley after he was dead. I—I suppose I was ashamed, for both Mama and me." She began to cry silent, acid tears.

He held her tightly, letting her sob it out, rubbing her back reassuringly. "Oh, *querida*, you feel ashamed? After all that's been done to you, you're the last one who should feel shame. When I heard, I felt sick, knowing what he'd done, what hell your life in the parlor house must have been after Lyla became ill."

"I knew Elizabeth told you. You talked when you were delirious," she murmured.

He continued soothing her. "She told me what you did for your friend. I know what it cost you, Amanda. You have more honor and courage than anyone I've ever known, my wife. Oh, Amanda, I'm sorry I added so much hurt, so unfairly. I love you. I want to be your husband. I will cherish and respect you for the rest of our lives. We know each other now. There can be no more deception. All our false pride, our weakness is out in the open. Can you give me your trust, your love?" He held his breath as she slowly raised her head from his chest where he was cradling her.

The radiance of her tear-streaked face gave him an answer no words could ever duplicate. "I have always loved you. I was a sixteen-year-old housemaid when you came to Lyla's and I was beguiled even then. Remember the mud-covered 'filthy urchin from the garbage scow' who ruined your linen suit and fought with Helen?"

"So that's why . . ." his voice trailed off in amazement as his mind slipped back all those years. He thought of their introduction at the opera. Even then he had felt he had met her before seeing her that day at the track. "Something drew me to you the first time I laid eyes on you. It must have been my boyhood affinity for mud!" He chuckled incredulously, then turned serious. "I'll always love you, whether your hair is brown with mud, or gold, or gray, *querida*."

She stroked his cheek softly, her eyes filled with wonder, thinking of their odyssey, all they had endured to reach this moment. "I could never stop loving you, never let any other man—oh, Esteban!" She clung to him and wrapped her arms tightly around his neck.

Their kisses intensified as the afternoon grew late. They had talked for hours. Now the time for words was past. Still holding her in his embrace, he rose from the confines of the sofa, pressing her tightly to his lower body as she clung to him, returning his fierce, deep, hungry kisses.

"Please let me love you, *querida;* it's been so long, so long," he breathed the words hoarsely as he ran his hands through her hair, down her back, feeling her passion rise with his.

Her answer was a sobbed, "Yes, oh, yes."

Then she stopped, placing one small hand on his right side softly. "Your side. I might . . ."

He laughed exultantly. "I heal remarkably; remember what Dr. Murray said?"

In a slow choreography of caresses, they moved toward the bed. He unbuttoned and slid off her silk riding shirt and the camisole beneath, cupping her freed breasts in his hands, bending his dark head to kiss each one. She gasped and arched against the demands of his mouth. Then he loosened her heavy linen skirt and slip, letting them drop to the floor. He pulled off her boots and stockings, then quickly shed his light trousers in one lithe movement.

It was as if they were transported back in time, she lying on the bed of the rocking ship, clad only in lacy underwear, he standing over her, looming like a bronzed statue. Only this time she wasn't that terrified girl, afraid of the consummation of their love. With no coaching she reached up to stroke his engorged shaft. He groaned and bent down, pulling the pantalets off her, then lay atop her, placing his weight to his left side, favoring his right.

They ran eager hands over each other, rediscovering the delights of soft and hard, smooth and hairy, that had been so long denied. She tenderly kissed the ridge of the saber scar, the area still bandaged from the bullet, the slash on his forearm. He teased and rubbed and licked at her hardened nipples, moving down her soft little belly and then caressing between her legs in that wet, hot place until she begged him to enter her. She was mindless in need, desperate to have him fill her.

He moved to comply, surprised to feel that despite her wet eagerness she was almost as tight as a virgin. God, he loved her! He vowed he would be as faithful to her as she had been to him. At first, he penetrated her slowly and gently. Then, as she gasped and arched against him, he increased the tempo, afire with the joy of pleasing her, appeasing her hungers after so long. Too quickly, her nails dug into his back and she sobbed in release, her whole slim body shuddering in climax. He held himself still in her for a few moments, kissing her neck and face, holding her until she calmed. Then he began to move again, gradually harder as she caught his rhythm, joining him in fierce delight once more. Again she convulsed in ecstasy, the bright red flush of orgasm spreading across her breasts, down her torso. He raised his upper body and watched her. Then he was able to hold back no more. He exploded deep inside her, gasping in exhausted, sated joy, utterly drained and weakened.

He rolled onto his side, unable to support his weight any

longer. Now that his sexual tension was released the effects
of his wound and fever were apparent. Gently she followed
him, stroking his chest, jaw, temple, easing him onto his
back, then cradling him in her arms to rest. This time she
pulled the covers over them and watched him sleep.

"Oh, my dark love, I adore you," she whispered,
tucking her head against his shoulder and dropping off to
sleep too.

Later that evening, Amanda woke, recalling that they
had been alone in the bedroom since noon. It was almost
full dark now. What must everyone think? She had to
chuckle; she was sure what Lupe thought. That crafty old
woman had planned it all!

Careful not to disturb her sleeping husband, Amanda
slid from the bed and threw on a robe. She'd see to Paul,
then bring a light supper to their room. Her plans for
silence were rudely curtailed, however, when she stepped
onto a sharp wooden block and let out a sharp cry of pain.
Paul's blocks, forgotten from the morning play session!

She looked up after massaging her aching foot to see
Esteban's amused grin. "Any broken bones?"

"I don't think so, but I may have splinters. In the
future, sir, you and your son will have to confine construc-
tion projects to his room or the courtyard."

"Yes, ma'am." His face was grave and serious.

When she went to the kitchen to fetch some supper, a
smug, knowing Lupe greeted her with a tray, warm from
the oven. Their dinner was ready and waiting. Oh, yes,
could she take Pablito in to say good night to Papa before
he went to bed?

When she took Paul to say good night, Esteban, who
had put on his pants and picked up the blocks, insisted on
tucking his son into bed himself. Lupe allowed herself one
last smirk, then glided off to her room. It had been a
profitable day.

Esteban and Amanda sat in the courtyard and enjoyed
their simple meal as if it were a banquet. Lupe had
mysteriously produced cold beer for the patrón. Afterward,

they slept long and well that night in the big bed, wrapped in each other's love.

The next morning, Amanda woke to butterfly kisses all over her face and neck. Then the covers were pulled down and she could feel warm lips and a scratchy stubble of beard as the kisses continued to follow the slowly retreating sheet. Each inch of her collarbones, breasts, and belly were nuzzled languorously as they were exposed. Finally, as she writhed in the heat of pleasure, she opened her eyes and reached up to pull Esteban across her, kissing him fiercely.

They were so occupied with saying good morning that they missed the loud commotion in the hall. Suddenly the bedroom door burst open and Travis Mitchell fairly flew into the room. Distraught, Lupe desperately pulled on his coattails in a vain attempt to drag him back.

"Oh, patrón, I am so sorry! I tried to stop him, but he would not listen."

Esteban sat bolt upright in bed, quickly pulling the sheet up. Amanda sat behind him, her hands pale on his dark arms, her head peeking over his shoulder as he shielded her with his body.

"Who the hell are you?" Esteban said in a cold, deadly voice. He was pretty sure of the answer before it came.

Travis Mitchell stared dumbstruck at the two lovers, obviously naked under the sheets. That face! He knew with a sinking certainty that those sculpted dark features could only belong to Paul's father.

"Travis, this is my husband, Esteban Santandar," Amanda said in a subdued voice from behind Esteban's back.

"My God, you told me he was dead! I came back this morning after riding like hell all night. I couldn't find out a damn thing about you in San Francisco and I'd decided to insist you tell me yourself. And what do I hear but you have a Mexican pistolero staying at your house, shot in a gunfight, for Christ's sake! I couldn't believe it. And then she," he gestured furiously at Lupe, "tells me you're asleep, at ten o'clock in the morning! What the hell was I supposed to do? To believe? I thought he was holding you by force! Obviously I was mistaken, madame. My apologies for the interruption, Mrs.—no, not White—Santandar?''

He tipped his hat with an angry, jerking gesture and turned on his heel to storm out, with Lupe behind him, carefully closing the door.

Amanda sighed raggedly. ''I hurt him terribly with my lies. I should have told him the truth when I first suspected he was beginning to care for me. I knew I could never return his love. Oh, Esteban, I always wanted to be what I'm not—a lady. I have to face the truth, accept what I am, no more sham.''

He held her in his arms as they knelt in the middle of the big bed. ''Be proud of who you are, Amanda! You *are* a lady, in every way that counts. More important, you're a brave, loyal woman, my wife, my love.''

Her eyes shimmered with the glitter of unshed tears, and he could read final freedom from guilt in their proud depths. *How lucky you are, Esteban Santandar,* he thought, *to have this golden lady love you!*

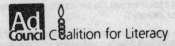